Caught by Love

The Steeles at Silver Island

Love in Bloom Series

Melissa Foster

ISBN: 978-1948868723

Cover Design: Elizabeth Mackey Designs
Cover Photography: Sara Eirew

PRINTED IN THE UNITED STATES OF AMERICA

A Note from Melissa

I have been itching to write Archer Steele's book since I first met him a few years ago. He's such a strong, sexy, resilient hero, but his guilt over the past goes so deep, he can't see the love at his fingertips. I knew he was going to need an equally strong heroine who understood the type of emotional pain he was going through, and Indi Oliver is definitely that woman. She's as passionate about everything she does as Archer is, and they butt heads as often as they bump other body parts. I laughed and I cried while writing their story, and there were times I wanted to shake them both, but it only made me love them more. I hope you enjoy Archer and Indi as much as I do.

If this is your first Love in Bloom novel, all of my stories are written to stand alone or to be enjoyed as part of the larger series, so dive right in and enjoy the fun, sexy ride. For more information on Love in Bloom titles, visit www.MelissaFoster.com.

On the next two pages you will find a Steele family tree and a map of Silver Island. You can also download your own copies of those documents and more here: www.MelissaFoster.com/RG

I have many more steamy love stories coming soon. Be sure to sign up for my newsletter so you don't miss them. www.MelissaFoster.com/Newsletter

FREE Love in Bloom Reader Goodies

If you love funny, sexy, and deeply emotional love stories, be sure to check out the rest of the Love in Bloom big-family romance collection and download your free reader goodies, including publication schedules, series checklists, family trees, and more!
www.MelissaFoster.com/RG

Bookmark my freebies page for periodic first-in-series free ebooks and other great offers!
www.MelissaFoster.com/LIBFree

STEELE FAMILY TREE

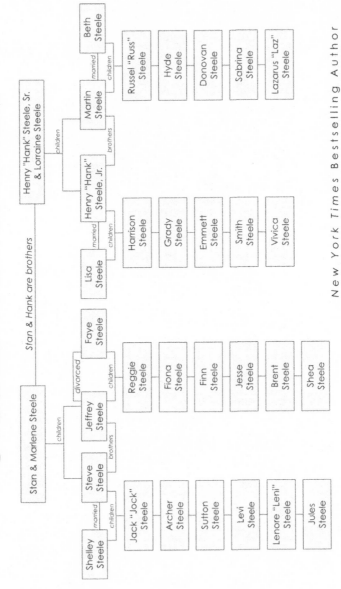

Henry "Hank" Steele, Sr. & Lorraine Steele

Stan & Marlene Steele

Stan & Hank are brothers

children

Shelley Steele — *married* — Steve Steele
Jeffrey Steele — *divorced* — Faye Steele
Lisa Steele — *married* — Henry "Hank" Steele, Jr.
Martin Steele — *married* — Beth Steele

Steve & Jeffrey brothers
Hank Jr. & Martin brothers

Shelley & Steve children:
Jack "Jock" Steele
Archer Steele
Sutton Steele
Levi Steele
Lenore "Leni" Steele
Jules Steele

Jeffrey & Faye children:
Reggie Steele
Fiona Steele
Finn Steele
Jesse Steele
Brent Steele
Shea Steele

Lisa & Hank Jr. children:
Harrison Steele
Grady Steele
Emmett Steele
Smith Steele
Vivica Steele

Martin & Beth children:
Russel "Russ" Steele
Hyde Steele
Donovan Steele
Sabrina Steele
Lazarus "Laz" Steele

New York Times Bestselling Author
MELISSA FOSTER

SILVER ISLAND

Wildlife
Refuge

Rock
Harbor

Fisherman's
Wharf

Seaport

Brighton
Park

Rock Bottom
Bar & Grill

Seaport
Primary

Trista's   Happy End

Silver Island
Airport

Rock Harbor
Primary

Lovers
Cove

Top of
the Island
Winery

The
Bistro

Silver
Monument

Silver
House

Majestic
Park

Silver Island
Community
College

Brighton
Bluffs

The Sweet
Barista

Silver
Harbor

Scoops

Silver Island
High

Sunset
Beach

Silver Haven
Primary

Marina

Silver
Haven

Fortune's
Landing

Chaffee

Fortune's
Cove

Bellamy
Island

Cuddlefish
Cove

Chapter One

I CAN'T BELIEVE I slept with him again. Eight hours into the new year, and I've already blown my most important resolution. Indi Oliver tipped her face up to the warm shower spray on Archer Steele's boat, trying to wash away the regret of their latest hookup, but that regret was chased by the titillating memories of Archer's strong hands on her skin, his gruff demands echoing in her head, and the rush of lust billowing inside her again with nothing more than the thought of him.

This has got to stop.

The shower door opened, and she willed herself not to look at the scorching-hot beast of a man as he stepped in behind her. She tried to ignore the spine-tingling desire clawing up her skin as he pressed his hard body against her back. His greedy hands slid up her belly, palming her breasts as if he owned them, teasing her nipples so exquisitely, a moan escaped. Damn him.

He nipped at the base of her neck, growling, "Where do you think you're going? I'm not nearly done with you."

"Archer..." She hated how needy she sounded, but she had no control around him.

"That's it, baby. Say my name again. You know what that does to me."

Did she *ever*. He was so arrogant, he wanted her to acknowledge who was giving her pleasure every time they were together. As if anyone else had ever been able to make her feel the incredible way he did.

He ground his hips against her, one hand slipping between her legs, taunting her, masterfully zeroing in on the magical spot that had her eyes closing, her head falling back against his broad, muscular chest. She really liked being with him. He felt so good, so safe and real. But she knew better. He might be authentically Archer, not fake and full of pretense like the Big Apple models and actors she did hair and makeup for, but he definitely wasn't *safe*. Her best friend Leni's older brother was the playboy of Silver Island, a world-renowned vintner who took what he wanted and made no apologies. He lacked the charm of his other siblings, but *damn*. What he lacked in charm, he made up for in raw sexuality. He was rough and greedy, bigger than all of his brothers, like pure sex on legs with his military-short dark hair and trim beard, which made him look a bit menacing and amped up his badass allure. Everything about Archer was *big*, from his thick thighs and barrel chest to his bulbous muscles and formidable cock. Indi secretly thought of him as *Hurricane Archer*, because she could feel a storm brewing inside him at all times. Sometimes it was pent-up desire wafting off him like a gale-force wind, but at other times another force seemed to stack up inside him and pulse in the air around him. She didn't know what that was, but it called out to her with the same vehemence as the testosterone he wore like aftershave, getting under her skin in the best *and* the worst ways.

"I have to go," she said half-heartedly, struggling against her hunger for him.

"I think you mean you have to *come*."

He squeezed her nipple with one hand, teasing between her legs with the other, and her traitorous body nearly combusted. "We're less than ten hours into the new year, and I've already blown my resolution not to sleep with you."

"Nice to know I made resolution status."

His cockiness was as frustrating as it was scintillating. He chuckled against her neck, quickening his efforts between her legs, sending rivers of pleasure slithering through her. She went up on her toes, and he pushed his fingers inside her. His thumb pressed on that bundle of nerves that wreaked havoc with her ability to think or feel anything but the orgasm building, pounding, swelling inside her, consuming her entire being. *"More...don't stop...oh God, yesss."*

His thumb stilled, and a whimper escaped as he gritted out, "Say my *name*, Indi." He underscored his demand with a bite on her shoulder and withdrew his fingers.

She grabbed his wrist, holding him where she needed him most. "Archer, *please*—"

"Fuck." He spun her around, pinning her back and hands against the cold, wet tile, and crushed his mouth to hers. His hard length pressed enticingly against her belly. Ever since they'd first hooked up, their connection had been so intense that they'd both been eager to ditch condoms early on, and they'd taken steps to make that happen safely.

They feasted on each other as if they hadn't just spent the night ravenously devouring each other every which way they could. *This* was what she craved. The unrelenting, all-consuming passion that practically oozed from their pores every time they were in the same room. She knew he was all wrong for her. Knew she had to stop this madness since she was thinking about moving to the island and opening her own business. The last thing she needed was her name connected to a man who everyone knew would never settle down, but as he tore his mouth away, dipping his head to suck her breast, those thoughts fractured and she cried out, swept up in the pleasure coursing through her. He dropped to his knees, spreading her legs wide, and then his mouth was on her, his scruff abrading her thighs, obliterating everything other than the whipping thrills of being caught in his torrent as she shattered against his mouth. Her fingernails dug into his shoulders, and his name shot from her lips like a curse. He stayed with her as her body bucked and shook, until she went limp against the wall.

He rose to his feet, lifting her into his arms, then lowering her onto his thick shaft. Renewed lust zinged through her as he pumped and ground. Why did he have to feel so damn good? His eyes remained trained on hers as she rode him like a fucking bronco. As if he could read her mind, he smirked victoriously. She lowered her mouth to his, kissing that arrogance off his lips, swearing this was the very last time she'd have sex with Archer Steele.

ARCHER NEVER LET women spend the night on his boat, but he was insatiable for Indi, and what better way to start the day than buried eight inches deep in the gorgeous petite blonde? He'd never met a woman who was as sexually brazen as he was, until Indi. She was a tigress in the sack, and he fucking loved it. His fingers itched to be tangled in her long silky hair again as he took her from behind. He ached to see those crimpy curls bouncing on her bare breasts as she rode him hard and fanned out on his pillow as he drove into her until she cried out his name in the throes of passion.

His cock jerked with the memories.

Fuck.

He pulled on his jeans, getting a kick out of her as she rushed around the cabin putting on her heels, while simultaneously finger-combing her damp hair and grumbling about needing to call Leni and being late to meet Charmaine. Charmaine Luxe was a local real estate agent. She was showing Indi retail space for her hair and makeup business. She was so damn cute, it made him want to make her even later.

"I can't believe I'm showing up in the dress I wore last night."

Archer's twin, Jack, who went by the nickname "Jock," had married the love of his life, Daphne Zablonski, last night. Indi was supposed to stay at their parents' house with Leni after the wedding, but this wasn't the first time she'd ended up in Archer's bed, and it damn well wouldn't be the last. "Want to borrow some sweats?"

"No, I don't want to borrow sweats," she snapped. "That's just what I need, to show up in *your* clothes. Where's my phone? I have to text Leni and let her know I'll meet her at the first property. She's going to kill me."

"Relax. She knows you're with me."

She gave him a deadpan look. "*That's* the problem. I told her not to let me end up here again. I swear it was the tequila."

"Yeah, *the tequila.*" His words dripped with sarcasm. Indi hadn't been drunk last night, and neither had he. When Daphne's sister, Renee, had flirted with him, Indi's baby blues had caught fire, and she'd turned up the heat to pure, unadulterated *vixen*. Archer didn't know if the supremely organized and fiercely confident blonde had done it out of a sense of competition or jealousy, and he didn't care. She'd landed exactly where he'd wanted her.

"I have the worst taste in men. No offense, but you're not exactly husband material."

"You got that right."

"Exactly, which means everyone knows we're just hooking up, and that won't bode well for my reputation or my business if I move here."

He cocked a grin. "And yet you keep coming back for more." He snagged her phone from the floor by the bed and closed the distance between them. She scoffed and reached for the phone, but he closed his hand around hers. "Don't beat yourself up for wanting more of the best thing on this island."

"*Ugh.* You are so arrogant."

He tugged her against him, and damn, she felt good. "You know you love it."

"In the *dark*, maybe." She pushed out of his arms, yanking her phone free. "In the light of day, it just kind of makes you a jerk."

He chuckled and pulled on a Henley. "If that were true, I doubt you'd be here."

She rolled her eyes. "I have to go." She began typing out a text while she walked out of the cabin, stomping past her coat lying on the couch.

He shoved his feet into his boots, grabbed her coat, and snagged her around the waist as she headed up to the deck.

"Archer, I have to—" She spun around and saw her coat. "Oh. *Sorry.* Thanks."

"Don't be so hard on yourself, darlin'. Women line up to

get into my bed."

"Not this woman." She took her coat, furiously putting it on. "Not anymore. It was fun, but I'm done."

"Isn't that what you said last time?" He grinned.

"I mean it this time. I need to concentrate on my business. I don't have time for"—she waved toward his body—"you and your big body and orgasmic tricks."

"As I recall, you enjoyed my orgasmic tricks several times last night." He hauled her against him again, grabbing her ass. The stairs brought them nearly eye to eye. "Especially that thing we did when you held on to the headboard."

Her eyes flamed, and her cheeks reddened.

"You like my mouth, my hands, my—"

"Stop!" she said anxiously.

He pressed his cheek to hers, speaking huskily into her ear. "What's the matter, gorgeous? Getting wet for me again?" He slid a hand beneath the back of her dress into the lace panties he'd taken off her with his teeth last night, earning a needy sigh as his fingers slid through her wetness. A low growl fell from his lips. "Let me fuck you one more time, right here on the steps."

She swallowed hard, her eyes screaming *yes!* even as she pushed out of his arms. "*Goodbye,* Archer." She turned and hurried up the stairs.

He was right behind her as she blew through the door, the brisk air assaulting them. Silver Island was off the coast of Cape Cod, and winters could be brutal. "I'll drive you to meet Leni. You can't walk all that way in those heels."

"City girl, remember?" She waved over her head as she headed down the ramp to the dock.

He followed her down. "Come on, darlin'. I'm not going to let you freeze."

"*Let* me?" She laughed incredulously, glancing over just as he hauled her into his arms and threw her over his shoulder. Her legs flailed, and she screeched, "*Archer!* Put me down! I'm not your property…"

She was so damn stubborn, bitching the whole way to his truck. He tossed her into the passenger seat, talking over her griping and huffing. "I'm just being a gentleman."

"More like an ass," she snapped, her gorgeous blue eyes shooting lasers.

"As I recall, your hot little hands were all over my ass last night—and the rest of my body—so quit your bitching and buckle up, buttercup, or you'll be even later." Ignoring her scalding stare, he closed the door and went around to the driver's seat. She glowered as he started the truck and drove out of the marina parking lot. "Main Street?"

She thumbed out a text, anger emanating off her. "*Yes.*" The word snapped like a whip.

"Just need to make one stop." Archer reached across the seat and squeezed her thigh.

"I'm not getting down and dirty with you in your truck."

He chuckled, loving her feistiness. "That's not on my agenda this morning, but now that you mention it…" He waggled his brows, earning an eye roll.

Indi texted furiously as he drove down the quiet streets toward the Sweet Barista, a café owned by Keira Silver, one of his buddy Grant's younger sisters. As much as Archer enjoyed the hustle and bustle of summers on Silver Island, he reveled in the tranquility of winter, when locals meandered at an easier pace, there were no lines at restaurants and cafés, and women didn't throw themselves at him every time he walked down the street. Who knew that could ever get old?

As he parked in front of the Sweet Barista, Indi gave him an incredulous look. "Seriously? You're stopping for breakfast? Can you just drop me off first, please?"

"This'll only take a second." He threw his door open. "Want to come in?"

She looked down at her dress and pulled her coat tighter across her chest. "Definitely *not*."

He climbed out of the truck and headed inside. Keira eyed him from behind the counter as she finished with a customer, her light brown hair framing her face. As the customer walked away, he stepped up to the counter. "Hey, Keira."

"I didn't expect to see you this morning. You and Indi looked like you were going to tear each other's clothes off before you even got out the door last night. Guess she took off on you again." The Silvers had all been at the wedding.

"Hardly," he grumbled, but the truth was, Indi wasn't like other women. She never tried to coerce him into staying longer or letting her linger. Indi never stuck around, which had been just fine with him at first, but lately he couldn't get enough of her, and it pissed him off that she shrugged him off so easily. "Give me two of your froufrou lattes my sisters rave about and two muffins or pastries chicks like."

Keira arched a brow. "Did Renee join you two last night?"

"*Focus*, Keira. *Coffee*. I'm in a hurry."

"Okay, okay, Mr. Mysterious."

A few minutes later he strode out to the truck and handed Indi a coffee and the bag of pastries. "Sorry I made you late this morning."

"*We* made me late this morning." She sipped the coffee, closed her eyes, and moaned. "But this apology latte is amazing. We're forgiven."

She smiled, and it tweaked a knot in his chest. She peeked into the bag, her face lighting up. "Are these blackberry, lemon, and thyme muffins? How did you know they're my favorite?"

The appreciation in her eyes was too damn beautiful to tell her the truth, but it slipped out anyway. "I didn't. Keira did."

She sipped her coffee, that soft smile remaining. "Other guys would've lied about that."

"Other guys suck." He drove to Main Street and spotted Leni in front of the empty retail space where Silver Island Salon used to be. Her arms were crossed, and she looked sharp in jeans, a suede jacket, and boots. He pulled up by the curb, and Leni's keen eyes locked on him as she stalked over to his window, her auburn hair bouncing with every determined step. He steeled himself for the shit she was about to give him as Indi climbed out of the truck as usual, without any parting words.

"Did you have to make her late?" Leni said harshly but quietly. "Charmaine has been waiting inside for ten minutes."

He handed her the other latte. "Sorry."

Her brows knitted as she accepted the cup and sipped, her scowl softening. "Oh, you're *good*."

"No shit. Why do you think we're late?" He chuckled and drove away, toying with thoughts of Indi moving to town and warming his bed more often—and his truck, his boat, and just about any other place the feeling hit them. She was fooling herself with that *last-time* bullshit.

It was starting to look like a damn good year.

Chapter Two

IT TOOK EVERYTHING Indi had not to watch Archer as he drove away, even though she was dying to know if he glanced back to see her one last time. He was infuriatingly hot *and* stubborn, but that stubbornness had saved her from freezing her butt off, and that, along with breakfast, was kind of sweet.

Pushing thoughts of the burly sex machine away, she tried to focus on why she was there. Indi was a makeup artist by trade, and a few years ago she'd developed Indira, her own skin care and cosmetics lines, which she currently sold online and in department stores. She was finally ready to take the plunge and open her own boutique. She looked at the sign Leni's youngest sister, Jules, had hung on the door of the empty retail shop. A VERY SPECIAL SHOP IS COMING SOON. Jules owned the Happy End gift shop at the end of the block. She was Silver Island's unofficial entertainment coordinator, matchmaker, and pep squad all in one. Her shop had red-framed picture windows and two iron giraffes out front, which she dressed up every day. Today they wore red hats and purple scarves. Jules had survived cancer as a child, and she spread positivity, love, and support like confetti to everyone around her. She'd been trying forever to talk Indi into moving to the island and starting her business.

All the Steeles were supportive of the idea. Not for the first time, she thought about how her friends' parents were warmer and more supportive of her than her own parents, which was one reason she wanted to move to the island.

"Girl..."

Leni's voice pulled her from her thoughts. She was shaking her head and looking at Indi in the way only a best friend could. The look said, *I can't believe you did it again* and *Of course you did it again. Don't worry. I've got your back.* She'd met Leni almost seven years ago at a fashion show where Indi was doing hair and makeup and Leni was handling PR. Leni had encouraged Indi's dreams from the moment they'd met, and she had single-handedly helped Indi make a name in the industry by having her high-profile clients use and promote Indira products. She was a no-holds-barred friend. The kind who would tell her if she looked frumpy in outfits, had toilet paper hanging off her heel, or if she needed to stop hooking up with her brother, which, judging by the expression on Leni's face, was what she was about to say.

Indi held up her hand. "I know, and we're done. That was the last time."

"That's what you said two hookups ago." Leni lowered her voice. "We don't have time to talk about my brother's hold over you. I told Charmaine you went to see if you left your bags on the ferry, which you didn't realize you'd lost until this morning. Got it?"

"Yes, but then how did I get the dress to wear to the wedding? Did I come to the island wearing it? And how did I do everyone's hair and makeup before the wedding without my supplies?"

"Smile and don't overthink it." Leni dragged her inside.

"She was at the wedding," Indi whispered. "She saw me in this dress." Her thoughts fell away as she took in their surroundings. Brick walls and dark hardwood floors gave the space a unique feel, and exposed metal beams on high, wooden-slatted ceilings gave it an edge. There were two sinks in the back, and three salon chairs with mirrors along two walls. It would take some modifying, but it had a certain charm, calling out to her in a way she didn't know retail space could. Kind of like Silver Island had the first time she'd stepped foot on the sandy oasis with Leni several years ago. She'd never forget walking down Main Street for the first time, with its quaint shops and colorful awnings. Window boxes had overflowed with flowers, WEL-COME signs hung by every door, and people sat on painted benches eating ice cream. Nearly everyone had smiled or said hello as they passed, so different from life in the big city. She'd felt the stress of trying to appease her parents and working in a busy city, in an industry where authenticity was as hard to come by as gold bars, fall away. In the years since, she'd found a warm community on Silver Island, with more friends who had become like family than she could have ever hoped for. More importantly, the Steeles had shown her what a family should be like. They'd had their own trials and tribulations over the years with Jules's cancer and a rift between Archer and his twin, Jock, that had lasted a decade, but they'd weathered those difficult times supporting one another, as families should.

Now she had the chance to become part of the special island and community that had given her hope for all the things she'd never found in the city. She'd been dreaming of opening her own boutique for so long, she had goose bumps. Charmaine was right last night when Indi had pulled her aside at the wedding to talk about properties and told her this one would be perfect.

Charmaine came out of a room toward the back, a knowing smile curving her lips as she approached. "If I had a dress as sexy as that, I'd wear it every day, too."

Indi was thankful for her attempt at discretion, but if she hoped to make a go of things, she wasn't about to tiptoe around her choices. She'd just make better choices in the future. "I'm sorry I'm late, and thank you for *that*, but we all know I left the wedding with Archer. It was a one-time thing."

Charmaine and Leni exchanged disbelieving glances.

"Okay, a *few-times* thing, but it's over. I'm going to focus on finally making my dream come true and giving Indira products the boutique they deserve."

"Damn right, you are." Leni nodded reassuringly. "You've run that business out of your apartment for way too long."

"I don't see why you can't do Archer *and* the business," Charmaine said supportively. "I mean, he *is* just about the hottest thing on this island, and opening a business can be stressful. I'd give anything to have a distraction like him waiting for me at the end of my long days."

"If you're into guys who will never give you more than a good time, go for it," Leni said.

Indi gave her an incredulous look.

"*Aha.* You're *not* done with him, just as I thought." Leni grinned.

Indi rolled her eyes, trying to play it cool, but this was the trouble with hanging out with her best friend. Leni knew all her secrets. Indi didn't *intend* to sleep with Archer again, but history had proven that when his dirty texts rolled in, or his rough voice came through the phone promising all the naughty things he did so well, or she caught his seductive wink from across a room, her resolve always faltered. She told herself she was going to be stronger this time, and she damn well meant it. But that didn't mean she wanted Leni throwing gorgeous, leggy Charmaine into his path.

Leni sipped her latte. "Look, I love my brother. He's a great guy, an amazing uncle to Joey and Hadley, and he's made the vineyard far more successful than it would have been without him." Joey was Leni's twin brother Levi's daughter, and Hadley was Jock and Daphne's little girl. "But you know he's wicked arrogant, and yes, in all fairness, he's an award-winning vintner, and as Charmaine said, he's a hot commodity on this island, so he's got reasons to be that way. He's never going to settle down, and I don't want you to get hurt."

"I'm not going to get hurt. We're just hooking up. Or we *were*. Can we please stop talking about Archer?"

"Of course," Leni said. "I guess you could do worse. You could have hooked up with Wells."

"I would *never* go out with a guy who two-timed you," Indi exclaimed. Leni had gone out with Wells Silver when they were in high school. He'd cheated on her with another of her close friends, Abby de Messiéres, and Leni had never let him, or anyone else, forget it. Abby lived in New York now, and when the three of them got together, Wells always came up in conversation.

"Sometimes I wish I'd grown up here so I was *in the know* with all the gossip," Charmaine said. "But then I realize I'd probably be part of that gossip, and I'm glad I'm a transplant."

"I'd like to stay far away from that grapevine, too," Indi agreed. "So how about we focus on this incredible space and not the various players who live around it?"

"Yes, let's." Charmaine went into a well-practiced sales pitch about the use of the space and potential layouts for the boutique. She went over utilities and the changes in foot traffic during peak and off seasons.

When she started to give Indi a pitch about the island, Indi interrupted her. "You can save the sales pitch about the holiday parades, the flotilla, and other events. I've been coming here for years, and as I said last night, this is definitely where I want to open my boutique. And this *space*. It's incredible. Would I be allowed to take out a few of the salon chairs and counters and maybe paint the bricks white? Freshen it up a bit?"

"I'll have to check with the owner about painting the brick, but you can definitely take out the chairs and counters as long as you repair the floors and walls."

"Are you sure you want to take them out?" Leni asked. "This was the only salon on this part of the island. You could be giving up valuable income that you won't have to work hard to earn."

"I know, but I don't want to run a big salon. I enjoy cutting hair, but I don't want it to be my main focus. My heart is in skin care and cosmetics and doing hair and makeup for special events. I think three chairs will be enough for customers who come in to get ready for events, and I want to add displays on the other side."

"What if you have a larger group, like a wedding party? Will three chairs be enough?" Charmaine asked.

"I usually meet larger groups of clients at the venues so they don't mess up their hair on the way over. I think three is plenty. I've been dreaming about opening a boutique for so long, I can picture lighted wall units with glass shelves over there." She pointed across the room. "Pretty displays for the hair products on this side of the room and makeup and skincare over there and in the back, or maybe the other way around. I can see mother/daughter makeovers and girls coming in to get ready for homecoming dances and proms. I can't wait to teach young girls how to apply makeup and help women learn about why using the right hair products can mean the difference between frizz and curls or flat and full of body. And, Leni, I know you're worried about me losing the built-in income from the salon, but I make more money off my products than I ever would cutting hair, and I'll be a lot happier doing it because I can *finally* meet the women whose lives my products are touching. My head is literally *spinning* right now with ideas. I can offer gift baskets for special occasions, sales and events for each season. The possibilities are *endless*."

Charmaine sighed. "You make *me* want to open a boutique."

"She really has been talking about it forever," Leni said. "I just can't believe she wants to move to the place I couldn't leave behind fast enough."

"That's *not* true. You love it here, and you know it." Indi knew Leni loved living in the city, but she was always raving about the island.

"Shh," Leni said conspiratorially. "Don't tell anyone."

Charmaine chuckled. "Let me show you the rest of the space."

She showed them the office in the back of the shop, with natural light pouring in through the windows and an enormous stockroom and separate closet.

"There's so much space," Indi said. "It really is perfect."

"Why don't we take a look at the apartment upstairs," Charmaine suggested, heading toward a door near the back of the space.

"I got so excited about this area, I forgot there was an

apartment included in the rent."

"All of the buildings on this street have either apartments or retail space above them. But don't get too excited," Charmaine warned as they followed her upstairs. "It's not very big."

She led them into a spacious living area with the same brick walls and wood-slatted ceiling as the retail space. Natural light flooded in through large picture windows in the kitchen and dining areas. The living room and kitchen were separated by a nice-size bar, and the dining area had floor-to-ceiling shelves on one wall and an arched entryway into the kitchen. Indi couldn't believe Charmaine thought the apartment was small. She'd obviously never lived in New York City. "This is twice as big as my studio apartment."

"And twice as nice, for a third of the cost," Leni added.

Charmaine opened the bedroom door. "Between you and me, the rent on this place is a steal for Silver Island. The owner is anxious to get it leased."

They looked at the bedroom and bathroom. Indi pictured her bed by the window, her dresser by the closet, and her pretty towels hanging in the bathroom. When they went back into the living room, she mentally laid out her love seat and other furniture, imagining leafy plants basking in the sun by every window. It already felt like home, unlike her apartment in the city, where she still felt like she was living in someone else's space.

"Why don't I go downstairs to call the owner about painting the bricks and let you two chat."

Charmaine headed downstairs, and it was all Indi could do not to squeal. She bounced on her toes. "*Leni.* This feels perfect. What do you think? What am I not thinking of?"

"That you won't have your favorite taco shop or coffee shop

right around the corner."

"So I'll find a new favorite food. Trista's Café is a few doors down, and the Sweet Barista isn't far away. What else?"

"It's a big move. You've lived in the city that never sleeps your whole life. Silver Island is going to take some getting used to when you're here for longer than a few days."

"I know. Instead of Broadway shows and street vendors, there are movies and cute little restaurants. I know I have to deal with the whole Archer thing, but being around your family and all the friends I've met over the years sounds so good to me."

"Stop looking at me with puppy-dog eyes." Leni smiled. "You know I support whatever decision you make, even though if you move here, it'll mean you're farther away from me."

"I'm sorry, but thank you!" Indi hugged her. "Now let's talk about the layout for the boutique."

As they brainstormed, the more ideas they came up with, the more the boutique came to life and the more excited Indi became. Her phone rang, and when she pulled it out of her coat pocket, her mother's name appeared on the screen, replacing her excitement with the inescapable feeling of not being *enough* for her parents.

Leni must have seen something in her expression, because she said, "Your mom?"

Indi nodded.

"Let it go to voicemail."

"She'll just keep calling. Give me a sec." She stepped aside to answer the call. "Hi, Mom."

"Indira, honey, we missed you last night at the annual New Year's Eve bash at the club. James was asking about you. I hope you'll give him a call."

I'm fine, Mom. How are you? My friends' wedding was magical. Thanks for asking. Similar nonexistent conversations played in Indi's head every time her mother called. "It's been five months since James and I broke up. He needs to get over it, and you need to stop encouraging him." James Rutherford was a family friend, and they'd had an on-again, off-again relationship since high school that was full of good intentions but void of sparks or passion. They'd gotten together again about a year ago, but Indi had finally ended it for good around the same time she'd made the decision to stop trying to be something she wasn't and get the heck out of New York City to live the life *she* wanted, where *she* wanted to live it.

Leni mouthed, *James?* Indi nodded, and Leni shook her head.

"Oh, honey," her mother said in the dismissive tone Indi hated. "He's not the type of man who gets over a woman, and surely you don't want him to. You two got along famously."

"We're friends. Of course we get along. We've known each other forever, but as I told you five months ago and a hundred times since, I need more than he can give."

"What else could you possibly want? He is financially secure, and he adores you."

Oh, I don't know. Love, laughter, and heart-stopping passion. "I don't need a man for financial security, and I'm a little busy right now, Mom. I don't have time to talk about James."

"Are you back in the city? James is here talking with your father. We could all have dinner together."

Indi was *done* with her mother's games. "Mother, I have no interest in having dinner with James, and I'm still on Silver Island, looking at space for my boutique."

Silence stretched between them, and when her mother finally spoke, her tone was tight. "I thought you gave up that silly idea."

"I have no idea why you'd think that since I've never wavered from my intentions, and it's not—" She stopped herself from justifying her dreams. Why did she always backpedal with her parents? She reminded herself for the umpteenth time that she no longer needed her parents' approval. "Was there something you needed, Mom? I really have to go."

"Yes. I wanted to make sure you were coming to brunch on Sunday."

Indi's stomach clenched, anxiety crawling up her spine. Their family got together once a month for brunch, rain or shine, at The Grand, of course. The Grand was the oldest and most exclusive social club in the city, with an eighty-thousand-dollar initiation fee and annual dues of thirty thousand dollars. Her family, along with several other families from her parents' highbrow circle, had been brunching there for generations.

It was all for show, and Indi hated the very premise of it. But she missed her sister, her niece and nephew, and her brother—trophy wife, overblown ego, and all. The truth was, whether Indi wanted to admit it or not, some part of her still held out hope that her parents might come around and see her success for what it was. She hated that, too. "I'll be there, but I really have to get off the phone now."

As Indi ended the call, Leni put her arm around her. "Do you want some ice water for the smoke coming out of your ears?"

Indi straightened her spine and squared her shoulders. "What I want is to sign the lease. Where's Charmaine?"

"You're going for it? You're really going to move here and open your business?"

"Damn right I am, and assuming I get approved for the lease, I want to get it going right away. The sooner I can get started, the better."

Leni squealed and hugged her. "I'm totally psyched for you!" Her expression turned serious. "But what about Fashion Week? It's only six weeks away. Are you sure you can handle making this big of a change with that on deck?"

"Absolutely. I've been doing Fashion Week for years. I know how to prepare and what it takes."

"Indi, you're talking about a *huge* move. Opening a business is no small feat. We have to strategize your marketing plan to get the word out, and you have to hire someone to do the renovations. Levi can probably give you recommendations." Levi owned Husbands for Hire, a renovation company, but he'd moved off the island years ago. He and Joey lived in Harborside, Massachusetts.

"I know it's a big endeavor, but I'm ready for it. I think I mentally left the city a long time ago. I just realized that I'm going to need to keep my furniture in the city until after Fashion Week so I have a place to sleep while I finish out my contracts. Do you think Charmaine can find me a short-term furnished apartment? Or maybe your parents will let me stay with them until I can move here."

"You're not going to believe this," Leni said. "But Jules *knew* you were going to take this place. She gave me a key to her apartment before she and Grant left for Spain and said you can stay there until you're all moved in here." Jules's fiancé, Grant Silver, had surprised her with a trip to Spain, and they'd left that morning.

"You're kidding. See? This was meant to be."

"I think so, too. But you've booked a few events after Fashion Week. What's your long-term plan for your apartment in the city? I know you switched to a month-to-month lease a few months ago, but are you going to keep it?"

"It's too expensive. I'll have to let it go after my sixty days' notice. I guess I'll stay with Mare while I finish the events I've already committed to." Her sister, Meredith, also lived in Manhattan.

"Or even better, stay with *me*."

"You wouldn't mind? I love my niece and nephew, but I'd rather stay with you than impose on Mare and her husband."

"*Yeah*," Leni said sarcastically. "It'd be a real burden hanging out with one of my besties."

"You're a godsend." Elation bubbled up inside her. Nothing had ever felt so right. Archer bullied his way into her thoughts, stirring desires that made her heart race. How did he do that? She tried to push that yearning away, vowing to stay the course. From this moment on, her sole focus was building the life she'd always wanted. No more hookups with Mr. Arrogant, no more running late because of sexy showers or lost panties someplace between the beach and his boat. This was her chance to become the woman she'd always wanted to be and to show her parents, and the world, *exactly* who that was.

"Let's do this." She took Leni's hand and headed for the stairs.

Chapter Three

ARCHER MADE HIS way through the wine cellar of his family's winery early Wednesday morning. Top of the Island Vineyard spanned sixty acres to the west of his parents' house and had been in his mother's family for generations. Archer had never wanted anything more than he'd wanted to become a vintner. From the time he was a little boy, he'd been enthralled by the sights and smells of the winery and vineyard. He'd followed his grandfather and his father around the property, carrying tools and soaking in their life lessons about family, work ethic, what it meant to be a man, and facts about wines and vines, all of which were far too complicated for a little boy. But he'd been so inspired by the passion in their voices, it had made him want to understand those lessons and become a part of the business even more. While most of his siblings had left the island for college or other endeavors, he and Jules had remained anchored to the small towns of their youths, and to this day, there was no place else he'd rather be.

He usually found solace in the winter months, when things slowed down, and in these quiet moments, without the noise of racking, filtering, and bottling. But this morning it was too quiet. He craved the sounds of wines being moved from barrel to barrel, allowing them to stabilize and the tannins to soften, and the chatter of the staff to distract himself from thoughts of Indi. She'd been lingering front and center in his mind a hell of a lot more lately. He hadn't even entertained the idea of being with another woman in months. It was a good thing he was taking his boat out of the water this weekend to store it for the rest of the winter, because he couldn't look at the damn thing without seeing her gorgeous body there for the taking and those big baby blues pleading with him for more. He swore her feminine scent had seeped into the mattress. But it was more than her beauty and their hot sex that was gnawing at him. She didn't look at him the way other women did, like they couldn't believe he was with them. Indi looked at him like she *knew* she was worthy, like *he* was the lucky one, and hell if that wasn't exactly how he felt. He liked her sassy mouth and innate confidence. She was whip smart, which he admired, because beauty without brains was exciting for about five minutes.

Why the hell am I thinking about this shit?

Fucking hell.

She messed with his head in ways no other woman ever had, and it intrigued him as much as it annoyed him. It was time to put her back in the OSZ—only sex zone. No afterthoughts meant no catching feelings. He walked around a rack of barrels and pulled out his phone, thumbing out a text that would put her right back where she belonged. *What're you wearing?*

As usual, her response rolled in quickly. *I'm just getting in the shower. Why?*

A slow grin slid into place as he responded. *I need a visual. I'm thinking about bending you over one of these barrels next time you're in town.*

A message bubble popped up with an eye-rolling emoji

followed by *I told you we're done hooking up and I meant it.*

"No, you didn't." He thumbed out, *Can you feel me gripping one of your hips from behind? My other hand tangled in your hair, tugging just hard enough to make it sting as I drive my cock deep inside you?* He hit send, aroused at the thought of being inside her again. He stared at his phone, anticipating her sexy response. She always gave it right back to him, and man, he dug that. Silent seconds turned to minutes without a response, and he gritted his teeth.

She was toying with him.

He was tempted to send another text, but Archer Steele didn't chase women. He pocketed his phone and was heading out of the barrel room when another text rolled in. His pulse sped up as he pulled out his phone. Jock's name flashed on the screen, and he cursed. Not because it was Jock but because it wasn't Indi.

He read his brother's text. *You coming to Mom's for breakfast? I want to see your ugly mug before we leave for our honeymoon.*

Archer typed, *On my way*, hitting send as another text from Indi popped up. *Dream on, lover boy. We're done.*

"Like hell we are." He gritted his teeth and headed outside.

He drove one of the golf carts they used around the property over to his parents' rambling, cedar-shingled, two-story. His childhood home had a gazebo anchoring one side of the spacious front porch and memories anchoring his heart to the past. His grandfather had passed away years ago, but his grandmother, Lenore, lived in the carriage house out back. For the millionth time in the last six months, relief washed over him. Relief from ending a decade-long rift between him and Jock that never should have happened in the first place. A decade of so much anger and hurt, he wasn't sure he'd ever come out of it. He still carried a shitload of guilt about that, but here he was, parking the golf cart beside Jock's car, looking forward to seeing the twin brother he'd lost for far too long.

He and Jock were the oldest of their siblings, followed three years later by their sister Sutton. Two years after her, Levi and Leni were born, and finally, three years later, Jules came along. *Jules.* The baby sister he couldn't protect from an awful disease. She'd suffered greatly but had never let her pain dim her sweetness or her bright outlook on the world. He loved all of his siblings, but Jules had a special place in his heart, just like Jock did. He and Jock had been best friends and troublemaking cohorts until they were in their early twenties, when Jock was finishing college in New York City and Archer's best friend, Kayla, whom he trusted and loved like family, had moved there for work and had gotten together with Jock. Archer had been happy for them, and months later, when they found out Kayla was pregnant, he was thrilled. What could be better than his two best friends building a life together? Kayla had continued to call and text him at all hours, just as they always had, and his relationship with Jock was stronger than ever. Jock had written a book while in college, and when it became a bestseller, Archer had been the first to congratulate him. Then one awful night, while Jock and Kayla were out celebrating Jock's success, tragedy struck. In one horrific moment, a truck ran a red light, killing Kayla, and, a few hours later, Jock lost their baby, too.

Archer had been blinded by the pain of losing Kayla, by Jock's agony of losing his girlfriend and child, and by the shock and fear of almost losing his twin. He hadn't known what to do with the rage, which had twisted into barbs of blame and had shot out at Jock like bullets. He'd said and felt unthinkable things that consumed his every thought, chaining him to the past. Until ten long years later, when Daphne came into Jock's life, and his brother, the man he blamed for all of their pain, the man who had betrayed Archer's one request to take care of Kayla, had found the strength to do what Archer couldn't and had faced those demons head-on. Fists and accusations had flown, but with every punch, every vile word, they'd smashed through their hurt and anger, clearing a path to mending their broken hearts, and over the past few months they'd worked together instead of dredging the abyss between them even deeper, and they'd found their way back into each other's lives.

Thank fucking God.

The front door opened as Archer climbed out of the golf cart, and three-year-old Hadley toddled out. "Unca Archer!" She clutched her favorite stuffed owl in one hand, her honey-colored pigtails flouncing beside her sweet face. Jock was on her heels, futilely trying to put his little girl's coat on her as she made her way down the steps. "*No*, Daddy Dock."

Archer's heart filled up at the name she called Jock. She had trouble saying *J*s. Archer wondered if she'd eventually call him Daddy Jock, or just Daddy. It had taken a hell of a lot for his brother to get past his grief and open his heart to another woman and child, and Archer felt guilty about that, too. Jock was a damn good father and husband, and he deserved all the love Daphne and Hadley had to give. Daphne ran the events for the winery, and there was no missing how much she loved his brother.

Archer jogged over and scooped up his adorable niece. "Hey now, squirt. You listen to your daddy. He loves you, and he takes good care of you."

Jock nodded his appreciation, but his jaw was tight, a tell-tale sign that he was stressed. He was everything Archer wasn't, and vice versa. They were both tall with dark hair and eyes, but Archer was built for a fight, with calloused hands from working the vines and boxing, while Jock was fit but much leaner, his hands soft, like his heart. He had a writer's hands, and there was an air of dignity about him that Archer couldn't emulate if he'd wanted to. His brother was thoughtful and chose his words carefully before speaking, like their father did. Even his voice was tempered, while Archer didn't have much of a filter to slow him down before he spewed whatever shit was in his head. His interactions were gruff and blatantly honest.

He looked at his scowling niece, lips pursed, brows knitted. She was so different from Levi's daughter at that age. Joey was eight. She'd been a colicky baby, but she'd quickly outgrown it, and Archer swore she'd been smiling ever since. But as his mother always said, *Life would be a bore if we were all the same.*

Hadley had one arm around Archer's neck, her little fingers pressing into it. She might not be big on smiling, but she smiled a hell of a lot more now than she had when he'd first met her.

"Go on, now," Archer said firmly. "Let your daddy put your coat on."

Her gaze darted to Jock, and she stuck her arm out, allowing him to do it.

"Attagirl." Archer kissed her temple.

She shoved her owl toward his face. "Kiss Owly."

Jock chuckled.

Archer grimaced and kissed the damn stuffed animal, earning a toothy grin from Hadley.

She wriggled in his arms. "Down." He set her feet on the grass, and she plopped onto her butt, playing with her stuffed toy. He eyed Jock. "Rough morning?"

"You could say that." Jock lowered his voice. "Daph is frantic about leaving her for a week, and I've got to admit, I'm not thrilled at the idea, either. It seemed reasonable for our honeymoon, but now I'm kind of torn."

"Dude, she's three. You should be torn. But she'll be fine. Better than fine. You know Mom and Dad will spoil her rotten while you're gone, and hopefully, you and Daphne will be doing your own spoiling, if you know what I mean. Take your gorgeous wife on her honeymoon and remind her why she's got the best husband around. Make love to her until she can't remember what day it is, and then do it some more, because once you come back home"—he nodded toward Hadley—"it's sticky fingers, bedtime stories, and whispered promises in the dark so you don't wake your little one." Archer clapped a hand on Jock's shoulder. "You both deserve this."

"Thanks, man."

"Sure. Besides, with you gone, there's more bacon for me. Now quit being a pussy, and let's go inside." He looked at Hadley and cringed, silently chiding himself for his language. "Pussy *cat*. Quit being a pussy cat." He offered his hand to Hadley. "Let's go eat, squirt."

The house smelled like it had every day of his life, of meals made with as much love as the embraces their parents lavished on them. He had no idea how his family had put up with him for all those years when anger ruled his every move, but he was damn thankful they had.

They left their coats in the closet by the door and followed the sounds of hushed voices and giggles into the kitchen. The counters were covered with platters of eggs, bacon, and sausage. Freshly baked muffins were cooling on a rack by the oven, and their father's arms were wrapped around their mother from behind, his face buried in her neck. The women on the island called Steve Steele a silver fox because of his salt-and-pepper hair, trim beard, and fit physique, but he only had eyes for his wife. Their mother, Shelley, was a big, beautiful woman with long auburn hair, bangs that gave her a youthful look, and a heart as big as her personality. Their parents had never shied away from open affection, and while Archer could count on one hand the times he'd heard his parents arguing, he couldn't remember a single time that those arguments had lasted more than a few minutes. Those were just some of the reasons Archer would never jump aboard the marriage train. He wasn't cut out for that type of relationship. He wasn't warm like his parents or siblings, and he wasn't the kind of guy who did romantic shit or whispered sweet nothings. He was wired differently than the rest of his family. Their wire was smooth coated, while his was barbed.

Hadley toddled over to their father, arms shooting toward the ceiling. "Up, Gwampa! Up!"

"Hey, sunshine." His father picked her up and kissed her cheek.

His mother leaned in to kiss Hadley and tickled her belly, earning a burst of giggles. "How's Grandma's big girl?"

The kitchen door opened, and his grandmother walked in, as fashionable as ever with her blond pixie cut, wearing a thick black cardigan, a black blouse, and black slacks. Her black-and-gold leopard-print scarf matched her gold earrings and necklace. Grandma Lenore was in her late seventies. She had a wicked rebellious streak Archer admired and more energy than someone half her age. "Just in time." She winked at Archer as she snagged a piece of bacon from a platter.

"Good morning, Mom," his mother said.

"It *is* a good morning." His grandmother reached for a muffin, and Archer noticed a faint PYTHONS stamp on her hand. His grandmother and her friends, who called themselves the Bra Brigade because they'd been sneaking off to sunbathe in their bras since they were teenagers, thought nobody knew that when they said they were going to play bingo on the Cape, they really went to a strip club called Pythons.

His mother smacked her hand. "We're eating in a minute."

His grandmother rolled her eyes, and Jock said, "You have to grab them when she's not looking, Gram."

"Sorry I'm late." Daphne breezed into the kitchen, her blond hair swaying and her jeans and sweater showing off her voluptuous curves. "Hey, Archer."

"Hi, Daph." He leaned down and kissed her cheek. She was perfect for Jock, and much too sweet for Archer's taste, but he couldn't help razzing his brother. "Ready to nullify that wedding and take off with the better twin for a weekend of debauchery?"

Jock gave him a scathing look.

"Heck *no*. I married the best Steele there is." Daphne quickly added, "No offense, Steve."

Their father chuckled. "No offense taken, darlin'."

"Damn right you married the best." Jock pulled her into his arms, stealing a kiss.

Daphne blushed. "You didn't let Archer near our luggage, did you? I don't want to find snakes in my suitcase."

Archer chuckled. He and his brothers had a reputation for playing pranks on one another and on their parents and friends. The first time Daphne had come to the island, he'd put a rubber snake in her bedroom, and Daphne had shrieked when she'd found it. But snakes in a suitcase were child's play compared to the mayhem they'd caused in the past.

"Don't worry, babe. I guarded it with my life." Jock pulled her in for another kiss.

"As well you should." Their mother gave Archer a warning look before hugging him. "You look a little tired, sweetheart. Did you sleep okay?"

No. I was too busy thinking about Indi. "I'm fine."

"Mm-hm." She patted his cheek. "If you say so."

His father bounced Hadley in his arms. "He's probably still recovering from the long weekend."

"Recovering from his night with a certain makeup artist is more like it," his grandmother added.

He was used to them giving him shit about Indi, but he didn't want to hear it today. He was having enough trouble getting her out of his head.

"You must have done something right, since Indi leased the space on Main Street." Daphne reached for a piece of bacon and took a bite. "I'm excited that she's moving to the island. I have some great ideas to help her spread the news, and it'll be fun having another friend around."

What the hell? Why hadn't Indi told him she'd signed the lease and was moving to the island when they'd texted earlier? He tried to process that new information as his mother and Daphne chatted about referring clients who booked weddings and other events at the winery to Indi, and Jock and their grandmother carried the food to the table.

His father set Hadley down to toddle after Jock, and she climbed onto her booster seat. "I want Gwandma's muffins!"

Jock looked seductively at Daphne. "Daddy wants Mommy's *muffins.*"

"I bet he does." His grandmother chuckled.

Daphne blushed a red streak and began filling a plate for Hadley, going on about feeling like she'd forgotten to pack something.

As they discussed a laundry list of items she'd packed, Archer stewed over Indi, growing more irritated by the second.

His father nudged his arm. "You look a little shell-shocked."

Archer gritted his teeth.

"You want to talk about it?"

"No." His father was as stable and robust as a good Cabernet Sauvignon. He'd taught Archer many life lessons, most of which Archer had fucked up in one way or another, like what it meant to love unconditionally and to duke out his frustrations in the boxing ring instead of on other people's faces. He had no doubt his father would have something wise to say about this situation, but right now there was only one person he wanted to talk to, and she was across the fucking ocean.

"Then let's sit down and eat," his father suggested. "Everything's easier to deal with on a full stomach."

"I gotta take care of something first." He turned to head out the side door, and his father grabbed his arm, his eyes as serious as his grip.

"Ten seconds can save you a world of grief."

Archer scoffed at his father's age-old advice to count to ten before reacting—*It gets the crazy out and allows you to think before you speak*—and stalked out the kitchen door.

His father had tried to talk some sense into him after the accident, when Archer had stopped speaking to Jock. Hell, so had everyone else, but Archer had been too angry to listen. He'd been working on that the last few months, and sometimes he tried that ten-second rule, although he rarely made it past five.

He pulled out his phone and called Indi, pacing the yard as

it rang a second and third time.

"Hey," she said when she finally answered. "I'm about to meet a friend for coffee."

"Just one question. Why the hell am I finding out about you moving to the island from my family and not from you?"

She was quiet for a second. "I didn't think you wanted or needed to know all of my business."

His jaw clenched tight. "Darlin', I've been *all* up in your *business* for months."

"You know what I mean. We had fun, but we're done hooking up, so why do you care if I'm moving there or not?"

He didn't know why, but he fucking did. "Because I like to know what's happening on my island."

"*Your* island? Wow, your arrogance knows no limits. I hate to break this to you, but it's not your island, and I'm not yours to harass."

"Jesus, Indi. I'm not harassing you. I just want to know what's going on."

"What's going on is that I'm going to meet my friend James for coffee."

A pang of jealousy gripped him, and he cursed the unwanted emotion.

"I don't have time to argue with you. Goodbye, Archer." The line went dead.

He stared at the phone, anger and something else simmering inside him. *The hell with it.* He was done giving a shit what she did.

Chapter Four

INDI SHOVED HER feet into high heels, frantically double-checking her supplies for the bridal party that was waiting to get dolled up for their main event. It was Saturday afternoon, and she hadn't been scheduled to arrive at the hotel for another hour and a half, but the mother of the bride had called asking if she could fit in three more people. Indi was scheduled to do the bride's hair and makeup, and makeup only for the rest of the bridal party. She always allotted a little extra time, which might allow for *one* extra makeup session if she didn't get too distracted by *helpful* bridesmaids. But the woman was frantic and had gone on to explain that three of the bride's cousins who had backed out of being in the bridal party because they'd had a falling-out with the bride had shown up that morning with heartfelt apologies, crying rivers of tears, and had smoothed things over.

Indi to the rescue.

Or so she hoped.

She put on her coat, shouldered her bag, and as she reached for her wheeled supply case, she spotted her phone on the couch. *Geez.* She really was frazzled to have almost forgotten her phone. She snagged it, and her heart tugged at another unread message from Archer on the screen. He'd texted a number of times since Wednesday morning when she'd hung up on him, and it was torture not reading them, but going cold turkey was the only way she'd ever move on. She hadn't realized how tangled up in him she'd gotten until she'd asked why he cared if she moved to the island. In the split second before he'd responded, she'd had a fleeting hope that he'd tell her it was because he cared about her. *That* was when she'd realized she'd lost her mind and had gotten in too deep with the one man who could never reciprocate in the ways she needed.

His island. She scoffed. The only thing he cared about was making sure he knew her whereabouts so she didn't cramp his style.

Well, the heck with him. They'd had their fun, and it *was* fun. It was exciting and passionate beyond belief. In the bedroom, Archer was everything she'd craved and fantasized about when she'd been with James. But she hadn't broken up with James or signed a lease that would completely change her life and possibly alienate her even further from her family just to be someone's sidepiece. She was taking charge of every aspect of her life and heading into her business venture with a clear head and eagle-eyed focus.

She shoved her phone into her bag, grabbed the handle of her supply case, and headed out the door—nearly smacking into the burly, arrogant vintner, clad in a fur-lined brown leather bomber jacket, jeans, and work boots. *"Archer? What are you...?"* The flutter of excitement in her chest was quickly smothered by reality. They'd hooked up at her place before, when he'd shown up out of the blue. At first it was just for sex, but somewhere along the way he started taking her out for dinner and drinks first. She wasn't going there again, and she didn't need to be chewed out for not telling him she was moving to the island. "If you're here to yell at me, I don't have time for it."

His expression remained rigid, tension tugging at his jaw as his gaze traveled over her red lips, to her simple dangling diamond earrings, and slowly down the plunging neckline of her short black dress beneath her open coat. "Where are you going all dolled up?"

"Work, and I'm late." She pushed past him and began dragging the case down the stairs. "How'd you get into the building?"

"I told a nice old lady I was your boyfriend. Give me that."

He reached for the handle of her supply case, putting his large, rough hand over hers, and her stupid body heated up in ways only he had ever caused. "I've got it. Thanks." She tried to tug the case down the steps, but he tightened his grip, holding it hostage on the third step down. She met his steely gaze. "I've done this a million times. I'm fine."

"I know you are, but only an asshole would let a woman carry this thing down a flight of stairs."

"Based on our last conversation, I'd say you're right on track. Now can I go, please? Why are you even here?"

His eyes narrowed. "You won't answer my texts or take my calls. What the hell did you think I'd do?"

"What you always do. Find some other woman to screw, hit on me when I'm in town hoping to get laid, then wash, rinse, and repeat."

His nostrils flared. "You have no idea what you're talking about."

A dozen silent retorts darted through her mind, but why bother arguing? He wasn't her boyfriend, and he was no longer her lover. She had more important things to worry about than if she'd hurt his ego by hanging up on him. "I don't have time to argue about your sexual proclivities. I had three unexpected bridesmaids added to my schedule, and the bridal party is a mess of heightened emotions. There's not enough time to do what needs to be done, and if I don't leave *now*, they'll all walk down the aisle with puffy eyes and splotchy skin."

"I've got my truck. I'll drive you."

"Fine. It's quicker than hailing a cab." She gave him the name of the hotel, and tried to pull the case down a step. He loosened his grip just enough for *him* to pull her hand free.

"I'm carrying your bag, because I'm not a total prick."

"If you say so." It was a cutting remark that she didn't really mean, but she was flustered, late, and still unsure why he was there.

Anyone who knew Archer knew the only things he was one hundred percent of the time were an A-class vintner and a ridiculously gorgeous, infuriating man. Other than that, as far as she could tell, he was about sixty percent unfiltered, arrogant prick and forty percent protector of his friends and family who did the right thing regardless of the consequences. She had absolutely no idea why that tipping of the scales was so appealing.

There was obviously something wrong with her.

He said things in bed that could make a whore blush, but then he'd do something like pay a visit to someone who wronged his sister and make sure the guy would never do it again. Indi had witnessed that side of him firsthand a few years ago when she and Leni were visiting Leni's parents for a long weekend. Leni had met a guy while they were out the night before, and she'd just gotten back from a date with him. Archer had overheard Leni saying the guy, a tourist from Connecticut, had gotten too aggressive with her. Archer had wasted no time tracking him down and tearing him apart. He'd gone so far as to escort the guy off the island with threats of being buried six feet under if he ever returned. Indi didn't condone violence, but there was something to be said about being loved and protected so fiercely.

"You need help at this thing?" he asked as he put her case in the back seat.

"I'll be fine." She wasn't sure she would, but she didn't want him, or anyone else, to know that. She watched him stealing glances at her as he drove, his jaw muscles bunching, as if he had something to say but refused to say it.

He lifted his chin. "Why are you looking at me like that?"

"I don't know. I guess I'm trying to figure out why you're really here."

"Because I was a dick on the phone, and I wanted to say I was sorry. You didn't deserve that."

Her thoughts stumbled. She knew apologies didn't come easily to the man who had held a grudge against his brother for years, and that made this one even more special. "Thank you. I'm sorry I hung up on you, but you caught me on a bad day. I was on my way to meet my ex to straighten a few things out because my mother wouldn't get off my back about him, and I was—I *am*—sick of people trying to control how I act and what I do."

His chest expanded with a deep inhalation, hands gripping the steering wheel tighter. "You need me to take care of your ex?"

"What? *No.* Didn't you hear the rest of what I said?"

"Yeah, but it's bullshit. I've never tried to *control* you," he said sharply.

She couldn't resist showing him how wrong he was, even if what she was about to say wasn't a bad thing. She lowered her voice. *"Say my name, Indi. Stroke harder. Get on your knees."*

He scoffed. "You dig that shit, and you know it."

"Yes, in the *bedroom*. But we're not a couple, Archer. I don't answer to you or anyone else, and now that I'm moving to the island and building my business there, I can't be one of your bed bunnies. I have to protect my reputation."

He tightened his grip on the steering wheel as he pulled over in front of the hotel. "Indi—"

"Let me finish. This is important, and I'm stressed about today's event. So, please just let me say this so I can get in there. You're my best friend's brother, and I love your family probably more than I love my own, which is sad, but it's the truth. I don't want to mess that up." The muscles in his jaw flexed repeatedly, but she didn't let it slow her down. "I really like you, Archer, even if you infuriate me sometimes. But we went into this with our eyes open. We knew there was going to be an end to it, and I need to know that we can still be friends without it being weird between us. Okay? Can you be cool about this?" She shouldered her bag as the doorman came to help her out of the truck.

"Yeah, we're cool." His tone was gruff.

He threw open his door and climbed out, getting her supply case from the back seat, and wheeled it around to her. Looming over her like the mountain of a man he was, he nodded at the doorman, who stepped discreetly away.

"Thank you for coming to apologize, and for the ride."

His jaw tightened. "You know we're not done, Indi."

"Ohmygod. It's like you didn't hear a word I said."

"I heard everything you said. But we both know no one else can satisfy you like I do."

"You are the *most* bullheaded man I know." It didn't matter that he was right. She didn't want to hear it.

A slow grin curved his lips. "I'm not denying that, so don't pretend you don't love it."

Her jaw dropped, and she grappled for a response, but before she could find words strong enough to put him in his place, he spoke.

"Now go in there and show them how awesome you are before I toss you in the truck and find a dark alley to have my way with you in."

She snapped the handle of her supply case from him, trying to hide the heat crawling up her chest and neck, and stalked inside, heart racing, body vibrating, images of her and Archer naked in his truck assaulting her.

ARCHER WASN'T ABOUT to let that be the end of their conversation, and although Indi had downplayed how frazzled she was over her job, he'd seen her tells. She'd fidgeted with the gold ring she wore on her right hand, and her leg had bounced nervously during the whole ride, and it wasn't because of their close proximity. Those tells were different, softer. A flutter of her lashes, a hitch in her breath. He'd seen those signs the second she'd opened her apartment door. But then his calm, cool-headed girl outside the bedroom and firestorm-between-the-sheets vixen had tried her best to put him in his place.

Good luck with that, darlin'.

Now, to help you shine...

He tipped the valet, grabbed a few bottles of wine from the case in the back seat, and headed inside. A quick stop at the reception desk told him where to find Indi, and a few minutes later he knocked on the door. A cute brunette answered it, wearing a red robe with *Bridesmaid* written in script above her right breast. Her eyes lit up as she ogled him, but it was the chaos going on behind her that caught Archer's attention. A gaggle of women in red silk robes were surrounding a blonde in a white robe—the bride, he assumed—while Indi worked on her hair. The women were all talking at once. "I know she wants an updo, but she looks better with her hair down." "An updo with tendrils framing her face is perfect." "Her cheeks look heavy when her hair is down." A collective gasp sounded, and the bride's face contorted in the mirror like she was going to cry. The other girls sent harsh glances and even harsher words at the brunette who had said her cheeks looked heavy with her hair down. The brunette burst into tears, and two women put their arms around her, consoling her as she professed her apologies. "I didn't mean her cheeks look fat. Her cheekbones just look higher when her hair is up."

Holy hell. Women were vicious.

While the girls argued and consoled, Indi spoke reassuringly to the bride, but in the mirror, Archer noticed the tension around Indi's eyes and jaw. Damn, she was good.

"I didn't know this room came with a wine boy."

The bridesmaid's flirtatious tone jerked him from his thoughts, bringing his attention back to the woman standing before him, and he turned on the charm. "You can call me Wine Boy if you'd like, but I prefer Archer." He winked, earning a wide smile. "Archer Steele, assistant extraordinaire to your fine makeup artist. What's your name, beautiful?"

"Anything you want it to be. Get in here." She opened the door and announced, "Ladies, meet Indi's assistant, Archer."

All eyes turned toward him as he stepped into the room, sparking whispers of appreciation. Indi wasn't kidding about puffy eyes and splotchy skin. A few of the women looked like they'd been up all night, with dark circles under tired eyes. Indi would have to be a miracle worker to cover that shit up.

The women headed for him, calling out hellos and introducing themselves, just as he'd hoped, giving Indi space to work in peace. Although the look in her eyes was a bit scathing. He tossed a wink her way, but it did nothing to ease her anger.

"Let me relieve you of that wine." A blonde took two of the bottles from him and her friend grabbed the third.

"Thank you," he said, eyes still locked on Indi, who clearly didn't want him there.

"You do hair and makeup?" another woman asked.

"There's not much I don't do." He felt his lips tip up as Indi rolled her eyes. *You know it's true.*

"He can mess up my hair any day," someone said, causing an uproar of laughter.

"Now, now, ladies. Don't get me fired before I even get started. Why don't you pour yourselves some wine while I talk to the boss, and then we'll get to know each other better." He ignored their flirtatious comments and closed the distance between him and Indi.

"*What* are you doing?" she whispered.

"Getting them off your back so you can do your job."

Surprise and guarded appreciation rose in her eyes. "You just happen to carry wine in your truck?"

He glanced at the bride, who was pretending not to listen.

"I figured if an apology for being late to work didn't do the trick, I'd bribe you with your favorite wine." To the bride, he said, "She's a great boss, but she's touchy about punctuality."

The bride laughed softly.

"You're a lucky lady. Indi's a master at everything she does. Her hands should be patented." He cocked a grin. "What do you need me to do, boss? Have you moisturized and prepped these beautiful ladies yet?"

"Have I...?" Confusion riddled Indi's brow. She grabbed his arm, turning their backs to the bride and whispering, "Do *not* mess this up for me."

"I would never screw with your work."

She scowled.

"Relax. I've got this. How do you think Jules learned to do makeup? When your baby sister wants to practice doing makeup on you, you let her do it, or you hear about it all night long."

Her eyes narrowed. "Seriously?"

"I swear." He made an *X* over his heart.

"You are *full* of surprises, but if you're lying..."

"No need for threats." He leaned in, whispering for her ears only, "Just wait until you see what surprises I have in store for us later." Heat rose in her eyes, and she took a step back, giving him a warning stare. He took that as a win and turned his attention to the eager wine drinkers. "Okay, ladies, who wants to be moisturized and primed first?" causing an outburst of *Me*'s and *I do*'s.

The next few hours passed with animated conversations, dodging innuendos from the single bridesmaids, and admiring Indi's professionalism and expertise. She'd done his mother's and sisters' hair and makeup many times throughout the years, but they were family, not women he noticed in any great detail, and he'd never actually *seen* her in action, working her craft like the professional she was. She paid complete attention to each woman as she worked on them, assessing their skin type and hair and eye color before picking out palettes. She made her work look effortless, but he could see the gears in her brain churning as she shaded and contoured, making each of them look like a runway model. There wasn't a puffy eye in sight. She even made the mother of the bride look about a decade younger than she had when he'd walked in, and she'd finished them *all* just in the nick of time.

The women gushed over each other, thanking Indi and Archer, though he did little more than prep their skin and keep them occupied as Indi worked her magic. Indi helped them get out the door, making sure nobody forgot anything, a gorgeous smile plastered on her face.

When the last of them left the room, Indi leaned her back against the door and sighed. "I can't believe we made it in time."

"*We* didn't. You did, and damn, Indi. You're pretty amazing."

She pushed from the door and began gathering her supplies. "Thanks. I couldn't have gotten it done in time without you."

"You could have, but I was glad to help. It gave me a chance to see you in action." He couldn't resist adding, "With your clothes *on* for a change."

She planted a hand on her hip, stunningly sexy in a short, formfitting black ribbed dress, despite the smirk on her face. "Don't think just because you helped me, I'm going to—"

He tugged her against him, silencing her with a rough, hungry kiss. She was right there with him, kissing him like she'd been thinking about it all day, just as he had. But then she pushed back, breaking their kiss, cheeks flushed. *"Archer..."*

It was a halfhearted retreat, so he hauled her close again. "Don't worry. I'm not going to strip you naked and bend you over that table, although the idea did cross my mind."

Her eyes narrowed, but the flames simmering in them were inescapable.

"I just had to get that out of my system."

"It's *never* out of your system," she countered.

"And that makes you one lucky chick. Come on, I'll buy you dinner."

She looked at him skeptically. "Really?"

"Sure. Then you can take me back to your place and take advantage of me."

She scoffed. "Don't count your chickens."

"Darlin', it ain't chickens I'm counting on. It's *dessert*." He swatted her ass.

She jumped out of his arms with a surprised squeak. "We'll see how dinner goes."

"Good plan." He helped gather her supplies. "Maybe I'll change my mind by the time the bill comes."

"Yeah, like *that's* going to happen."

"We'll have to see how cute the waitress is."

"God, you never stop, do you?"

"I think you know the answer to that." He tugged her into his arms again and kissed her slow and sensual, until she went soft against him, and then he kissed her longer, because she was right. Reining in his desire for her was like trying to stop a surging storm.

Chapter Five

THEY STUMBLED INTO Indi's apartment, devouring each other's mouths as they tore off their coats. Archer whipped off his shirt and went for her dress.

"Zipper!" she said anxiously.

He growled, "*Fuck*," and spun her around, quickly unzipping her dress and pushing it to the floor. He sealed his teeth over the curve of her neck and sucked hard. His teeth dug into her skin, sending zings of pleasure skating through her as he reached around and unhooked the front clasp on her bra, tearing that off, too. She started to toe off her heels, but he said, "Leave them *on*." Oh, how she loved that!

His hand dove between her legs, teasing her through her thong, while his other hand found her nipple. As they moved toward the couch, he knew just how to touch her to drive her wild. Anticipation stacked up inside her at the thought of him taking her from behind. She loved his aggression and his innate sexuality and confidence when they were getting down and dirty.

She gripped the back of the couch *tight*, breathless and needy for the man she'd sworn off only hours earlier. But they'd fallen right back into their dirty-talking, taunting banter over dinner, and that was another thing she craved. His spontaneity and complete focus on her when they were together. With his hand between her legs under the table, he'd teased her until she was so wet, she'd thought she'd come with the waiter right there beside their table. But then Archer had withdrawn those talented fingers, smiling triumphantly. She'd given that right back to him, stroking him through his jeans as he'd ordered their drinks, and then she'd gone further, whispering in his ear that she wished she could slink beneath the table and take his cock in her mouth. He'd clenched his teeth so hard, it had to hurt.

She needed him *now* more than she needed to keep her promise to herself, and she was going to enjoy every second of it.

As he stripped off her thong and worked his jeans open, she told herself this was *definitely* the last time. He shoved his jeans down and drove into her in one hard thrust. She cried out at the thrilling sensations shooting from her scalp all the way to her toes and every delicious spot in between. He thrust harder, taking her deeper, until she could barely breathe for the pleasure consuming her. Greed and need intertwined, thundering like a rampant drum inside her and escalating in intensity with every pump of his hips.

"You feel so fucking good." He fisted one hand in her hair, and she dug her fingers into the couch as he tugged her head up. His other hand clamped around her hip, and he slowed his pace to a mind-numbing rhythm, stroking over that secret spot inside her with deathly precision. He knew just how to take her to the edge and hold her there. She moaned and panted, chasing the orgasm that was just out of reach.

"*Faster*," she pleaded.

"Hell no." He thrust even slower. "You don't make the rules after keeping me in the dark about your move."

She looked over her shoulder, his dark eyes staring arrogantly and greedily back at her. "If I'd told you, you wouldn't be here, and *this* wouldn't be happening."

He slid his hand from her hip to between her legs, teasing the nerves that made her toes curl. Lust coiled deep in her belly. Her nipples throbbed. Her insides ached. "Maybe not *here* or *now*, but don't fool yourself. This was always going to happen."

He withdrew until the head of his cock lingered on that sensitive spot inside her, playing her like a song he knew by heart. *Archer, please*, hung on the tip of her tongue, but she bit it back, unwilling to say his name. She rose onto her toes, as she'd learned to do when he moved that way, heightening the sensations, and covered his hand between her legs with her own, trying to push her fingers past his to give herself the relief she needed most. But he grabbed her wrist.

"You'll come when I'm good and ready for you to come."

She glowered at him. "I hate you right now."

"I don't fucking care." He let go of her hair and her wrist and wrapped one arm across her chest, lowering himself over her back, still thrusting slowly. His other hand moved to the apex of her sex, driving her out of her mind. "Your body sure as hell doesn't hate me."

"Shut up."

He chuckled and sank his teeth into her skin, then quickened his efforts, causing a storm of sensations to crash over her. His name flew from her lips as she trembled and bucked, and then she was floating, cocooned by his strong arms and body, his lips moving over her heated flesh. Her body jerked with aftershocks, and his breath coasted over her ear. "I fucking love the way you hate me."

Laughter tumbled from her lips, and she gasped when he withdrew from between her legs and turned her in his arms, his rigid cock pressed against her belly. Restraint and appreciation stared back at her. Before he could say a word, she gave him a challenging stare and said, "My turn. Take off those damn boots and clothes and get on the bed."

INDI STEPPED OUT of her heels and strutted sexily around the open-cubed shelves that separated her bed from the rest of the apartment. Nothing turned him on like a woman who knew what she wanted and went after it. Especially when that woman was Indi Oliver, just conservative enough in public to make everyone believe she was a good girl. But he'd seen past that facade years ago. It was hard to miss the way her baby blues lingered hungrily on him like a platter of ribs before a lioness, despite his being an angry asshole most of the time. But she'd refused to give him the time of day. Four months ago, something changed. He'd felt a shift the night of his grandmother's birthday party. His sister Jules had tricked them into dancing together, and while Indi had always rebuffed his advances, that night she'd flirted back, giving him hell as much as she'd taunted him. She'd gone for a drink with Wells and some of their other friends after the party, and when he'd shown up, the flirting continued. He didn't know what had changed, and he didn't care. The sexual tension between them was white hot, and he went for it, asking if she wanted to get out of there. He could still hear her eager response. *I thought you'd never ask.*

She'd let her vixen flag fly high that night, and it had only flown higher every time they'd been together since.

He stripped and went to his hot little temptress. She stood beside the bed, arms crossed beneath her breasts, her gaze sliding down his naked body. He ached to take her six ways to Sunday. She was petite all over, with a sweet waist, narrow hips, and not more than a palmful of breasts. She was nothing like the curvy women he used to get down with, but he'd never been more attracted to anyone.

She lifted her chin, eyes moving to the bed. "On your back."

He'd give her control, for now...

He stripped the comforter to the foot of the bed and lay on his back. She straddled his torso, and he grabbed her hips, salivating for a taste of her. She put her hand between her legs, teasing herself until her fingers were slick and she was writhing in his grip. He lifted her to move her onto his rigid length, and she said, "You'd better be moving me over your mouth."

Fuuck. She was his every fantasy come true.

Following her command was no hardship. He'd happily suffocate between her legs.

Using hands and mouth, he devoured her, teasing and groping until her legs flexed, and she cried out. Her sex pulsed, her essence spreading over his tongue. Before she came down from the peak, he lifted her up, lowering her onto his cock in one swift move. They moaned and clawed at each other as she rode him wildly. He gritted his teeth against the mounting pressure inside him, searing her gorgeous image into his mind, breasts bouncing, hips grinding, eyes closed, lips slick and parted. He'd never seen anything so beautiful. But this wasn't enough. He needed *all* of her and tugged her mouth down to his, feasting as his hips pistoned. He tangled his hands in her hair, holding her mouth to his as they surrendered to their all-consuming passion. Fire and ice burned through his veins, and fucking fireworks went off inside him. A spectacular explosion of colors behind his closed lids seemed to pulse through him. She was the only woman who had ever caused those sensations. It was just another thing about her he didn't understand but craved like a drug.

He thrust and groaned, eating up her mewling sounds, as they rode their erotic highs, until they had nothing left to give. He gathered her in his arms, rolling them onto their sides, their bodies still connected. She buried her face in his neck, her softness excruciatingly perfect against him. This was the only time his world went quiet, the guilt of his past nowhere in sight. But he knew he had only about sixty seconds to revel in the serenity he didn't deserve. Then Indi would head into the bathroom, and when she returned, she'd be back to smartass remarks and sexy banter.

Not that he minded.

Any more than sixty seconds of serenity and he'd probably lose his mind.

Like clockwork, she drew back, looking as drunk on him as he was on her, but as usual, she snapped that gloriously sweet look off her face and climbed out of bed. He watched her disappear into the bathroom and propped himself up against a pillow. There was something cool about knowing what she was going to do next. It alleviated the hookup awkwardness that he used to hate.

His gaze moved over the tight space that served as Indi's bedroom. The cream-colored dresser with hand-painted flowers on it matched a tall and narrow chest of drawers. The flowers picked up the accents in the curtains and the fluffy comforter bunched at the foot of the bed. Like the living room furniture, they appeared simple but well made, and he'd bet the drawers were as organized as the open-cubed shelves separating the bedroom from the living room, which were neatly filled with books, brightly colored binders, baskets, and plastic containers with Lord knew what inside them. Her apartment was understated, like her. She could doll herself up with excessive makeup and clothes that made her stand out, but she didn't. She dressed sexy and smart, and that alone made her rise above the rest. She had a few paintings and plaques with positive sayings on the walls, and the last time he was there he'd noticed pictures of Indi with friends, many with his sisters, and some with fashion models at different events. He'd wondered about those, because she wasn't a showy person. But even more curious was her lack of family photos.

Indi came out of the bathroom, all delicate curves, her pink nipples pebbling as her gaze slid down the length of him. "You're not dressed."

"You don't miss a thing, do you?" He propped his arm behind his head, drinking her in as she pulled open a dresser drawer, giving him a great view of her heart-shaped ass. His fingers itched to touch her again.

"Don't you have to get back to the island?" She pulled a T-shirt from the drawer and put it on. It didn't cover her ass.

His cock twitched greedily. "Nope. The only thing on my agenda is getting my boat out of the water at noon tomorrow. We have *all* night." He pulled her down to the mattress beside him.

"I heard there's a storm coming. Don't you have to batten down your hatches or something?"

"The storm won't roll in until late Monday. The only hatches I want to batten down are yours."

"*Archer*," she complained half-heartedly, like usual.

"What?" He rolled over her, pinning her beneath him. "You got a late booty call with *James*?" He felt that damn snag in his chest at the thought of her with another man. Yet another thing that drove him crazy about her. Before Indi, he'd never given a second thought to the women he'd hooked up with. But everything was different with her. She was the only woman he trusted enough to have sex with without a condom, and *man*, she'd put him through the paces with that one. He'd had to get tested for every disease under the sun, and they'd both sworn not to ride bareback or go down on anyone else while they were hooking up.

She cocked a grin. "Jealous?"

"Hell no."

"Then why ask?" She arched a brow.

Because I want to hear you say he's just a guy you work with…and he's gay. He gritted his teeth, blood boiling. "Just want to know who you're fucking."

A flash of something he couldn't read—Hurt? Disappointment? Anger?—appeared over her face, bringing a dose of guilt. But in the next second that look was gone, and she wriggled out from beneath him, repositioning herself with her back against the headboard.

"James is my ex-boyfriend, and I'm *not* sleeping with him."

He remembered that was the name of the guy she'd met for coffee the morning she'd hung up on him. She'd had to straighten something out with him. Archer's protective urges surged.

"But you and I don't do sleepovers, so you can go." She

started to get up, and he tugged her back down.

"What world are you living in? You spend the night on my boat every time you're in town."

She rolled her eyes. "Well, we don't do that *here*."

"Hm." He fluffed a pillow and put it behind his back, settling in beside her. "I like this bed, and I like you, so tonight we are." He gave her thigh a squeeze. "Now tell me why you had to straighten that guy out."

"Don't pretend you care about that."

"I'm not pretending. There are only two reasons to meet with an ex. Because you're banging him or he pissed you off. You said you're not banging him, so I need to know if I should pay him a visit."

She shook her head, laughing softly. "You're such a Neanderthal. Plenty of people remain friends with their exes. James is a *family* friend, and I'm perfectly capable of handling him."

"What was the issue?"

She looked at him for a long moment, as if she was trying to read his interest level.

"Indi, I'm in your bed. I obviously care."

"You said you never catch feelings for women you hook up with."

Did she remember every damn thing he'd ever said? "I don't, but I've known you for years, and you're Leni's best friend. It's different. Tell me, or I'll find out for myself."

"God, you're a pain."

"No shit. Now give me the lowdown on this guy."

She rolled her eyes, pushing the sheet toward him. "At least cover yourself up."

"Can't handle the distraction?" He covered his dick.

"Why do I bother with you?"

"Because I can make you come six times before I do. Stop procrastinating and tell me about the situation with your ex."

"It's not so much a situation with *him* as it is with my family. They're not like your family. My parents are all about appearances, and they're old-fashioned. They believe men should take care of women, and women should look pretty, have babies, take care of their husbands, and go to charity functions and luncheons."

"I can get behind the taking care of their men thing, but are you saying they think women shouldn't work? Are they filthy rich or something?"

"You could say that."

He arched a brow, realizing he knew very little about Indi's life outside the bedroom. "Spill it, Oliver."

"I can't believe Leni never told you this. My great-grandfather was the founder of Oliver Aviation Enterprises, OAE. My father is the president of the company."

"Are you shitting me?" OAE was one of the largest aerospace companies in the world. His family was fairly well off, but they weren't even on the map compared to the money she was talking about.

"I wish I were. Not that I begrudge my family's business, but my parents think my career is *cute* and *frivolous*. They can't wait for me to get married and start cranking out grandbabies, like my sister and my brother's newly pregnant wife."

"What is this, the 1950s?" He scoffed. "I don't get it. Being a stay-at-home mom is great for some women, but not *you*. You're like *me*. We have fire in our bellies. We need problems to solve, new endeavors to conquer, and you get that with every person you work on as a makeup artist. Tying people like us down only fires us up and makes us more determined to break free. How can they not see that in you?" That fire, her unwillingness to hold back or follow the crowd, was one of the first things he'd noticed about her. She spoke her mind regardless of what others thought.

"I don't know. I guess I'm surprised that you do."

"Are you kidding? With a mouth like yours, it's hard to miss."

"Ohmygod." She bumped him with her shoulder.

"You're also incredibly talented, as I witnessed today. I can't believe they want you to give that up just to pop out a bunch of kids."

"I do more than hair and makeup. I have my own skincare and cosmetics lines."

"What do you mean, your own lines?"

"I mean, I saw a need for better products and I filled it. Like with everything, there are quality high-end products, and then there's everything else. The midline all-natural products that were available were mediocre or overpriced. I created a line of high-quality, organic, and affordable skincare products and cosmetics that are suitable for everyone, from teenagers to grandmothers, and I sell them through my company, Indira."

Holy shit. He knew she was smart, amazing in bed, and fun as hell to be around, but he'd had no idea she was also highly ambitious. That made her even more attractive. "That's incredible. How did I not know about your company?"

"You never asked. It's not like we have the kind of relationship where we talk about our lives."

"That's true, but most people brag about their successes."

"You don't," she pointed out. "You got pissed when I called your boat a yacht, which it *is*."

"That's a fair point. I hate when people use what they own

and their jobs to gain recognition, but I want to know about *you*." He hadn't realized how much he wanted to know about her until just now, and as different as that was for him, he was going with it. "Why did you become a makeup artist in the first place?"

"That goes *way* back to when I was a kid. You don't want to know that stuff."

"Yeah, I do."

She looked at him weird, like she didn't know why he was interested.

"Come on, you know all about the shit I've gone through."

She sighed. "Okay, it's kind of boring. As kids, we went to a lot of high-profile events with my parents. My mom would take me and my older sister, Meredith, to get our hair and makeup done. Mare is beautiful. She has thick, curly hair the color of rich dark chocolate. It's not kinky like mine. She has natural spiral curls that women pay lots of money to have. She's fair skinned, like me, but she has freckles, which give her a little something special that sets her apart, and she has *big*, gorgeous hazel eyes. I've always been envious of her natural beauty."

"I think you're selling yourself short. You're smokin', babe."

"Thanks, but she's stunning. Unfortunately, the stylists always straightened our hair, and they'd cover up her freckles and try to make her eyes stand out less, and then they'd enhance my eyes and cheekbones, which I hated, because I have an oval face, and it's supposed to look softer."

He liked hearing what she thought of herself. He'd never noticed the shape of her face, but he'd always thought her entire being was soft and feminine.

"Our faces would break out for two weeks after every event, and I always thought they made us look fake. Mare is five years older than me, and we used to sneak my mom's makeup into our bathroom and do each other's faces. We got in a lot of trouble for that." She smiled, shaking her head. "But we had fun, and by the time I was a teenager, I had scoured the internet and watched a million YouTube videos, learning everything I could about hair and makeup. I wanted to bring out Mare's natural beauty, not cover it up, and I wanted products that were light and breathable and wouldn't make our skin break out." She shrugged. "That's how it all started, and I'm really proud of my Indira products."

He loved knowing that it had all started out of love for her sister. "You should be proud. How did you come up with the name Indira? It's striking and memorable." *Like you.*

"That's my real name, but I don't ever use it. It's too fancy."

He looked at the beauty before him, her eyes warm and her heart open, so different from the wild lover he knew her to be. "You're right. You're definitely more free-spirited *Indi*, but Indira is a classy company name."

"Thanks. I thought so, too. Want to hear a secret that's kind of cool?"

"Always."

"My logo for Indira is just the word written in gold script and it's actually my handwriting. It was Leni's idea."

"That is cool."

"I know. I love it."

"So, how'd you get started with Indira?"

"On a hope and a prayer." She laughed softly. "I started the company right here in this apartment five years ago, and for a long time I lived with boxes of products stacked up everywhere and filled every order myself. Now I have a distributor that does it for me. But I only sell online and through salons and other stores. That's why I want to move to the island and open a boutique."

"Why not open it here? You'll get a lot more foot traffic than you would on the island."

"And I'd pay five times the rent and work five times as hard. I love what I do, but I also want a life, and I don't want it in this fast-paced city where my family is always on my case. I haven't even told them I signed the lease or that I'm moving."

"It doesn't make sense to me that your family wants you to give up the business you've spent years building to become some jackoff's arm candy." He wanted to have a face-to-face with her parents and set them straight.

"You don't understand. Let me explain it a different way. I do hair and makeup for fashion shows, photo shoots for ads, and all sorts of other media. Most wealthy, high-profile people sit in the front row at fashion shows. They would never work behind the curtains. Well, my parents would never set foot anywhere *near* a fashion show. They feel it's silly and beneath them. Besides, it's not like I'm Estée Lauder, earning billions."

"Who gives a shit what you earn? You *built* a company. That takes intelligence and hard work. It's not fucking cute or frivolous. It's admirable, and they should be so proud of you that they shout it from the rooftops."

"Thank you, but that would be *your* family. Why do you think I hang up pictures from events I've worked on—my first Fashion Week, my first *Cosmo* cover, and the others? Usually parents display their children's accomplishments, but mine would *never* do that. They're not about unconditional love and support. They love me, but the depth of that love is definitely conditional."

What the hell kind of parents did she grow up with? "What

does *that* mean?"

"It means they would love me more if I lived life by their rules, like my brother and sister do. My brother, Simon, works for my father and got married last year to a gorgeous model who wants nothing more than to kiss his ass, spend his money, and have his babies, and Mare married an amazing man, who *also* works for my father, and they have two beautiful kids. Mare seems happy, but she went to college hoping to go to law school and gave it up to live the life our parents wanted. And my brother will make a great father, and I think his wife, Anika, will be a good mom. But I swear everything my parents do has a scheme behind it. They introduced Mare to Bruce, her husband, at Christmas her senior year of college and found a hundred reasons to bring them together after that. And then they pushed for their engagement right after graduation and urged Simon to propose to Anika shortly after they'd met so she *wouldn't get away*. Then they threw them a huge engagement party that was covered by all the high-society media outlets. Like I said, it's all about appearances. Family get-togethers only count if other people see us."

"That's fucked up." He sat up taller, muscles tensing. If anyone deserved to be loved conditionally, it was *him*, not kind, generous Indi.

"It is messed up, but it's not all bad. My sister encourages me to stay true to myself, which I appreciate. She just can't do much where my parents are concerned. She would have made a great attorney. She's level-headed, and she does a great job of encouraging her kids to be themselves. They're good kids, too, which says a lot about her and Bruce's parenting skills. Chantal is seven, and she's the best big sister to my four-year-old nephew, Terrence, who's a real handful."

"I'm glad Mare has your back." He was also curious about her relationship with her brother, but he didn't want to get too far from where their conversation had started. "But how does all of that play into whatever you needed to straighten out with your ex?"

"Because my parents think James is husband material. He works for my father, which gives them some control over him, and he's handsome, wealthy, and a nice, stable guy."

"If he's so great, why'd you break up with him?"

She lowered her gaze, fidgeting with her gold ring. "Because I wanted more than he could give."

"Meaning?"

"Meaning lots of things," she said a little sharply.

"That's not an answer. How long did you go out with him?"

"Most recently, about six months, but we have a lot of history together, and my family refuses to believe it's over."

"Six *months*? That's a long time." He must have been special to her, which brought another pang of jealousy. "He can clear that up with them, can't he?"

She shrugged, her eyes flicking up to his. "He's kind of still hung up on me."

Of course he is. Indi was not the kind of girl a guy walked away from. Hell, look at *him*. For years, when he'd come onto her and she wouldn't take his bait, he'd tried—and failed—to get her out of his head. An uncomfortable thought dawned on him. "You sure *you're* not still hung up on *him*?"

"Oh God, yes. We're friends, and I'll always care about him, but not like that. I tried to make it work, tried to be partially who my parents wanted me to be. But I couldn't."

"Why not? You said you had a lot of history together. Did he hurt you?" Archer needed answers.

"No, he'd never hurt me. We grew up together, and after years of people trying to set us up, I finally gave in. We started going out our senior year of high school, and we were on and off for a few years, while I went to cosmetology school and he was at college."

"Holy shit, Indi. A few *years*?"

"Mm-hm. I know how it sounds, but it wasn't like we were madly in love or anything. I didn't feel that toward him. And then I started my career and he was working for my dad, and it was kind of like dating a friend. I was comfortable and he was good to me, but I realized I was a little lonely even when we were together. We didn't have a lot in common beyond family and everything that came with it, which as you now know, isn't a happy connection, and I didn't feel the type of sparks and chemistry my friends talked about. So I ended things. He had a difficult time with the breakup and transferred to the Colorado office, and we saw each other here and there. Then he moved back last year, and my parents were all over me about giving up my *silly* business and getting on with my life."

Archer gritted his teeth. *Silly, my ass.*

"They were pushing James on me, and it wasn't like the guys I was going out with were all that great. I thought maybe things would be different, and I gave it one more shot. But I realized a few months in that nothing had changed, except that James started talking about a future with me that I didn't want. That's when I ended it for good and started thinking about getting out of the city and living my life my way."

The changing tide…

"And I did the right thing. Thanks to you, I know what true passion feels like, and I'm not going to settle for anything less than the whole package. But to be honest, the whole dating thing scares me. I mean, how do you know who you can trust? I know I can trust James, but his friend Todd has been engaged forever to Jordan, a great girl who lives in Maryland. I've met her a number of times, and he *still* hit on me every time he saw me, whether or not James was there."

Fucking dirtbag. "You should tell her what he's doing, and James should have beat his ass."

"James is *not* a fighter. He saw what Todd did as a joke, but it wasn't. I know if I'd given in, Todd would've been all over me. I was going to tell Jordan, but James got furious and said I shouldn't put myself in the middle because I'd be ruining her life."

"What the hell does that mean?" James had sounded like a nice guy, until now.

"She has no family. Her sister went missing years ago, and her parents died in a car crash. But I think she might have a feeling that something is off, because she's postponed the wedding a bunch of times. I feel bad for not telling her, and you know what? I'll never keep my mouth shut for a man again because I don't ever want to be the girl who finds out too late that her guy is chasing every skirt he sees." She smiled and touched his hand. "I think that's why it's so easy to be with you. I trust you, which I know is weird, considering your squirrely reputation, but you've always been up front about who you are and what you want. It doesn't matter that you're the farthest thing from husband material a girl could find, because you're not even a contender, and I'm good with that. In fact, doing this with you is way easier than dating. If I wasn't moving to the island, I'd probably continue letting you be my boy toy."

What the hell? He didn't want to be a contender to be tied down, but he didn't like being written off so easily, either.

Unfamiliar emotions twisted him up inside. He needed to redirect them away from all of this emotional talk to something he could handle. He threw off the sheet and shifted over her legs, kissing her stomach. "You know damn well I've ruined you for other guys." He clutched her hips and kissed her inner thigh, inhaling the scents of soap and sweet, sexy Indi.

"You're *good*," she said coyly. "But I wouldn't go *that* far."

"No?" He slicked his tongue along her center and sucked her clit between his teeth.

Her hips shot off the mattress, and she grabbed his shoulders. "Oh, dear Lord."

"You can call me Lord, but I still want to hear you say my name."

"Just don't stop, Archer, Archer, *Archer*." She pushed his head between her legs.

He teased her until she was writhing and clawing at his skin, pleading for more. Her head tipped back, and her back arched. *So fucking gorgeous.* "Watch me make you come."

The most hypnotic eyes he'd ever seen hit him with the heat of a thousand suns, and those uncomfortable feelings tried to claw their way up to the surface again, but he fought against them the best way he knew how. He devoured her into a frenzy, soaking up every last drop of her pleasure as she pulled his hair so hard, he thought it might rip from his skull, and then he buried himself deep inside her and didn't stop until neither of them had energy left to think.

Chapter Six

INDI LAY IN Archer's arms, his warm body curled around her, thinking about when they'd first hooked up, the night of his grandmother's birthday party. He'd been fit to be tied over Jock's returning to the island with Daphne and Hadley, and it seemed everything had set him off. And there she'd been, riding her own emotional roller coaster, having recently broken up with James and seriously considering saying *fuck it* to her family's overbearing ways and moving out of the city. She'd never forget the way they'd gotten caught up in a storm of sexual banter, and before they'd landed in his bed on his boat, he'd said, *You'd better be sure you want this before you get in my bed, because when we're done, you're out the door, and I'm on to my next conquest.* She'd secretly wanted him for so many years, she'd been blinded by desire and had responded with, *No worries there. I've already got my next conquest in my sights.* It was a blatant lie, but he'd responded with cavemanlike vehemence, which had been a massive turn-on, and said, *It better not be Wells Fucking Silver.* He and Wells were good friends, but if she'd learned anything about Archer Steele, it was that he saw everything as a competition, and he never lost. He'd held her just like this that night, like he was never going to let her go.

But she'd taken the upper hand and had left while he was sleeping, heading back to his parents' house, where she and Leni had been staying.

The next morning, before she left the island, his whole family had gathered at his parents' house for breakfast, and he and Jock had gone head-to-head in their backyard. She'd never seen two grown men fight the way they did. It was terrifying, but somehow she'd known they'd needed it. Archer had shown up on her doorstep in the city five days later, looking fit to be tied again. She'd wanted to comfort him, but she'd known he wasn't the type to allow someone else to comfort him. At least not in the sense that most people were, with tender words and gentle embraces. She'd said, *I thought you were on to your next conquest*, to which he'd said, *What do you think I'm doing here? Time for an encore, darlin'. Clothes off. Let's get to it*, reeling her in for a second night of the most glorious sex she'd ever experienced. She'd fallen asleep in his arms just like this, but she'd woken up when he'd left an hour later with nothing more than a *See ya around.*

The pull between them was so strong, she'd ended up on his boat again a few days later, after they'd exchanged a slew of dirty texts. Even Leni hadn't known she'd gone to see him. Only that time when she'd tried to slip out in the middle of the night, he'd tightened his hold on her and growled, *We're not done. Just need to power up.* He'd slept like a baby, and by morning he was powered up all right. *Whew.* She got turned on just thinking about their trysts. She snuggled deeper into the curve of his body. His arm tightened around her middle.

"Damn, you smell good in the morning." He kissed the top of her head.

So do you. He smelled manly and familiar, and…

Her eyes flew open. What the heck was she doing? This wasn't an *oops, I did it again* moment. She'd been stone-cold sober last night. She pushed from his grip and climbed out of bed, pulling on a T-shirt. "You have to go."

"Why?" He stretched languidly, arms spread wide, biceps flexing as he pulled his arms back, expanding his chest.

She caught herself staring and threw his jeans on the bed. "It's already nine thirty. You have to go get your boat out of the water, and I have to get ready to meet my family for brunch." Her stomach burned at the thought.

He sat up, suddenly fully awake, jaw muscles bunching. "How about I go with you?"

"Absolutely not." He would hate everything about The Grand *and* her parents, and her parents would look down upon a man in jeans and work boots with the Chinese symbol for *wolf* on his neck, who swore like a sailor and said whatever inappropriate thing popped into his head, no matter how good a man he was. She tossed Archer his shirt. "Hurry up and get dressed. I have to be at The Grand at eleven."

"The Grand?" He scoffed. "Can I get a shower first? Or do you want me walking out of here smelling like sex?" He pushed to his feet, his cock dangling enticingly between thick thighs.

Her mouth watered. *Ugh. Seriously? What is wrong with me today?* Silently chastising herself, she stalked into the bathroom, grabbed a clean towel from the linen closet, and shoved it into his hands. "Hurry up."

"Alone?" He said it like the very idea of it was appalling.

"It's faster, and I can't be late."

He tugged her against him, sudden worry filling his eyes. "Why do you play their games?"

"What are you talking about?"

"You know what I'm talking about. You're not a *Grand* girl. You're a ribs or tacos and mojito girl, who licks her fingers when she's done eating and slips off her heels under the table when she thinks nobody's looking."

Shocked he'd noticed, she was touched in ways she shouldn't be. Or at least in ways she shouldn't let herself be, because it made him harder to resist, and she needed to focus on getting through brunch with her family and then moving and setting up her boutique, *not* how good he made her feel by truly seeing her, when it couldn't ever lead to something real.

"That's an awful long silence, darlin'. Do you need someone to tell you it's okay *not* to play their games? Because I'm telling you. You don't need to please anyone but yourself, and you don't need anyone else running your life."

If only it were that easy. She didn't dare tell him that she still hoped her parents would change and want to spend time with her just because they loved her.

Archer's eyes remained trained on her. "Especially not people who devalue your dreams."

She hadn't realized he'd been listening so closely to the things she'd told him. The painful truth in what he'd said hit hard, and she didn't know how to react. She had the strange urge to defend her parents. *She* had a right to say those things, but hearing him say them felt a little like a betrayal, and *that* was messed up. It was all too much, and she didn't have time to digest or dissect it, so she stepped out of his grip, ignoring what he'd said altogether.

"Go get ready or you'll be late to take care of your boat." She knew his boat was everything to him, and she was counting on the fact that he wouldn't leave it in the water to be bullied by Mother Nature.

He grumbled, "Fuck it," under his breath, hauled her over his shoulder, and headed into the bathroom.

"*Archer!* I don't have time!"

"One way or another you're leaving here with a smile on your face."

She couldn't help but laugh. Freaking Archer. Everything was a competition.

And everything he did made her want more of him.

TO SAY THE Grand was opulent would be an understatement, with its mahogany walls, expensive chandeliers, and four-course brunches. The food was always perfectly prepared, the waiters knowledgeable and trained in the art of table service, and the barely there serenade of classical music underscored the elegance of the exclusive club's patrons. Indi and her family were seated at their usual table near the stone fireplace and beautifully draped windows. She sat across from her parents, between Meredith, who in this setting was as graceful and amiable as Indi was uncomfortable and outspoken, and Simon, their father's doppelgänger and protégé, who played the games their parents expected but used to be a secret goofball who snuck Indi out at night to run around the neighborhood with him. She missed those days.

Simon's wife, Anika, a leggy and poised former model, sat to his left. Meredith's children sat between her and her loving husband, Bruce. Chantal was sweet as sugar at seven with her father's shiny dark hair and hazel eyes, and Terrence, a rascal with a mop of untamable light brown curls and a giggle that made Indi's heart sing.

"We're thinking June is the perfect time to go..." Her mother was telling them about a trip to Greece they were planning with James's parents.

Indi had her mother's coloring, though her mother's hair was straight and cut just below her ears, and her soft blue eyes never looked at Indi the way most mothers looked at their daughters. She'd always been beautiful and carried herself like she was being watched, even when it was just the family in their home. Her father was classically handsome with sharp cheekbones, an angular nose, and more salt than pepper in his hair. He had an aristocratic air about him and turned heads wherever he went, but he only had eyes for her mother, as proven in the way he was gazing lovingly at her as she reminisced about the last time they'd visited Greece. Indi wondered what happened to that warmth when he turned those same eyes on her.

There was a time when Indi had idolized her parents and had wanted to be just like her mother. But she'd been only a child, dressed up and fawned over as they showed her off at events and dinners, and had mistaken the attention for love. That unsettling reality had hit when she was around six or seven and began noticing the difference in how she was treated at those events and when they walked in the door at night and in the time between events. She and her siblings had been taught to be respectful of adults, seen and not heard unless an approving nod from her father was given. As the youngest and only fair-haired sibling, Indi had always gotten the most attention. People commented on her big blue eyes and beautiful blond hair, how sweet she looked in her dresses, and how her parents should prepare themselves for a long line of suitors at a young age. By the time she was old enough to understand what they meant, her parents, and it seemed everyone around them, were already aligning her future with James's.

Indi fidgeted with her ring, her leg bouncing nervously under the table in her black slacks. As she slipped her feet out of her heels, Archer's voice trampled through her mind. *You're a ribs or tacos and mojito girl who licks her fingers when she's done eating and slips off her heels under the table when she thinks nobody's looking.* A little thrill ran through her at the secret she hadn't realized he'd noticed. He'd surprised her a lot these last twenty-four hours. He'd really stepped up yesterday, helping her at the event. She smiled at the memory of Archer applying moisturizer to the ladies' faces. The women had been all over him, and he'd been charming and suave, not his usual brash, unfiltered self. She'd never seen him like that, and if she thought he was appealing just the way he was, well, that side of him only drove the attraction deeper. She wondered what other hidden talents he was keeping locked within his badass self. Her mind trickled back to what he'd said about how they were alike, with fire in their bellies and a drive to create. It was funny. She'd thought they didn't have anything in common outside the bedroom. She was starting to realize how wrong she was.

"Indira, your mother asked you a question."

Her father's voice snapped her from her thoughts. Everyone was looking at her expectantly. Maybe she should have let Archer come to brunch. At least then she'd have someone in her corner. "I'm sorry. I didn't hear the question."

"That's okay, dear," her mother said. "We were wondering if you'd consider joining us in Greece."

A flutter of cautious hope rose inside her. "You want me to go with you?"

Meredith shot her a warning glance, as if she knew something Indi didn't.

"Yes," her mother said. "I happen to know that James will be there for at least two weeks of our stay, and he asks about you quite often."

I should have known. James hadn't said anything to her about the trip when they'd met for coffee, but it wasn't like she'd given him the chance. She'd told him flat out when she first sat down that she would always care for him, but she was not interested in anything more. He'd been disappointed but hadn't pushed it. Now she tried to quell her irritation, but there was no holding back. "Is that supposed to make me *want* to go? I've told you a hundred times that we're not getting back together."

"I know, Indira, but I just don't see why not," her mother insisted. "You two are so good together."

"We're good *friends*, but that's it. I want *more*. Why can't you understand that?" *Do I have to spell this out for you? I want to be with someone like Archer, who is spontaneous and challenges me in and out of the bedroom.*

Her father said, "We just want what's best for you."

"If that were true, you wouldn't be pushing James on me. You'd support my career and my dreams."

"Mom, Dad, I think Indi knows what's best for herself," Meredith said in a way that was both careful and firm, and Indi knew it wasn't easy for her to stand up to their parents.

"I agree." Simon smiled supportively at Indi. "If she's not into James, I can set her up with another of my single friends. I know lots of great guys."

"Ohmygod," Indi muttered. "I don't *need* a man. What I need is—"

"Mama, who is *he*?" Chantal asked.

They all followed her stare, and Indi's thoughts skidded to a halt. Archer was striding toward the table, stone faced, eyes locked on Indi, still wearing his leather bomber jacket, jeans, and work boots. Her pulse sprinted. What the heck was he doing there? Everyone was watching him, probably wondering how he'd gotten past security, given the strict jacket-and-tie dress code.

As he approached the table, her parents' confusion morphed to appalled expressions. Her siblings looked curiously between them, Anika eyed Archer appreciatively, and Terrence practically shouted, "He's as big as the Hulk!"

Indi gulped air into her lungs, wondering what she'd done to deserve this kind of hell.

ARCHER WAS FULLY aware of being scrutinized by every overdressed person in the place, but the only one he gave a damn about was Indi, who had been deep in conversation with her parents and had looked like she'd been spitting nails when he'd walked in. Now she looked like she'd like to spit those nails at *him*.

"Sorry I'm late, darlin'. I had to take care of a few things." One phone call to Leni had given him an earful about Indi's parents and all the ammunition he needed to put them in their places. Not only did he have to research Indi's business, but the storm had gained strength overnight and had already earned a name. Winter Storm Agador was barreling up the coast and would hit the island by nightfall. He should have gone home to get his boat out of the water, but instead he'd called his buddy, boatbuilder Brant Remington, to secure his boat until he could get there. His father, Roddy, ran the marina. Archer knew his boat was in good hands. He leaned down and kissed Indi's cheek, whispering, "You didn't think I'd let you face the firing squad alone, did you?"

"I thought I said you didn't have to come," she said through a forced smile. "I thought you had other plans."

"Nothing comes before you, babe." If looks could kill, he'd be flat out right now, but he didn't care.

"Indi, aren't you going to introduce us to your friend?" asked the wholesome-looking, freckle-faced brunette with a mass of curls, who could only be Meredith.

"How come *he* doesn't have to wear a tie?" the curly haired little boy chimed in, and Meredith quickly shushed him.

"I'm Archer, Indi's occasional assistant." He ignored the dark look Indi was giving him and smiled at her sister. "You must be Meredith. I've heard a lot about you. It's too bad you didn't have a chance to pursue law school. Indi said you'd make a great attorney, but it looks like you've been blessed with something much better than legal briefs." He looked at her adorable little girl wearing a pretty pink dress. "You must be Chantal, the best big sister in the world."

"Yes, sir." Chantal beamed at him.

"That's *Archer* to you, little lady. *Sir* would be my father." Archer walked over to the little boy who looked far too uncomfortable in dark slacks, a dress shirt, and a bow tie and held out his fist. "Touch your fist to mine, buddy. That's called a fist bump. It's what *cool guys do.*"

Terrence grinned, hand fisted, and glanced at his father, who nodded his approval. The curly haired boy touched his tiny fist to Archer's, and Archer said, "Attaboy, Terrence."

Bright eyed and smiling, Chantal held up her fist. Archer chuckled and touched his fist to hers. *"Nice."* The approving glance Meredith shared with Indi didn't go unnoticed. "You have a beautiful family, Bruce." Archer shook his hand, loving the shock in Indi's parents' faces and the softening of Indi's beautiful blue eyes as he moved around the table to greet her brother and sister-in-law, putting his hands on their shoulders. "Simon, Anika, congratulations on your pregnancy. Family can be *such* a blessing."

"Thank you." Simon gave his wife's hand a squeeze.

Only *then* did Archer turn to Indi's parents, showing them that he didn't find them more important than the others, and he sure as hell wasn't going to try to impress them.

Her father pushed to his feet, an air of *why is this working-class man interrupting our brunch* wafting off him. He was a few inches shorter than Archer, with narrow shoulders, condescending eyes, and dressed in a suit that probably cost a few grand. Clearly aware that all eyes were still on them, her father extended his hand. "Sy Oliver."

Archer shook it, impressed with the old man's grip, and nodded at Monica, Indi's mother, but he remained tight-lipped. He wasn't about to lie and tell her parents it was a pleasure to meet the people who made Indi feel like she wasn't *enough.* "You have a very talented and kind daughter, and it is an honor to watch her in action." He cast a coy grin at Indi, whose eyes widened. *That's right, babe. It's an honor with and without our clothes on.*

"You're Indira's *assistant?"* Sy looked curiously at Indi as a waiter set another chair and place setting beside her.

"That's right, among other things." Archer could practically feel the floor shaking from the force of Indi's bouncing knee.

"May I take your jacket, sir?" the waiter asked. "Shall I bring you a menu?"

Archer shrugged off his jacket and handed it to him. "No menu, thank you." He sat down, eyeing Indi. "I'll share with this sweet darlin'."

"You mentioned *other things*? Are you two…?"

Archer said, "Yes," at the same time Indi said, "No."

Her sister stifled a laugh, her brother looked concerned, and her parents did nothing to hide their displeasure or their confusion.

Archer covered Indi's hand with his, giving it a reassuring squeeze. "We don't like people to know we occasionally mix business with pleasure."

Indi's eyes narrowed, but she turned a confident smile on her parents. "What he means is, we've been on a date or two."

"I see," her mother said disapprovingly. "Is he the reason you don't want to go to Greece?"

"Greece?" Archer held her mother's uncomfortable gaze.

"Yes, a good friend of hers may be going to Greece with us this summer, and we'd like her to come along."

He looked to Indi for an explanation.

"She's talking about James." The irritation in her voice was palpable.

"Ah, yes. The husband-material guy."

"Ohmygod." Indi closed her eyes for a beat and reached for her glass of water.

Sy cleared his throat. "Indira and James went out for a very long time."

"Yeah, she told me." Archer draped an arm across the back of Indi's chair. "But she's done with him. Why drive a Lexus when you can take a spin in a Bentley. Am I right, darlin'?"

Indi nearly spit out the water she was drinking and covered her mouth as she composed herself. "I've told them that James and I are not well suited for the long term."

"That's one way to put it." Archer shifted his attention to her father. "But even if she wanted to go with you to Greece, I don't know how she'd fit it in with her new endeavor." Indi glowered haltingly, but he would not be deterred. It was time she took control of this situation with her parents, and he was just the person to nudge her in the right direction. "Have you told them your exciting news yet?"

"Not yet," she said through gritted teeth.

"News?" her father asked.

Her siblings sat forward in their chairs, their gazes moving between Indi and Archer as if the news pertained to *them*. Worry wrinkled Indi's brow, her leg bouncing faster beneath the table.

Archer placed his hand on her thigh, stilling it, and gazed deeply into her eyes. "It's the most spectacular news I've heard all year. Tell them, darlin'."

Her beautiful, worried eyes moved over her sister and her husband, who looked eager to hear her news, and Simon and Anika. Simon appeared concerned, while Anika merely looked curious. Indi glanced nervously at Archer, and he nodded in encouragement. She straightened her spine as she met her parents' scrutinizing gazes. Archer squeezed her thigh, knowing she had it in her to stand her ground but also knowing firsthand how it felt to go up against his own parents.

"I've signed a lease for retail space and an apartment on Silver Island. I'm going to open a boutique, and I'll be moving there in late February."

Archer wanted to cheer the confidence in her voice, but he

was too busy watching her parents exchange a glance that clearly translated to *not this again*. His muscles tensed, and he reminded himself that ten seconds could save Indi some grief.

"Surely you're kidding," her father said.

One...two...

"Why would she kid about something like that?" Meredith asked supportively.

Three...

"*Indira*," her father said sharply. "I will never understand this rebellious streak of yours, but this just proves what I've always thought. You are not well suited to run a business. No businessperson in their right mind would move from the most profitable business hub in the US to an *island* to open a business unless they were selling surfboards, and even then it's questionable."

Motherfucker. Archer's hands curled into fists. *Four...*

Indi looked like she might cry, but she lifted her chin confidently and said, "I'm sorry that you believe I'm unfit and that you see my choices as rebellion."

"I'm with Dad on the move, sis," Simon said. "Silver Island is nice, but it's not going to offer you the same year-round income you'd get in the city. Have you run the numbers?"

Six...seven...

"She'll never find a worthy husband on an island, either," her mother added condescendingly.

Fuck it. As her father opened his mouth to speak, Archer cut him off, ignoring her mother's ridiculous comment for the moment. "You're a successful businessman. I find it hard to believe that you don't know the difference between rebellion and determination, which tells me that your eyes have been closed to your daughter for a very long time. Did you know that within the first year of business Indi signed Bergdorf's, Nordstrom, *and* Neiman Marcus to carry her products? Or that she negotiated unprecedented discounts with her distributor and her manufacturer?"

"Archer." Indi touched his arm. "Just let it go."

"No. They need to hear this." He turned his attention back to her parents. "Do you even *know* your daughter? Have you bothered to ask Indi *why* she's so passionate about skincare and cosmetics? She's more than a pretty face. She's a brilliant, capable woman. Has it even crossed your mind that your daughter might not be interested in finding a husband right now?"

Her father seethed. "How dare you come in off the streets to interrupt our family gathering and speak to us like that."

"I realize you're not used to people being blatantly honest with you, but someone has to open your eyes before you lose your daughter altogether. She's twenty-eight years—"

"Twenty-nine," Indi interrupted.

Shit. "She's an adult. She doesn't need your permission to build a business or move out of the city, or anything else. But it sure as hell would be nice for her to get your support."

Her father pointed across the table. "You don't know a damn thing about this family."

"I've seen all I need to know." Archer pushed to his feet, softening his tone for the children, who looked frightened, which only added to the piles of guilt on his shoulders. "I'm sorry, kids, but life isn't always pretty. Sometimes you have to stand up for friends and speak the truth loudly just to be heard." He turned to Indi. "Let's get out of here, darlin', unless you want to continue dodging barbs and justifying your dreams to deaf ears."

Indi looked nervously around the table, but he saw her gathering strength from Meredith's supportive nod as she pushed to her feet and lifted her chin.

Her father's eyes narrowed. "Indira, *sit down*. We are not done speaking with you."

Archer leveled him with a dark stare. "You haven't even begun speaking to her. You've only spoken *at* her, like a bully." He put a hand on Indi's back as she hurried out of the restaurant, collected their coats, and headed outside. Clouds had moved in, bringing gusts of wind and spitting rain, but he felt the impending storm.

"I can't believe you did that." Indi stalked away from the entrance and paced, pulling her coat tight around her. "I shouldn't have left. Nobody walks out on my father."

"That's why he bullies people. He'll respect you more for standing up for yourself and walking out than he would if you'd stuck around and let them browbeat you."

"You don't know my father. What if you're wrong?" Her eyes teared up. "You aren't exactly a relationship guru."

He gritted his teeth against the pain those tears brought. "You're right. I suck at relationships, but I know bullies, and the only way to stop them is to stand up to them."

She paced. "You might have just cost me my family."

"Damn it, Indi. Nobody held a gun to your head. You could have stayed." He didn't mean to snap, but he was pissed at himself for going off and furious with her parents for the shitty way they treated her. Thunder roared, and she looked up at the darkening sky. He went to the curb to hail a cab. "I'm not *James* or another one of your father's cronies. If you think I'd sit back and watch them berate you, then you don't know me at all."

"I didn't *ask* you to come here."

"No shit." As a cab pulled over, he bit back, *Just because you won't ask for help doesn't mean you don't need it.* "I'm sorry for how that played out, but it had to be said." He opened the cab door just as the skies gave way to driving rain and helped her into the car. "Winter Storm Agador is supposed to hit the coast by nightfall. Get home and stay there."

"How're you getting back to the island?" Her eyes widened. "Ohmygosh. Your *boat.* Archer, you shouldn't have come."

He ground his back teeth together. He'd never left his boat in someone else's hands. But going back to Silver Island would have been trying to outrun one storm to protect the only material possession he'd ever cared about, when every iota of his being had wanted to plow headfirst into another storm, to protect the woman who was starting to matter even more.

"I wanted you to know that someone had your back." He closed the door, and as the cab pulled away from the curb, a beautiful mix of conflicting emotions stared back at him.

Chapter Seven

"YOU SHOULD HAVE seen our parents' faces when Archer blew through the restaurant and kissed Indi's cheek like they'd been dating forever. I'm sure I looked just as floored as they did. I mean, she could have clued *me* in." Meredith sat back in her wool slacks and pristine blouse, smiling at Indi. It was late Wednesday afternoon, and they were in Leni's office, filling her in on what had gone down at brunch, before discussing marketing plans for the boutique.

Indi hadn't heard a word from her parents, but Meredith had called Sunday evening to make sure she was okay, and they'd talked for a long time. Indi had nearly cried when Meredith told her she'd support her in any way she could.

"But the way he stood up for Indi..." Meredith sighed, pressing her hand to her chest. "I've never seen anything like that. I love my husband, and he's very masculine, but your brother is *all* man."

Indi's chest constricted thinking about Archer. She hadn't heard from him since he'd sent her off in the cab. She knew he had to get back to the island and take care of his boat, but in the days since, he hadn't even sent one dirty text. He'd never gone two days without texting her. She'd thought he couldn't stand the idea of her *not* thinking about him—out of sheer arrogance, of course. But now she wasn't sure what to think.

"I thought our father was going to blow his top when Archer called him a bully," Indi added.

"He'd never cause more of a scene like that," her sister pointed out. "But as I told you, after you left the restaurant, he complained to the manager for letting Archer in and found out exactly who Archer really is. I know you said he was a winemaker, but I had no idea he was a world-renowned vintner, and Dad was clearly floored by that information. He swept the whole thing under the table and ordered brunch like nothing had happened."

"Archer may not look the part, but he's the best there is. Indi, have you heard from your parents?" Leni asked.

"No, but you know how they are. They're waiting for me to apologize or tell them I changed my mind or something. But that's not going to happen."

Leni's expression warmed. "I'm sorry it's always so hard with them. I think they mean well, even if their beliefs are so far out in left field, I can't even pretend to understand them. Honestly, if you'd let me, I'd have given them a piece of my mind years ago."

"For years I've told myself that they just see things differently than we do," Meredith said. "I've rationalized their behavior, but they've gotten worse with Indi."

Leni looked at Indi. "Whatever you said to Archer about them must have really ticked him off."

"To be honest, I didn't know he'd listened so carefully. I still can't get over Archer telling them he was my assistant. I kept wondering if our parents would figure out who he really was, but then I realized he never said his last name."

"Of course he didn't," Leni said. "My brother doesn't believe in using his success to gain the upper hand. But I have to admit, when you mentioned he'd said that, it threw me for a loop. Knowing Archer, he meant it sexually, like he's your orgasm assistant."

Indi laughed. "Any other time, I'd say you were right. But it was partially true. When he showed up to apologize on Saturday, I was on my way to an event and they'd added three extra clients to my schedule, so I was nervous about getting them done on time. Archer dropped me off and showed up fifteen minutes later with three bottles of wine, laying on the charm like he'd been working as my assistant for years. It was quite a sight, actually, seeing him like that instead of all arrogant and playboyish. And he prepped the women's skin for me. You never told me that he knew about moisturizers and makeup."

Leni chuckled. "You can thank Jules for that. She's had him wrapped around her finger since she was a little girl. There's nothing he wouldn't do for her. And as far as standing up to your dad goes, if anyone knows how to handle a bully, it's Archer. He acted like one for years after the accident. Try navigating holidays when your brothers aren't talking to each other. We told you about that, right, Mare?"

"Mm-hm." Meredith nodded.

Indi thought about the rift between Jock and Archer often, wondering if it would be easier to just stop talking to her parents. But she knew how hard it had been on Leni and the rest of his family, and she wouldn't want to do that to her siblings or niece and nephew.

"Thank God Jock finally got sick of his shit and had it out with him. Archer doesn't avoid family get-togethers anymore, and even though he'll always be gruff, at least anger no longer billows off him like the wind." Leni sat back and crossed her legs, looking professional in a black skirt and pale-blue blouse. "More importantly, since when does my brother spend the night at your apartment?"

"He *doesn't*," Indi insisted. "It was a one-time thing. He showed up to apologize for acting like a jerk when he found out I'd signed the lease, and one thing led to another. You know how he is."

Leni cracked a grin. "I know how you two are *together*. Heck, anyone within a ten-mile radius of you two can see the sparks."

"I can attest to that," Meredith added. "The way Archer went all Johnny Castle and 'Nobody puts Baby in a corner' on my parents, I think there's a lot more going on than Indi is owning up to."

"There's not," Indi and Leni said in unison.

"Trust me, my brother isn't the kind of guy that'll ever settle down. But he is a fighter. He stands up for what he believes in, and he protects the people he cares about." Leni's brows knitted. "Although, he's never left his sacred island to pursue a woman as far as I know, and yet he came all that way just to apologize to you." She crossed her arms, drumming her fingers on her forearm.

"We're talking about *Archer*. He came for sex." Even as Indi said it, she didn't fully believe it.

"Women flock to him like moths to a flame," Leni reminded her. "Do you really think he had to come *here* to get laid? Archer *never* leaves the island."

"That's not true. You told me that when you came here for college, he took you all around the city to make sure you knew where everything was so you wouldn't be nervous or get lost."

Indi remembered how proud Leni had been when she'd told her that. It was right after Indi had first met Archer, when she'd made a comment about him being a bit of a jerk. Leni had agreed but had followed it up by giving her a diatribe about all the wonderful things he'd done for her and her siblings.

"He did," Leni said. "But when is the last time you saw him visit me or heard about him visiting Sutton or Levi?" Her older sister, Sutton, was a reporter and lived in Port Hudson, New York.

"It's been a long time since I've been single," Meredith said, "but even I know that booty calls don't include helping you at work or a showdown with your family. He obviously wasn't here just to have sex."

"Well, considering I haven't heard from him, I'm pretty sure he won't be coming back." That probably shouldn't have bothered her as much as it did. Even more so than her parents' behavior. It was normal for them, but this wasn't typical for Archer. Was he angry that she'd said he shouldn't have come to brunch or that he'd shown up at all instead of taking care of his boat? She hoped it wasn't damaged in the storm, which hadn't been as bad as the weather reports had predicted, but there was some flooding along the coast. Maybe he was sidetracked with the boat or the winery. Or maybe they were finally over.

Her stomach knotted.

Wasn't that what she wanted? To protect her reputation when she moved to the island? That's what she needed to do, but she hated the way they'd left things. "I should thank him."

"For not coming back?" Leni asked.

Indi blinked several times, realizing she'd said it aloud. "For standing up to my family. I was in shock when we walked out, and I didn't exactly leave things on an appreciative note."

"Well, you'll be on the island in two days. I'm sure you'll see him then." Leni pushed a folder across the table. "But now that I'm all caught up on Sunday's nightmare, it's almost six, and I have a dinner meeting with a client at seven thirty, so let's go over the ideas I have for marketing your new boutique and talk about schedules."

They went over mock-ups of revisions to Indi's website, online advertisements, flyers, and pamphlets to distribute to other businesses on the island. "I was also thinking about your social media posts. You do a great job of creating valuable content, but now that you'll have a boutique, I think we should kick it up a notch. Bellamy has more than a million followers, and she's working with several of my clients to market their clothing, shoes, and other products, but she hasn't signed a skincare or cosmetic sponsor yet."

"Who's Bellamy?" Meredith asked.

"Bellamy Silver. I've told you about her," Indi reminded her. "She's a lifestyle influencer, and Jules's best friend. The cute brunette who works part-time for Jules and wants to go on a reality show."

"Oh, yes." Meredith shook her head. "I must be getting old. Why anyone would want to do a reality show is beyond me."

"For some people, it's a great way to get discovered," Leni explained. "But Bellamy has lived a pretty sheltered life. I don't believe it's the right fit for her."

"Her brothers would *never* let her do it, anyway," Indi said. "I can see Grant, Wells, and Fitz locking her in an attic, like Rapunzel. I don't even think Keira would let her do it. She's a supportive big sister, but she's sworn off men. There's no way she'd let Bellamy put herself out there like that."

"Exactly. Grant took the bull by the horns and sent her to

me. I've been expanding her sponsorships in new directions."
Leni's eyes lit up. "She's on the cusp of something big. I can feel
it. I think she's perfect for the face of Indira. She's beautiful,
naturally engaging, articulate, and her skin is flawless."

"That's because she's been using my products for three
years," Indi said proudly.

"And that makes her talking up your products even more
believable," Leni exclaimed.

Indi's mind raced with ideas. "If she agrees to be the face of
Indira, can we get close-ups to put on the walls of the boutique
and use her pictures in brochures? I should have samples of my
spring cosmetics line early next week. The timing is perfect."

"*If* she agrees? You're offering to make her a name in the
skincare and cosmetics industries. She'll be thrilled." Leni jotted
something down in her notebook. "We can give her a quick call
to gauge her interest, if you'd like."

"Yes! If you have time."

Leni pulled out her phone. "There's always time to put a
deal together." She held up her index finger as she made the
call. "Hi, Bellamy. I'm sitting here with Indi and her sister,
Meredith." Leni paused, then said, "Bellamy says hi."

"Hi," Indi and Meredith said in unison.

Leni spoke into the phone. "Indi is going to be opening a
boutique down the street from Jules's shop." She paused,
listening. "Of course you do. I bet everyone on the island knows
by now. Indi has an exciting offer for you. How would you like
to be the face of Indira?"

Bellamy shrieked so loud, Leni pulled the phone away from
her ear, and they all laughed. Indi did a little happy dance and
hugged Meredith.

"Great," Leni said. "I'll get back to you with all the contractual details, but Indi is coming to the island Friday to get things going, and we'd love to schedule photo shoots for marketing materials. What's your availability over the next few weeks?" She took notes as she listened.

When Leni ended the call, Indi ran around the desk to hug her. "Thank you! It makes me so happy to use someone we know." She went back to her chair. "Uh-oh. Something just dawned on me. Are you sure I can afford her? I should have asked before you called."

"I wouldn't have called if you couldn't afford to hire her," Leni said. "We'll have to craft a solid deal, because once the press release goes out announcing her as the face of Indira, her sponsorships will go up tenfold."

"Wow, really?" Meredith asked.

"Yes. Skincare and cosmetics sponsorships are some of the most lucrative. But don't worry, this is her springboard. It won't be too pricey. It's the *next* contract that will pay out the nose— once she's gained an even bigger audience. Her promotional posts are fairly expensive, but the return on investment has been outrageous for most of my clients, and her demographics are perfectly in line with Indira's. There are no discounted sponsorships, because each one builds on the next, but I think we can get a discount on posts, since she's practically family now that Jules and Grant are engaged."

"I don't want to pull those kinds of favors. If you say she's worth it, I'll pay the going rate."

"It's Silver Island," Leni said flatly. "She'll be offended if you don't pull favors when you can."

Meredith arched a brow. "The island sounds a lot friendlier than New York."

"What have I been telling you for the last few years?" Indi

loved many things about the island, but the people were at the top of the list.

"You'll see for yourself at Indi's grand opening. I'm planning an extravaganza like no other."

"You are?" Indi shouldn't have been surprised. Leni was always two steps ahead of her. "I don't know when I'll be opening the boutique. I'm hoping by April, but I'll have a better idea once I get a handle on the build-out. I left a message for Levi to see if he can do a walk-through with me soon to discuss the renovations. I want to talk with him about what to expect before I hire someone local."

"That's smart, and you know he'll push you to the top of his priority list," Leni said. "He's excellent at space design, and he'll make sure you know what to expect. It's too bad you won't be open for Winter Walk two weeks from Saturday."

"What's Winter Walk?" Meredith asked.

"It's something Silver Haven retailers started a few years ago to keep tourism up after the holidays," Leni explained. "It's like a beefed-up, hyped-up sidewalk sale. It's turned into a major event, with live music and special games and events for the kids. People come from all over the island for it. Jules hires three extra people to help for the weekend because she does twice as much business as usual. She was worried about being away with Grant this time, but she comes home late Saturday night, so she'll be there on Sunday."

Meredith looked at Indi and said, "That sounds like too big of an opportunity to miss out on."

"I'm thinking the same thing. I forgot about Winter Walk. The boutique won't be open, but I can set up tables and give out samples and cards with my website information so people can order online, and I can sell my starter packs. They're perfect for something like that. I'll put in an order today." Indi pulled out her phone and added it to her to-do list.

"That's a great idea. The same people come back year after year for island events. It'll be a good time to get to know some of them." Leni looked over her notes. "Tara usually takes pictures for the Silver Island website and the local newspaper for that event. I'll make sure she takes some of you so we can use them in marketing pieces. And speaking of Tara, she's been doing all of Bellamy's local photo shoots, and she's absolutely amazing. Are you okay with hiring her to take your promo shots of Bellamy? They work really well together."

"Sure." Indi turned to her sister. "Tara is the mayor's daughter. I've told you about her. She's friends with Jules and Bellamy."

"Give me more." Meredith wiggled her fingers.

"She's the cute blond freelance photographer who I think has a thing for Leni's twin, Levi."

"She *definitely* has a thing for my brother, although she'll never admit it," Leni agreed. "Talk about a reality show. She and Levi are one in the making. But that's another story."

"Wait." Meredith held her hand up. "You can't say something like that and not explain it. It sounds juicy, and I never get juicy gossip."

"It's complicated, so listen carefully because we're on borrowed time," Leni warned. "Levi had his daughter, Joey, with Tara's older sister, Amelia, but Amelia didn't want to give up pursuing her career as a travel writer to be a mom, although she loves Joey to pieces. Tara has always been a big part of Joey and Levi's life, even though they live in Harborside, not on the island."

"Basically, Levi's a single dad, and we all think Tara would like to change that," Indi added.

Confusion riddled Meredith's brow. "Okay, but why would her sister have to give up pursuing a career just because she had a child? Plenty of mothers work."

"They were really young. It's complicated." Leni softened her tone. "I don't mean to rush us through this, but we need to get back to nailing down the marketing and advertisements before my next meeting."

"Sorry," Meredith said.

"No worries. Believe me, if I had more time, I'd grab a bottle of wine, draw you a family tree, and let you in on *all* the island gossip. But we're on a deadline. So that'll have to wait." Leni glanced at Indi. "Let's talk trends. Women are going crazy for how-to videos right now. I was thinking we could do a series of short videos where you do Bellamy's skincare routine or makeup for different occasions and walk the viewer through the process. I was also thinking about getting a model in her forties or fifties, so we cast a wider net."

Indi loved that idea. "That's perfect. Age and lifestyle have a big impact on our skin, and our routines have to change with it."

"I don't know much about marketing," Meredith said. "But as a thirty-four-year-old mother of two, I'm lucky to get a shower some mornings, and by the end of the night, the last thing I want to do is spend half an hour on a facial routine. If Indi hadn't shown me how to do my face in five minutes or less, I'd be a mess. Couldn't you do special videos for moms, and maybe use regular women instead of flawless models?"

"I *love* the idea of a series just for moms, but there are bene-fits to using influencers other than their looks. Actors, models, and other influencers typically have enormous followings, which helps expand Indi's market to people she'd have a hard time reaching otherwise."

"Why can't we do both?" Indi asked. "Use professionals, as you suggested, but also include regular women in the series. We wouldn't be losing any marketing opportunities, and we might actually increase exposure by word of mouth to people who don't follow influencers. I wonder if we could feature women from Silver Island, like your mom and her friends, or your grandmother. Do you think they'd consider something like this?"

"I think they'd do anything for you." Leni jotted down notes. "Plus, we can cross-promote some of the local businesses by featuring the women who work there. We might even be able to share the marketing costs. I bet Margot Silver would be interested. Not that the Silver House needs more marketing, but she loves to promote local businesses, and you know Jules and Keira would do it."

"I think we're onto something." Indi turned to her sister, getting more excited by the second. "Mare, would you consider doing the mom series with me?"

"Me?" Meredith shrank back in her chair.

"*Yes.* It was your idea. *Please?* Unless you're afraid Mom and Dad will give you a hard time?"

"You know they will," Meredith said softly. "But I'll do it. If Archer can stand up for my little sister, I sure as heck should be doing a better job of it."

Tears sprang to Indi's eyes. "Really?"

"Absolutely. I just want you to be happy."

Indi hugged her, her heart soaring. "Thank you."

"Why do girls *always* cry?" Leni teased, and they laughed. "Now that *that's* settled, how would you feel about having

Bellamy do a photo shoot of a yacht scene in early spring, wearing a cozy sweater to make women dream about snuggling with a man, and reel in the yacht clubbers?" Her eyes flicked to Indi. "I know a guy you can probably convince to let you use his yacht."

Considering I haven't heard from Archer, I wouldn't count on using anything of his in the future. She kept that to herself and said, "You've never steered me wrong, so I'll do whatever you think is financially feasible. Do you know if Archer's boat survived the storm?"

"Beats me, but if it didn't, we'd probably hear him raging from here." Leni chuckled.

As Leni went over more ideas, budgets, and timelines, Indi's mind lingered on Archer, guilt and longing twining together into a painful knot. He'd put himself out there for her more than once without concern for his boat, his reputation, or anything else. She wasn't ready for him to walk away.

She pulled out her phone and sent him a quick text. *Hey stranger.*

His response was immediate. *What's up?*

Her nerves flared at the curtness of his answer. She typed, *Are you busy?*

She glanced at the ad copy Leni put in front of her but couldn't concentrate as another text rolled in. *Just thinking about all the things I want to do to you.* He added a devil emoji.

Relief and excitement swept through her as she thumbed out, *I'm sorry for getting upset. Thank you for standing up to my family. When I didn't hear from you, I figured you were mad at me.*

Another message popped up. *I was giving you time to cool off before showing up on your doorstep.*

Her smile morphed to a smirk as she thumbed out, *What were you planning on doing once you got here?*

"Who are you texting?" Leni asked.

Indi jerked her attention from her phone to Leni and Meredith. "Sorry. I was just"—*flirting with your brother*—"answering a client." Her phone vibrated with another message. *I'll be there at eight to show you.* Heat slithered through her as another text bubble appeared. *Prepare to be naked and on your knees.*

So much for one last time…

Chapter Eight

ARCHER LOCKED UP the winery Friday night and climbed into his truck. He started it up, and the headlights illuminated the vineyard. The vineyard had always been special to him, but he wasn't thinking about anything except Indi at the moment. They'd disappeared into the vines to get away from the rest of the partygoers during his family's annual Field of Screams Halloween event. That was the night he'd found out just how much Indi liked to push the envelope. He'd wanted to take off for the boat, but she'd coaxed him into fooling around in the vineyard. And under the cover of night, with the din of other couples braving the Field of Screams in the distance, they'd had wild, passionate sex.

That was *hot*.

Almost as hot as Wednesday night, when he'd shown up at her place and she'd answered the door wearing a bathrobe. When she'd dropped the robe *and* her inhibitions, she'd stood before him naked, save for a pair of pink knee pads. They'd laughed as much as they'd fucked that night. In fact, he laughed a hell of a lot when they were together. With his mind on Indi, he pulled out his phone to see if she'd responded to the text he'd sent half an hour ago. He was worried about her. Had she heard from her family yet? Her parents pissed him off. If he thought it'd do any good, he'd go talk some sense into them, but he had a feeling nothing spoke to them but money and prestige.

Still no response.

Damn it.

As he drove out of the parking lot and headed to his parents' house to check out their leftovers from dinner, he wondered why his sexy little vixen wasn't returning his texts on a Friday night. She'd pulled the old *This is the last time; I have to protect my reputation* crap again, but they both knew she'd never stick to it. He didn't know why she even bothered saying it. But with three sisters, he knew better than to try to figure out women.

He drove down his parents' driveway and was surprised to see Tara and their niece Joey climbing out of Tara's car. Tara was a twiggy blonde, a real sweetheart of a girl, with a heart so full of Levi and Joey, there was no missing how much she cared about them. Tara waved.

As he climbed from the truck, Joey sprinted toward him in her purple down jacket and black leggings, her cinnamon hair bouncing around her pretty freckled face. She'd come a long way from the colicky infant Levi had brought home from the hospital. Levi had been only twenty years old, still living in their parents' house, and he was exhausted twenty-four-seven. Archer had left his boat and moved into his old bedroom for a couple of weeks to help his brother out. When Joey would wake up at night, he'd let Levi sleep and wear a path in the hallway with baby Joey on his shoulder. When she'd fall asleep, he kept walking for hours, night after night, because every time he'd set her down, she'd let out a blood-curdling wail.

"Uncle Archer! We're having a girls' night." Joey launched

herself into his arms. "We went skateboarding and had dinner at Monster Burger." She was a total tomboy. When she wasn't sporting biker boots and a fur-lined leather bomber jacket, she was wearing jeans and skater sneakers or sports jerseys and baseball caps. It kind of made sense, since Levi was a member of the Dark Knights motorcycle club in Harborside. Joey had grown up around big, burly bikers who all treated her like their daughter.

Archer ruffled her hair, holding her up with one arm. "I hope you wore a helmet."

"Aunt Tara won't let me skateboard without one."

"That's right." Tara smiled. "Hi, Archer."

"Hey, Tara. Where's Levi? I didn't know they were coming."

Before Tara could answer, Joey said, "Dad's with Indi, checking out her new store. I'm spending the night at Aunt Tara's, but we're having dessert with Grandma and Grandpa first. Want to have dessert with us?"

"I can't, sport," he said, chewing on the fact that Indi hadn't even told him she was coming to the island. He kissed her cheek and set her down, heading back to his truck.

"You're leaving?" Joey called after him.

"I need to take care of something. Sorry."

Archer drove to Main Street, getting more ticked off by the minute. He'd *thought* they'd had a phenomenal time on Wednesday night. Maybe even the best time they'd ever had, and she pulled this shit? Levi might be the right guy to check out her new space, but seriously? *He* was the one who'd tasted every inch of her body two nights ago, and she couldn't send a text saying she was going to be on the island? What the hell?

He counted down from ten to cool himself off as he parked

at the curb and blew through the doors of Indi's new retail space—*Seven, six, five*—

Three sets of eyes turned toward him, and jealousy obliterated every other thought. Indi stood in a curve-hugging sweater, skintight jeans, and knee-high leather boots between tall, dark, and cocky as hell Wells Silver, the owner of Rock Bottom Bar and Grill and Archer's friend—even though Archer had beat the hell out of him for cheating on his sister when she was in high school—and Ryan Lacroux, Silver Island's most lusted after police officer. Ryan lived next door to Jock and Daphne. He looked like a movie star, with short brown hair and chiseled features, and he was raising his drug-addicted brother's little boy, Ritchie. Archer swore single women saw that guardianship as an aphrodisiac, and he'd be damned if he'd let Indi be one of those women.

"What the hell is going on?" He closed the distance between himself and Indi, ignoring the smirks Wells and Ryan were exchanging.

"Dude…?" Levi walked over from the other side of the room. "How about a hello?"

Archer ignored them all, eyes locked on Indi. "Guess I didn't get my invitation to the party."

"Excuse us for a moment." Indi grabbed his arm, tugging him away from the others, whispering vehemently, "What is *wrong* with you?"

There was no calming this runaway train. "I was balls-deep in you two nights ago and you didn't think to let me know you were coming to the island? I gotta find out from my frigging niece and walk in on *this?*"

She gasped. Wells coughed to mask a laugh, and Levi murmured, "Oh shit. Come on, guys. Let's go measure the sidewalk."

As they hurried out of the store, Indi seethed, "What the hell do you think you're doing coming in here and talking to me like that?"

"I didn't say anything that wasn't true. Why didn't you let me know you were coming?"

She put her hand on her hip, eyes shooting daggers. "Why *would* I? Are you suddenly a renovations expert?"

"There's *nothing* I can't do." Jealousy clung to him like a second skin, fueling his anger. "I get why Levi is here, but do you really need a reverse harem?"

"A reverse—"

"Why'd you call Wells? You *know* he's dying to shine the floor with your back. And Ryan? *Really?* You don't even like pretty boys."

"You're such a jerk." Her hands curled into fists. "Wells was on his way to Rock Bottom to meet Keira and Fitz, and he stopped in to invite me, and for your information, Ryan just got off duty and was welcoming me to the island. It's what *nice* people do. Not every man thinks with his dick."

He spoke through gritted teeth. "If you think Wells doesn't want a piece of you, you're crazy."

A challenging grin slid across her face. "If I want to screw Wells, that's *my* business, not yours. In fact, if I want to sleep with every man in this town, there's not a damn thing you can do about it."

He loomed over her, leaning so close her breath became his. "That'll do wonders for your precious *reputation*."

"It couldn't do *half* the damage you could."

Archer's chest felt like it was going to explode. He *hated* the vile things he was saying, hated fighting with her at all, but he'd never felt like this before, and he had no idea how to handle it.

Levi opened the door and peered in. "Is it safe for me to come in, or are we hiding a body?"

Archer couldn't take it anymore. He gritted out, "She's all yours. I'm outta here," and took off before he did any more damage.

INDI SAW RED as Archer stormed out. She wanted to scream and tear something apart, but Levi was walking cautiously toward her, looking at her like she was a land mine and one wrong vibration might set her off. As Archer's brother, he must have had a lot of practice.

"Are you okay?"

"*No.* What is wrong with your brother?" She paced, trying to calm herself down. Why did she have to be attracted to the jerky brother? Levi was a big, handsome man. He was thoughtful and careful with people's feelings and a wonderful father. If she was smart, she'd be attracted to him instead of his explosive brother.

"What he said in front of us and how he said it was wrong. But he's a good man, Indi, and you don't strike me as the type of person who would've gotten close to him if you didn't know that."

"It's hard to remember *why* right now."

"I get that. But you've known him for years. You know *exactly* how he is. What you may not know is that he wasn't always like this. He's never backed down from a fight, but he didn't always cause them."

Indi crossed her arms, fighting tears of frustration as she met his sympathetic gaze. "Then why now? Why with me?"

"I haven't talked to him, so I don't know why he'd feel threatened by me and guys he's known forever."

She scoffed. "Archer is never threatened by anyone or anything."

Levi opened his mouth to speak, then clenched it shut without saying anything right away, his jaw tightening, much like his brother's, but not angrily. This was restraint. As if he was holding back his thoughts. "All I can tell you is that he must really care about you to lose his shit like that."

"You could have fooled me. That was embarrassing."

"For *both* of you," Levi pointed out. "Everyone thinks Archer is made of stone. But if you ask me, he just showed us he's human after all. You two obviously have something going on, and from what he said when he walked in, it sounds like you blew him off. This is the first time I know of that anyone has had the upper hand with him."

"I don't feel like I have the upper hand, and I don't want it. He said some awful things to me."

"I'm sorry he did that. He's a passionate guy, and he definitely needs to learn to think before he speaks, but for what it's worth, he hasn't exactly had many relationships to practice those skills."

"We aren't in a relationship."

"Well, I don't know which one of you is confused, because it sure seemed like there was something more between you."

She couldn't go there, because she'd been thinking the same thing the other night when Archer had come over and they'd had so much fun. They'd laughed, fooled around, ordered food for dinner, and then had made out some more. He hadn't stayed over, but the night had been as perfect as it could have been. "I'm sorry. I can't talk about this. I know you mean well, and I appreciate it. It's just…I have so much on my plate right now, I can't think straight, and I really need to get things going with this space."

"Of course. I think I've got all I need to work up an estimate. You said you want to do the painting yourself?"

"Yes. I love painting, and I want to feel like I'm part of the process, not just paying someone to get it done."

"That's great. I wish there were more people like you in the world. I think we're all set. I'll get the estimate to you tomorrow morning. What do you say we head down to Rock Bottom and take Wells up on those drinks?"

"I hope he has a pitcher of mojitos ready for me, because I'm going to need it."

Chapter Nine

ROCK BOTTOM BAR and Grill was located at the marina and offered a casual, rustic atmosphere with outdoor dining during the spring and summer, including dockside ordering for boaters. It was one of the hottest night spots on the island, and the place was hopping. Indi sat between Keira and Ryan at the bar while Levi and Fitz stood. Bellamy had been there for a little while, and they'd toasted their new partnership, but she'd taken off to spend time with Tara and Joey, and Wells was at the other end of the bar flirting with two very attractive women. She was glad the guys hadn't mentioned Archer's outburst. She didn't need everyone in the place knowing about what had happened.

Indi had hoped being there would distract her from her thoughts. But she was having no such luck. She should have known she'd have a shit day, since it had gotten off to a rough start. Simon had called to go over her lease, her finances, and her plans. She wanted to believe he was checking on her because he cared, but the way her parents had always treated her made her feel scrutinized and second-guessed, and the conversation had been stressful. She still hadn't heard from her parents, and when she'd told Simon that, he'd asked why it surprised her. He had a point. Her parents would go on pretending that last Sunday had never happened, and she just couldn't handle that. She needed to deal with them head-on, but she wasn't any more prepared for that than she'd been for Hurricane Archer to blow up in front of their friends.

How did their fun, no-strings arrangement get so complicated?

She couldn't stop thinking about the things Levi had said. Archer *was* a good man, but did good men say mean things to women? She knew the answer, because good women said mean things, too. Why couldn't she just let him go and move on? The pit of her stomach burned. There were plenty of eligible bachelors on the island. They may not make her heart race the way he did, but...

Ugh. What am I doing?

She spotted Wells heading their way, stopping to flirt with a cute brunette. *Men.* Were they always looking for something better?

Wells broke away from the brunette with a flirtatious touch of his hand on hers and headed for Indi and the others. "Hey, guys. Who's ready to celebrate our latest Silver Island transplant and business owner?" He put his hand on Indi's shoulder, holding up his glass. "Here's to Indi's new venture."

Indi clinked glasses with the others as they cheered and congratulated her.

"Thank you, but I have a long way to go." She sipped her mojito.

Fitz, another good-looking bachelor, held up his glass. He and Keira were fairer haired than their siblings, and while his other siblings had each branched out on their own, Fitz helped run the Silver House with his parents. "Here's to adding one more beautiful woman to our dating pool."

The guys toasted, while Keira and Indi exchanged an eye roll.

"Don't get too excited," Indi warned. "I'm staying on dry land for the foreseeable future." She hoped one day to have a family of her own, but not at the price of having someone telling her what to do or how to live. For now she had a boutique to kick off, an apartment to paint and move into, and at some point, a bridge to mend with her family. If that was even possible.

Keira bumped her with her shoulder. "Smart move, sister."

Indi looked across the room just as Archer came through the crowd, his broad shoulders wrapped in leather. He turned the head of nearly every woman in the place as he scanned the room, his dark eyes landing on *her*. Indi's pulse quickened. *Please come over and apologize. Get rid of these awful feelings.* His jaw tightened, a storm of anger and something that looked a lot like regret swimming in his eyes. But those eyes she knew so well, the eyes she saw in her bedroom late at night when she was alone with her thoughts, shifted away from her, and he headed to the other end of the bar, sidling up to the two women Wells had been flirting with earlier.

Hurt and anger warred within her as the women eyed him lasciviously. Archer lifted his chin, saying something that made them smile and share a *he's mine* glance between them. He called the bartender over, those dark eyes hitting Indi like bullets as he held up three fingers, ordering drinks. Her chest constricted, but the sting of his actions bullied past her bruised heart, and full-blown anger took over.

"Don't tell me Archer ruined you for all men." Wells leaned in and lowered his voice. "One night with me, and everything will look better in the morning."

She wanted to tell him that Archer didn't have that power, but she was too livid to say a word.

"Oh *please*." Keira pushed her light brown hair out of her eyes. "One night with you and she'll be hightailing it across the globe."

"If she does, it's only because I'm so hot it'll take Antarctica to cool her down." Wells high-fived Fitz.

Indi watched Archer doing shots with those other women while stealing glances at her. *Yeah, I see you, you big jerk.* She should take Wells up on his offer and show Archer that he didn't have a hold over her, but her stupid heart was still trying to climb over the hurt and anger, keeping her from doing anything else. He was the *only* man whose words had the power to rile her up like that, and that infuriated her even more.

Ryan nudged her, drawing her attention. "Not all men are like that. Some of us actually want a commitment and aren't afraid to show our feelings in a calm and rational way."

She didn't have the heart to tell him that she'd been with a man like that, and she'd been just as unhappy as she was tonight, but for different reasons. She tried not to look at Archer, telling herself she didn't care what he was doing. But she'd never been a good liar, and when it came to Archer, she had very little self-control. He was ordering another round, his piercing stare searing a path to her. She swallowed hard, willing herself to break their connection, but she was no match for the electricity arcing between them.

"Men are *all* dysfunctional in one way or another." Keira's voice broke through Indi's uncomfortable bubble. "Give me a cupcake over a guy any day."

Ryan leaned forward to see around Indi. "What do *you* have

against men?"

"Where should I start?" Keira sighed. "They're either too basic or obnoxiously aggressive, they all think they're better in bed than they really are, and…"

As Wells, Fitz, and Levi joined the debate of the pros and cons of the male race, Indi fought her own internal battle, trying to force her feelings for Archer away, but they flapped around her like a flock of birds, their wings slapping at her, unwilling to be deterred. She couldn't look away as Archer handed the girls shot glasses, then held his up and toasted with them, earning giggles and flirtatious smiles, their hungry eyes watching him as he downed his shot—his eyes darting back to Indi. She couldn't just sit there and watch him, and she sure as hell wasn't going to stoop to his level and start flirting with their friends just to get back at him.

She pushed to her feet. "I'm going to the ladies' room."

ARCHER WATCHED INDI moving through the crowd like a woman on a mission, while every asshole in the place checked her out. Fire burned in his chest, his hands curling into fists.

The brunette he'd bought shots for touched his shoulder. "How about we take this party back to our hotel room?"

"No thanks. I'm outta here." He tossed a few twenties on the bar and blazed a path through the crowd, catching up to Indi as she turned the corner, heading down the narrow hallway that led to the bathrooms and Wells's office. "Hey." He hadn't meant to bark at her, but his emotions were all over the map.

Indi spun around, her eyes shooting venom. "Leave me

alone."

"Don't you think I would if I could?" He closed the gap between them, his body brushing hers, pulse racing, heat thrumming between them despite their anger. "Do you think I *like* feeling like this? Being an asshole to you at all, much less in front of my brother and friends? You make me so fucking crazy I can't think straight."

"*I* drive *you* crazy? You make me insane, and the way you treated me today was—"

"It was *wrong*. It was shitty and uncalled for, and I'm surprised you didn't slap the hell out of me."

"Believe me, I *wanted* to."

"If I ever do that again, please grab the nearest bat and beat the hell out of me. I should *never* have disrespected you like that. I'm an asshole, Indi, and I'm so damn sorry."

"You *are* an asshole. Do you have any idea how it felt to have you tell everyone that we had sex?" Her lower lip quivered, but she lifted her chin defiantly. "You made me feel *cheap*."

That gutted him. He didn't think as he hauled her into his arms, heart hammering, emotions bleeding from his veins. "I'm so sorry. Cheap is the last thing I'd *ever* want you to feel."

"Then why'd you say all those things?" Her tortured eyes sliced through him.

"I don't know. I've been trying to figure that out, but everything about us is confusing. We're so fucking hot, so *good* together, and I know you think so too, but then every single time, you say it's the last time. I never believed it, and I didn't think there was any way in hell *you* believed it, either. But then I heard you were in town, and you didn't let me know you were coming, and when I saw you with the guys, I lost my mind. I thought maybe I'd fucked up, and you'd meant it this time."

"I *did* mean it. I meant it every time I said it, but then you text or call, and—"

A woman came out of the ladies' room, and he tightened his hold on Indi, unwilling to let her escape. He tugged her into Wells's office and locked the door. When he pulled out his phone and thumbed out a text, she glowered at him.

"If I'm interrupting your busy schedule, I'll leave." She reached for the door, but he grabbed her wrist.

"The hell you will. I was just texting Wells to let him know we're talking in here because we're not leaving this room until we figure this shit out." He pocketed his phone.

"*God*, Archer. How did we get here?" She paced, frustration wafting off her. "It was just supposed to be sex and fun, but then we started texting all the time, and I was sneaking back to the island, and you started showing up in New York, taking me out for dinner, staying over. I couldn't help but feel more for you despite knowing I shouldn't. Then last weekend, you didn't just step up for me; you held the *world* at bay. Nobody has ever done that for me before, and it made me like you even more, so I pulled away to keep from falling harder and getting hurt."

"You did the right thing. I know that in my head. I'm not looking for marriage and babies. Hell, I'm not even looking to be anyone's boyfriend, and I know you want all those things at some point down the line." He stepped in front of her, stopping her from pacing, his heart breaking at the conflicting emotions in her eyes. He knew he had too much guilt on his shoulders to be the man she deserved, and he should let her walk away, but he wouldn't do it. He *couldn't* do it. "But sometimes the right thing isn't the best thing. At least not for us right now. I don't know what we're supposed to be, but it's never been just sex and fun with you, and that makes me nuts, because I don't know what to do with it. But I know this. I hated being the last one to know you were on the island, and when it comes to you, I'm a jealous bastard. The thought of you with any other guy makes me want to kill someone."

"Do you think I like the idea of you being with other women?" she snapped. "That's why I wanted to end things when I got serious about moving to the island. You're right, I'm not looking for a boyfriend or a husband right now, especially not from you, but I also didn't want to be seen as your good-time girl and have everyone around here feeling sorry for me because you're out there sleeping around."

He gritted his teeth. "Then what the hell are we arguing for? I haven't been with anyone else since we first got together."

Her eyes narrowed.

"Why do you think I've been coming to the city? Because I like taking the fucking ferry?"

"You *really* haven't been with anyone else?" she challenged.

"That's what I just said, and you know I don't lie. Now, can we stop fighting and get to the makeup sex?"

She smiled and shook her head. "You're unbelievable."

"So you've told me." He cocked a grin. "I like it better when you're naked when you say it, but it's all good."

She rolled her eyes. "This is serious, Archer. Now that I know you're not sleeping around, I'd be into continuing our arrangement, but I don't want to do that if you're going to disrespect me the way you did earlier."

"No shit, darlin'. I've already caused enough hurt for a million lifetimes. The last thing I want to do is cause more, especially to you." The truth stung, but she needed to hear it, and he needed to say it. "I'll do everything within my power not to make that mistake again. But you know I'm messed up, Indi.

Everyone on this island knows it. I've made a career of making sure women don't catch feelings for me, and I sure as hell never caught feelings for any of them. I don't know how to deal with this shit. I've never been jealous a day in my life, but I was ready to rip Wells's arm off when he put his hand on your shoulder out there, and that's fucking wrong."

A soft laugh fell from her lips.

"You think that's *funny*?"

"Not the idea of you hurting Wells. Just that it sounds like you actually *like* me."

"What the hell does that mean? Have you been screwing me and thinking I *didn't* like you? I'm an asshole, but I'm not *that* asshole. And quite frankly, you're too good for that."

She stepped closer. "No, I mean you *really* like me."

A rush of relief brought a surge of emotions that nearly bowled him over. Trying to push past that rocky terrain and regain footing on familiar landscape he knew how to navigate, he grabbed her ass, pulling her against him. "I like *this*." He nipped at her neck. "And *that*."

She put her arms around his neck and went up on her toes, whispering, "Admit it. You like who I am, and that's a little scary for you."

He gritted his teeth. "Nothing *scares* me. Things piss me off, and I say shit that I instantly regret, but *never* out of fear. I want to learn not to do that with you, but short of a muzzle, I have no clue where to start."

She laughed. "Considering I like your mouth in *play*, it sounds like we need a safe word."

"What the hell are you talking about?"

Her fingers moved lightly down the back of his neck, taking the edge off the stone-guarded beast inside him. "We need a way to stop you in your tracks," she said, sweeter than he deserved. "Because I *won't* be the battleground for your crazies, but I will try to help you get them under control."

Relief that she wasn't kicking him to the curb hit hard. He hated that he needed help with a damn thing, but she didn't deserve any more outbursts, and for her, he'd gag himself if that's what it took. *"Fine."*

Her face brightened with his agreement, and damn, that twisted him up inside. "Okay. How about this? When you go off, I'll say *bananas*, and you have to stop no matter how mad you are."

He raised a brow. "Bananas?"

"Yeah. It fits perfectly for when you act like an ape."

"I'll give you a banana," he said with a laugh. He pulled her in for a kiss, but she put her hand on his chest, stopping him.

"Do we have a deal?"

"Yes. Now shut up and kiss me."

She giggled, and he sealed his mouth over hers, feeling like he could breathe for the first time since they'd argued. He kissed her ravenously, earning hungry moans and the press of her hot little body. When he deepened the kiss, she opened her mouth wider, allowing him to take more. He ground his hard length against her, and she was right there with him, moving as if she were possessed by a tide, meeting every rock of his hips with one of her own in a sensual rhythm.

"You drive me insane," he growled, backing her up against the wall.

"Same."

He crushed his mouth to hers, feeling her smile against his lips. Her greediness for him was like gasoline to their inferno. She was his sustenance, the only thing that had ever centered him, and he needed more. Needed a deeper connection as much as he needed air in his lungs. He kissed her more demandingly, pinning her arms above her head, and gripped both wrists in one hand. "*Yes,*" she urged as he pushed up her sweater and yanked the cup of her bra down, lowering his mouth over her breast.

She bowed off the wall. *"Archer."*

The plea in her voice was urgent, needful, and so fucking hot he sucked harder, earning a long, low moan that made his cock throb. He tore open the button of her jeans and pushed his hand into her panties, working that sensitive bundle of nerves that made her go wild.

She panted and rocked. "*Faster*…suck harder…*ohmyg—*"

He captured her cries in a possessive kiss, wanting *all* of her. Every sound, every scratch of her nails and greedy plea. As the last shudder rolled through her body, he quickened his efforts, sending her up to the peak again, and pushed his fingers inside her to feel every pulse of her climax. He loved the heat and taste of her, the way she let herself take and ask for pleasure. As she came down from the high, he released her wrists and tangled his hands in her hair, angling her mouth beneath his, meeting her hazy gaze for only a second before kissing her breathless. Because those beautiful eyes saw something in him that others didn't, giving her the power to do things to him he couldn't allow.

He got lost in her mouth, in her willingness to help him, and when she drew back, whispering his name, trusting and full of desire, it tugged at something deep in his chest, drawing his eyes to hers again. She could ask him to do just about anything right then, and he wouldn't think twice. But she didn't ask for anything. She just turned them so his back was against the wall and opened his jeans as she sank lower, whispering, "Watch me."

She dragged her tongue up the length of his cock, teasing over the broad head. Her eyes never left his as she fondled his balls with one hand and fisted his length with the other. She knew just how to make him lose his mind, those eyes drilling into him as she lowered her mouth over his shaft, working him like she loved every second of it as much as he did.

"*Christ*, Indi." He sank lower against the wall, allowing her to take him deeper.

What a sight she was, bold and beautiful, her delicate hand following her mouth, those gorgeous eyes locked on him. He fisted his hands in her hair, holding tight as he pumped his hips. He'd held back the first time she'd gone down on him, and she'd brazenly said if he ever did it again, it would be the last time she blew him. She grabbed his ass, eyes pleading for more. A growl rumbled up his chest as he thrust faster.

Appreciation bloomed on her cheeks. She matched his rhythm, tightening her grip, sucking harder, determined to make him lose his mind. He fucking loved that. Heat seared through his veins, muscles flexing as he fought off his release, wanting to savor every second of her touch and the sight of her pleasuring him. Those were only a few of the images he drew upon late at night when she was in the city and he was tied to the island. Then there were the sounds of his cock moving in and out of her lips, her moans and mewls. *Fuck*, he was going to lose it. She moved one hand to his balls and tugged just hard enough to shatter his control. He gritted out her name like a curse, clinging to her hair as he found his release and she took everything he had to give.

Victory shone in her eyes as she licked him clean and

dragged her finger along her glistening lower lip, then sucked it off. *Man*, she fucking owned him. He hauled her up to her feet, taking her in a rough kiss, fighting the feelings pounding through him. He chased them away, using his hand to make her come again, to hear his name wrapped in her pleasure, only it didn't chase them away. It drove those feelings deeper, made the ache for her more intense.

She collapsed against him, and he gathered her in his arms, breathing her in. Being with Indi stirred a torturous internal battle between what he felt and wanted and what he deserved. But the thought of being without her was even more brutal. He needed to take control of his runaway emotions, to bring this back to just sex, to reclaim the upper hand.

He brought his glistening fingers to her lips, painting them with her arousal, reveling in the challenge rising in her eyes as her tongue slid over the wetness. He crushed his mouth to hers, feeling her smile, as if she'd gotten exactly what she wanted. She challenged him on every level, and damn, he loved that.

He held her gaze as he closed her jeans and fixed her bra. "You're coming home with me."

"I was counting on it."

Chapter Ten

INDI WASHED THE shampoo from her hair as Archer stepped out of the shower and began toweling himself off. This was the first time she'd been in his three-bedroom cottage, and it felt nothing like his boat. Nothing like *him*. She watched him drying his chest and shoulders, pushing the towel down his stomach to the python between his legs. They'd already fooled around, and still her body pleaded for more. It wasn't only the thought of sex that was turning her on. It was the way he was watching *her*, the same way he'd looked at her last night and again this morning when they were lying in bed, like he was trying to figure something out, and she held the answers.

Or maybe like he'd made the biggest mistake of his life last night, confessing that he was jealous over her, and wondering if he should take it back. That was too uncomfortable of a thought, even though it was probably more accurate, so she clung to her first explanation.

He wrapped the towel around his hips, a slow grin curving his lips. "Keep lookin' at me like that and I'll be late for work."

"I don't know what you're talking about. I was admiring your choice of towels." She ducked her head under the water one last time, and he reached into the shower and smacked her ass. She glowered at him.

He walked out of the bathroom chuckling.

She heard him getting dressed as she finished her shower, grinning like a fool. After they'd jumped over those painful hurdles last night, creating new boundaries that didn't say they were a couple but gave her peace of mind, it was hard to remember that their arrangement couldn't lead to anything more. But he'd made that perfectly clear, and for now she was okay with it. She had too much on her plate to nurture a new relationship anyway, and why would she, when being with Archer gave her so much pleasure?

She dried off and wrapped a towel around herself, admiring his bathroom. It was nice, with a tile floor, a double sink, and a big shower. But the walls were white, the towels beige with starfish on them, and the faucets and cabinets were ivory and oak. She knew he rented it out during the spring and summer and stayed on his boat until the threats of storms and ice were too strong. But the cottage *felt* like a rental, not like his boat, which wasn't decorated with much more than a few family photos and blue and white accessories, but it felt rugged and nautical, like him. Even though he was a vintner, he always reminded her of a take-charge sea captain.

She finger-brushed her teeth and opened the cabinet below the sink in search of hair products or at least a hair dryer. Of course she didn't find either. Why would she? Archer was a guy's guy. She'd have to do her hair when she got to Jules's apartment. She flipped her head upside down and scrunched up her hair as best she could, then headed into the bedroom. The room was empty, the bed was neatly made, and there was no sign that they'd been there other than her phone sitting atop her clothes, which were neatly folded on the chair by the closet—

Archer's doing, not hers.

Several things suddenly became clearer. Archer wasn't a control freak in the general sense of the word, at least not that she'd seen. He might have gotten his feelings hurt by her not telling him she was coming to town, even if he hadn't put it that way to her, and jealousy had brought out the worst in him, but she didn't think he was trying to control her. She had a feeling *scary* had been replaced with *pissed off* in his vocabulary, and he sure didn't like to *feel* out of control. Or, she realized, have his life change without his approval, like his thinking she'd decided they were truly over and hadn't made it clear enough to him. She wondered if that went back to when he lost Kayla, or if he was like that before the accident. He'd never said much about his relationship with Kayla, but Leni had told her they'd been best friends and Archer had lost his mind when she'd been killed.

She dressed in the clothes she'd worn last night, stepping into the uneasy feeling that came with it. Even though she took comfort in Archer's admission about not sleeping around, there was no denying how much she hated leaving in the same clothes she'd worn the night before.

Her stomach growled as she grabbed her phone from the chair and made her way out of the bedroom, following the savory smell of breakfast through the living room, which was also decorated in beiges and whites, with nothing nautical or otherwise *Archerish* in sight. The kitchen was just as unremarkable, with a table for six and oak cabinetry. There was, however, a delicious man standing at the stove, wearing a white T-shirt, the material straining over his barrel chest and muscular biceps.

He dragged his eyes down the length of her, his lips curving up. "You're a sight for tired eyes. Have a seat. I made breakfast."

It took her a second to process this turn of events. They didn't sit down to breakfasts together, and he sure as heck had never cooked for her before. "Um…okay. I didn't even know you could cook."

He gave her a wry smile and transferred scrambled eggs from a pan onto two plates, alongside slices of toast and several pieces of bacon. "I told you there's nothing I can't do."

So arrogant, except she knew better. He might be good with his hands, but emotions were a whole different story. She slid into a seat at the table, where two steaming cups of coffee were waiting. "What did I do to deserve breakfast?"

"An old friend told me it might make you stick around longer, and I want to talk about your plans." He brought their plates to the table and sat across from her.

"What friend were you talking to about me?"

"Nobody." He shoveled eggs onto his fork. "What are your plans for the boutique? How long are you staying on the island, and where are you staying?"

"Slow down, cowboy." She crossed her arms, waiting for him to finish his mouthful of eggs. "You have to answer my question if I'm going to answer yours."

He sipped his coffee, looking annoyed. "I didn't talk to anyone about you. Roddy saw you leaving my boat one morning and made a comment about it."

The first time Indi had come home with Leni to meet her family, she'd also met Roddy, his wife, Gail, and the three of their children who lived on the island. She'd since met the two who didn't live there. She'd met the Silvers at the same time, because the three families were *that* close. Roddy and Gail were very down-to-earth and easygoing, reminding her of hippie throwbacks. She liked their family a lot, and she'd seen Roddy more than once when she'd left Archer's boat early in the morning. He'd always greeted her pleasantly, despite having caught her on several walks of shame. She didn't know how she felt about him saying something to Archer, but there wasn't anything she could do about that now.

"Don't look so worried," Archer said. "It was a while ago, right after Halloween, and he basically told me I was an asshole for taking off and leaving you there."

Her mind reeled back in time to the only day Archer had left the boat before her, when he'd flown out of bed to check his vines after the Field of Screams. She remembered it vividly, because when he'd come home to an empty boat, he'd sent her a text telling her she'd missed out on a second round of great sex, and he'd followed it up with a phone call, giving her a blow-by-blow description of what he'd wanted to do to her.

"I know you're worried about your reputation," Archer said, bringing her back to the moment. "But, if anything, he was protecting you. Don't make it into something it's not."

"I won't."

"Great, so what's your plan?"

"Well, I'm staying at Jules's apartment for now, and I'm here for the next few weeks to get the boutique set up. It all happened so fast, but I've got my arms around it. I'm working with Leni for marketing, and I've hired Bellamy as the face of Indira and Tara to take her pictures…" He was listening so intently, it made her even more excited. "Levi and I went over the layout, so now I can order cabinets and displays and chairs for the hair-washing stations. I need to order storage shelves for the stockroom, office furniture, and mirrors. There's so much to do. I want to start painting tomorrow. I know people usually paint *after* the other renovations are done, but I don't want to wait, and Levi said it would be fine."

"You're brave as shit, you know that? Moving away from everything and everyone you know to open a boutique."

She'd been so busy trying not to think about the demeaning things her parents had said about her career and the boutique, she hadn't had time to even contemplate something like how brave she was. It felt great to hear Archer say it. "I do feel brave, thank you. But it's also a little scary."

"Most things worth your time are, or you're not thinking big enough."

Was *he* included in that assessment? She took another bite, pushing away those thoughts.

"What about your work in the city?" He ate a mound of eggs.

"I have to go back for a couple of small events this month, and then again for Fashion Week, which starts on Valentine's Day. That's going to be grueling. I'm hoping the boutique will be mostly done by then so I can really concentrate on the show."

"That should be plenty of time. How *grueling* is Fashion Week?"

She shrugged, watching him eat as determinedly as he did everything else. "Oh, you know, just busy and chaotic. Nothing I can't handle."

"How often will you go back to the city once the boutique is open?"

"Not often. I have to finish up the contracts I've committed to through March, but other than that I'll be here full time." She ate a piece of bacon, curious about how interested he was.

"Are you keeping your apartment in the city?"

"No. I already gave notice. I need to be out by the end of

March, but I hope to be moved to the island by the end of February, so I have time to get settled before the grand opening. I'm looking forward to building a life here, where people aren't always rushing from one thing to the next, and I'll be dealing with customers instead of models and fashion icons." She took a bite of eggs. "*Mm*, this is good. Thank you."

"You're welcome. When are you planning on opening the doors?"

"I'm thinking about April first. Levi thinks the work can be done by the middle of February, but Leni needs time to set up my online marketing, and April gives me time to spread the word. I'm going to announce the grand opening on the Silver Island website and advertise in the newspaper—print and online."

"Don't forget to make flyers and give them to local businesses. That's how every place around here gets started."

"It's already on my to-do list. But first I have to hire a contractor. Levi said he has friends in Seaport who can do the work, so once I get his quote, I'll call them. He said they're super busy this time of year, but as a favor to him, they'd probably fit me in." She bit into her toast.

"He's talking about the Battle brothers, but you don't need them. While I was making breakfast, I talked to Levi about the work you want done. The guys and I can take care of it."

"The *guys?*"

"Brant, Grant, Jock, my old man. Whoever's around." He finished the last of his toast, guzzled his coffee, and sat back.

"You guys can do flooring and install lights and salon chairs? There's a lot of work to be done, and you already have a full-time job."

"It's the slow season. I wouldn't have said I'd take care of it if I didn't think I could fit it in."

She set down her fork, studying him. Had she made a mistake about his controlling ways? "What are you doing, Archer? Is this about me hiring a contractor? Are you going to be jealous of *any* guy who comes into my life, because—"

"*No*," he said firmly, eyes narrowed. "What the hell, Indi? You're moving to *my* island. This is what we do here. We take care of our own. I'd do the same thing if *any* of my brothers' or sisters' friends moved here." He pushed to his feet and cleared his plate, then leaned against the counter and crossed his arms, the muscles in his jaw flexing. "I knew I shouldn't have said that shit last night."

"*Yes*, you should have." She went to him, feeling horrible for assuming the worst. "I'm sorry. I'm just not used to you taking this type of interest in my life, and I guess yesterday made me overly sensitive."

"Yesterday *sucked*, and I'm sorry I was an ass, but I said I was going to try not to be one anymore with you, and I meant it. Think about it, Indi. You live in another state. You have an entire life I know nothing about. Do you really believe I'm so jealous that I'm going to try to control who comes in and out of your life? Or do you think I got jealous because Wells has been hitting on you since you first came to the island?"

Wells hit on everyone, but she could see how that would send Archer off the rails, because if a woman flirted with him the way Wells usually flirted with her, she'd be seeing red, too. "You're right. I'm sorry I jumped to conclusions. I guess you're not the only one who needs to think before they speak."

An arrogant grin lit up his handsome face. "I can think of a few ways you can make it up to me."

"Only a *few*? Maybe I should start taking applications for a more creative friend with benefits."

"My ass you should." He lifted her up and plunked her down on the counter, wedging himself between her legs.

"Thought you weren't jealous," she teased, loving when he took control in *this* way.

"I'm *not*. I'd just hate to see some asshole waste his time trying to measure up to me." As he lowered his mouth to hers, her phone rang. He cursed under his breath.

She pulled her phone out of her pocket and saw Meredith's name on the screen. "It's my sister."

"Take it. I'll clean up." He lifted her off the counter and set her on her feet.

She answered the call as he cleared the table. "Hi, Mare."

"Hi. I'm going over my schedule, and I really want to plan time to come to the island to see your new boutique and apartment. I was thinking about coming for Winter Walk, to help you out, unless you'd rather I didn't."

"Are you kidding?" Happiness bubbled up inside her. Archer looked over with a curious expression. "I'd *love* that. There's not much to see yet. I'm ordering the display cabinets and everything later today, and I'll start painting tomorrow, but I have no idea when things will be delivered or what shape the place will be in when you come."

"I don't care. I just want to put my feet on the same ground where you'll be living and see the place you're so excited about. Do you need me to bring anything from your apartment?"

"No, thanks. I brought tons of stuff. I'm *so* excited that you're coming! I can't wait for you to see the island." Indi lowered her voice. "Has Mom or Dad said anything about me?"

Archer looked up from washing dishes, his face a mask of concern, those jaw muscles bunching again.

"No, and I doubt they will. They've always dealt with family conflict by sweeping things under the carpet. I don't see that changing anytime soon."

"Then they go in for the kill when you're stuck sitting across a table from them."

Archer's jaw clenched.

"I'm sorry they're so hard on you," Meredith said thoughtfully. "Do you want me to talk to them?"

"No, definitely not. Thanks, though. I'll figure something out."

"Okay. I'm here if you want to talk about it. How are things with Johnny Castle?"

Indi glanced at Archer, and her heart beat a little faster. "Patrick Swayze has nothing on him."

They talked for another minute, and when she ended the call, Archer dried his hands, his expression serious. "Everything okay?"

"Yes. Mare is coming in two weeks to see my place and help with Winter Walk. I forgot to tell you I'm going to put out tables and give away free samples and sell my starter kits."

"That's a great idea. I'm glad Mare's coming. What's happening with your family? Have you spoken to your parents?"

"No. They haven't called."

His jaw tightened. "And your brother? Has he reached out to you?"

"Yes, but he's hard to read sometimes. I couldn't tell if he was supportive and worried, or if he thought I was making a huge mistake."

"It's never a mistake to go after your dreams." Archer took her by the wrist and pulled her closer, his expression softening. "You need to talk to your parents and try to fix this."

"You saw how they treated me," she said sharply. "How can you say that?"

"I did see it, and I hated it. But I lost years with my brother and screwed up my family, and I can never undo that damage or get those years back. I don't want that to happen to you."

"They should come to me. I'm their *child*. Your family didn't turn their backs on you and Jock."

"I know, and I was banking on the fact that your parents would see the light and come crawling back to you by now. I hope I didn't fuck things up beyond repair for you."

"You didn't. You don't know them. They just act like conflicts never happened. They don't try to understand or fix them."

"Then you need to take the bull by the horns. I'm not saying you should kowtow to them or live your life the way *they* want you to. Tell them you're not changing your plans, and let them know how important it is that you're accepted for who you are. But maybe sitting down with them privately, not in a restaurant or at an event where they're trying to uphold some social standard, would work."

"I've done that a million times, and you basically did that at brunch. My family doesn't work that way."

"Then *make it* work that way. Don't let your stubbornness be your downfall."

"You're one to talk." She realized how cutting that was and softened her tone. "I'm sorry. I shouldn't've said that."

He shrugged. "Why not? It's true."

"I still shouldn't have said it. I can't imagine how hard that whole thing with Jock must have been for you. If you ever want to talk about it, I'm a pretty good listener, and I'd like to understand what happened."

"There's nothing to tell. I've got to get to work."

He turned to leave, but she caught his hand. "Archer, you can trust me. I'd never judge or betray you."

He gave her one curt nod and strode out of the room. She watched him heading for the front door, wishing she hadn't driven her rental car to his place, so he could give her a ride to Jules's apartment and she could try to get him to open up to her.

But wishing was for fairy tales and fools.

He grabbed his keys from the table by the door and waved over his shoulder. "See you later."

This sure as heck wasn't a fairy tale.

ARCHER WAS SCREWED. The winery had always been his escape, the place he could empty his mind and get lost in the world of vines and winemaking. But he'd been trying to concentrate on schedules and budgets for hours, and all he saw, all he could think about, was Indi. She'd gotten so far under his skin, it was like she'd become a part of him, and for the first time ever, he'd actually considered opening up and talking about all that had gone down with Jock and the heartache and guilt he carried about Kayla. But not a day went by that he didn't battle those demons, and no woman, especially not Indi, needed to come second to the nightmare that lived in his fucked-up head. He hated the way he'd left that morning, but he couldn't have the conversation she'd wanted, and he couldn't bear seeing the disappointment in her eyes.

He forced thoughts of the accident away. He might not be

boyfriend or husband material, but he sure as hell could help make her dreams come true. He pulled up the notes and schedules he'd come up with earlier for the work Indi needed to have done and reviewed them one more time.

His father peered into his office. "Got a minute?"

"Sure." Archer minimized the documents and spreadsheets. He'd already told his father about helping Indi with the work at the boutique, and his father had agreed to lend a hand.

A tease rose in his father's eyes. "Do I need to report you to HR for looking at inappropriate material?"

Archer scoffed. "I don't need porn, Dad."

"So I hear." He sat in the chair across from the desk.

"Goddamn Levi," Archer grumbled.

"Levi didn't say anything. Tara said you took off when Joey told you Indi was with Levi, and we missed you at breakfast this morning. It doesn't take much to put two and two together. I guess things are heating up with Indi?"

Archer didn't respond. He loved his father and knew he'd always been there for him, even when Archer didn't deserve it. But he wasn't in the mood to talk about whatever this was between him and Indi.

"Does this long silence mean there's trouble on Rocky Ridge?" his father asked.

"Most people would say trouble in paradise."

"Not anyone who knows *you*." His father smiled. "Want to talk about it?"

"There's nothing to talk about."

"I'm not buying that. This is a small island, son, and you've been coming and going a lot more in the last few months. Don't think for a minute that your lady friend has gone unnoticed on her late-night and early-morning ferry rides."

"Shit. Who do I need to shut down from spreading those rumors?"

"Nobody. I took care of it months ago."

That surprised Archer. "I appreciate that."

"You can thank your grandmother. She gave the order. I just did the rest." He grinned. "She wasn't about to let gossip derail what she says is a match made in the most stubborn parts of heaven."

Archer barked out a laugh. "She's lost her mind."

"I don't know about that. Not many women are equipped to handle the rugged peaks and craggy valleys of Rocky Ridge. But Indi holds her own, and I've seen the way she looks at you. It reminds me of the way your mother was when we first got together."

"Then you've lost your mind, too, old man. We both know I'm not equipped to handle a real relationship."

"I don't know any such thing, son. You might have gotten your mother's fierce and stubborn streaks, but you also got her warm heart. You just don't show it in the same ways she does."

You've got that right. I push people away to keep from hurting them.

"You show your heart by fighting for the people you love."

"I didn't do that for Jock." Archer's chest constricted with the admission.

His father leaned forward, holding his stare. "You lost too much in the accident to fight for anything but your own survival."

Archer's throat thickened with emotions. His family rationalized for him, forgiving him despite his faults and all the tragic mistakes he'd made. But Archer knew the truth, and there was no way in hell he'd ever forgive himself.

He tried to shove that darkness down deep, but he needed a fucking sledgehammer. He pushed to his feet, feeling like he couldn't breathe. "Did you come in here for something important?"

"Yeah. You might want to clear your schedule for next month's *Wine Aficionado* gala." He stood and pulled an envelope out of his back pocket, handing it to Archer. "Open it and check out the nominees for Winemaker of the Year."

"You know I don't care about that stuff." He tossed it on the desk and reached for his jacket.

"Your name is on that list, Archer. That's quite an honor. Your mother and I will be attending the gala. We'd really like you to go with us to accept the award we all know you'll win."

"No thanks." He put on his jacket. "I don't make good wine to win awards. I do it because I enjoy it. It's in my blood, and I know I'm making Grandpa proud."

His father put a hand on his shoulder. "You make us all proud, but not because of the wine you make. Because of the man you've become."

Archer wanted to tell him to save that praise for his sons who deserved it, but he wasn't in the mood to argue. All he wanted was to get out to the vineyard and breathe fresh air into his lungs to try to chase away his demons.

They walked out of the office together, and his father said, "Jock and Daphne get home tomorrow. I bet he'll help with the work at Indi's."

"I know. I'll talk to Jock he gets back. I called the other guys to let them know I might need their help. Wells and Fitz are in, depending on the day, because of work, but Brant's able to help, and he's checking to see if Roddy's free."

"You guys have been friends for a long time."

Practically since birth. "What's your point?" He always had one.

"Those sure sound like real relationships to me, and you've maintained them for a lifetime."

Archer shook his head.

"Where are you going? Out to the vines?"

His dad knew him so well. "Yup."

"Your grandfather used to say there was no stronger relationship than the one between a vintner and his vines."

His grandfather's deep voice trampled through his mind. *Take care of the land so it can feed your vines, and then care for them like you would newborn babies. And for Pete's sake, hand harvest to make the best wine you can, because anything else isn't worth your time.*

"You've nurtured that relationship since you were about yay high." His father held his hand at his waist. "Seems to me you can handle all types of relationships. Hope you find what you're looking for out there."

Archer pushed through the back door, embracing the sting of the crisp winter air. He trudged across the courtyard, heading for the vines, standing bare as bones like rows of skeletons. But looks were deceiving. The vines were very much alive, storing carbohydrates in their trunks, expanding their root systems, and soaking up nutrients from the soil.

Fond memories trickled in as he walked among the vines. Memories of running through the vineyard with his brothers and friends, their parents chasing them off, and of his grandfather, a tall, lean man with weathered skin and the largest hands Archer had ever seen, teaching in his gruff way. And then the painful memories came, of sneaking out at night with Kayla and hiding in the vineyard, telling ghost stories and conjuring childhood plans of world domination, and riding their bikes all around the island when Jules was little and undergoing cancer treatments. He and Kayla always ended up right back there in the vines. His safety net. He closed his eyes against the sadness swamping him. His gut twisted into painful knots, his mind sprinting back to the morning and the way he'd walked out on Indi.

He fucking sucked.

He rubbed his knuckles, which were calloused from years of beating his frustrations out on the heavy bag without gloves. He thought about calling a buddy to go a few rounds in the boxing ring in his parents' garage, but he knew that wouldn't help. There was only one thing, one *person* who could turn this mood around.

He pulled out his phone, thumbing out a dirty text to his sexy, stubborn girl. His thumb hovered over the send arrow as Indi's voice whispered through his mind, sweet as honey and real as rain—*Archer, you can trust me. I'd never judge or betray you*—drowning out his urge for sex.

What the hell was happening to him?

He pocketed his phone and headed for his truck.

INDI SAT IN one of the salon chairs in her newly leased space with her laptop on her knees, ordering the last of the display cabinets. She submitted the order and looked in the mirror, feeling great about all she'd accomplished. Her gaze moved over her kinky blond hair and the blue sweater she'd changed into at Jules's apartment. She looked the same as she had a month ago, but so much had changed. She was *really* doing it, starting a life on the island, away from her parents and the hustle and bustle of the city. In a few weeks she'd open the doors to her dream boutique. At least she'd stuck to *one* New Year's resolution, even if the rest of her life was confusing. She'd spoken to Leni earlier, and she'd been as floored about Archer making Indi breakfast and wanting to help with the renovations as Indi had been. Indi didn't tell her about the way her bullheaded brother had shut down and walked out when she'd brought up the past, because after thinking about it all morning, she wasn't sure she had the right to expect him to open up to her in that way. Just because she wanted something deeper didn't mean he had to give it to her, especially since he'd been clear about his boundaries.

The front door opened, and she was surprised to see her brawny brooder walking in with a to-go cup in his hand. His powerful legs ate up the distance between them. Her pulse quickened at the entrancing way he was looking at her, almost like he needed her. But Archer never needed anyone, so she had a feeling that was wishful thinking.

She got up and set the laptop on the chair. "Hi."

"Hey, darlin'." He leaned down and kissed her.

Her chest fluttered when he called her that all gravelly and tender instead of the tense way he sometimes said it.

He handed her the cup. "I'm sorry for being a jerk this morning and walking out. You didn't deserve that."

Lord have mercy. Who was this caring man? "Is this another apology latte?"

He shrugged, smiling adorably.

"Thank you." She looked down at the steaming cup in her hand, and her heart warmed along with it. "I might have to buy stock in the Sweet Barista if you keep this up."

He took off his jacket and tossed it on a chair. Then he reached for her hand as he sat in the empty chair and pulled her onto his lap. "Tell me something good. Tell me about your day."

She liked slipping through this crack in his armor, and she was tempted to ask what had changed, but she didn't want to risk him shutting down again, and she *was* excited to share her news. "I had the *best* day. I found gorgeous scalloped mirrors and the prettiest cabinets and displays on clearance at one of the distributors. I also ordered the cutest office setup. It wasn't discounted, but it was too perfect to pass up. I'm waiting to confirm delivery dates, but the salespeople assured me that I could get it all within two weeks. Let me show you."

She reached for the laptop, but he snagged it first and set it on her lap. As she showed him everything she'd bought, explaining why each piece was perfect and what she had planned for them, he listened intently, asking questions and commending her choices. She noticed him watching her instead of the laptop screen, and everything felt different. Even the way he was holding her. It wasn't possessive as much as it was like he *needed* her, and she had to ask, "What's going on with you? Did something happen?"

He was quiet for a moment, his jaw tensing, brows slanting, like he was fighting something inside or struggling to get the words out. "I just like hearing your voice."

It was unlike him to say something so sweet, and his voice was gentle again, but the way his fingers curled tightly around her leg told her those words hadn't come easily, and she carefully gathered them up and tucked them away. "I like hearing your voice, too."

He kissed her then, deep and slow, his hand moving to her

hip, giving it a seductive squeeze. "Let's get out of here."

And just like that, her sex fiend was back.

As she got up to put her laptop away, he said, "I want to hit the paint store so we can get started tomorrow. Why don't we grab dinner at Rock Bottom, and we can go over the schedule I came up with."

She was stunned. He was delaying sex *and* taking her to dinner? Was this his way of taking her on a date? They'd gone to dinner in New York, where nobody knew them, but they'd never been out one-on-one on the island. She wondered if his boundaries had changed. She was having a hard time tamping down the hope blooming inside her, but she kept her cool. "Sounds good."

They left the store, and when she turned to lock the door, he put his arms around her from behind, speaking gruffly into her ear. "We'll have *dessert* at my place."

Her body tingled with desire. She headed for her rental car, but he drew her to his side. "This way, darlin'. You're riding with me."

This sure felt like the start of a date.

He opened the passenger door and as he helped her in, he said, "After tonight I should be the *only* asshole on this island flirting with you."

Her *sex fiend* had been joined by the *arrogant competitor*, and they were strutting around to the driver's side like a gorilla beating its chest.

Was it bad that she liked it?

Chapter Eleven

ARCHER ADMIRED INDI'S ass bopping from side to side in her paint-splattered overalls as she sang another one of the annoying pop songs he'd been forced to listen to since losing a coin toss for control of the playlist. It was Sunday, and they'd been painting all day. Her hair was piled on top of her head in a messy bun, her feet were bare, and she was wearing only a sports bra beneath overalls. She might be petite and a bit of a glamour girl, but she was scrappy. She'd been working just as hard as he had, and when he'd suggested they take a break for lunch, she'd called him a slacker and ordered pizza so they could work while they ate. She was the coolest woman he knew, and just being around her took him out of his own head. No one else had *ever* been able to do that.

She was also funny as hell. Last night at the paint store she'd joked about painting the stockroom red so she could claim to have a red room, and that had led to kinky sex talk that had them both in hysterics. By the time they'd gone to dinner, the bad memories that had plagued him all afternoon had been drowned out by laughter and great conversation. When they'd gone back to his place, his only thoughts were about the beautiful woman in his arms and how thankful he was that she put up with him. He was looking forward to painting with her the next couple of days.

Indi spun around, singing into her paintbrush like a microphone, jarring him from his thoughts. She was adorable, wiggling her shoulders as she sang into that damn paintbrush. Her beautiful eyes sparked with trouble waiting to happen as her pitch climbed and she sang about wanting to be his girlfriend and being a *motherfucking princess*. Lucky it was only a song, because he'd be the worst boyfriend on the planet. He had too many demons. But whatever this was between them was pretty cool. If only he could stop getting all twisted up in her every time they were together.

"What's the matter, tough guy? You don't like Avril Lavigne?"

No, I like you too fucking much. He went back to rolling paint on the wall and kept his thoughts to himself.

She pointed her paintbrush at him. "I'll have you know that's one of Jules's favorite songs, and I love Jules, so now it's one of my favorites, too. I might have to play that song a *lot* over the next few days, so get used to it."

Did she have to bring up Jules? He'd done a great job of *not* thinking about her being halfway across the world. "At least you know the words." Jules loved to sing, but she was notorious for singing the wrong lyrics.

"I *love* the way she sings, and you laugh at her lyrics, so you must like it, too."

He dunked the roller in the paint, focusing on the job at hand to try to take his mind off the hot little number waving her paintbrush at him as she went on about Jules and the discomfort stacking up inside him over his baby sister growing up.

Indi hummed to the beat of another song as she painted. "Admit it, Archer. You like the way she sings."

"I love my sister, so yeah, I can handle her singing and other quirks." Jules had quirks that went beyond her inability to learn song lyrics. She was too trusting, saw the good in everyone, and she was happy all the damn time. And as if it wasn't enough for *her* to be happy, she spent her life trying to spread her sunshine to those who needed it. Needless to say, she'd spent countless hours trying to pull Archer out of the darkness that had swallowed him up after the accident, and in rare and brief moments, it had worked.

"She's definitely quirky, but that just makes me love her more." Indi began swinging her hips to another song. "Leni always said it would take a special person to fall in love with her. I never really believed in fate, but between Daphne and Jock and Jules and Grant, it's hard to believe their coming together was anything else. I'm glad Jules has Grant. I hope they're having an amazing time in Spain."

"He'd better be taking care of her," he grumbled, focusing on painting to keep from barking at her.

"Don't you trust him? I thought he was one of your best friends."

"He *is*, and I do trust him, but they're too damn far away."

"Why? It's not like they're gone forever. They're coming back the weekend after next, and she *is* a grown woman. Believe it or not, Jules can take care of herself."

He kept his eyes trained on the roller as he pushed it up the wall. "No shit, but she's still my baby sister."

Indi leaned her face in front of him, so he had no choice but to look at her. "*Aw*, are you having trouble letting your baby sister spread her wings?"

He gritted his teeth. "You could say that."

"Why is it so hard for you with her? Was it hard with Sutton and Leni?"

When he didn't respond, she stepped between him and the wall. Anyone else would have taken the hint and stopped poking the bear, but not Indi. She was always trying to get into his head.

"Talk to me," she said cheerily. "Maybe I can help."

He knew she wouldn't let it go until he gave her something. "It wasn't as difficult with my other sisters."

"Why not?"

"Because Jules is different, and I've been taking care of her for years."

"She is different. Sutton and Leni come across as resilient and tough enough to handle anything, but Jules is strong. She just exudes a different energy. But how have you taken care of her?" He clenched his jaw, but she didn't relent. "I mean, in what ways?"

"In *every* way. I'm the only one who stayed on the island. I'm the one she came to when someone hurt her feelings or she was pissed off, scared, or lonely. *I'm* the one whose boat she's been hiding out on since she was fifteen, who helped her get her business going and held her on the days when she wasn't sure she could handle it. And now I'm supposed to just step back and hope Grant loves her enough to keep her safe and happy?" *Fuck.* He tossed the roller onto the tarp and paced. "I don't mean that. I know he adores her, but it's hard to let go sometimes, and she's so far away right now, it takes everything I have not to bug the shit out of her by texting and checking up on her."

Indi set down her paintbrush and stepped into his path with

a soft expression.

"*What?* Does that make me a pussy?"

"No," she said sweetly. "It makes you a little irresistible, which is worrisome, but I can handle it."

He scoffed. "Don't worry too much. I'm still an asshole."

"I know you are." She waved her finger at him. "In fact, I'm counting on it, but I like that you're not a jerk to Jules."

"You know what she's been through. I'd kill anyone who was a jerk to her."

"I believe that. It must have been really hard for you when she was sick."

"Yeah." He crossed his arms. "I couldn't be around her much."

"Why not?"

His chest constricted. He was about to redirect the conversation like he usually did, but her eyes implored him like pools of truth serum, drawing out his painful secrets. "Because I suck."

"Come on, Archer. We both know that's not true."

"In this case it is. Jules used to be afraid of monsters. I guess most kids are, but even when she was just a tiny two-year-old she'd climb out of her toddler bed and come find me when she was scared. I'd make a big show in her bedroom, pretending to look for monsters and scare them away. I'd put her back in her little bed and lie beside her until she fell asleep. When she got diagnosed with cancer, she kept asking me to scare the fucking *cancer monster* away." A lump lodged in his throat. "She was so small and so trusting, and I couldn't do a damn thing to protect her." He closed his eyes, hands fisted, and lifted his chin toward the ceiling, trying to count, to keep his emotions at bay, but even now, years later, the pain was still too raw, the guilt all-consuming, and it burst from his lungs like a slew of curses. "I was too fucking weak to watch her go through it, and I'll *never* forgive myself for that." *Or so many other things.*

Indi's arms circled him, and she pressed her cheek against his chest. He tried to pull away, but she tightened her hold. Years of self-loathing and blame rose to the surface, making his skin feel too tight. "*Indi,*" he warned.

"Shut up. This hug isn't for you. It's for the eleven-year-old boy who believed he should be capable of protecting his baby sister against anything."

Fuuck. He clenched his eyes shut, willing the burn of tears away, his entire body flexing, fighting the kindness he didn't deserve.

Indi pressed a kiss to his chest, tightening her hold on him even more. "This hug is for you. For carrying a burden you never deserved."

His head fell forward, arms engulfing her.

"And for being the kind of brother I wish I had."

His protective urges roared at the way she said it. "*Damn it,* Indi. What the hell?"

INDI ACHED FOR Archer. She'd seen glimpses of that tender side of him but had never imagined he carried so much guilt and pain. Everyone thought he was guarded and angry because of the accident and the awful years that had followed, but now she wondered what else was being overlooked. He sounded so angry, she worried his ego was taking too big of a hit and tried to ease his pain. "Don't worry, I won't tell anyone you're human."

"Fuck that." He broke away, pacing again, nostrils flaring. "I wondered what was up with your brother. I couldn't get a good read on him the other morning, but I had hoped he was being cautiously supportive. Did he *ever* stand up for you or protect you?"

It took her a second to process his redirect. "Not in the same way you protected Jules, but he was there for me in other ways. *Archer…*" She reached for his hand, but he continued pacing, shoulders rounded, hands fisted. He was like a ball of rubber bands, strung so tight it might take years to undo the bindings.

He eyed her without slowing down. His lips were moving, but she couldn't tell what he was saying to himself.

"You don't have to change the subject. We can talk about how you felt back then or how you feel now."

"There's nothing to talk about. If there's one thing I've learned, it's that you can't change the past." He stopped pacing, the tension around his jaw easing. "Please let it go, darlin'. You don't want to swim with those sharks."

"What if I do want to?"

"I won't let you." He took her hand, pulling her against him. "You're a beautiful woman on the cusp of an amazing future. Don't fuck it up by trying to make this into something it's not. I'll never be the spill-your-guts guy you need. I'm the asshole who won't give up poker night for a woman and won't feel bad about it." He palmed her ass and squeezed, sending heat rippling through her despite the seriousness of their conversation. "But I can be the guy who helps this boutique come alive and makes you feel good *all night long*."

He kissed her, swatted her butt, and picked up the roller,

going right back to painting. She wanted to tell him to stop being so macho and let her in, damn it. That the big-hearted man beneath all those bindings was worth fighting for. But she knew that would only get his defenses up even more, so she let it go, hoping one day he'd realize she didn't scare that easily.

She watched him in his tank top, biceps flexing, chest heaving, those keen eyes locked on the roller. She imagined him mentally wrapping more rubber bands around himself to cover the fissure he'd exposed, locking down that vulnerability even tighter. But she cared too much about him to let him stew in the self-imposed hell he'd created.

She dipped her paintbrush in the paint can and playfully called out, "Hey, Archer."

He looked over, and she snapped her wrist, sending paint flying onto his face and chest. She held her breath, heart pounding, as his eyes widened, then narrowed. He wiped his cheek with his fingers, then looked down at his hand. She pressed her lips together to stifle a giggle at the incredulous look on his face.

"Oh, you're in big trouble now. This is *war*."

He dropped the roller and sprinted toward her. She squealed and bolted across the room, darting through the open door leading up to the apartment. She made it up four steps before he caught the back of her overalls, yanking her into his arms. They cracked up as he tore the paintbrush out of her hand. She squirmed and laughed, trying to break free as he dragged the paintbrush down her neck.

"Archer! *Stop!*"

"If you can't take the heat, don't light the match." He swept one leg behind her knees, taking her carefully down to her back on the steps, and straddled her, pressing the insides of his knees to the outsides of her arms, pinning them against her body without putting any weight on her. Their eyes connected like metal to magnet, his triumphant grin igniting flames in his eyes.

"You're mine now, Oliver."

Sparks skittered beneath her flesh at the wicked truth in his words.

He unhooked her overall bib and peeled it down, his gaze sliding to her chest. He licked his lips, and ran his fingers over her sports bra, bringing her nipples to taut peaks, sending titillating sensations tingling through her.

"Hm." He dangled the paintbrush above her cheek. "Where to start?"

"Don't you *dare*."

He laughed and tossed the paintbrush over his shoulder. Thank goodness they'd put tarps on the floors. He rose onto his knees, still trapping her arms by her sides as he opened his jeans and withdrew his cock, giving it a few tight strokes.

Holy cow. Her entire body flamed at the sight of that big hand working him to his full length. "Did you lock the door?"

"I thought you liked pushing the limits."

"I do! But, Archer, I can't—"

"Don't worry, darlin'. It's locked." He whispered, "*This time*," and stroked himself faster.

She must really be messed up, because that made her even hotter. Her eyes were riveted to his thick fingers moving along his cock. Her sex clenched greedily, but she was salivating for a taste of him. *"Archer."*

"You want this?" He pivoted forward, dragging the head of his cock along her lips. She thrust her tongue out, but he drew back. "I like you needy." He cupped her jaw and pushed his thumb into her mouth. She closed her lips around it, sucking it like she wanted to suck him.

"That's it, baby." He withdrew his thumb, replacing it with two thick fingers. "Suck like it's my cock. Let me feel how badly you want me."

She sucked and licked, lifting her head to get all the way to his knuckles, and moaned, knowing how it turned him on.

"Christ, you're sexy." He fisted his cock again, stroking himself as he went up on his knees. "Push your overalls and panties down."

He didn't have to ask twice. She could barely breathe for the excitement mounting inside her as she followed his dirty demand.

She leaned her elbows on the step behind her. As he steadied himself above her with one hand on the wall, she guided his cock toward her mouth, holding his gaze the way they both loved.

"You're so fucking sexy." He reached behind him with one hand, teasing between her legs. "Damn, baby, you're so wet for me."

Lord. The way he talked made her even greedier.

His jaw went tight as he pushed his fingers inside her and thrust his hips, fucking her deep in both places. She stroked him with one hand, holding his hip with the other as he worked her so perfectly, her entire body hummed. Her eyes fluttered closed, and he growled, "I want to see it in your eyes." Her eyes flew open just as her climax hit. He pulled out of her mouth, those dark eyes holding her hostage as he swept an arm beneath her, holding her off the stairs as he aligned their bodies and drove into her. Sensations exploded inside her, and she cried out. He pumped faster, eyes boring into her as her orgasm ravaged her. He dipped his face beside hers, growling and cursing, his every sound drenched with pleasure as he found his own release, taking her right up to the peak again. Their bodies shuddered and jerked as they soared to new heights.

With his arms around her, he repositioned them, so he was sitting on the step and she was straddling him, their bodies still connected. He held her tight, his face buried in her chest. His breath came in warm puffs against her flesh, bringing rise to goose bumps. He always felt so different after sex, like he was finally at peace. It was in those moments that her mind played tricks on her, weaving unattainable fantasies of a future with Archer filled with steamy sexcapades, double dates, and maybe even a family of their own one day.

She ran her fingers through his hair, thinking of his confession about Jules and his words that had followed. *Don't fuck it up by trying to make this into something it's not. I'll never be the spill-your-guts guy you need.*

There it was. Their cold, harsh reality.

As she did whenever they were together, she forced herself to peel away from him, tucking those feelings down deep, and pushed to her feet. "I'll be right back."

She hurried upstairs to the bathroom in the apartment to try to beat her stupid heart into submission.

Chapter Twelve

BY WEDNESDAY NIGHT, Indi hurt in places she didn't know she could hurt. Who knew that three days of painting could leave a person feeling like a rag doll? Well, four days of painting, coordinating next week's deliveries, and three super-sexy nights with Archer. It was totally worth it. Archer was helping her paint, and it was taking longer than they'd anticipated because painting bricks was tricky. They'd figured out how to give the bricks a cool, distressed appearance that she loved. The more difficult part was what spending all that time with Archer was doing to her. They made a great team. They were having so much fun every day and they fit so well together at night, it was a little too easy to imagine more. That was why tonight, exhausted after painting all day, she planned on taking a shower at Jules's apartment and going to bed alone.

But Archer had other plans.

With promises of a low-key evening of popcorn and a movie, he'd coaxed her into grabbing her things and showering with him at his place. It was after eight, and they were just finishing up their shower. She'd convinced him to let her wash his face with her facial cleanser. She massaged it over his cheekbones, and he wrinkled his nose. "Try to stay still."

"It's gritty, and it smells like flowers," he complained.

"So?"

"I'm a dude."

She giggled. "Is *that* why you have that thing between your legs and I don't?"

He smiled coyly as she washed his nose and chin. "Careful, it's likely to bite."

"If that thing grows teeth, it's never coming near me again." She went up on her toes and kissed him. "Close your eyes."

"I like where this is going." Archer closed his eyes.

She washed his forehead, down the bridge of his nose, and under his eyes, loving their new, relaxed playfulness. "Okay, you can rinse your face."

"*Wait.* No happy ending?"

"My body needs a break. Everything hurts, and I thought we were going to watch a movie."

He rinsed his face, then pulled her closer and kissed her. "We are. Your turn." He spun her around, so her back was to him, and caressed her butt.

"Archer, I just said I needed a break." She was glad they'd decided to take a painting break for a day or two before tackling the apartment, which she also wanted to brighten up, but there was no rest for the weary. She had a busy day lined up for tomorrow.

"I let you put flowery shit on my face. Relax and trust me."

She tipped her face up to the water while he poured body wash into his hands and began washing her shoulders. His hands were strong and somehow also gentle as he massaged her tight muscles. She sighed, letting her head tip forward as he worked his way down her back and along her sides. He massaged her butt, and she was sure he'd make a move, but he never even tried. He continued working the knots out of every muscle in her body, right down to her fingertips.

She'd thought those moments after sex were special, but when her sex-craved man made no move toward sex and just took care of her? *That* was dangerous territory.

After they showered, she towel-dried and combed out her hair as he threw on sweats and a T-shirt. She changed into her yoga pants and sweatshirt and was putting moisturizer on when he peeked into the bathroom.

His gaze swept over her. "*Mm-mm.* You could make a snow-suit look hot. Want to skip the movie and see how those pants look on the floor?"

Yes. It was ridiculous how much she wanted him all the time. They'd gotten so much closer so fast, it was too easy to fall back into his arms like that and get lost in them. She needed to at least *try* to protect her heart.

She hated denying herself the pleasure he'd bring, the feel of lying in his arms, their naked bodies warm and intertwined. But she planted her hand on her hip and gave him her best not-interested look, which she imagined looked as fake as it felt. "You promised me a low-key movie night, not another night of hot sex, and I *know* you're a man of your word."

"Yeah, yeah," he relented, and leaned in for a quick kiss. "If only I could be a dick *and* a liar."

She laughed and shoved her things into her toiletries bag. "Your mama would be so proud."

His expression went a little serious. "What do you want to watch? I'll get the movie started."

"I don't care. You choose. What's your favorite movie?"

"*A Nightmare on Elm Street*, but I'm pretty sure it'll scare you."

"*Ha!* That shows how little you know about me." She'd never watched *A Nightmare on Elm Street*, but she didn't scare easily, and she liked scary movies, so she was pretty sure she could handle it. "Queue it up. I'll be right out, and I'll make the popcorn."

Half an hour later, they were sitting on the couch in the living room, eating popcorn and watching the movie. Archer put his arm around her and pulled her closer. "Are you scared yet?"

"Hardly. Creeped out, maybe, but not scared. I mean, come on. The guy wears a glove with knives for hands. Do you really think anyone would do that in real life? But I am enjoying the story, and I love seeing the eighties hairstyles and clothes."

He chuckled and kissed her temple, hugging her against his side. "You are one cool chick."

She tucked her legs beside her and rested her head on his shoulder. They'd never watched a movie together, and snuggling on the couch with him was nice. He set the bowl of popcorn on the coffee table and kissed her head. "Let's lie down."

He lay down, tucking one arm beneath her head, the other around her belly. He was so warm and big, so relaxing, her eyelids got heavy. She tried to stay awake, but she must have zonked out, because the next thing she knew, she was waking up, and the credits were rolling.

"Oh *no*. I missed it?"

"You were exhausted." He kissed her cheek. "We'll watch it another time."

"I'm sorry. What a hot date I am, huh? I'd better get going." She tried to sit up, but he tightened his hold on her.

"You're not going anywhere."

"*Archer*, I'm really too tired to fool around."

"Stay." He nuzzled against her neck. "We'll just sleep. I promise." He scooped her into his arms.

"*Archer...?*"

"Enjoy it, Oliver. This is the only ride you're getting to-night." He pressed his lips to hers and carried her into the bedroom.

Talk about dangerous territory. She probably should have stuck to her guns and gone to Jules's because she was already in too deep, but how much damage could one more night do?

Chapter Thirteen

ARCHER BRUSHED HIS teeth and washed up early Thursday morning, trying to wrap his head around the shit going on inside him. He dried off and set the towel on the sink, catching sight of Indi's toiletries bag on the counter and her toothbrush next to his. His gut clenched. He and Indi had spent most of the last few days joined at the hip. If he wasn't at the winery, he was with her, painting, grabbing dinners, and falling into each other's arms at night. They woke up every morning tangled up like long-lost lovers, enveloped in her intoxicating scent. It was everywhere—on him, in his sheets, in the fucking air—and he liked it way too much. He didn't know what he was thinking, telling her to stay every night, when he knew he could never give her what she deserved. He *wasn't* thinking. That was the problem. Around her, it was easy not to think and to let his emotions lead instead. He'd been so caught up in her, he couldn't stand the idea of *not* being with her, and that was as messed up as the feeling he had now of needing to reclaim his space, his independence, his fucking *mind*.

He leaned his palms on the sink, staring into the mirror, gritting his teeth at the idiot looking back at him. *You had to get greedy. Now look where we are.*

He was Archer Steele, not some pussy-whipped idiot who couldn't make it through a single night without his woman. He hadn't even worked out all week. He needed to take control of this situation before she got hurt.

Pushing to his full height, he took a deep breath, mustering the strength to do what needed to be done. Feeling more determined and in control, he strode into the bedroom and tried to ignore the tug in his chest as he drank her in. She looked like an angel with her delicate features, so beautiful without makeup, curled up on her side, her hair fanned out on his pillow like spun gold that had gotten caught in a machine, all kinky and sexy. Man, he loved her hair.

Guilt tightened around him like a noose, and he turned away, telling himself again that he was doing the right thing as he pulled on sweatpants and a T-shirt. They'd committed to exclusivity, *not* practically moving in together. She'd understand. She had to.

He sat beside her and ran his hand down her hip. *One night.* He just needed to make it through one night without her.

She rolled onto her back, eyes fluttering open, her sweet smile tightening the knots in his gut.

"Good morning," she said sleepily. "I guess I'm showering alone this morning. Are you going in to work early?"

"No. I'm going to work out." Maybe he could pound out his frustrations on a heavy bag.

She fluttered her lashes seductively and hooked her finger into the waist of his sweatpants. "I can give you a great workout, and you wouldn't even have to leave the bedroom."

She ran her hand down the front of his sweatpants, awaking the beast that had gotten him into this trouble in the first place. He put his hand over hers, moving it to his leg.

Damn, he hated this. "There's nothing I'd rather do right now than *you*, but I've got to work out before I lose my mind."

"I get it."

He doubted she did.

"Want me to lock up when I leave?"

"Yeah, that'd be great, but, *uh*, what are you doing today?" *Way to procrastinate, asshole. Just rip the bandage off and get it over with.*

"I have a busy day now that we're almost done painting. This morning I'm going over my schedules for Fashion Week, making sure I have enough supplies on hand for the event and coming up with the initial inventory list for the boutique. Then I'm getting together with Bellamy and Tara to take pictures of Bellamy for the walls of the boutique and for some marketing pieces. Bellamy has a list of high-profile influencers she's become friends with. We're going to come up with an evite she can send them for my grand opening."

Her excitement made it even harder for him to let her down. Especially since he knew he'd want to hear how her day went later. That thought was accompanied by a claustrophobic feeling, giving him the push he needed.

Before he could get a word out, Indi said, "I'm also going to run a few ideas I have by Leni to see how I should pitch them to local businesses, including your winery."

"What kind of ideas?"

"Cross-promotional. I don't want to say anything more until I have all the details worked out." She stretched, arching her back, and the sheet fell away, exposing her bare breasts. "If it goes well, I'll tell you about it tonight."

He gritted his teeth against the heat simmering inside him and pushed to his feet, needing to put space between them before he gave in to his primal urges. "Yeah, sorry, but tonight's a no-go for me. I'm playing poker with the guys, and I think I'm going to just chill afterward."

"Okay." Her eyes narrowed. "Why do you sound so weird?"

"I don't *know*. We've been together every night. I just need some space." His words came out harsher than he'd intended.

Hurt and confusion rose in her eyes. She threw the sheet off and got out of bed, collecting her clothes. "I'm sorry if I'm cramping your style."

Fuck. He scrubbed a hand down his face. "Indi—"

"Why did you ask me to stay over if you were feeling suffocated?" She tugged on her clothes like she was at war with them. "I said I'd leave, *remember*? But you were all, *You're not going anywhere.*"

"Because I *wanted* to be with you," he said angrily. "But then I saw your toothbrush, and it freaked me out."

"Well, excuse the hell out of me." She stalked into the bathroom, grabbed her things, and came out waving her toothbrush at him. "You won't have to worry about this scary toothbrush anymore." She shoved her feet into her boots. "It's a good thing you're great in bed, because you really can be a dick. Enjoy your *space*. I'll see you when I see you." She spun on her heels and stormed out.

"Fuck." He grabbed a sweatshirt, his keys, and his phone, thumbing out a text to the guys on his way to the front door. *Poker tonight. My place 7:00.* As he sent the message, he heard Indi's rental car peeling away from the curb.

By the time he reached his parents' house, he was fit to be tied. Jock's car was parked out front. He hadn't seen him since he returned from his honeymoon, but Daphne had been flitting around the winery on cloud nine. Archer headed into the garage. Jock was working the speed bag on the other side of the boxing ring. Jock and Archer had always gotten in each other's faces, even when they were young. Their father, who had boxed in college, used to have to pry them off each other. One winter he got sick of it and had the boxing ring installed. He taught them and their closest friends, Brant, Grant, Wells, and Fitz, how to box. Jock and Archer had boxed competitively when they were in high school, and in the years since, they'd installed various pieces of exercise equipment, free weights, a heavy bag, and a speed bag in the garage. It had been Archer's savior during the decade when he and Jock weren't speaking to one another, and this morning, he sure as hell hoped it would help shake the eight-hundred-pound gorilla off his back.

"Hey, man. Poker tonight at seven, my place." Archer took off his sweatshirt and tossed it on the weight bench. "How was your honeymoon?"

Jock's smile lit up the whole damn garage. "It couldn't have been better." He grabbed a towel and scrubbed it down his sweaty face. "I wouldn't trade Hadley for anything in the world, but having Daphne all to myself was incredible. I am without a doubt the luckiest guy around."

"Then why are you here at the crack of dawn instead of showing her how lucky she is?" He made his way around the ring to the heavy bag.

"She knows, trust me. I'm here because I gotta work off the feasts we enjoyed every night." Jock patted his stomach.

"Dude, it was your honeymoon. There shouldn't have been any calories in what you were eating."

Jock chuckled and shook his head. "I had to refuel at some point." He set down the towel and started hitting the speed bag. "How've you been? I heard you and Indi have been seen around town together. What's up with that?"

"Nothing. I'm helping her paint the place she leased." Archer began hitting the bag, welcoming the sting of the leather against his calloused hands.

"The gloves are on the shelf."

Archer went at the bag harder. "Don't need 'em."

Jock stopped hitting the speed bag. "What's going on? Want to talk about it?"

"Nope." He continued punching the bag, relieved when Jock let it go and went back to working out. Talking wouldn't fix it. He was a broken motherfucker, and Indi deserved better. He couldn't get the sound of the hurt in her voice out of his head. He punched the bag faster, trying to beat the guilt away.

He didn't know how long he pounded that bag, but when Jock touched his back, he was drenched with sweat, heart thundering, anger and guilt still shouting in his ears like the devil. "*What?*" he snapped.

"You're bleeding." Jock motioned to Archer's hands and gave him a towel.

Archer looked from his split knuckles to the blood on the bag. "Shit. Hand me the spray and that rag from the shelf, will you?"

"I've got it." Jock grabbed the spray cleaner and a handful of paper towels and began cleaning the bag. "What's going on with you?"

"Nothin'." He snagged another clean towel and wiped his face.

"I'm your twin. You can't bullshit me. If there were something wrong with the winery, Daph would have told me." Jock tossed the paper towels in the trash and set down the cleaner. "I know your boat is safely stored for the winter, and nobody in the family is having issues, which leaves girl trouble."

Archer gritted his teeth.

"Come on, Archer. We used to talk about girls all the time. Maybe I can help."

You can't help. Nobody can. My shit runs too deep. "We're not fifteen anymore. Let it go."

"No." Jock held his gaze. "I did that once, and it cost us a decade."

"Well, this has nothing to do with us." It was a lie. Every damn thing Archer did was wrapped in layers of guilt about the grief he'd caused their family, but he wasn't about to lay that on Jock. "I'm asking you to back off."

"Fine, but Indi's a great girl, and if she digs your ugly ass, then maybe you should let her in. Look how happy Daphne and I are. If I hadn't opened up to her about all my grief and the guilt I carried about Kayla and the baby, and you, I wouldn't have her or Hadley in my life. Hell, bro. I still wouldn't have *you* in my life."

Archer fisted the bloody towel in his hand, a lump lodging in his throat. "What makes you think I'm not letting her in?"

Jock gave him the knowing look he'd been giving them since they were kids. "Several bloody knuckles and a decade of silence."

Before Archer could get out from under his emotions enough to respond, Jock put a hand on his shoulder and said, "Come on. Let's get those hands cleaned up so they don't get infected."

"Do I have to call you Daddy Dock, too?" Archer kidded as they headed inside.

"No." Jock opened the door to the house. "You can call me *sir.*"

Archer shoved him, and Jock spun around, the two of them falling into a play fight, calling each other names as they stumbled into the kitchen. They stopped in their tracks at the sight of their mother crying at the table. Their father was kneeling in front of her, holding her. Archer's heart nearly stopped. The last time he'd seen his mother crying like that was at the hospital after the accident.

Their father looked over, grief-stricken. "Why don't you boys go have breakfast at your place?"

Their mother turned away, wiping her eyes, and their father's gaze moved to Archer's bloody hands. "You need help?"

"No. What happened? Is Jules okay?" Archer asked, he and Jock stepping closer.

"She's fine," their father answered.

"Grandma?" Jock asked.

Their father shook his head. "Lenore is fine, too."

Archer's mind scrambled for answers. Their mother looked over, her red-rimmed eyes and pink nose cutting him to his core. "Then what's going on? And don't tell me *nothing*." He went to her, a threatening stare locked on his father. "Did you do something?" His parents rarely fought, and even when they did, his father was careful with his words. He would never lay a hand on her, but Archer was at a loss for what could be going on. As they held each other's stare, silent warning raging between them, he wondered if they were two men protecting the same woman or if his father was protecting himself. That thought came with a bite of guilt.

"No, honey." Their mother wiped her tears with a handful of tissues. "I—" A sob stole her voice.

"Are you sick?" Archer's gut seized.

"Mom...?" Jock went to her other side.

Their parents exchanged a long look that told of years of love and support, adding more guilt to Archer's shoulders. Their father would never hurt her, and he shouldn't have even asked.

Their father put his hand on hers. "Maybe you should tell them."

She nodded, struggling against her tears.

Their father looked at them with the most serious expression. "Not a word of this leaves this room. Do you understand me?"

Fuck. This is bad. One look at Jock told Archer he was thinking the same thing.

They agreed, and their mother clung to their father's hand, her lower lip quivering, her voice a thin, shaky thread. "It's Ava."

Ava de Messiéres was one of their mother's closest friends. She ran the Bistro, a restaurant down the road from the Silver House, on Sunset Beach. Ava's husband, Olivier, had passed away many years ago, leaving Ava to raise her two daughters, Deirdra, who was Sutton's age, and Abby, one of Leni's best friends, alone. Unfortunately, after Olivier died, Ava lost herself at the bottom of a bottle of alcohol, and her girls had paid the price. Her business started failing, and Archer's parents, along with the Silvers and Remingtons, did what they could to help keep it afloat, hiring the Bistro to cater events, paying far above what they should have, and sending their children over to help wait on and bus tables, free of charge. Their parents took Abby and Deirdra under their wings as much as the girls would let them. Now Abby was a chef in New York City, and Deirdra was a corporate attorney in Boston.

"She's..." Their mother closed her eyes, and their father squeezed her hand. She reopened her eyes, and fresh tears rolled down her cheeks. "She's got cancer. She's dying." Sobs burst free, and their father embraced her.

Archer felt like the oxygen had been sucked from the room. He was slammed back in time to the crushing pain when he'd learned Jules had cancer and to the devastation of losing Kayla. He was gutted for his mother, and for Deirdra and Abby. He grabbed the back of a chair as he tried to drag air into his lungs.

"Can't she get treatment?" Jock asked.

"It's too late," his father said. "She's been sick for a long time, but she never said anything, and with her drinking, we never realized there was more going on. She doesn't have much time left."

Archer's hands fisted. "Do Dee and Abby know?"

"No, and you *can't* tell them or anyone else." Their mother looked at them with pleading eyes.

"Is *she* telling them?" Jock asked.

"No," she said softly.

"What the hell, Mom?" Archer fumed. "They *need* to know. She's their *mother*."

"That's not our decision to make," their father said firmly.

"I don't give a damn. Ava isn't thinking straight. Dee and Abby have a right to know." Archer paced. He'd have given anything to have had a warning about the accident so he could have had a chance to say goodbye and say all the things he and Kayla never had a chance to.

Their mother pushed to her feet, visually steeling herself against the tears streaking her cheeks, putting on a brave face for her sons. "Listen to me, baby. This decision might not be one you or I would make, but we have to respect Ava's wishes. You know how much Ava has put the girls through with her drinking. Their lives have not been easy."

"I sure as hell do, but this is going to make it worse." It didn't matter that the girls had endured a shitty childhood, or that Deirdra could barely stand coming back to see her mother for more than a few hours, and that was only out of a sense of obligation. They still deserved to know what was going on. He glowered over her shoulder at Jock, whose gaze was locked on the floor. "Aren't you going to back me up on this?"

Jock lifted his face. It was sheet white. *Fuck.* He was probably thinking about Kayla and their baby, who Jock had named Liam in the moments before he'd died.

"I agree she's making a mistake." Jock's expression turned apologetic. "But I have to assume she knows what's best for her family."

"Are you fucking kidding me?" Archer hollered.

"Watch your language," his father warned.

"Ava has been drunk for most of their lives, and you think she knows what's best for them?" Archer seethed. "She's put them through hell. She should be doing everything she can to fix that before she loses the chance. And who's going to pick up the pieces when they find out? *You*, Mom? How is that fair?"

"I think we all know life isn't fair." Their mother touched his cheek, holding his angry stare, not the least bit intimidated by it. She'd never shied away when he'd lost his temper, no matter how hard he'd tried to get her to. "But Ava is my friend and I love her despite her failings, because that's what we do in this family. We support each other, and you of all people know that we don't have to agree with a decision to abide by it."

He lowered his eyes, gritting his teeth against the guilt swamping him.

"Look at me, honey." When he did, she said, "I tried to convince Ava to tell them, but she has her reasons not to, the same way you had your reasons to keep your distance from Jock. I need you to respect her wishes and keep this within these walls. Nobody else can know."

"We're just supposed to act like everything is normal when our friends' mom is dying? You're not even going to give Leni any warning so she can be there for Abby?"

"No, I'm not, and neither are you. I shouldn't have told you and Jock, but I know you'd have torn this kitchen apart before you'd walk out without answers." She lifted her chin and feigned a smile. "When I leave this house this morning, I will leave my tears behind. Nobody will know that one of my best friends will be gone in the next few weeks, or that she'll take a piece of me with her." Tears welled in her eyes, bringing a lump to Archer's throat. "I need you to promise me that you'll do as I asked."

He felt like he was going to explode and cry at the same time. He nodded curtly in a silent, reluctant promise and put his arms around her, holding her tight. "I'm sorry she's sick."

"I know, baby. Me too."

"I love you."

She pulled back and pressed her hands to his cheeks. "I love you, too."

Archer looked at his parents. "If you *ever* do this to us, I will never forgive you." He stormed out to the garage, grabbed his jacket, and got the hell out of there.

Ten minutes later he was at the marina, wishing his boat were still in the water as he threw open the door to Roddy's office. Roddy had always been like a second father to Archer, letting him knock around the marina, teaching him about boats and rescues, and calling Archer on his shit, in his own laid-back way. Like when he'd seen Indi leave his boat early one morning and had caught Archer coming home to see her a few hours later, he'd said, *Gotta love island life, where everyone knows your name and your dirty little secrets. Next time try offering to buy her breakfast instead of taking off at the crack of dawn.*

"I need the keys to the rescue boat."

Roddy raked his thick, collar-length gray-brown hair away from his face and pushed to his feet, concern written in his furrowed brow. His laid-back demeanor was now replaced with seriousness. "What's the problem? I didn't get any distress calls."

"Nothing you need to worry about."

Roddy came around the desk, wearing the same frayed jeans he'd worn forever and a HARBORMASTER sweatshirt that had seen better days. He stroked his beard, eyeing Archer the way he'd been doing since Archer was a kid, like he was trying to read between Archer's lines. "You want company on this excursion?"

"No." This wasn't the first time Archer had come in for this reason, and though every time he hoped it would be the last, he knew better.

Roddy arched a brow. "Should I *care* that you don't want company?"

"You damn well better." Roddy had a way of diffusing situations, and he'd been able to dim Archer's fuse a few times over the years, but nothing would extinguish the explosion building inside him.

"A'righty, son." He reached into the key cabinet. As he set the key to the boat in Archer's hand, he closed both of his hands around Archer's. "How long?"

This was the caveat to taking the rescue boat. What he was really asking was how long until he should assume the worst— that Archer had been so upset he'd lost control of the boat—

and come after him. "Forty-five minutes."

Roddy nodded. "Be careful out there."

Archer headed out to the boat. He piloted slowly out of the harbor, then opened up the engine. Tortured by thoughts of Indi, his mother, Dee and Abby, and what felt like every one of his many wrongdoings, he welcomed the icy spray that soaked him as he climbed in knots to the perfect speed and reveled in the burn of the crisp air as he rode the crests of the rough waves away from the island, leaving the rest of the world behind.

Twenty minutes out, he cut the engine, fisted his hands, and opened the valve to his anguish, letting it roar out in deafening volume.

Chapter Fourteen

ARCHER'S COTTAGE WAS alive with jovial banter as he dealt another hand of poker. He sat at the dining room table with Jock, Brant, Fitz, and Wells. They'd been playing cards, and getting into trouble together, since they were kids. Usually Grant was with them, and before they'd moved off the island, Brant's brothers, Rowan and Jamison, had also joined them. The group changed from time to time depending on who was around, but the sense of camaraderie remained strong, even in the worst of times, like during the years when Jock's chair had been empty, a constant reminder of Archer's failings and the loss of his two best friends.

Archer had lost Kayla because of a stranger, but losing Jock had been his own doing. He looked across the table at his brother, who seemed to be handling the news about Ava much better than he was. Archer's mind was a tsunami of guilt, worries, and frustration, and he was just trying to stay afloat, but every thought dragged him under—the way Indi had stormed out, his mother's grief, how Ava was handling things with her daughters and the mandate that he not tell anyone. Even the discomfort of the way he'd handled things with Indi's parents crept in, followed by his grandfather's voice, rough and to the point. *A man should treat his grapes like he treats his woman. Nurture the world around them so they have what they need to flourish, and observe every little thing so you know what needs attention before it becomes too big of an issue to fix. Remember, boy. If the roots get damaged, the grapes can't thrive.* Nothing was off-limits to his messed-up mind, including the fact that he'd been fighting the urge to call Indi all day, just to prove to himself he could go without her, and *that* was killing him the most.

Fitz tapped the table beside Archer's cards. "You okay there, buddy?"

"Yeah." Archer picked up the cards, barely registering them.

Was he being selfish with Indi? Should he let her go so she could find someone who knew all the right things to say and wasn't buried under guilt? He gritted his teeth as he looked around the table at the guys who never would have lost their cool. He imagined Fitz was the type of guy Indi's parents would go apeshit over, with his suit coat hanging over the back of his chair. His dress shirt was open, the sleeves rolled up to his elbows, and his tie hung loose around his neck. Fitz knew how to play the games the rich liked to see. The games Archer had no patience for. Hell, her parents might get off on a clean-cut restaurateur like Wells, too, until he opened his mouth and said inappropriate shit.

"You are *all* going down with this hand." Brant set down one card and motioned for Archer to deal him another.

The blue-eyed boatbuilder, whose dimples and charm won him dates with the hottest women on the island, also had a great reputation, but Indi's parents would probably disregard him simply because he worked with his hands. *Assholes.*

"Sorry, Brant, but the only one I go down on is my wife,"

Jock teased, sparking a round of jokes.

Archer wished he had Jock's temperament. Why was it that he could finesse the hell out of a business deal, but when it came to the people Archer cared about, his mouth often got him in trouble?

They played out the hand, and Brant gloated about his win.

Fitz gathered the cards, eyeing Archer. "I'm dealing this time. Your head's not in the game."

Tell me something I don't know.

"Are we still on for next Saturday?" Brant asked, looking expectantly at Archer.

It took Archer a minute to remember he'd texted them after they'd firmed up delivery dates for the cabinets and the rest of the supplies Indi had ordered. "Yeah. Everything's being delivered before then, so we should be good to go."

"What time do you want us there?" Jock asked.

"Whenever you can make it. I'll be there early, by seven or eight. I really appreciate your help."

"Wish I could be there," Wells said. "I look tough with a tool belt. I could milk that with the ladies."

Fitz scoffed and dealt the cards. "You couldn't look tough if you wore a Hulk costume."

Brant chuckled. "Speaking of costumes, I was telling a friend about the prank Grant played on your father over the holidays. How're you Steeles going to top that?"

"Remember when you guys took Levi to the store and told him it was Free Snickers Day?" Fitz shook his head. They'd been kids, and Jock and Archer had taken off while Levi had stuffed his pockets and gotten caught by the store owner. "You guys were cruel."

"We were not. Someone had to prepare him for the real

world," Jock said. "Besides, he got us back. He put itching powder in every pair of our underwear. We found out later that our father helped him do it, too."

They all cracked up, except Archer. He loved a good prank, but as he listened to the guys tossing out ideas for future pranks, all he could think about was Indi. They played another hand, and Archer tried to concentrate on the game, but as the conversation turned from pranks to sports to women, his patience with himself, for being there instead of where he wanted to be, shredded like a fast-fraying thread.

Wells raised his brows at Archer. "Now that Archer's off the market, the dating pool is a little fuller."

"Shut the fuck up with that off-the-market bullshit," Archer warned.

"Are you and Indi on the rocks already?" Fitz asked.

Archer's hands fisted beneath the table. It was nobody's fucking business what he and Indi were doing.

Wells leaned casually back in his chair, checking out his cards. "If she's getting tired of your grumpy ass, I'll be happy to comfort her."

"Fuck this. I'm out of here." Archer pushed to his feet and grabbed his jacket.

Wells stood up, hands splayed. "Dude, I was only kidding."

"No shit," Archer gritted out. "I got something to take care of."

He headed for the door, and Jock caught up to him. "Is this about earlier? Because I'm sorry—"

"It's *not*." Archer opened the door, meeting his brother's concerned gaze. "It's about my whole fucking life."

INDI ADDED MORE shading to Bellamy's cheeks as Tara videoed them. They were in Tara's photography studio, and they'd already taken pictures of Bellamy for the interior of the boutique and put together the evite for Bellamy's influencer friends so she could invite them to Indi's grand opening. Bellamy, a petite brunette with a jagged bob and big brown eyes, sat with her back pin straight, speaking to the camera. This was the fourth, and last, makeup application for the evening and the eighth video they'd made. Bellamy had explained the dos and don'ts of social media videos for influencers, which were slightly different than they were for other people, and the first rule of thumb was not to overdo her excitement. That wasn't an issue tonight. While Indi was excited to be working with Bellamy and Tara, and as proud as she was thrilled with her new spring cosmetic line and the gorgeous pictures for the walls of the boutique and the brochures Tara had already taken, she was also wrestling with thoughts of Archer.

"For those of you who missed my earlier videos in this series, you're getting an exclusive behind-the-scenes look at Indira's spring cosmetic collection. In the other videos you'll see..." Bellamy spoke with the grace of a movie star and the engaging ease of the girl next door. "All Indira products are organic, and I swear by them. They're light and long lasting, and they have never damaged my skin or caused breakouts..."

As Bellamy chatted up the products, Tara moved stealthily around her, shooting the video. Tara was a beautiful blonde with natural highlights and gorgeous curls who did very little to make herself stand out. She was a little shy, and Indi got the impression she was most comfortable behind her camera.

"Before we go, let me introduce you to the mastermind behind Indira, Indi Oliver." Bellamy looked at Indi, as comfortable as if they were having a chat in her living room. "Indi, I am in *love* with the new spring line."

Indi put on her best *casual* smile. "Thank you. I am, too," she admitted with a soft laugh.

"Can you tell us when this line will be released to the public?"

"Yes. The complete spring cosmetic line will be available April first at all Indira distributors *and* at my new Indira boutique on Silver Island, which opens the same day. But I will be giving out free samples and I'll have a limited number of products for sale during Silver Island's Winter Walk a week from Saturday."

"This is so exciting." Bellamy looked at the camera. "Not only will we *finally* have a boutique solely for Indira products, but you can get free samples in just *two weeks*. I'll be picking up my freebies, and I know where *I'll* be on April first." She turned back to Indi. "Will you be giving demonstrations during the grand opening of the boutique?"

Indi had spoken to Leni earlier about her ideas, and they'd discussed ideas for the grand opening, but they hadn't even thought about demonstrations. She'd need to hire people to help her on the floor if she was doing demonstrations, but what a *great* idea. "Yes. I'll be doing demonstrations throughout the day."

Bellamy looked into the camera. "You heard it here first, my beauties. Mark your calendars, and come out to celebrate Winter Walk and the grand opening of Indira's boutique right here on beautiful Silver Island, just a short ferry or plane ride from New York and Boston. But remember, these are going to be *major* events, so be sure to book your ferry or your flight soon. I hope to see you there!" She gave her signature wave and waited for Tara to end the video.

"God, you're good." Tara went to get her other camera off her worktable. "I don't think Silver Island is prepared for the onslaught of people these videos are going to bring."

"I hope you're right," Indi said.

"Didn't Leni tell you what happened when I wore a Swank sweater?" Bellamy reached for a hand mirror. Swank was a unique and eclectic clothing shop in Provincetown on Cape Cod.

"No." Indi began putting away her supplies. "What happened?"

"The business blew up. They sold out of the sweater in less than three hours of my post going live and got a quarter of a million dollars' worth of orders in the following two weeks."

"Are you *kidding*?" Indi didn't think there was any chance she'd see sales anywhere close to that, but she hoped for the best. "Leni said the return on investment was high, but unless they paid you a fortune, that's insane."

"They didn't pay me. It was just a sweater I ordered online." Bellamy admired herself in the mirror. "I swear you're some type of makeup savant. You make me look less baby faced but not too vamped up. I wish you could do my makeup every day."

Bellamy moved so quickly from one subject to the next, it was as though the missed income opportunity didn't faze her at all. She and Tara both seemed more interested in enjoying their work than in making money. It was a refreshing change from the people she usually worked with.

"Swank is the luckiest company around," Indi said. "And

thanks for the compliment, but you don't have a baby face. You have a youthful face, and that's a good thing. You'll appreciate it when you're older and wrinkle free."

"If I look half as good as my mom does when I'm her age, I'll be happy." Bellamy stuck her tongue out at herself in the mirror and giggled.

Bellamy's mother, Margot Silver, was indeed beautiful and probably the chicest woman on the island, next to Archer's grandmother. Margot carried herself with an air of elegance, similar to Indi's mother, but Margot was far more down to earth, and like Shelley Steele, she had been warm and lovely to Indi since the very first time they'd met, when she'd tried to set Indi up with her sons.

"Let's get the last set of pictures." Tara took the mirror from Bellamy. "I promised Joey I'd FaceTime with her tonight."

"Are you FaceTiming Joey's hot daddy, too? Indi can do your makeup and you can knock his socks off," Bellamy said as Tara positioned her for the shoot.

Indi would love to get Tara in her chair. With her natural beauty, she could be in front of the camera instead of behind it.

Tara blushed a red streak. "I am not FaceTiming with Levi." She fidgeted with the camera, looking down, her blond hair falling like a shield around her face.

"Mm-hmm. *Right*. She's totally into him," Bellamy said, earning a glare from Tara. "She stays at Levi's house in Harborside when he needs help with Joey, and she spends oodles of time with them when they're here."

"I'm Joey's *aunt*, and sometimes Levi has big projects that last into the evenings, so if I'm free, or if I have a photography gig in Harborside, I stay with them and take care of Joey." Tara looked at Indi. "Joey loves acting as my assistant, so when Levi's busy, she comes with me. She's tagging along with me at Winter Walk while Levi helps Archer do the work in your boutique."

"That sounds fun," Indi said.

"Yes, it does, but *come on*, Tara. You can admit you're into Levi. I mean, who isn't? He's *hot* and wicked cool, and I love his motorcycle." Bellamy flashed a coy smile at Indi. "Then again, Archer's got that bad-boy thing going on, too, doesn't he?"

"More than you know," Indi said under her breath.

"Are you and Archer together?" Tara asked tentatively. "My brother said he saw you two having dinner at Rock Bottom the other night."

"*No.* I mean, *kind of.* It's complicated." *To say the least.*

"I think everything about guys is complicated and confusing," Tara said.

Bellamy whipped her head to the side, eyes wide with mischief. "I think the next time you're with Levi, you should just kiss him! That'll take care of any confusion."

"Bellamy! Can you please look at the camera and stop talking about me?" Tara took her by the chin, repositioning her face.

Bellamy giggled.

Indi was glad for the change of subject. She continued putting away her supplies as they took pictures.

"Lower your chin, Bell." Tara clicked away as Bellamy moved through poses. "Now turn your face a little to the left. Good. Look past my right ear."

Indi's phone vibrated with a message from Archer. Her heart raced. She felt crappy about storming out that morning, but she'd been hurt, and the sucky part was that she knew she had no right to be hurt just because he wanted space. It wasn't an unreasonable request, especially for a lifelong no-strings-attached guy like Archer, and she'd been worried about spending too much time together anyway. But it was the *way* he'd said it, like she'd tried to move in or something.

She read the message. *Where are you?* Most guys would at least say hi, but she was used to Archer's blatant ways. The man didn't think before he spoke, and most of the time she appreciated his honesty and his brashness didn't bother her. Like everything else he did, when he spoke, it was *always* with purpose. That gave her pause, remembering when he'd come to the boutique the other night when he'd just wanted to hear her voice.

She lingered in the goodness of that memory for a moment.

Men were confusing, all right, but Archer took confusing to a whole new level.

She thumbed out, *Getting ready to leave Tara's studio. Why?* She waited for his response, but minutes passed without one, and her mind took a dark turn. Was he just checking up on her while he played poker with the guys? She'd put a stop to that. She wasn't *his* to check up on. But for some stupid reason, she wanted to be.

"Okay, we have almost everything we need," Tara said. "Indi, can I get a few with you and Bellamy?"

"Sure." They stood arm in arm as Tara took pictures. Indi wondered if her smile looked as off as she felt.

"Can we get some with all three of us?" Bellamy asked. "I'm making a memory book of my influencer journey, and being the face of Indira is one of the best things that's ever happened to me."

The joy in Bellamy's voice snapped Indi from her thoughts. Why was she letting Archer put a damper on what should be an exciting time with friends? She vowed not to let anything with

Archer get in the way again.

"I'm glad you're excited," Indi said. "Because your acceptance of the role is one of the best things that's ever happened to *me*, too. We should go out and celebrate tonight."

"Yes!" Bellamy exclaimed. "We can't let my amazing makeup go to waste. Rock Bottom has a great band playing. Tara, can you join us after FaceTiming Joey?"

"I'll do one better. I'll FaceTime her after we take these last shots, so I can head over with you. It'll be a quick call," Tara promised. "She likes to tell me about her day."

This was just what Indi needed to forget her brash and confusing *space* needer.

Chapter Fifteen

INDI HAD A great time with the girls, and while she was in the moment, she *almost* forgot her troubles with Archer. But an hour and a half later, alone with her thoughts as she drove away from Rock Bottom Bar and Grill, it all came rushing back. He'd never even bothered to respond to her text, and that made her even more annoyed with him.

She parked behind the building and retrieved her small makeup case from the back seat. As she walked around to the door on the side of the building that led up to Jules's apartment, she realized she hadn't slept there once since coming to the island. She'd gotten so used to falling asleep in Archer's arms, it felt strange knowing she was going to sleep alone. She'd lived alone her entire adult life. How could that change so fast?

She pulled open the door, startled when Archer pushed to his feet from where he was sitting on the steps. She sighed heavily. "What are you doing here? And why'd you text me asking where I was and then leave me hanging like I don't matter? I thought you wanted *space*. You really need to decide what you want, because you're giving me whiplash, and I—"

"Bananas," he said calmly.

She shook her head. *"What?"*

"Bananas. Isn't that our safe word?"

"Yes, but…?" *Oh God.* He was right. She *was* going a little bananas.

"Don't worry. You can yell at me later. I deserve it." He drew her into his arms and pressed a kiss to her temple. He tightened his hold on her, burying his face in her hair. "I need you, babe."

He was *too* serious, too solemn. "What's wrong? Did something happen?"

"Yeah." He gazed down at her with troubled eyes. "I woke up."

She didn't know if that was good or bad, but he needed her, and that was all that mattered. "Let's go upstairs and talk."

They went up to Jules's apartment. Indi set her makeup case down by the door, getting more nervous by the second as Archer paced, wringing his hands. "Do you want something to drink?"

"No thanks."

"Do you want to sit down?" She motioned to the couch, and he followed her over, the muscles in his jaw bunching. "What did you mean—" she asked at the same time he said, "I'm sorry for—" and they both quieted. "Go ahead," she urged.

"I'm sorry I hurt your feelings this morning."

"I shouldn't have overreacted. I understand wanting space. We're both used to living alone, and we've been spending a *lot* of time together. It was just the way you said it, almost like an accusation. And after you made me feel so wanted the night before, it really hurt."

"That's the thing. I *did* want you there, and I *like* waking up with you, but I'm not used to having anyone in my space. And when I say anyone, I mean *anyone*, Indi. You're the only woman other than Jules I have ever let stay overnight on my boat or in my cottage." He almost smiled but never made it past a pained expression. "I *swear* I wanted you there, but I saw your stuff on the counter, and I got freaked out."

She noticed he didn't say *scared*, and she wondered if he'd claimed not to be scared about anything for so long, he'd forgotten what it felt like. There was so much honesty in his voice, so much emotion in his eyes, she felt like he'd peeled off a layer of himself, and she was the only person allowed to see the rawness beneath. She tried to lighten the mood and ease his discomfort. "That toothbrush was pretty scary."

"I shouldn't have said anything about the toothbrush. I have a habit of being brutally honest, and I know it's cutting sometimes."

"So I've noticed."

"I know you have, and I hate that I ever say things that hurt you. I've mastered the art of pushing people away, but as I told you, I don't know how to do *this*. To be with someone I care about." He held her gaze, his words tethering them together. "I should have just said I was playing poker and couldn't see you. I get that now. I should have tried harder. I should've slowed down and thought it through. I've spent so many years pushing people away, slowing down isn't second nature to me yet."

"I'm not going to disagree. I like that you're honest, but cushioning certain things would be less hurtful. You could have said the same words but in a gentler way."

He began pacing again. "I feel like one of those assholes who's always apologizing for the hurtful shit he does."

"Telling me you need space doesn't make you an asshole. The way you said it was just hurtful."

"*Still.* I don't want to hurt you. I need to get my arms around that if I'm going to be with you."

He rubbed the back of his hand, and she noticed cuts on his knuckles. "Archer, were you in a fight?"

"No. It's from hitting the heavy bag this morning."

He must have really gone off on it to have split his knuckles so badly. "Maybe you should wear gloves."

"That would defeat the purpose." He pressed his hands to his thighs.

"Do you do that a lot?"

He shrugged. "I've been doing it for years."

No wonder his knuckles were all calloused.

"I don't want to talk about my hands. A lot of shit went down today, and all I wanted was to be with you, see your face and hear your voice."

"Why didn't you call me?"

He leaned his forearms on his knees, wringing his hands again, his gaze locked on the floor. "Because I've never needed anyone before, and…" His voice was rough and raw. "It's hard for me."

She was in awe of the courage it must have taken for such a virile man, who believed he could save everyone around him, to admit he needed her. She looked at him wringing his hands, this man who had spent years in a battle with his twin, and somewhere deep inside she knew what he'd said wasn't exactly true. He might not have known he needed Jock, but she was sure he did, because she'd noticed the difference in him once they'd started mending that broken bridge.

"I understand," she said softly.

"That's just it. You *can't* understand." He pushed to his feet, pacing. "You don't have any idea what goes through my mind a hundred times a day. I don't even know if it's fair to be here with you right now. But if there's one thing I know for sure after today, it's that I *want* to be here. I want to be with *you*, Indi. Not the guys, not anyone else. Just you."

As elated as that made her, she was worried about him. "Why? What happened?"

"We got some bad news, and it brought everything else to a head."

Now she was even more worried. "What kind of bad news?"

His jaw clenched. "I can't give you specifics. I promised my parents. Sorry."

"You're scaring me a little. Is one of them sick or something?"

"No. One of my mom's close friends is, and she doesn't have long to live."

"Oh, *Archer*." Sadness welled inside her. "I was just with Bellamy and Tara. Please tell me it's not one of their parents."

"It's not. I don't think you know her. She's been part of our lives forever, but not close, like the Remingtons or Silvers. She's an alcoholic. She has two daughters that don't live on the island. We used to help out at her restaurant."

Indi's stomach sank. "Are you talking about Abby's mom, Ava?"

"*Shit.* I forgot you knew Abby."

"Don't worry. I won't say anything. I know Abby's relationship with her mother is strained, but she's probably devastated."

"She doesn't know."

"*What?* Why not?"

"It's Ava's choice, and we can't say anything." He continued pacing. "It's been tearing me up all day. No one was supposed to know, but Jock and I walked in on my mother bawling her eyes out this morning, and she had to tell us."

"I feel so bad for Abby and her sister, and for your parents."

"Yeah, it sucks. My parents are in an unthinkable position. They have to pretend nothing is wrong while my mom's best friend is dying and then pick up the pieces after she's gone." He cursed under his breath, wearing a path in the floor. "They're always stuck dealing with other people's shit. They dealt with mine for years. When they told us what was going on, it stirred up all the shit that went down when Kayla died. I'm pissed that Ava won't tell Abby and Dee. I would give *anything* to have had a chance to say goodbye to Kayla and make some sense of all the things we never got to say to each other."

Indi went to him, but he kept his distance and looked up at the ceiling, fists clenched. "It's fucked up, and it's all my fault." He lowered his chin, shoulders rounding as if they'd become heavier with the confession.

"You can't take that responsibility. You weren't driving the truck that hit them."

"I might as well have been," he said through gritted teeth.

"Why would you say that?"

"Because it's *true*."

"Arch—"

"*Stop it*, Indi. It's the truth." His words were sharp, but she knew that anger wasn't aimed at her. "Kayla had been texting me all night, asking me to come meet them. She said she needed to talk, but I was hanging out with the guys and the last thing I wanted to do was to go into the city. I hate the fucking city, always have."

But you came to see me. Did he think about the accident every time he'd come to see her? The magnitude of that possibility hit hard, but she tucked it away for now, focusing on

Archer as he began pacing again.

"If I had been there, she and the baby might still be alive. She was one of my best friends and had been from the time we were kids, and I couldn't make the time to go see her. She trusted me, and I fucking blew it."

It crushed her, knowing he was carrying so much guilt—about Kayla, about Jules, about his parents dealing with their rift. What else did he blame himself for? "I can't imagine how it feels to lose someone you care about, but you can't know if going to meet them would have made a difference. They still might have gotten in the car at the same time and gotten hit by that same truck at the same red light."

"But it *could* have made a difference." He shook his head as he paced. "And you want to know how selfish I am? I never admitted that to Jock or anyone else. Not after the accident or even last fall when Jock and I had it out. I was so fucked up after Kayla was killed, I couldn't deal with the thought of never seeing her again, and I blamed *Jock*. How messed up is that? He'd not only lost his girlfriend, but also his baby, and I told him he was dead to me." His damp eyes found hers. "How could I do that to my brother? My *twin*? To my family?"

Tears slid down her cheeks. "You were grieving."

"That's no excuse. So were they. I was so lost, and I missed her *so* much. I missed everything about her. Our stupid talks, the three a.m. texts, her ridiculous cackle of a laugh. I even missed the way she called me on my shit. I wanted her to be *alive*, but that would mean I could have lost Jock, and I didn't want that, either." He held up his hands beside his head, shaking them. "All that shit was in my head twenty-four-seven. I couldn't look at my own brother a year later, two years, five, *ten years* later, without being dragged right back under. And then Jock dropped another bomb that threw me for another fucking loop."

She couldn't imagine there being more.

"Last fall when Jock and I finally had it out, he told me that Kayla was in love with me. They'd planned on coming home the next morning and telling me." His voice cracked. "That's probably why she wanted to meet me that night, to tell me sooner."

"Oh, Archer." Tears spilled from her eyes. "Were you in love with her, too?"

"No, and I didn't believe Jock at first. Kayla and I were *friends*. But then he pointed out that we talked *all* the time and shared everything, and the more I thought about it, the easier it was to see. Back then, I wasn't such a closed-off dick. We'd text three times a day about stupid shit that didn't matter."

"You trusted her as much as she trusted you." The impact of that broke her heart for him. She felt like she was finally seeing *all* of him, his demons and his devastation. It explained so much about who he was and how he reacted to situations. "That's why you push women away, isn't it? So they don't catch feelings you can't return?"

ARCHER SCRUBBED A hand down his face, trying to wipe away the vulnerability clinging to him like a second skin, but it was inescapable. He'd asked for it, had sought Indi out and had sat on her steps for nearly two hours waiting to apologize and open up to her. "That's part of it. I'm drowning in guilt, Indi, and nobody deserves to be taken down with me."

Indi stepped closer, holding his gaze. "Then why are you here, telling me all of this?"

"Because when I'm not screwing things up by saying the wrong things, I think we're pretty great together. I'm hoping that now that I've laid all my shit on the table, you might see beyond my mistakes and want to help me figure out how to get past the guilt, how to stop being the closed-off asshole who says the wrong thing and move forward instead of telling me to fuck off."

A small smile appeared on her beautiful face, giving him hope that she wasn't sick of his shit yet. "You've held a lot in for a very long time. It's not going to be easy to move past."

"Nothing in my life has ever been easy."

"Do you want to know what I think about the things you just told me?"

"Have at it." He drew his shoulders back, readying himself for an onslaught of more guilt, which he'd surely deserve.

"It makes me sad that you blame yourself for everything, but I can see how you would twist it that way in your head. You're the guy who thought he should be able to save his sister from cancer, so it makes sense that you believe if you'd have gone to see Kayla, you could have saved her, too. And from what I've seen and heard, your family has already forgiven you for everything that happened."

"They have, but I have no idea *how* they did, so it makes it hard to trust it."

"Maybe that's because you haven't forgiven yourself."

His muscles tensed. "I can't do that."

"Why not?"

"Because I caused too many people too much pain."

"That might be true, but you've been paying the price for

years, and you're no longer causing them grief, so why continue to carry the burden? I think you need to forgive yourself in order to let it go, and maybe the way to do that is to own up to the things that you feel you've done."

"I just did."

"Not to *me*. To them. Tell Jock about the texts."

"And give him a reason to hate me?" *No fucking way.*

"Archer, he just got you back. I doubt he's looking for a reason to push you away again."

He swallowed hard, thinking it over.

"It might be a difficult conversation, but nothing is as hard as secretly carrying that big of a burden. You feel guilty about not going to the city when Kayla asked you to. Have you ever thought about apologizing to *her*? Or explaining your reasons?"

"How can I do that? She's gone."

"I don't know, exactly. But I think you have to get the guilt out or you'll never be able to move past it. Maybe you could go to the cemetery and try talking about it. I'll go with you if you want me to. Or is there a special place you two used to go?"

"Yeah, the vineyard. That's where we first became friends."

She smiled. "Now, that's a story I'd like to hear. Unless it's too hard to talk about."

"You don't want to hear about her."

"Archer, I care about you, and you *really* cared about Kayla. I know who you are now, but she knew the little boy who scared away monsters for his sister. She knew parts of you that I wish I'd known. I love that you had a special connection with her and that she had you, the great protector and prank puller, by her side. What fun that must have been. Of course I want to hear about her."

His throat thickened as she spun her magic, taking his self-loathing down a notch by making him think differently. "I'd like to talk about her. It's been so long since I have, and I feel horrible about that."

"Do you want to sit down?"

He nodded, and they made their way to the couch. "You'd've liked her. She didn't put up with my shit and she loved anything scary. Movies, stories, pranks."

"How did you guys first become friends?"

"She lived down the street from us, so I always knew her, but one night my parents were having a party at the winery and all of us kids were running around the vineyard. I saw her hiding behind the trees at the edge of the vineyard, and when she saw me, she made her voice real deep and said, *Get outta here. I'm fighting ghosts.* And then she lunged into the darkness doing karate chops." He laughed. "We were only like six years old, and I'd never known anyone who'd fought real ghosts. I wasn't about to give up my only chance to get in on it, so I pretended to fight off a gang of ghosts, and from then on we were thick as thieves."

He told her about how they'd snuck out at night and hidden in the vines and how since Kayla didn't get an allowance, he'd always shared his with her. She teared up when he told her about riding their bikes around the island to keep from going home when Jules was sick, and he admitted that while the vines were their safe place, being with Kayla during that time had been his. He told her about pranks they'd pulled on their siblings and how they'd throw pebbles at each other's windows in the middle of the night to sneak out and talk, and how when she went to college, she still called all the time about stupid stuff, and they'd laugh. "She's probably the only girl other than you who could make me laugh."

"No wonder you were so lost after she was killed. She sounds really special. You said you weren't in love with her, but did you ever feel more for her, or try to date each other?"

"No. We were each other's first kiss, which is *why* we never hooked up."

Indi leaned in. "Was it that bad?"

He laughed. "We were only twelve, so there wasn't much to it, but it was like kissing my sister. We laughed about it, and I thought she felt the same. It didn't make anything weird between us. She told me about the boys she crushed on, and when she started dating, I used to threaten the guys to make sure they didn't hurt her or try anything."

"I bet she loved that."

"She gave me hell for it, but that didn't stop me." He smiled with the memory. "When her prom date got sick, I took her to the dance."

"That's the sweetest thing. I bet you looked cute in a tux."

"You know it," he said arrogantly. "And she looked pretty all dolled up, but we both wore our sneakers."

"Really?" Indi laughed. "I love that."

"Yup, and afterward, when everyone was making out and going to parties, we went and got pizza and took it out to the vineyard. We made a stupid fort and stayed there all night telling ghost stories and talking about what it would be like when she left for college. She loved it here, but she had big dreams of studying fashion and working in the industry. We watched the sunrise together and then had breakfast with my family."

"That sounds like a wonderful night. She must have been so happy. You were a really good friend to her. What was it like when she went away? Did you miss her?"

"Oh *yeah*, but she texted me at all hours of the day and night, telling me shit I didn't want to hear about the guys she was dating and her classes, parties. But she didn't love school, so she got her associate's degree and came home. But she didn't give up her dreams. She worked at an upscale retail store in Chaffee, and we researched what it would take for her to get a job in the fashion industry, and she applied to a *million* jobs. It took almost two years, but she finally got an entry-level job with a company in New York. She and Jock got together soon after that."

"How'd you feel about that? Was it weird?"

"No. I was thrilled. What could be better than my two best friends getting together? You know that first kiss I told you about? I never thought about it after it happened, until Jock told me she was in love with me. Since then, I've thought about every conversation we ever had, every laugh, every time we held hands when she was sad or went for a run when I was pissed, and I realized that any other guy would probably have fallen in love with her. I don't know what that says about me, but I feel bad about that, because she deserved to be truly loved."

"But she was truly loved, as your friend, and it sounds like you were always there for her. I think she was lucky. She got all those great years with you, sharing the good and bad and everything in between. You can't help who you fall in love with, but I think you loved her as a friend."

"I did. I don't know if it was enough, but I hope it was." He took her hand in his. "I feel pretty lucky right now, being here with you, talking about all of this. It feels good to talk about her, and it helps. I didn't know talking could do that." Maybe she was onto something, and talking to Jock would help, too.

"I'm glad you trust me enough to talk to me. What you've

shared with me explains a lot about what you've been going through, and I know it wasn't easy for you."

"I more than trust you, Indi." He pulled her onto his lap and kissed her. "I tried like hell not to catch feelings for you, to save you from all of this, but I'm catching them like a net."

"Nets have holes," she pointed out.

"So do I. But maybe you can help me close them."

He leaned in for a kiss, and she yawned, and then laughed. "I'm sorry. We've had a few busy days and late nights, and I guess they're catching up with me."

"Is that your way of kicking me out? Because I know I said I wanted space, but I'd really like you to come home with me tonight."

"Why don't we just stay here?"

He looked around the apartment, remembering when he'd helped Jules move in. He could still see her happy little face as she flitted from room to room. "Sleeping in my little sister's bed with you feels all kinds of wrong."

She giggled. "We don't have to *do* anything."

"We both know how that'll go. You'll press your sexy little body against me, and I'll combust." He kissed her neck, relief and something much deeper swelling inside him. "Come home with me, darlin'."

"Can I bring my scary toothbrush?"

He grabbed her ribs, and she squealed, trying to climb off his lap, but he shifted her onto her back on the couch, grinning down at her smiling eyes. "After everything I just told you, you still have to give me shit?"

"You like when I give you shit." She leaned up and stole a kiss.

"I like everything you do." He lowered his mouth to hers in

a slow, sensual kiss. The shards of his past no longer felt quite as jagged. He reveled in the taste of her, in the feel of her forgiving heart against his chest as her arms circled him and he took the kiss deeper, sparking the passion that always took hold. He wanted to strip her bare and lay her out, worship every inch of her body, and pay homage to the beautiful woman within. But somewhere in the back of his mind was the uncomfortable thought of being on his sister's couch, and he forced himself to break their kiss.

She came away breathless, her cheeks flushed, and he came away lost in her, his heart full. There was a sliver of fear tangled up in all that goodness. Could he really do this? Say and do the right things? Learn to count to ten every time he needed to? Move past the ghosts that had haunted him for what felt like forever and be the man she deserved?

He gazed into her eyes, their sizzling connection as hot as ever, but it was deeper now, *rawer* and *realer* than anything he'd ever felt. His grandfather's voice rumbled through his mind— *Why pussyfoot around when you can jump in with two feet?*— filling him with that indestructible feeling he'd possessed before the accident, and he knew that for Indi, there was nothing he couldn't do.

Chapter Sixteen

INDI PULLED UP to the winery Tuesday afternoon for a meeting with Shelley and Daphne, taking in the cedar-and-brick building, the covered pavilion in the back, off to the side, and acres upon acres of vines that were winter bare but still breathtaking. Over the years, Indi had been to many birthday parties and community events on the winery grounds, and she knew the property well. The U-shaped building was warm and inviting inside with a mix of stone and rich dark wood, and in the back, there was a slate courtyard with a built-in bar and fire pit in the space between the two sides of the building. She had many good memories there with Leni and her siblings and friends and of dancing with Archer when Jules had thrown them together at his grandmother's birthday party. It was funny how she felt more of a connection to this property and the people who owned it than to her own family's business and her parents.

She parked next to Archer's truck, and butterflies fluttered in her belly. Even though there hadn't been any uprisings over the last few days, things felt different between them. *Better.* She could tell that the act of opening up to her had taken some weight off his shoulders, and that made her happy, but there was still an uneasy edge she saw flashes of sometimes when she caught him staring off, looking like he was trying to solve world peace, or every now and again, looking at her the same way.

As she cut the engine, her mind tiptoed back to Saturday evening, when Archer had gone to the marina to help Brant and Roddy with something. Indi had taken the opportunity to try to give him space by claiming she had a lot of work to take care of and said she would catch up with him the next day. It was the truth, although she didn't have to do the work at night. She'd been at Jules's apartment jotting down ideas for holiday events and sales for the boutique and answering emails from her New York clients, trying *not* to think of Archer, when there was a knock at the door. She'd known it was him before she'd even answered the door. Archer had stood on the doorstep looking like the rugged and delicious man he was, sexy jaw muscles bunching, dark eyes boring into her, and he'd said, *Hey, gorgeous. You too busy for me?* Her heart had done a happy dance, and she'd wanted to toy with him the way she did sometimes, but his struggle was so obvious, that push-pull of wondering if he should've shown up or not, she'd just grabbed the front of his jacket and hauled him into a long, slow kiss.

A bang on the window startled her, and she gasped. Archer opened the car door. "You going to sit there all afternoon, darlin'?"

"Hi. I didn't expect to see you." She climbed out of the car, and he tugged her against him.

"Did you really think I'd let you come here and not collect a kiss?"

He lowered his lips to hers, holding her tighter as he deepened the kiss. His tongue swept through her mouth, rough and possessive, stoking the embers that never seemed to go out for him, leaving her a little dizzy. "*Boy*, I like kissing you."

"I like kissing you." He nipped her lower lip and gave it a tug. "*Feasting* on you." Heat slithered through her core, and he ground his hips into her. "And being buried so deep inside you, you feel me the next day."

"*Yes please*" came out in one long hot breath.

A raspy laugh tumbled from his lips, and he gave her butt a squeeze. "Come find me after your meeting." He glanced at her car. "We need to get you a vehicle. Renting has got to cost a fortune."

She was still hung up on finding him after her meeting, imagining sneaking into his office and doing dirty things on his desk. It took a second for her to catch up and respond. "I'll find something at some point."

He nodded, kissed her senseless again, and then sauntered off toward the back of the winery, like he hadn't left her weak-kneed, her mind drenched in dirty thoughts. She took a moment to pull herself together before heading inside.

Shelley was hurrying down the hall toward the reception area when she walked in, smiling brightly. She was beautiful in black slacks and a gray wrap sweater, her auburn bangs sweeping across her brows. If Archer hadn't told Indi about Ava's illness, she would have no idea that Shelley was on the cusp of losing a friend.

"I was just coming to meet you." Shelley hugged her. "Daphne is on a call, so why don't we wait in my office?"

"Sure." She followed her down the hall. "Thanks for making the time to talk to me today."

"Oh, baby. I'll always make time for you."

As they went into her office, Indi felt a stab of longing to be loved like that by her own mother.

Shelley's office was as bright and cheery as she was, with an array of family photos and vibrant pictures on the walls. There were black-and-white photographs of her parents in front of the winery, and of Shelley, a pudgy little girl of five or six, wearing overalls and the unmistakable smile Indi had come to love, holding her grandfather's hand among the vines, and pictures of Archer and his grandfather, and several with various groupings of his siblings.

As she took off her coat, she noticed two more pictures of Archer on the wall by the table where she and Shelley were settling in. She had seen them a handful of times over the years, but it was like she was seeing them for the first time. There was one of him standing in the wine cellar with his father and his grandfather, surrounded by wine barrels. Archer looked to be about seventeen or eighteen. He wasn't as heavily muscled as he was now, but he stood shoulder to shoulder with the other men and was equally broad. His face was clean shaven, and she took a moment to notice his strong jaw, so much like his father's, and his proud smile, almost identical to his grandfather's. She wished she'd known him then, and she wished she'd known Kayla, the girl who had been such a big part of his life. The other picture was of Archer and Jock when they were probably eight or nine, standing in front of a big tree, each holding a can of soda. Their shirts and shorts were dirty, and they'd been caught laughing, their mouths wide open, eyes bright. They looked so carefree, she could almost hear their laughter ringing in her ears. She ached at how much of that youthful freedom they'd both lost, and she was a little sad for herself, too, for *never* having experienced it for more than a few brief moments.

Shelley leaned across the table, speaking low and conspiratorially. "Before Daphne comes in, I just want to say that while I try never to meddle in my children's lives, my boy sure seems happier lately, and after everything he's been through, it makes this mama's heart all kinds of delighted. Thank you. And that's not meant to put pressure on you."

"I know it's not. I'm glad you said something, because I wondered if I was the only one who felt things changing for him."

"We all feel it, sweetheart."

"I'm so sorry to keep you waiting," Daphne said as she breezed into the room, breaking the intimate moment. She looked pretty with her blond hair pulled back in a low ponytail, wearing a royal-blue sweater that brought out her eyes. She sat down and plunked a folder on the table. "Shelley, that call was a referral from your nephew Reggie."

"Really?" Shelley lifted her brows. "I'll have to give Reg a call and thank him."

Indi had met the Steeles' cousins from Trusty, Colorado, a few times. Reggie was the oldest of his six siblings, and Leni worked for Reggie's youngest sister Shea's PR firm.

"If this comes through, you should send him a *big* present," Daphne said excitedly. "He referred two sisters who are looking for a venue for their double wedding this fall. I gave them my best sales pitch, and since Indi said to keep her in mind for events, I told them we work with Silver Island's *premier* makeup artist." She gave Indi a hopeful glance. "I *might have* thrown in that you're from New York City, you're known for working with top models, *and* you'll be behind the scenes at Fashion Week. I hope that's okay."

"It's more than okay, because it's all true," Indi said. "Great sales job, Daph. I hope it comes through."

"Me too," Daphne said. "I know we have a lot of work to

talk about, but before we start, I have to ask. How excited are you to move here? I mean, I *just* made the move a few months ago, and I remember being scared and excited and I can tell you with one hundred percent certainty that I made the right decision."

"You don't have to convince me," Indi said. "I'm nervous but not really scared, because I've been thinking about it for a while. I never felt like New York was *it* for me, but the very first time I came home with Leni, I had this peaceful feeling, like I could breathe for the first time, and that feeling has just gotten stronger ever since." She drew in a deep breath, exhaling slowly. "My parents still aren't talking to me, so there's *that*, but we've always had a rocky relationship."

"Oh, honey." Shelley reached over and patted her hand. "I'm sorry to hear that."

"It's okay. I haven't fit into who they think their daughter should be for a long time, and I'm coming to grips with the fact that they will probably never feel any differently."

"I can't imagine how hard that is," Daphne said.

"I'm getting a little more numb to it with every incident, and this time I'm *not* crawling back for their approval."

Shelley sat back with a serious expression. "My dad was a tough cookie. A lot like Archer, gruff and to the point. But I always knew he loved me for me. If there's one thing I've learned, it's that parenting is hard, but so is being a daughter."

"You can say that again," Daphne agreed. "I never know if I'm doing the right thing with Hadley."

"You're a great mom, sweetheart," Shelley reassured her. "The thing is, we try to raise confident children, but part of that is encouraging them to speak their minds. That doesn't mean we agree with, or like, when they blaze their own paths. Most of my children left the island, and my heart broke each time one of them left. But I'd never hold them back, because I want them to be unafraid of life, and to be happy. I also believe if you love your children enough, they'll find their way back. They might not move back home, but they'll come around enough to take the pain of missing them away."

"That's why Jock and I visit my family so often. I miss them, but I love it here."

"I don't think my parents ever miss me," Indi admitted.

"Don't be so quick to judge," Shelley gently warned. "Every family shows their love differently. Look at the Silvers. Margot and Alexander live in separate houses. To an outsider, they might look like they're worlds apart, but their love for each other and their children is endless. I'm sure we look like the perfect family. But, Indi, you saw, and Daphne, you've heard, how difficult it was for us to manage the rift between Jock and Archer. Our family walked on eggshells on the rare occasions they were both on the island."

Indi felt protective of Archer but also sad for their whole family. "Everyone must have been so mad at Archer."

Shelley's brows knitted. "I can only speak for myself, but I wasn't angry with him. How could I be? He lost a big part of himself when he lost Kayla, and he's never been good at managing his emotions. Archer is a fighter, just like my father was, and fighters are quick to act and slow to forgive. The trouble is, fighters beat themselves up far worse than they do anyone else, and sometimes it takes a long time to move past that."

"If you don't mind me asking, what was it like for you all those years?" Indi asked.

"It was sad," Shelley said. "The boys I carried together in

my womb were at odds. I was heartbroken for them. But they're *my* boys, so I did the only thing this mother's heart allowed. I loved them, and I gave them the time and support they needed to figure things out. I never expected it to take a decade and end in a fistfight, but *hey*, whatever it takes, right?"

Indi was missing the love part from her mother, and Shelley must have sensed it, because she said, "I don't know what's going on in your parents' minds, but I have to believe they're hurting, too. Parental love is different from anything else. It doesn't just end. Sometimes people can shut off those feelings, but if you ask me, they are still alive inside them. Maybe they're fighters, too, and they just need more time to sort things out."

"Maybe." Indi doubted it, but she didn't want to go down that path and ruin the rest of her day.

Shelley softened her tone. "In any case, I'm here if you want to talk, if you need a hug, or if you want me to make you a seven-course meal of just desserts so you can drown your feelings in sugar."

"Thanks, Shelley. That means a lot to me." To lighten the mood, she added, "I might just take you up on that sugar overload thing."

Daphne said, "I'll help with that one," making them all laugh.

On that happier note, Indi said, "*Okay.* Enough about me and my parental woes. I'm thrilled to be moving here and excited about the chance to work together on events, so let's talk business."

"We're excited, too," Shelley said. "And before I forget, Leni mentioned that you're doing Winter Walk, which is smart. It'll be great exposure."

"I'm looking forward to it. My sister is coming to help me

for the day. I hope you'll both stop by and meet her."

"Of course! I can't wait," Shelley said.

"Hadley and I will be spending a lot of time at the park that day, since Jock is helping Archer at your boutique. We'll definitely stop by," Daphne said.

"Leni also mentioned that you might be looking to hire two part-time employees. Are you?" Shelley asked.

"I haven't started looking yet, but yes. I think that'll be enough to get me started until I see how much help I need during the summer. I'd really like to find people who have some experience with makeup or skincare, which I know might be hard. Leni suggested I put an ad on the Silver Island community board's website."

"That's a great idea," Shelley said. "You might also want to talk to Jules when she gets back. She has a part-timer named Noelle who might be interested. Noelle is a pistol, not a wallflower, and she is phenomenal with customers. I know she narrates erotic romance novels. I'm not sure if she has any skincare or makeup experience, but her makeup is always perfectly downplayed, except for the red lipstick. That's her signature look."

"She sounds great. I'll ask Jules what she thinks."

"You'll *love* Noelle," Daphne said. "I also have a friend in my mom group who's looking for something. Her name is Macie Walsh, and she works part-time at Whit's Pub in Seaport, but I know she worked at the makeup counter of Cotton's Department Store for a few years. She's really sweet and good with people."

"She sounds great. Why don't you see if she's interested, and if she is, give her my number. You guys might have just saved me a lot of time—thanks."

"Something I'm learning is that word of mouth works for everything around here," Daphne said. "Now, let's get down to business. Indi, what's your timeline? I know you want to open the boutique on April first, but when do you want to start branching out and doing events?"

"I think I'd like to give myself a month of running the boutique before actually doing events, but we can book them during that time. Does that sound okay?"

"Anything you're comfortable with is okay with us," Shelley answered.

They spent the next hour talking about ways they could work together and cross-promote their businesses. Indi took notes as they brainstormed, and it seemed like every idea led to another. She debated mentioning the video series she wanted to put together, but she held off until she could get a better handle on her timeline and focused on the things she knew she could get started with. "I can give you a stock of samples to give to your clients so they can try the products, and I'll offer a discounted service to anyone who signs up within two weeks of booking an event with the winery. That will give them time to consider their options but also a deadline."

"That's a fabulous idea," Shelley said.

Daphne jotted down a note. "A lot more people are doing video meet and greets these days because of their busy schedules. Would you be open to joining in on some of them if your services fit the event?"

"Absolutely. I'd love to. The more face time with potential customers, the better, as far as I'm concerned."

"We feel the same way," Shelley said. "How about discounts for referrals from friends as a package deal if they hire both companies?"

"Yes, definitely," Indi said.

"I love that idea." Daphne jotted it down on her list.

"Well, ladies, I think we've come up with some great ideas," Shelley said. "I'm so glad we're doing this together."

"Me too," Daphne and Indi said in unison.

They talked for a few more minutes, and after thank-yous and promises to follow up with each other, Indi was riding high as she left Shelley's office. She pulled out her phone and texted Archer on her way down the hall, excited to share her news and, hopefully, more of those steamy kisses.

ARCHER COULDN'T SIT still and do paperwork for another minute. He got edgy in the winter when his vines didn't need tending to as often and he was stuck indoors. It didn't help that Indi was front and center in his thoughts, making it even harder to concentrate. He glanced out his office window and pushed to his feet, itching to get out there and clear his head. He pulled on his bomber jacket and grabbed his vibrating phone from the desk, reading a text from Indi as he walked out of his office. *I just finished. Are you free?*

His first thought was that his day just got a hell of a lot better, but on its heels was the other side of reality. He wasn't even close to *free*. Being with him came at a price that they were both all too aware of. Things might be easier now that he'd lain all his cards on the table, but he was walking a tightrope, and Indi's heart was on the line. The underlying threat of being pulled into the abyss of guilt and barking at her or saying something asinine when he should count to ten would remain until he got out from under it. He'd been thinking about what she'd said about forgiving himself, but even the thought brought more guilt. He didn't have an answer, but he needed to figure this crap out and find a solution, because losing Indi was *not* an option he could live with.

He pocketed his phone and saw his beautiful girl coming down the hall, gorgeous in a forest-green jacket, the black jeans he'd tried to rip off her the minute she'd put them on that morning, and sexy fur-lined boots that gave her a naughty edge. He hoped her elated smile meant the meeting had gone well, but at the same time, he hoped it was caused by seeing him.

He strode toward her, a rush of happiness, horniness, and something else he didn't dare define filling him up like smoke from a fire. "Hey, darlin'."

She put her hand on his chest, brows knitted. "You're leaving?"

"Just taking a walk to clear my head."

"Darn." She frowned. "I guess that means no desk sex."

"The hell it does." He took her by the arm and headed back toward his office.

"Stop. I was kidding." She laughed, lowering her voice. "Your mother is right down the hall."

"So?"

"So I am *not* doing that with her in this building."

"Fine. But we're coming back after hours one night because now all I'm going to be able to think about is you bent over my desk."

She went up on her toes and whispered, "Is there a couch in your office, too?"

"You're killing me." He took her by the arm, hurrying toward the back door.

She giggled, walking fast to keep up. "Where are we going?"

"For a walk in the vineyard. I need air."

The second they were outside, he drew her into his arms. Her eyes glittered, which did funky things to his insides. He kissed her *hard*, trying to chase away the feelings that were becoming more familiar every time they were together. But he loved kissing her, and it drove those feelings deeper, making him want to run toward them, not away. The trouble was, he wanted to do a hell of a lot more than kiss her.

He tore his mouth away. "Let's walk before I get carried away and get us both in trouble. How'd your meeting go?"

"Give me a second to catch my breath. Geez. Your kisses need to come with warning labels. Or ice baths. Or *both*." Her cheeks were flushed, and she held on to his arm as they walked toward the vines.

Chalk all of that up to more things he liked about being with her.

"We had a great meeting. Daphne and your mom are really creative. We got a good start and came up with great ideas. More importantly, I think we'll work well together. I feel lucky that your mom trusts me to work with your clients."

"Of course she trusts you." He led her away from the building and down a row of vines.

"You make it sound like a given, but this is big. We're talking about your family's business. Your legacy. Everything that happens here reflects on all of you, and I am honored to be given a chance to be part of it."

Hell if that didn't touch him so damn deep it almost hurt.

"Why were you coming outside to clear your head?"

He looked past the vines. On clear days like today, he could see all the way to the other side of the island, and at night the lighthouses shone in the distance. "I just think better out here."

"It doesn't get old, does it?"

"I've been staring at these views for as long as I can remember as I walked the vineyard with my father and grandfather. They taught me to nurture the land and care for the grapes before I even knew that's what they were doing, and it's still the place that calls to me the loudest."

"So that's how it all began? Your love of the vineyard? With you and your dad and your grandpa?"

"This place has been in my mother's family for generations. It's in my blood." They walked to the end of a row of vines, and Archer put his arm around her, turning them to look at the vineyard. "The view of the island is gorgeous, but *this* is spectacular. We literally reap what we sow. The land, the vines, the wine. They all speak to me in a way nothing ever had." *Until you.* "I've never wanted to work anywhere else, which is probably because this place was my grandfather's passion, too."

"I don't know much about him, but I've heard your grandmother make jokes about how alike you two are."

"Yeah, he was an ornery bastard, too."

"You're not a bastard."

He arched a brow. "You've told me more than once that I can be a dick, and you're absolutely right."

"Yes, but that's different from a bastard. To me, a dick is a jerk, someone who says annoying things or doesn't cushion what they say when they should. But a bastard is someone who purposely hurts people."

He gritted his teeth, holding her tighter, hoping like hell she wouldn't take off when he pointed out the truth. "Then my grandfather was an ornery dick, but I'm afraid I'm both, darlin'. I'm pretty sure I said those things to Jock after the accident to hurt him. Part of me wanted him to hurt as much as I did, and I was too messed up to realize that he already was."

She looked at him with a mix of sadness and empathy. "Okay, maybe you were. But you weren't in your right mind, and I don't think you'd say those types of things to him or anyone else now. Do you?"

"I sure as hell hope not. I'd like to think I left that guy behind after Jock and I duked it out."

"I will never forget that day, mostly because I'd never seen men fight like that but also because we'd hooked up for the first time the night before."

"That day was a bitch, but it changed my life for the better, and that night with you changed my life just as much. You worked your sorcery and got under my skin. But we're not going to talk about that, or you'll end up on your back in these fields, and this time we don't have a dark night to hide us from prying eyes." He leaned down and kissed her. "Seriously, though. I'd like to think I left that bastard behind."

Her expression turned pensive. "What about all that stuff you said to my father? Did you say it to hurt him?"

"No. I told him the truth because he needed to hear it. I thought it would open his eyes to what he was doing to you. He's your *father*. He should protect you at all costs. Every child should be able to count on their father not only to have their back but to be three steps ahead at all times to ward off trouble before it hits. That teaches kids to think ahead, so they can protect themselves as adults. But having your back should never change, no matter what your age. And *your* father should be so damn proud of you, he can barely contain it, because you're fucking amazing."

"Thanks for believing in me." She put her arms around his

middle, hugging him. "Is that how your father raised you? Did he tell you those things about how to love your children?"

"No. My father *showed* me with his actions. My grandfather is the one who drilled them into my head with words. From the time I was a little boy, we'd walk through these vines, and he'd be talking about grapes one minute and about life or what it meant to be a man the next. Even when I was too little to understand, I desperately wanted to, because he was so passionate. He wasn't big on talking, so when he did speak, I listened to every word, and when we were out here, it was almost like he was talking to himself, because he was so direct."

"That's where you get it from."

"Probably. I remember asking my dad about the things my grandfather had said nearly every night."

"Did he explain them?"

"Sometimes, but usually he'd say I needed to ask my grandfather. When I got older, he told me the reason he didn't explain it all to me was that he didn't want to misconstrue whatever lessons my grandfather was trying to teach me. But I never asked my grandfather what he meant, because he got annoyed if we asked too many questions. He'd tell us to use our noggins and figure it out. So I listened more closely until I figured it all out myself."

"Still, that was thoughtful of your father to think of your grandfather first."

He half scoffed, half chuckled. "Maybe. Or maybe he was afraid my grandfather would give him hell if he explained it wrong. You never know. My grandfather could be a dick, after all. But you're right. It was thoughtful of him no matter what the reason."

"I hope you know how special your father is and how lucky

you are to have him. I'd give anything for a dad like him."

"I know, babe." He kissed her temple. "He's a hell of a man. He has always loved us unconditionally, and he taught us well. I know most kids idolize their fathers, but my grandfather was my hero. I remember when I was a little kid, he looked bigger than life. He was the toughest, smartest man I knew, and he loved my grandmother, my mother, and all of us, *and* this land, so fiercely, he grouped us and the land together and called us his *loves*."

"It's no wonder you feel so connected to this place. It sounds like you spent all your free time here as a kid. Did Kayla and your grandfather get along?"

"Kayla loved him. She was always bugging the heck out of him, asking a million questions, climbing onto his lap and shit." He laughed. He hadn't let himself think about all the good times in so long, it felt good to think about her now. "He used to tease her and say shit like, *Don't you have someplace to be?* She'd say, *Just here with you.* He'd roll his eyes and say, *Come on, kid,* and grumble as she took his hand."

"That's sweet. It's nice that you shared him like that."

"I guess. I miss them both. I'd give anything to see them one more time." *I've got a lot of apologizing to do.*

"How old were you when your grandfather passed away?"

"Eighteen." He kept his arm around Indi as painful memories rolled in, and he began walking again, this time along the edge of the vineyard. "I'll never forget my grandfather's last words. We were out here pruning the vines."

"You were *with* him?"

His throat tightened, but he wanted her to know *all* of him, so he forced the words to come. "Yeah. He was asking me if I was sure I didn't want to go to college, like Jock."

"He wanted you to?"

"I don't think so. I think he didn't want me to feel like I had to stay. But I set him straight and told him this was what I wanted and that I'd make him proud. He said I made him proud every day of my life." Archer got a little choked up. "Something about the way he said it sounded weird. *Final*, you know? I looked over and he was crouched beside the vine, like I'd seen him a million times before. I said *Thanks, Gramps*, and he grabbed his chest and tried to stand up but stumbled and fell onto his back. I ran over to him, hollering for help, and called nine-one-one. He was having trouble breathing, but he grabbed my shirt, pulling me down to him, and said, *Take care of my loves*. He usually had a deep, powerful voice, and it was so frail, like it took all his energy to choke out the words. It seemed impossible to have come from him. And that was it. His lights went out. I tried CPR, but I couldn't revive him."

"Oh, *Archer*." She hugged him. "I'm so sorry."

"He asked me for one thing, and I fucked it up."

"Please don't do that to yourself. He wouldn't want you to think that."

He fought the urge to get the hell out of there. *Don't fucking leave* ran through his head like a mantra. He wrapped his arms around her, anchoring himself in place. "It's messed up, Indi. I can't believe the damage I've done, the hurtful things that I've said. He'd be ashamed of me."

"No, he wouldn't. You said he was just like you. If anyone would understand what you were going through, it was him. Look around us." She motioned toward the vineyard. "You've taken care of *these* loves, and you fixed things with your family. It took time, and you might not feel like you're done fixing it, but you are doing everything he asked."

He clung to her words, wanting to believe them. "But is it too little too late?"

"Fixing things with your family wasn't a *little* feat. It was enormous and complicated, and it's never too late to make a positive change."

He gazed down at her, feeling too many things to pick them apart. "What did I do to deserve to have you in my life?"

"I ask myself that *all* the time," she said teasingly, and he was thankful for the levity. "I have a feeling that when you look in the mirror, it's hard to see past the years of anger and hurt and the way you distanced yourself from everyone. But what I see is a man who overcame insurmountable pain to right his wrongs and pours his heart and soul into this vineyard. I see a brother who went to New York City, which he *hates*, to make sure his sister didn't just know her way around but felt like she owned the Big scary Apple. A brother who loved his niece and younger brother so much, he left his beloved boat to take care of the late-night feedings and walked his brother's colicky infant at all hours because the minute she lay down, her belly would hurt, and she'd cry. And don't get me started on Jules and her makeup."

God, this woman. "How do you know about Leni and Joey?"

"When I first met you, I told Leni you were hot but kind of a jerk, and she gave me a lecture about all the things you've done for everyone. I could go on and on, about you going to Port Hudson to strut around on campus with Sutton so everyone knew she had an older brother watching out for her and how when Jock first went to college, he missed you, so you continued pranking him by doing things like sending a care package with blow-up dolls that popped out of the box, and when you went to see him, you guys went to a party, and you asked him in front of everyone if he'd stopped wetting the bed yet."

He laughed, having forgotten about that. "That was pretty funny."

"That was you going above and beyond to make sure your twin knew he wasn't alone." She wound her arms around him. "Don't you see, Archer? There's a reason your family and friends stuck by you when you were hurting. You're so much more than a man who said spiteful things and distanced himself from his family, and your grandfather has lots of reasons to be proud of you. I hope one day you can see that."

His chest constricted, thoughts and emotions pummeling him at breakneck speed. He couldn't hold on to any of them tight enough to put them into words. Instead, he framed her beautiful face between his hands and said, "All I see right now is you," and lowered his lips to hers, filling her with all his unspoken promises.

Chapter Seventeen

SILVER HAVEN WAS buzzing with activity in preparation for Winter Walk on Saturday morning, and Indi's boutique was just as busy, as Archer, Jock, Levi, and Brant worked with their fathers, coordinating and carrying out the work that needed to be done. They'd already put a table and chairs out front, and soon Indi would begin setting up for the sidewalk sale. Archer and Levi were uninstalling an old styling chair, while Jock and his father were installing the new chairs by the wash station, and Brant and Roddy were moving display cabinets into place. Indi hadn't expected to see Steve and Roddy, and when she'd said as much, Steve had said, *Darlin', this is what we do for family.* How a single sentence could nearly bring her to tears was beyond her, but with everything that had been going on between her and Archer, and knowing her sister was coming today, she was overly emotional.

Archer winked as he and Levi carried the old chair toward the back door. It had been only a week and a half since he'd shown up at the apartment after his poker night, but they'd gotten so much closer, it felt like a month. It wasn't like he'd gone from being gruff to sweet or turned into a guy who continued pouring his heart out. He was still the sexy beast who got her riled up with naughty texts and devoured her so blissfully, she could barely breathe, and he still glowered at every man who checked her out, as he had last night when they'd gone for pizza with Jock, Daphne, and Hadley. When he'd glared at them, she'd simply put her hand on his and whispered, *If you keep checking out the guys, I'm going to worry you're switching teams*, bringing his attention back to where it should be. She'd noticed him gritting his teeth a few times and looking up at the ceiling when they were having a heated discussion to keep himself from saying something cutting, and the one time a harsh remark had slipped out, he was quick to take it back. She hadn't expected him to be so aware so fast, but then again, she knew better than to underestimate the man who had once believed he had the power to change the fate of others.

He didn't need that power. He only needed to have enough determination to change his own fate, and hopefully one day, to forgive himself for the guilt he carried.

Her phone vibrated, drawing her from her thoughts. She was surprised to see James's name appear on the screen. She hadn't heard from him since they'd had coffee a few weeks ago. She answered the call as she walked toward the front of the store. "Hi, James. How are you?"

"I'm doing well, thanks. I saw Meredith the other day at the office with Bruce, and she mentioned she was coming to see your new place. You're really doing it, huh? Opening your boutique?"

"Does that come as a surprise? When we had coffee, I told you I had signed the lease."

"I don't know. I guess part of me was still thinking that Greece might be in your plans."

She couldn't tell if he was kidding but felt bad if he was still hanging on. "James, Greece was never in my plans. That was all in my mother's head."

"Can't fault a guy for wishful thinking. I hope the boutique is everything you've dreamed of."

She turned around and saw Archer come through the back door, heading her way. "I hope so, too."

"Maybe when you're back in the city we can grab a drink and catch up."

"Yeah, maybe," she said distractedly, caught in the hungry look in Archer's eyes.

"I look forward to it. Good luck with the boutique."

"Thanks, take care." She ended the call, and Archer leaned in for a kiss. He hadn't done that in front of everyone before, and it sent a little thrill through her.

"Everything okay?"

"Yeah, that was James. He was just calling to say good luck with the boutique."

His jaw tightened, and he turned to walk away.

"Archer...?"

He looked over his shoulder, eyes dark. "Trust me, walking away is better than whatever was about to come out of my mouth."

"He was just being nice," she called after him.

He lifted his arm, giving her a thumbs-up as he walked away, and she heard him grumble, *Nice, my ass.*

So, this is what progress looks like. She chuckled to herself and went to get her coat from the office so she could start setting up on the sidewalk. When she came out of the office, her sister and niece were walking through the front door. Happiness soared inside her.

"Aunt Indi!" Chantal ran over and hugged her.

"Hi. What a nice surprise. I didn't know you were coming with your mom." Indi looked at Meredith for an explanation, but Chantal answered before she could do anything more than smile.

"Mom said I could help you with Winter Walk," Chantal exclaimed. "Terrence wanted to come, but Daddy said he was too wild and he promised to bring him another time."

"That was probably wise of your daddy, but I'm really glad you're here. I need all the help I can get." She went to hug Meredith and said, "Thank you," just as Simon walked through the door. Indi barely had time to register her shock when she saw Archer striding toward them, eyes locked on Simon like a lion protecting his lioness. Levi nudged Jock, and they fell into step behind him like they either had to tame the lion or join him in a fight. She couldn't tell which. Steve, Brant, and Roddy were not far behind, although they were all smiles, like a welcoming committee.

"Hi, sis." Simon embraced her.

She held him tighter, catching Archer's gaze over his shoulder and smiling to let him know she was okay. "I can't believe you're here. After we talked on the phone, I didn't know what to think." Archer moved beside her, putting a hand on her back. She appreciated his silent support, although he still had a serious bead on Simon.

"I wasn't trying to hammer you," Simon explained. "I just wanted to be sure you had all of your ducks in a row, but then someone pointed out that I can come across like Dad sometimes."

Relief swept through Indi, and she could feel the tension draining from Archer, too. "It's okay. You're here now, and that's all that matters."

"It's good to see you again, Simon." Archer shook his hand. "Meredith, Chantal, I'm glad you're here. Let me introduce all of you to my brothers Jock and Levi." He motioned to each person as he introduced them. "This is my father, Steve, my buddy Brant, and his father, Roddy."

As everyone exchanged greetings, Archer pulled Indi closer, whispering, "I'm glad your brother got his head out of his ass."

"That's not the nicest way to say that."

He cocked a grin. "Yes, it is."

She shook her head, and the others' conversations came into focus.

"How old are you, Chantal? Ten? Twelve?" Jock asked.

Chantal giggled. "Seven."

"My daughter, Joey, is eight," Levi said. "She'll be stopping by later with her aunt Tara. I know she'll be glad to have another friend to play with."

"Did you hear that, Mom?" Chantal asked.

Indi caught part of Simon's conversation with Steve. "Six kids with two sets of twins? What was that like when they were growing up?"

"Like wrangling a pack of wild banshees who all covered for each other." Steve laughed. "I never knew who to punish."

They all laughed, and Indi wondered how many times Archer had taken the blame for his brothers and sisters.

"Are those real tattoos?" Chantal asked Levi. "I *love* tattoos, but Grandma said good girls don't spend time with boys who have tattoos because they're hoodlums. Are you a hoodlum?"

The guys stifled chuckles, Indi mumbled, "Of course she did," and Meredith warned, "*Chantal.*"

"I know you said we shouldn't listen to everything Grandma says, but she *did* say it at brunch after Aunt Indi and Archer left," Chantal said innocently. "Remember?"

"Yes, unfortunately, I do remember. I'm sorry, Archer," Meredith said. "My mother saw the tattoo on your neck, and she's from a different generation."

"Don't worry about it." Archer winked at Chantal. "I've been called worse."

Levi leaned down so he was eye to eye with Chantal. "Tattoos are just a form of self-expression, like painting your nails or piercing your ears."

"I know," Chantal said. "Mom told me. I want to get one when I'm older."

Now Indi was chuckling, and Meredith was rolling her eyes.

"On that note," Steve said lightly, "we should probably get back to work."

"How can I help?" Simon asked, shrugging off his coat.

Roddy clapped a hand on Simon's shoulder. "Do city boys know how to use power tools?"

"No, we're too busy polishing our shoes." Simon smirked. "But I've seen YouTube videos."

The guys laughed, and Meredith sidled up to Indi. "It was touch and go with the tattoo thing, but I think it's going to be okay." She pointed to Chantal, who was watching the guys as they joked around and gathered tools. "Someone is intrigued."

"They're an intriguing bunch." Indi glanced at Archer as he broke away from the group, glanced her way briefly, and headed for her niece. "Thanks for talking with Simon."

"I talked to him, but I never said anything about him sounding like Dad. I don't know who told him that, but it's definitely true." She followed Indi's gaze to Chantal and Archer talking a few feet away. Archer's arms were crossed, his chin low. "I wonder what that powwow is about."

Chantal nodded vigorously, and her whole face lit up as she took Archer's hand. Archer glanced at Meredith and Indi. "You don't mind if I introduce Little Miss to some hard work, do you?"

"*Please*, Mom?" Chantal pleaded. "I promise I won't get dirty."

Archer said, "Yes, she will. But a little dirt never hurt anyone."

"It's fine." Meredith smiled.

"Yay!" Chantal cheered, beaming up at Archer. "I know how to use power tools. Mommy lets me help with the electric mixer when we bake."

Archer chuckled. "Then maybe you can show me a thing or two."

They walked away hand in hand, and Indi's heart filled up at the sight of her big man's tender side.

"He's tough *and* good with kids? You were right. He's way better than Johnny Castle. Are your ovaries throbbing?"

"No, but other parts of me are." Indi forced herself to stop gawking at Archer. "Come on, let's get set up for Winter Walk."

They carried boxes out to the sidewalk, where retailers were preparing tables up and down Main Street. A colorful banner hung over the road announcing the event, and the old-fashioned streetlights were still draped in festive red, green, and gold from the holidays. WELCOME flags flapped in the breeze by shop entrances, and excitement hung in the air. Across the street, men were carrying musical equipment from trucks to the bandstand in the park, and the Bra Brigaders had shown up in force to help organize games and snacks for the children.

"This is so exciting," Mrs. Smythe, the woman who owned the cute clothing shop next door, said as she hurried back into her store.

Up the street, the optometrist and his wife were carrying a table out the front door of their shop, and just beyond, three teenagers were putting out trays of food in front of Trista's Café. Charmaine waved from up the street, where she and another woman were setting up out front of their real estate company.

Indi waved. "That's Charmaine, the Realtor who helped me find this space. I'll introduce you after we're all set up."

Meredith waved to Charmaine. "This town is adorable. I'm going to have to meander down to the bookstore and check out their sale later."

"Indi! What a beautiful day!" Bellamy called out from the corner, where she and two other girls were setting up in front of the Happy End gift shop.

"That's Bellamy Silver, the new face of Indira." Indi waved.

Meredith waved, calling out, "Hi! I'm Indi's sister. Congratulations!"

"Thank you!" Bellamy hollered.

Indi got a kick out of Meredith. Her sister was never that outgoing.

"Wow, she *is* gorgeous." Meredith reached into the box and began taking out starter packs.

"I know. We got the best pictures for the boutique." Indi began setting out samples. "Too bad you're not here for the weekend. You could have met Jules. She and Grant are coming home late tonight."

"I will *definitely* be back to meet her. It's no wonder you love it here. The energy is so different than it is in the city. Everyone is so friendly." She leaned closer and lowered her voice. "You didn't tell me Archer's brothers and friends were so hot. Even his father is a total hottie."

"Wait until you see Steve with Shelley. I've never seen two parents as in love as they are. They're always touching and kissing."

"I love that. What's the deal with Archer? He seems to touch *you* a lot for two people who are just casually hooking up."

"We're kind of transitioning into something more."

"Kind of?"

"We've been spending a lot of time together, and he's been opening up to me. I *really* like him, Mare. Neither of us was used to spending so much time, and so many nights, with someone else, which was weird at first. It's been interesting. We're figuring it out, but it took us by surprise. I mean, this wasn't supposed to happen, with *him* of all people. I was supposed to be focusing on work."

"You *are* focusing on work, and if you think about it, all relationships are weird."

Indi organized the samples on the table and set out cards for her website. "I guess that's true."

"You seem happy when you talk about him. Does that mean he has whatever James was missing?"

"There is *no* comparison. All I have to do is think about Archer and I get butterflies. Or pissed off."

"Welcome to life with a man," Meredith said, and they both laughed.

"When he wants something, nothing stands in his way, and I swear he has no filter. The things he says sometimes." She shook her head and told Meredith about the toothbrush outburst. "In all fairness, he's trying to fix the filter thing."

"It sounds like you're two peas in a pod. You rarely hold

anything back."

"I do think we're a lot alike, but I don't say mean things."

"Oh no?" Meredith smirked. "How about the time you told Simon his head was so far up Dad's ass, he couldn't speak without spewing shit."

Indi laughed. "That was *true*. You know how he was back then."

"Yes, I do, and I think what Archer said was true, too. I bet nearly every man thinks the same thing when he first sees a woman's things among their own. It's jarring. Remember how weirded out I got when Bruce and I moved in together?"

"I thought you'd lost your mind, complaining about his shoes not being lined up in the closet and taking up too much space. That was weird, and you called him a pig. Not everyone is anal about organization, and he's a great guy."

"My point exactly. Relationships are weird, and sometimes honesty doesn't come out nicely." Meredith set a starter pack on the table, eyeing Indi cautiously. "Should I worry about you getting too close since you said Archer isn't the type of guy who settles down?"

"I don't know. Probably. I know he cares about me, but he's dealing with a lot of heartache from his past, and he's got some issues he's working on." She looked through the window at Archer helping Chantal set a piece of wood flooring in place. "He's such a good person, Mare. He gives so much of himself, and he's loyal to a fault." *Going so far as taking on guilt he didn't earn.* "The crazy thing is, I can't resist him now, and I *know* he's holding back with me because of what he's been through. I can only imagine how incredible he'll be if or when he finds a way to put the past behind him."

"That sounds heavy. Do you want to talk about it?"

Indi shook her head. "Thanks, but it's not my story to share."

"Okay, but I'm here if you change your mind." Meredith arched a brow. "How are you holding up with the Mom and Dad thing? I tried to talk to Mom the other day, but she just changed the subject."

"Of course she did." Just as she'd done Indi's whole life. Indi tucked away the pain of being cast aside so easily by her parents and took stock in the things she was thankful for. She'd woken up in the arms of the man she couldn't stop herself from falling for, and she was surrounded by friends and family who were working hard to help her make her dreams come true. She had a lot to be thankful for, even if her parents didn't see it that way. "You know what? It's their loss. You and Simon and Chantal are on this beautiful island with me, and I'm not going to let anything, least of all our materialistic parents, put a damper on my excitement."

"Now, *that's* what I'm talking about."

Indi spun around at the sound of Leni's voice and was shocked to see her and Sutton, her tall, blond, porcelain-skinned older sister, carrying overnight bags. "Leni! Sutton! What are you doing here? Did you come to welcome Jules home tonight?"

Leni looked at her like she was nuts. "No, you dingbat. We're here for *you*." She hugged Indi.

"It's a nice escape from the wrath of my boss," Sutton said as Indi embraced her.

Sutton was a reporter for the *World Discovery Hour* show, an LWW Enterprises company. She'd moved up from her position as a fashion editor in another arm of LWW, and her lack of reporting experience was a bone of contention between her and her boss.

"Is he still trying to get you fired?" Indi asked.

Sutton rolled her eyes. "Every chance he gets. But I think I'm growing on him."

"I can think of several ways I'd like to grow on hot-to-trot Flynn Braden." Leni chuckled and hugged Meredith. "I didn't know you were going to be here."

"I thought I told you," Indi said, but now that she was thinking about it, she didn't remember telling her.

"Nope, which means my brother must be screwing you senseless," Leni teased.

Indi rolled her eyes. "Simon and Chantal came, too."

Leni made a *huh* sound. "Guess Simon's not a complete douche after all."

"*Leni*," Indi chided.

"Can we back up to our brother screwing Indi senseless?" Sutton turned a hopeful smile on Indi. "Does this mean you and Archer are doing more than sneaking off after the Halloween party? Because I've always thought if anyone could tame that man, it would be you."

The funny thing was, Indi wasn't trying to tame him. Archer was doing a good job of that all by himself.

Chapter Eighteen

MUSIC FROM THE park and the din of conversation added to the upbeat energy of Winter Walk. The morning had passed in a whirlwind of a constant flow of excited customers, who bought starter kits and asked dozens of questions about Indi's hair and makeup services. Many people had come from other towns on the island, welcoming her and Meredith to Silver Island and sharing their enthusiasm for the boutique and her products. It was only January, and three people had already signed up to have her do their hair and makeup for summer events. Between meeting customers and chatting with Leni, Sutton, and Meredith, Indi was having a blast. She'd been thrilled when Archer had come out to check on her, but Sutton had teased him about looking at Indi with puppy-dog eyes, and Leni had added, *More like a ravenous Neanderthal who wants to drag her off to his cave.* Leni's assessment was definitely more accurate. Archer had kissed Indi, growled at his sisters, and headed back inside, giving them all a giggle.

Now Leni and Meredith were handing out samples, Sutton was restocking the table, and Indi was finishing up with a customer. She put a card in a bag with two starter kits, for the woman and her teenage daughter, and handed it to them.

"Thanks again for stopping by."

As they walked away, Margot Silver and Gail Remington came through the crowd. They were all smiles as they approached the table, and Indi wondered if they knew about Ava. At first glance, Indi would never have put Shelley, Margot, and Gail together as besties. Shelley was a boisterous jeans-and-a-sweater type of gal, and Margot and Gail looked like they came from different worlds—Margot with her expertly applied makeup, perfectly coiffed blondish-brown hair, cut just below the diamonds dangling from her ears, and expensive designer coat, and Gail looking like she'd walked out of Woodstock with her earthy fashion sense and wild brown-and-gray curls that rivaled Meredith's. But looks could be deceiving. They were three of the warmest, most maternal and welcoming women Indi knew.

"With you four gorgeous ladies pushing the goods, Indi's boutique will *surely* be a hit." Gail hugged Indi. "Congratulations, sweetheart. We're so proud of you."

Indi soaked in her kindness. "Thank you."

"And isn't *this* a lovely surprise." Margot waved her finger at Leni and Sutton. "Shelley didn't tell us you girls were in town."

"Mom didn't know we were coming." Sutton came around the table to hug them.

"You haven't met my sister, Meredith," Indi said.

Meredith smiled. "Hi. You can call me Mare."

"Well, aren't you my younger, cuter, taller, thinner, doppelgänger with all those curls?" Gail said, making all of them laugh. "It's a pleasure to meet you. I'm Gail, and this is Margot. My husband and son are the dimpled duo helping out in the boutique." She opened her arms. "Now get in here and give me a proper Silver Island greeting."

"I *love* this island." Meredith did a little shoulder wiggle as she went to hug Gail.

"It's a shame my boys weren't able to help today. They're both tied up with work." Margot waved Meredith in for a hug. "By the way, are you single?"

"Back off, Margot." Leni shook her head. "She's *very* married."

"But the rest of you aren't." Margot raised her brows.

Gail leaned closer to Margot as Indi went to help a customer. "We're here to get samples for the Bra Brigaders, not to play matchmaker. Leave them be or they'll never come back to visit."

"And if my brother gets wind of you trying to hook Indi up with another guy, who knows what he'll do," Leni warned.

"I thought I'd heard rumblings about a budding romance that I need to be filled in on." Margot eyed Indi as the customer she was helping walked away.

Indi did not want to step into that gossip train. "You wanted samples, right?" She began filling a bag and held it out to her. "Here you go. It's so nice of you to make sure the Bra Brigade ladies don't miss out."

"Nice try, skinny Minnie." Margot took the bag. "But I want the scoop on you and Archer."

"The grapevine is already ripe with gossip," Gail warned. "But we need to hear it straight from the source to be sure they've got it right. Is it true? Is our Archer off the market?"

Meredith chuckled. "You weren't kidding. Gossip is *serious* business around here."

Sharing details with her girlfriends and sister was one thing, but Indi and Archer were still figuring things out. She didn't even know exactly *what* they were. How could she label it? They were exclusive, but not really boyfriend and girlfriend, and committed to monogamy, but not planning a future together. Archer's line in the sand about labels and not being boyfriend or husband material still held true. She went with a safe response. "Yes, we're seeing each other, but it's complicated, and *off the market* sounds a bit too serious."

Gail and Margot exchanged a mischievous grin, and Margot said, "Okay, we'll just go help uncomplicate things for you. *Toodles.*" She and Gail hurried across the street toward the park.

"*Wait!* Please don't say anything!" Indi called after them. Archer was dealing with so much, and he'd finally opened up to her. He didn't need people talking about them. She turned to Leni. "We have to stop them. I don't want them saying something that will upset Archer."

"Since when does Archer need protecting?" Sutton asked.

"Good point." Leni turned Indi around by the shoulders, so she was looking into the boutique. "But, more importantly, look at what my brother is doing for you."

Leni banged on the window, and the guys and Chantal turned around. Chantal waved, but the guys looked confused. Archer's eyes found Indi's like heat-seeking missiles, making her pulse quicken. His lips tipped up in a wolfish grin, doing all sorts of delicious things to her body.

"I don't think it's as complicated as you're making it out to be." Leni's brow wrinkled. "And I can't believe I just said something about Archer isn't complicated."

They laughed, and Sutton exclaimed, "Here come Daphne and Hadley."

Leni turned away, but Indi continued watching Archer as he went back to work, thinking about Sutton's remark. *Since when does Archer need protecting?* His family talked about how wonderful it was that he and Jock had made up, and they joked about how tough and gruff Archer was, but nobody ever mentioned the guilt he struggled with. Did they even have a clue?

Meredith sidled up to her. "You need to get Daphne in your videos. Her smile lights up the whole street."

"I mentioned it to her when we met her and Jock for dinner last night, but she's a little shy and she turned me down. But don't worry, I'm not giving up that easily." She turned around just in time to see Daphne step up to the table with Hadley in her arms. Hadley's little brows were knitted, her lips pursed.

Meredith whispered, "Her little girl doesn't look like she's having a very good day."

"Hadley always looks serious. I think she gets her scowl from her uncle Archer." Daphne was a divorced single mom when she'd met Jock, and Archer and Hadley weren't blood related, but they sure acted like they could be.

"You can say that again," Daphne said. "Although Archer smiled a lot at dinner last night." She glanced at Meredith. "Hi, you must be Mare. I'm Daphne."

"Hi. Your little girl is precious." Meredith wiggled Hadley's foot.

Hadley buried her face in Daphne's neck.

"Wait, you guys went on a double date?" Leni looked at Sutton.

"That sounds serious," Sutton said. "Archer doesn't date, much less double date."

"It was just dinner," Indi said casually, but it hadn't felt casual sitting in a restaurant with Jock and Daphne, with Archer leaning close, whispering sexy things and inside jokes. The fact that they even *had* inside jokes resonated differently now that things were changing between them. When they'd left the restaurant, he'd slung his arm over her shoulders, and even that had made her feel good. But she was trying to keep things in perspective since they had a lot on their plates individually and together.

A cute brunette approached the table, and Indi was glad for the distraction. "Hi. Welcome to what will soon be Indira, a skincare boutique."

"Hi. Are you Indi?"

"Yes."

"Oh, good. I was just down at the Happy End talking with Bellamy, and she was telling me about your products. I have had an awful time with makeup causing breakouts, and she said your products are all natural."

Thank you, Bellamy! As Indi talked with her, another wave of people came through, and Daphne took Hadley inside to see Jock. Just as she got another breather, Joey ran down the sidewalk. Her hair was pinned up in pigtails, and she had a PRESS badge hanging around her neck.

Joey hugged Leni and Sutton, gabbing a million miles an hour about everything she'd seen and done. Then she turned to Indi and said, "Aunt Tara told *everyone* about your new store."

"That's awesome. I'll have to thank her. Joey, this is my sister, Mare."

"Hi." Joey waved.

Meredith smiled. "Hi. It sounds like you've had a great day so far."

"I have! I'm Tara's helper. See." She held up her press badge.

"That's impressive," Meredith said enthusiastically.

"Tara's on her way down with Grandma Shelley and Grandma Lenore. They're bringing lunch." Joey peered through the door to the boutique. "Hadley's here? Who's that girl with Uncle Archer?"

"That's my daughter, Chantal. Want me to introduce you?" Meredith offered.

"I can do it!" Joey opened the door and yelled, "Chantal, I'm Joey!" and ran inside.

Meredith laughed. "She's adorable."

"Yeah. She's a trip. Chantal will love her. But fair warning, if they become friends, we'll probably have to watch them like hawks when they're teenagers. Levi is a biker, and so are most of his friends in Harborside, and Joey is probably the equivalent of a biker princess with their motorcycle club."

"*Oh boy.* Can you see Mom's and Dad's faces if Chantal goes through a leather phase?"

They chuckled, but inside, Indi was sad that her niece and nephew would ever be judged by clothing alone.

She pushed those thoughts aside and dealt with a few more customers before Shelley and Lenore made their way down the sidewalk carrying bags from Trista's Café and cardboard trays of to-go cups. Tara was a good bit behind them, taking pictures. Shelley wore a belted navy coat and a wide smile. Knowing how Shelley must be struggling with the news of Ava's illness, Indi realized that Shelley was just as good at hiding her grief as Archer was.

Shelley gasped when she saw Leni and Sutton. "I should have known my girls would show up to help Indi kick off her new adventure." She set down the bags she was carrying and pulled them each into an unusually long embrace.

There it was. The only fissure in her brave facade.

When she hugged Indi, Indi held her a little tighter. She might not be able to verbally support Shelley in her grief, but she could do that.

"Shelley, Lenore, this is my sister, Mare."

"I've heard so much about both of you," Mare said. "I feel like I already know you."

"Me too, honey." Shelley embraced her. "Welcome to Silver Island."

Archer came through the door and lifted his chin toward Indi, looking like he wanted to reach for her, but there were too many people in his way.

Meredith turned to Lenore. "I feel like I should bow down, meeting the infamous leader of the Bra Brigade."

"I *like* this gal," Lenore said. "Now that Indi's a real Silver Island girl, you'll both have to join us this summer on some of our Bra Brigade outings."

Archer scowled. "The only place Indi's going to hang out in her bra is on my boat."

The girls chuckled, and Leni said something about things not being very complicated.

Indi was shocked that he'd said something so possessive and *boyfriendish*, and she liked it! But she couldn't help riling him up. "*Excuse* me?" She arched a brow.

"You want to prance around the island in your bra?" Archer challenged.

Indi lifted her chin. "Maybe I do."

He scoffed.

"Calm your jets, Archer," Lenore scolded. "It's not like we're going to parade her up and down Main Street. *Sheesh.* You really are just like your grandfather." She lowered her voice. "Indi, honey, I've got a whip at my place. Stop by sometime and I'll show you how to use it."

Archer looked like he was ready to give his grandmother an

earful.

"That's a fantastic shot," Tara said from behind her camera as she took a picture of Archer. "I'm going to call that one *Man on Fire.*"

Everyone laughed except Indi and Archer. Indi hadn't meant for him to become the butt of someone else's joke. She went to Archer's side, feeling protective of the man who had been silently suffering for years and had stood up for her without hesitation and said, "Tara, that's a great title for the picture, considering Archer's the hottest guy on the island."

"Damn right." Archer tugged her into a kiss, causing the girls to *whoop* with surprise.

Leni rolled her eyes. "*We have to stop them*, she said. *It's complicated.*"

Indi giggled. "Archer is complicated. That's what makes him so special."

"There's nothing wrong with a complicated man. I was married to one forever, and we never had a dull moment." Lenore held up the trays of drinks she was carrying, looking playfully at Archer. "I'd ask who's hungry, but we already *know* you are. Too bad Indi is *not* on the lunch menu."

Archer chuckled, and as the others talked about lunch, he whispered, "Little does she know that I like midday dessert, and you're the *only* thing on *that* menu." He palmed Indi's butt, then reached for the trays. "Let me carry those, Gram."

He carried them inside, leaving her longing for something she couldn't have with so many people around. *God*, she loved that about him.

There was a flurry of activity as Indi wrote a note telling customers to take a free sample, while Leni and Meredith put the starter kits back in the boxes and stored them under the table so they could take a break to eat lunch. When they were done, they went inside. The girls joined the others, but Indi remained just inside the door, taking it all in as lunches were handed out and chatter rose around her. She could hardly believe her eyes. The wood floors were repaired and several of the display cases and cabinets were in place. The peach finish gave the room the flair she was hoping for. The new wash-station chairs looked incredible, and the scallop-edged mirrors gave the salon area a touch of elegance. Several of the lighted shelving units were also in place. They were definite attention grabbers, just as she'd hoped. The boutique was coming to life. Archer was talking with Jock and Roddy, stealing glances at her. He'd done so much, brought so many people together just for *her*. Emotions stacked up inside her as her gaze swept over Chantal, sitting on a tarp on the floor eating lunch with Joey and Hadley and Simon laughing with Levi and Brant. She hadn't seen her brother so relaxed in years. She heard Leni gabbing with Meredith and Daphne. Leni had supported her every dream from the day they'd met, and Meredith was her quiet supporter, carefully riding the line between Indi and their parents. The room was full of people who had come out to support her as if she were family. She felt well and truly blessed and tried to ignore the pang of sadness over the two people who hadn't come.

Simon broke away from the guys and came to her side. "You look pleased."

"Blown away is more like it. I'm so happy you're here."

"Yeah, well, I still remember that cool guy whose head wasn't so far up Dad's ass."

She laughed. "I don't remember saying you were cool."

"Maybe I made that part up." He bumped her with his

shoulder. "I want you to know, I get it now. These people make *me* want to move here. I'm happy for you, Indi, and I am sorry about Mom and Dad. If I could fix it for you, I would, but I've tried many times throughout the years, and Dad always shuts me down."

"You have? For me?" Her throat thickened, and she twisted her ring.

"Why do you think I used to sneak you out of the house? By the time I was thirteen I knew our family was messed up. But you know what they say—you can't pick your parents."

"Luckily, I have a cool brother. But why did you go to work for Dad if you feel that way?"

"Because I love the work, and if I'm going to spend hours earning money for a company, it might as well belong to our family." He looked down at her hand. "You still wear it."

"Every day, and I'll never forget what you said when you gave it to me for my sixteenth birthday." *It won't always be like this.*

He smirked. "Don't sneak out without me because Dad changes the alarm codes at night?"

"That too, but you said I was going to do big things one day, and I've always held on to that. It meant a lot to me that you believed in me." She hugged him. "I love you, Simon."

"Love you, too, sis." He nodded toward Shelley, heading their way. She'd shed her coat and looked cute in jeans and a red sweater. "Maybe Shelley and Steve can give Mom and Dad parenting lessons."

I wish...

"I just love this, don't you?" Shelley said excitedly. "I'm so glad I got to meet you, Simon. There's nothing like families coming together."

"I've enjoyed meeting your family, too," Simon said.

"Well, that's wonderful, but you'd better grab some lunch before my boys eat it all," Shelley warned. "I swear they have the appetites of elephants."

Simon chuckled. "I was just on my way to get some."

As he walked away, Shelley turned a warm, maternal gaze on Indi, a look she had never quite received from her own mother. "Oh, honey, look at this place. It's really coming to life, and it's all yours. *You* did this, baby girl. We are so proud of you and elated that you've chosen to put down roots on our island."

Shelley couldn't possibly know how much her words meant to Indi. "Thank you. I can't imagine putting down roots anywhere else," she said just as Steve walked up.

"What do you think, ladies?"

"I don't know what to say," Indi admitted. "I'm awestruck. The place looks incredible. How will I ever repay everyone for their hard work?"

"There's no repaying, darlin'." He put an arm around Shelley. "Right, love?"

"That's right." Shelley glanced at Archer heading their way. "You've already given our family something I don't think any of us thought we'd ever get."

"Our boy does seem happy, doesn't he?" Steve agreed.

Archer's eyes narrowed. "Why are y'all staring at me?"

"No reason." Shelley patted his cheek. "You done good, baby." She took Steve's hand. "Come on, college guy, let's give them some privacy."

Shelley had called Steve *college guy* since they'd first met. Indi had heard the story a dozen times. Steve was from Trusty, Colorado, and he'd gone to college with Alexander Silver and Roddy. They'd become fast friends, and one summer Steve came to the island with them and worked at the winery. Shelley had blown into her father's office angrier than a bear in a trap and had taken one look at Steve and said, *Excuse me, college guy, but I need to speak with my father alone.*

As they walked away, Indi said, "I love that she still calls him that."

"Yeah, it's kind of cool." Archer took her hand, leading her across the floor. "Come on. I want to show you the office."

"But we set it up yesterday, and you didn't do any work in there today."

His eyes darkened. "I'm about to do *something* in there."

"*Archer*," she whispered, turned on by the thought of sneaking away with him for a few minutes. As they made their way toward the office, a number of phones chimed, including Archer's.

Leni and Sutton said, "*Jules.*" Jules was the queen of group texting.

Archer froze, whipping out his phone as Levi said, "She and Grant caught a flight without a layover and should be back to the island by seven."

Archer let out a long sigh, the tension in his body easing like a balloon deflating.

"This calls for a celebration dinner," Shelley announced. "Everyone's invited!"

Archer took Indi's hand again, hurrying toward the office. "You okay with dinner at my parents' tonight?"

"I don't know," she teased, glancing around, glad no one was watching them. "Dinner with your parents is a *big* commitment."

He gave her a heated look as he opened the office door and tugged her inside. "Now you're just *asking* for a spanking."

Chapter Nineteen

ARCHER HAD BEEN alone for so long, and things were changing with Indi so fast, he should probably be freaking out as they headed up the walk to his parents' house. But he hadn't felt this comfortable with a woman since Kayla. Indi didn't judge him, and she really seemed to like who he was, despite his faults. Their connection was similar to the way he and Kayla had connected, but it was also completely different. It was so intense, it drove him to do, say, and *want* things he never imagined. He hadn't even been sure he was capable of being a good partner or building an intimate relationship that went beyond the bedroom. But Indi made him feel like he could do anything, and this afternoon, as he'd worked on her boutique with his friends and their families, telling them about how hard Indi was working to line up her marketing and strategize seasonal offerings and events, he was so damn proud of her, he wanted everyone to know it. And when she'd claimed him in front of everyone, telling them he was the best-looking guy on the island, he'd felt like a king—*her* king—making him even more determined to find a way to get past his guilt.

"Does it feel weird showing up with me like this?"

"Yes," he admitted. "But it's a good weird."

He leaned in to kiss her and heard the front door open. Jules sprinted down the front steps, squealing. "I knew it! My fairy magic worked!"

That smile, and the fact that she was home safe and sound, filled him with happiness.

Jules danced around them, bopping her head as she sang, "Marry me, Indi. We'll never have to be apart. Let's pick out a sexy white dress and walk down the aisle—"

Holy hell. *"Jules!"*

Indi stifled a laugh.

Jules stopped dancing and cocked her head. "What? It's 'Love Story' by Taylor Swift."

"Cut the wedding crap." He clenched his jaw. "Do I look like the marrying type?"

Jules stomped closer, glowering. *"Yes,* you do, *especially* when you're lip-locked with Indi."

Archer's eyes narrowed, and Indi mouthed, *Bananas.*

He looked at his sister, who had never hurt anyone in her life—and whom he'd let down—and counted to five, because ten took too damn long. "It's a good thing I love you, because you're annoying the shit out of me right now." He hugged her, pressing a kiss to the top of her head. "I'm glad you're back."

"And I'm glad you're with Indi." She hugged Indi. "He's all bark, no bite, so hang in there."

Indi eyed Archer. "I think he's got some bite in him."

"As long as he keeps his bites in the bedroom," Jules said cheerily.

"Jules!" He didn't want to even think about his baby sister knowing about bites in the bedroom.

Jules and Indi giggled.

Archer had a feeling it was going to be a very long night.

"Come on. Dinner's almost ready." Jules took their arms, escorting them to the house.

Indi's siblings and niece hadn't been able to stay for dinner, and the Remingtons had plans with Roddy's parents, so it was only Archer's family tonight.

As soon as they walked inside, Hadley and Joey ran over, with Leni trailing behind them, looking at Archer like she had a secret he wasn't privy to. Joey plastered herself against his leg, while Hadley's arms shot up. "Unca Archer!"

He hoisted Hadley into his arms and ruffled Joey's hair. "What's up, munchkins?"

Joey giggled, but Hadley gave Indi a serious stare and buried her face in Archer's neck. "*My* unca."

"I see your effect on females doesn't have an age barrier." Indi patted Hadley's back. "Don't worry, Had. I'm good at sharing with family."

He chuckled and kissed Hadley's cheek. "I'll always be your uncle, squirt."

"It's nice of you guys to finally show up. The girls are drawing pictures of the family and they needed to see your faces." Leni smirked. "Did you get *lost* in the shower?"

Indi gave her an imploring look that she hoped translated to, *Hey! Don't out us*, and Archer glared at Leni, but Jules whispered, "Go, Indi."

"How do you get lost in the shower?" Joey asked innocently.

"Aunt Leni was just being silly," Archer said.

Leni mumbled, "No, I wasn't." Then louder, "Who wants to finish their picture?"

"Me!" the girls cheered. Hadley wriggled out of Archer's arms and ran into the living room.

"Look at that. They stuck around about as long as all the

women before Indi." Leni chuckled as she walked away.

"Oh, there's my sexy hunk of deliciousness." Jules waved Grant over as Indi and Archer hung up their coats.

Grant pushed his shaggy brown hair out of his eyes as he sauntered over, his beard lifting with his smile meant especially for Jules. He was the oldest of the Silver siblings, ex–Special Forces, and had lost his left leg below the knee during an overseas mission with Dark Bird, a military contractor. He'd returned to Silver Island a changed, disgruntled man. Archer had thought nothing could pull his buddy from the darkness he'd fallen into, but then Jules had made it her mission to show Grant what he was missing out on, and he'd been a different man ever since. Archer was learning that the right woman really could work miracles.

"They're *really* together," Jules whispered loudly to Grant.

Grant chuckled. "Yeah, I see that, babe." He held out a hand to Archer, pulling him into a manly embrace. "No need to ask you how it's going."

"Right." Archer appreciated the lack of fanfare about him and Indi. "It's a good thing you brought my sister home in one piece."

"Archer!" Jules *tsk*ed.

"He doesn't mean it," Indi said quickly.

Grant and Archer exchanged a knowing glance, and Grant said, "Yeah, he does." He nodded to Indi. "Good to see you. Congratulations on your new place."

"Don't you just *love* love?" Jules attached herself to Grant's side, and he put his arm around her. "We have to go out on a double date. I know you're busy with the boutique, but how about Monday or Tuesday?"

As Jules pressed Indi for a time, Archer caught Grant's attention. "You sure you want to marry my pushy sister?"

Grant wrapped his arms around Jules. "More than I've ever wanted anything in my life."

"Aw." Jules smiled up at him. "See, Archer? Love is good. In fact, that's going to be my mantra around you from now on."

"On that note, I think I'll go see how Mom's doing." Archer reached for Indi's hand.

Jules slid between them. "You go see Mom. I'm going to borrow Indi and catch up on all the juicy gossip." She dragged Indi toward the living room.

He uttered a curse.

"Relax," Grant said. "She's just happy for you. She missed you a lot while we were gone."

"Yeah? It goes both ways."

"I figured as much. She told me about all the things you helped her through over the years. She idolizes you, man, and she's lucky to have you."

Grant headed for the living room, allowing Archer space to chew on the fact that he didn't deserve to be idolized, especially by Jules. He tucked that ever-present guilt down deep and went in search of his mother. She'd gone to see Ava that morning, and with everyone around, he hadn't had a private moment to check in with her this afternoon. He found her in the kitchen, taking a tray of chicken out of the oven. The counter was covered with dishes of vegetables, some type of casserole, bread, and pasta. His mother believed food soothed the soul and filled the heart with goodness. When he was growing up, it hadn't been unusual for her to whip up meals for all their friends. If ever there was a time that *her* heart needed soothing, it was now.

"Hi, lovey," she said as he walked into the kitchen.

He wrapped her in his arms, inhaling her familiar scent.

She'd comforted him so many times when he hadn't deserved it. He hoped he might bring at least a modicum of comfort to her now. "How are you holding up?"

"I'm *fine*, baby."

Her words were brave, her tone believable to anyone who didn't know what she was going through. But Archer was tuned in to that sort of silent sorrow, and he tightened his hold on her. "It's *me*, Mom. I know what it's like to lose a friend."

She sighed softly. "Yes, you do." She looked up, and her expression said, *I'm sad, but I'd never let you carry my burden.* "I'm sorry if knowing about Ava brings up sad memories about Kayla."

So that's where I learned to redirect. "I'm worried about you, Mom. Who else knows?"

"Just your father and Jock."

"What about Margot and Gail?"

She shook her head. "I can't go against Ava's wishes. It'll all be over soon."

A rush of emotions had him pulling her back into his arms. "What can I do to help?"

"Oh, my big-hearted boy. I wish I could tell you not to worry about me, but I know you will anyway. Just keep it between us, and be happy for all that you have right now at this moment, because life is too precious to waste." She pushed out of his arms and wiped tears from her eyes. "Now go get everyone to the table before I really start crying."

He wanted to say so many things, starting with *I'm sorry for what I put you through and the years I wasted,* and *Thank you for loving me despite my shitty attitude for all those years,* but all that came out was "I love you."

"I know you do, honey." She patted his cheek. "Now go get

that pretty little gal you've swindled into your arms and the rest of the crew, and let's celebrate."

A long while later, after eating too much food, hearing all about Jules and Grant's trip to Spain, and Jock and Daphne's honeymoon, Archer sat beside Indi, listening to her talk about her plans for the boutique. He was proud to be with her, but as he sat with his family, listening to their supportive comments, hearing the love they had for her, he realized he was also proud to be part of his family. He'd give anything for Indi's parents to be that way toward her.

"I want to do how-to videos featuring women of all ages and skin types." She looked at his mother. "I was hoping you and Lenore might be willing to take part in the series and let me do your makeup on camera."

"Finally, I get the modeling recognition I deserve," his grandmother said dramatically, making everyone laugh. "I would be honored, Indi. We mature women need makeup tips, too. Well, not *me* personally, but others."

"Mom." His mother shook her head. "It sounds like fun, Indi. I'd be happy to do it."

"Wonderful, thank you!" Indi exclaimed. "Mare is going to model for the series on quick tips for moms, and I was hoping Daphne might, too, but she'd rather not do it."

"What are Leni and me? Chopped liver?" Sutton teased.

Leni raised her wineglass. "I'm cool being chopped liver. I don't need to be in front of the camera."

"You're *not* chopped liver," Indi said. "With your travel schedule and your TV contract, I didn't think you'd be able to do it, and Leni has always said she'd rather be the one coordinating events than be in the limelight."

"I was only kidding. My schedule is insane." Sutton looked

at Daphne. "But you should do the video, Daph."

"I agree," Jules chimed in. "You totally should."

"I would feel funny putting myself out there like that," Daphne said softly. "I'm not a model. I'm a mom who eats too many carbs and likes them too much to stop." She held up a forkful of pasta.

"You're more beautiful than any model could ever be." Jock leaned in and kissed her.

Hadley said, "I want *kiss*, Daddy Dock!"

Everyone laughed as Jock gave his daughter a smooch. Archer loved seeing him so happy. He hadn't thought he could handle a relationship, much less a family of his own, but as he reached for Indi's hand, he wondered if maybe one day that would change, too.

"Seriously, Daphne," Leni said. "You're beautiful and relatable to so many other moms. You should at least think about it."

"If you won't do it for Indi and women in general, then do it for your daughter," his grandmother suggested.

"She's only three," Daphne reminded her. "She won't even know I'm doing it."

"Yes, but our children learn from us at all ages." His grandmother looked around the table. "If our girls grow up watching us shy away from putting ourselves out there, they might think they should do the same thing." She glanced at Archer. "It's the same for little boys with their fathers and grandfathers."

Archer thought about his grandfather's do-it-my-way attitude and the gruff, to-the-point way he used to communicate and his father's kind, easygoing manner. Jock and Levi had definitely patterned themselves after their father, while Archer had taken to heart and embraced everything about his idol. He chewed on that while Daphne agreed to think about doing the videos, and Jules asked about when Indi was moving to the island.

"I haven't had a minute to think about the actual move. Fashion Week starts on Valentine's Day, and the grand opening for the boutique is April first, but I hope to move in by the end of February or early March, if you're okay with me using your apartment for that long."

"You can use my place as long as you'd like." Jules snuggled against Grant's side. "I'm happily living in sin."

"Hey, now," Jock said.

"Yeah, we don't want to hear about that," Archer grumbled.

Levi cleared his throat and said, "There are little ears at the table."

"It's okay, Daddy. Sin isn't a bad word," Joey said. "Uncle Jesse has a shirt that says SIN NOW, PRAY LATER, and he told me that sin can sometimes be used instead of the word *ride*, like ride his bike now and pray later." Jesse Steele was one of Archer's cousins. Jesse and his twin, Brent, lived in Harborside and were also members of the Dark Knights motorcycle club.

They all chuckled.

Levi shook his head. "We'll talk about that later."

"I'll be more careful with my words," Jules promised. "But like I said, it's totally fine, Indi."

"Thank you. I'm *so* excited about the grand opening I can barely stand it," Indi gushed. "Leni and I are still getting it all mapped out, but I'm sending evites to all of my personal and business contacts next week."

"We'll send announcements out to the winery's mailing list, too," Archer added.

Indi and the others looked at him with disbelief.

"What? It makes sense, don't you think? There's a new business on our island. We should support it by offering a discount if they come out the weekend of the grand opening." He glanced at Jules. "You should do that, too. Your mailing list is huge."

"That's a fantastic idea," his mother agreed. "I'll ask Margot if she can do the same at the Silver House."

"*Archer*, that's a lot to ask," Indi said with a thread of embarrassment.

"You've been coming here and doing my mom's and my sisters' hair and makeup for years, and you've never asked for anything in return," he pointed out. "This is the least we can do."

Her eyes filled with wonder as his family agreed.

"It might not seem like it, babe, but I'm always thinking of you." Archer pulled her closer, whispering, "Usually of you naked." He kissed her blushing cheek and set a teasing gaze on Leni. "But you might want to think about new PR representation, since my sister obviously isn't on top of her game."

"Hold on a sec." Leni held up her index finger, brows knitted in concentration. She sighed. "Yeah, I've got *nothing*. I should have come up with that idea two weeks ago."

Everyone laughed.

"Oh my gosh, Archer, you're a genius!" Daphne exclaimed.

He arched a brow. "You're just now figuring that out?"

"No, seriously. We talked about ways to pull the winery's and Indi's resources together, but after hearing Archer's idea, maybe we're still not thinking big enough. Maybe we can come up with more ideas to drum up business for more shops on the island. Something like hosting a destination wine and wedding weekend for couples to sell them on having their weddings here."

Leni glanced across the table at Indi. "Indi recently pitched a *very* similar idea to me. Tell them, Indi."

Indi said, "I had suggested a Fall in Love on Silver Island weekend, but I like Daphne's way to brand it better. I thought couples could stay at the Silver House, get a tour of the winery, and the brides can get free makeovers from me."

"We can talk to the bakeries and restaurants about tastings, too," Daphne added.

"That's a fantastic idea," Leni said.

"I bet the Silvers and other businesses would be on board with it," Archer said.

"Don't forget Tara," Jules chimed in. "She's really making a name for herself as *the* local photographer—"

"Me too, as her assistant," Joey chimed in excitedly.

"Yes, you *are*. We're going to have to set you up with business cards," Leni said, and Joey beamed at her. "How do you feel about the idea, Mom?"

"I think it's a great draw, and we'd be bringing couples into the fold of the community, which gives them a bond to remember when they're making final decisions. Steve?" his mother asked. "What do you think?"

"I think Daphne and Indi just took the genius title away from Archer." Everyone laughed, and he turned to Archer. "Are you okay with this idea? You're part owner of the business. We need your approval."

"Just keep the masses out of my vines, and you can market your hearts out."

There was an uproar of excitement, and everyone chimed in on the discussion. As the evening wore on, Archer noticed his siblings giving him approving glances as they caught him and

Indi whispering or stealing kisses. His open affection surprised even him, and it was scary as hell, but it came without thought, and no part of him wanted to hold back.

"I have something to share," his father said, and everyone quieted. "We have a lot to celebrate tonight with Indi moving to the island and opening her boutique, and all of our children under one roof, which is always cause for celebration. But what you probably don't know is that Archer has been nominated for Winemaker of the Year by *Wine Aficionado* magazine."

There was a collective gasp among the girls.

"Way to go, Archer," Levi said.

"Attaboy," his grandmother said. "Your grandfather would be proud."

"Wow. Congratulations!" Jules squealed.

"That's a *huge* accomplishment. Congratulations," Indi said with awe.

Jock said, "I'm proud of you, bro."

"That's amazing!" Daphne exclaimed.

"Yeah, that's phenomenal," Sutton added.

"That's great. When is the awards ceremony?" Leni asked. "We can get some great promotions out of this."

"It's a gala, and it's in two weeks, but Archer has opted not to attend," his father explained. "Your mother and I will go and accept it in his place when he wins, which we all know he will."

"What the heck, Archer?" Jock asked. "Why would you miss that?"

Here we go. "Because I hate those events."

"So what?" Leni said. "It's not about the event. It's about your achievement."

Archer gritted his teeth. "No, it's not. It's about dressing up in a monkey suit so people can take pictures and act fake as sh—" He glanced at Joey and Hadley. "Fake as shitake mushrooms."

"They're not fake," Joey announced. "Daddy had them at a restaurant."

Indi put her hand on Archer's under the table, speaking softly. "What if you don't wear a monkey suit or pretend to be something you're not?"

"It's *expected*," he answered too sharply, and the room grew quiet.

"So what?" she said sweetly. "I remember a morning not too long ago when you stood up to my parents and told them that they should be proud of me and support me for *who* I am. Don't you deserve the same respect? You earned that nomination by putting your heart and soul into your vineyard and the wine you make, and you should be proud to accept it. Show up as *Archer Steele, winemaker extraordinaire*, wearing your jeans and work boots, or jeans and a dress shirt, or whatever makes you comfortable. No monkey suit, no fake airs. You taught me that it doesn't matter what anyone else expects; what matters is that you stay true to yourself. I'll go with you if you want, because there's nothing I'd love more than to see you honored for all your hard work."

"You're a damn fool if you turn her down," his grandmother warned.

Indi was looking at him like he was the farthest thing from a fool she'd ever seen, and he felt himself falling harder for the incredible woman who pushed all his buttons and made him feel so damn good. She thought he believed in her, but man, the way *she* believed in *him* was everything. His jaw clenched against that wave of emotions, but the part of him that *wanted* them pushed back, freeing his heart to expand and the words to come. "Fine. I'll go if you go, but I'm not wearing a freaking monkey suit."

There was a round of cheers, and Indi threw her arms around him and said, "Thank you!"

"Forget the whip," his grandmother said. "This one's got magic lips."

You have no idea, Grandma...

ARCHER HAD THOUGHT he was not the kind of guy who could become addicted to anything, much less a woman. But as they drove away from his parents' house, there was no denying that the woman who had captured his attention with her gorgeous looks and kept him coming back for more with her seductive smile, keen sense of humor, and sexual prowess had a hold on him.

"Okay, what's going on? You're too quiet," she said curiously. "Do you regret going to your parents' house together, or agreeing to go to the gala?"

He reached across the console and put his hand on her thigh. "Did I kiss you and touch you like I wasn't enjoying it?"

"No."

He brushed his fingers along her leg. "Did I act like I didn't want to be there with you?"

"No," she said breathily. "But you're so quiet."

"I've been thinking."

"About?"

So many things. He turned into the entrance to the winery. "What are we doing here?"

"You'll see." He parked and came around to help her out, backing her up against the passenger door. He brushed his lips along her neck, inhaling the sweet, sexy scent that infiltrated his dreams, turning them dark and dirty. "I've been thinking about all the things I want to do to you in exchange for going to the awards ceremony." He slicked his tongue around the shell of her ear, earning a sexy sigh. "Starting in my office."

Her eyes flamed. "Yes!"

He crushed his mouth to hers in a penetrating kiss that beat through him like a drum. They made their way inside, kissing and peeling off their coats on the way down the hall. When they reached his office, he locked the door behind them, stalking predatorily toward her. "Strip for me, darlin'." He loved the way her eyes remained trained on him, heat blazing between them as she tugged off her boots and wriggled out of her clothes, desire practically dripping from her pores. "*Christ*, you're beautiful." He pulled off his shirt, leaving his jeans on despite his throbbing cock, wanting to remain in control.

She ran one hand up her belly, palming her breast, and moved the other between her legs, her eyes darkening. "Lonely, too."

"The fucking hell you are." He took her in another passionate kiss, touching her ass, her waist, her breasts, wanting to pleasure all of her at once. He tore his mouth away, and she started to turn around and grab the desk, but he stopped her. "No, baby. I want you right here, like this." He guided her hands to the edge of the desk and nudged her legs open wider, daring her, "Don't move." He ran his finger along her lips. "You have the sexiest mouth. I love kissing it, fucking it, teasing it." He pushed his finger into her mouth, and she sucked it *hard*, a challenge rising in her eyes as her tongue played with his finger, sending all his blood rushing south. He pulled his finger out of her mouth and held her gaze as he dragged it down her chest and circled her nipple, feeling it pebble. He palmed her breast, and she sucked in a sharp breath.

"Mine," he growled, and lowered his mouth, sucking and teasing the hard peak, making her writhe and whimper. "Stay still, darlin'."

"*Archer*" fell breathily from her lips.

He teased between her legs, using his mouth on her other breast, earning more moans and mewls. When he pushed his fingers inside her, she grabbed his shoulders, and he fucking loved that, but he wanted to drive her wild, so he gritted out, "Hands on the *desk*."

"Damn you."

She clung to the edge of the desk as he continued driving her out of her mind, until she was panting, hips rocking, sex clenching. She gripped the edge of the desk so tight her knuckles blanched. "Archer, *please*—"

That was all he needed, to hear his name filled with desire. He reclaimed her mouth, using one hand to squeeze her nipple as he fucked her with his fingers and used his thumb on the place she needed it most. He tore his mouth away as she cried out his name, loud and untethered, and she rode his hand, her body clenching tight and perfect around his fingers. He tasted his way down her silky skin, slowing to nip and suck, her body jerking with aftershocks. Her chin fell forward as he dropped to his knees.

"You might want to hold on," he warned, and lifted her legs onto his shoulders, sealing his mouth over her sex.

"Oh *God*."

His tongue thrust into her wet heat, along her lips, and over her clit. He grabbed her ass, lifting her up, knowing just how to touch her, how to fuck and tease and make her come so hard, her thighs locked around his head like a vise. *That's it, baby.* A stream of indiscernible sounds sailed from her lungs, and he stayed with her, feasting on her sweetness until she went soft against him. He lowered her legs from his shoulders, rising to his full height, and kissed her hard and deep. He could feel her getting a second wind, rocking and groping, kissing him as ravenously as he was devouring her. Her *greed* for him was so intoxicating, it brought out the animal in him, and he growled, "I need to be inside you."

Her eyes narrowed, and without a word, she opened his belt, pulling him by it as she led him around the desk to his chair. "Pants *off.*"

Hell yes. She was the only woman he'd ever given control to, and the carnal pleasures she brought were worth every second. He quickly shed his boots and clothes, anticipation mounting inside him.

She pushed him into the chair with a devilish grin and sank to her knees between his legs, running her hands up his inner thighs. Christ, she was *hot.* She licked her lips. "You want my mouth on you?" Her voice was pure seduction.

"I want your *everything* on me."

"Now, *that's* a good answer." She took his hands and set them on the arms of the chair. "Don't move, and don't you dare come."

Fuuck. Just hearing her challenge made his cock jerk. "If you put your mouth on my dick, I'm going to come."

She ran her fingers lightly along the length of his arousal. "That's a shame. Guess you don't want my mouth on you after all."

She pushed to her feet, but he grabbed her wrist, pulling her back down, and gritted out, "*Fine.*"

Her victorious smile even turned him on. Man, she fucking *owned* him.

She lowered her mouth around his shaft, taking him to the back of her throat, working him fast and tight. He grabbed her hair, but she pushed his hands back to the arms of the chair, eyes shooting darts. She knew just how to make him lose his mind. He fought the need to come with everything he had, watching his cock slide in and out of her swollen lips as she moaned and stroked him to perfection. He gripped the arms of the chair tighter as she sucked and licked, driving him right up to the edge of madness. Every suck heightened his need to come until it pounded inside him, his entire body throbbing, aching for release. Her eyes were still locked on him, and she smiled around his cock.

"*Indi,*" he warned through gritted teeth.

She took his hand and placed it on his shaft. "Stroke it."

"You suck it and I will."

She shook her head. "I want to watch."

"*Jesus.*" He relented, stroking himself as she watched with eager eyes. "You're enjoying torturing me, aren't you?"

"Who, me?" She feigned wide-eyed innocence and rose to her feet, reaching between her legs, wetting her fingers with her arousal, and teasing her clit. "Better?"

"I want *your* hand on me."

"Since that's not going to happen..." She guided his other hand between her legs. "Make me come while you stroke yourself, and I *promise* to make you come."

"Fucking *hell*, Indi."

She giggled. "Too much for you?"

"*Nothing's* too much for me. But you're going to come so hard, they'll feel it across the world. Put your hand on your breast." He pushed his fingers inside her, using his thumb to move her fingers away from the place he knew by heart, and drove her wild. She caressed her breast, watching him stroke his rock-hard cock as he worked her into a moaning, pleading mess.

She rode his fingers, her eyes fluttering closed. "Don't stop. Oh *God...*"

"Open your eyes and watch what you make me do."

Her eyes opened, and she looked at the liquid bead on the tip of his cock. Pleasure glimmered in her eyes, and he applied more pressure to both of her sensitive spots. Her hips bucked, and her head fell back as she surrendered to her release. He grabbed her by the hips, lifted her up, and lowered her pulsing sex over his aching cock, and he swore the world tilted on its axis. Her eyes found his, her hair falling around her face like an angel. She was stunningly beautiful, trusting and demanding at once. He pumped his hips faster, feeling her orgasm ravage her as she rode him to the brink of release. She grabbed his shoulder with one hand, reaching behind her with the other, and teased his balls, sending his thoughts spiraling away. He wrapped her in his arms, holding tight, thrusting despite not withdrawing, taking her deeper, until she was all he felt, all he saw, all he ever wanted. She choked out, "*Yes,*" her voice so drenched with lust, it pulled him over the edge. He buried his face in her breasts as they soared through ecstasy. And as they came down from the peak, he had a burning desire, an aching need, to see her face. He looked up at her hazy eyes, their bodies slick from their efforts, and a trusting smile appeared.

"What?" she asked softly.

He knew what he *wanted* to say, but how could he tell her

she'd become so important to him, he couldn't see a future without her in it, when he still had no idea how to deal with the guilt of his past? If she was right and he needed to forgive himself, he had no clue where or how to begin. So he swallowed his confession and pressed a kiss to the swell of her breast. His feelings for her interlaced with his unresolved issues and came out as, *"Everything, darlin'. Just everything."*

Chapter Twenty

ARCHER WALKED INTO his office Wednesday morning, still brushing snow from his jacket sleeves. It had been snowing since the wee hours of the morning. They had about three inches already, and it was supposed to keep coming down. As he hung up his jacket, his mother peeked her head in.

"Hi, honey. Do you have a minute?"

"Sure."

She went straight to the window, looking cozy in a tan sweater and jeans. "This snow is something, isn't it?" She turned toward him. "I bet Indi's not used to driving in it."

"She's not. I drove her to work today." She was cute as hell that morning, standing by his truck, catching snowflakes on her tongue, bundled up in the hat, scarf, gloves, and winter boots he'd surprised her with when he'd heard it was going to snow.

"That's probably best until she's comfortable driving in snow. Speaking of which, we missed you at breakfast again. You know you can bring Indi with you."

And give up having Indi for breakfast? I don't think so. "Yeah, I know. We'll make it one of these days."

She put her hand on his arm. "I understand. I remember when your father and I were first seeing each other. We never wanted to be apart. You two are getting close, huh?"

"Is that why you came in? To pry information out of me?"

"Only partly," she admitted. Then her tone turned serious, and sadness welled in her eyes. "I wanted to let you know that Ava is gone. She left us last night."

"Shit. I'm sorry, Mom. Are you okay? Do you want to sit down?"

She smiled and shook her head. "No, baby. I'm okay. I was with her until the end, and I had all night to put things into perspective. I'm going to miss her terribly, but she's in a better place now. She struggled for so many years, disappointed in herself for drinking and for the burden she put on the girls. But her disease was bigger than her."

"I still think she should have told them. Do they know yet?"

"I called them last night, and I agree that she should have told them. But she wasn't strong enough. She could never forgive herself for all of her failings."

He knew something about that. "Do you think it would have helped if she had?"

"Oh, *yes*. Forgiveness is a powerful thing, especially when it's internal."

"Maybe she didn't want to forgive herself because she didn't think she deserved it, or she didn't know how." He wondered if his mother knew he was talking about himself.

Her brows knitted. "I think it was probably both of those, but the real problem was that she never *tried*. I think she was too scared to try."

"Why?"

"I'm only guessing, but if she tried and couldn't forgive herself, it would be one more failure in a long list of them and another disappointment for the girls. If she had tried, who knows what could have happened."

She paused as if she was letting her words sink in. Or maybe he was just too close to the issues they were discussing to think clearly. In any case, his mother's words echoed in his ears. *The real problem was that she never tried... Who knows what could have happened if she had.*

"Are you okay?" his mother asked. "She was my friend, but you always helped her when she needed it, and I'm sure you feel the loss."

"I'm okay. It sucks that she's gone, and I'll miss who she once was, but my bigger worry is for Dee and Abby. Does Leni know? She should be there for Abby."

"Yes. I called the rest of the kids this morning. I wanted to tell you in person so you could see that I was okay."

He appreciated that. "When is the service?"

"Saturday at ten. Ava didn't want any fanfare, just a small graveside service. Her girls aren't announcing it to the community, but I'm sure word will get around."

"It always does. Is there anything I can do to help?"

"Not specifically. But as I told your brothers and sisters, remember how precious life is. I think we can all learn something from Jules. I know she can be a little much, but she takes nothing for granted. She tells people she loves them, tries never to let things go unsaid, and she finds joy in every single day."

Thinking of his pushy, adorable sister, he said, "Maybe she's onto something, but don't get your hopes up. I'm not wired like she is."

"Really?" his mother teased. "I never noticed."

He hugged her, thinking about his mother's inner strength and determination to live a life full of love, hope, and forgiveness—all the things he'd like to learn how to embrace and nurture for the other woman who was on his mind: his sweet, resilient Indi.

MOST DAYS, INDI had to pinch herself to believe she was really opening her own boutique. It was already the end of January, and she was in her new office. She hadn't decorated it yet, but she loved the furniture she'd chosen and was happy to have an office at all after not having one for so many years. She was still waiting for the pictures for the walls of the boutique and a few finishing touches, but the lighting had been installed, and the pendant lights she'd chosen gave the store a splash of elegance. Inventory would start arriving next week, and by the end of the week she hoped to have two part-time employees. She'd spoken to Macie yesterday, and with Jules's blessing, she'd called Noelle this morning. She liked them both very much, though their personalities were completely different. Macie was as careful as Noelle was direct. They were coming in for interviews early next week, and if those meetings went well, she hoped to meet with both of them together. Despite the way her parents treated her, she'd learned a few things from them over the years. Most of which revolved around how *not* to treat her own children, but she'd listened to the lessons her father had given Simon around the dinner table while grooming him to work in the family business, and one piece of advice had stuck with her and was the reason she wanted to meet with Macie and Noelle together. *A company must be built with a strong team, whose strengths and weaknesses complement each other. One broken link can mean the downfall of everything around it.* She'd always wondered why that didn't carry over to their family, but she had too much to do to worry about that now.

She needed to find something to wear to the awards ceremony next weekend that wasn't too fancy, since Archer was dressing down, and she was only two weeks away from Fashion Week. She and Leni had wrapped up final plans for the grand opening, and her to-do list was packed. They were going to start rolling out grand-opening announcements tomorrow, so she was going over the evite list for the billionth time, and just like each of the times before, when she saw her parents' names and email addresses, her stomach pitched. She debated not sending them an invitation, but that felt wrong. Sometimes she could *almost* pretend they didn't exist, but then Archer would say something about reaching out to them, or she'd hear something that reminded her of them, and she was thrown right back to the painful reality of being a disposable child.

Tears burned her eyes, and she tried willing them away. She got up and paced. She'd been giving herself pep talks her whole life, and she tried that now. *I'm building a great life here with more support than I could ever ask for. Things with Archer are better than I ever imagined, and I'm happy. Those are the things that matter.*

Why couldn't her parents be happy for her?

That question had been running circles in her mind, driving her batty, making her sad, and making her so angry, sometimes it was all she could do to shove it down deep enough that it didn't bubble out. But how long could she live like this? Worrying, wondering, hating that she wasn't enough for them? Not much longer, that was for sure. It was too hard to carry the guilt of not being what they wanted and, at the same time, stand up for herself and go after what *she* needed.

How on earth did Archer live with the guilt of everything he'd shared with her, when she had a hard time with just this?

Except it wasn't *just* anything. It was her *parents*.

Knots tightened in her stomach, and suddenly it was too overwhelming. She was done. She couldn't struggle like this anymore. She grabbed her cell phone and called her mother, needing to clear the air and see where they really stood once and for all. No more rationalizing or waiting.

"Indira, *darling*. How are you?"

Her mother's voice tugged at her heartstrings, and her initial instinct was to soothe the ache and go along with her typical ploy of avoiding the crack that had turned into a ravine between them. But she couldn't do it.

"I don't know how I am, Mom. On the one hand, I'm ecstatic with my life here on the island. My boutique is opening April first, and everyone here is happy for me. But on the other hand, I'm sending out invitations to the grand opening, and I don't even know if my parents will come."

"Oh, *Indira*. Stop being so dramatic."

Indi closed her eyes, trying not to lose her cool. "You think wanting to know if my parents, who haven't spoken to me for weeks, are coming to the grand opening of my boutique, which they think is cute and frivolous but in reality is my whole world, is being *dramatic?*"

Her mother sighed. "Yes, quite frankly, I do, and *please* lower your voice."

"I won't lower my voice, Mom. Maybe you should ask *yourself* why I'm being dramatic, and then you might realize that it is, and has always been, the *only* way you ever see or hear me. Why can't you accept me for who I am and support my dreams?" Her voice escalated, and she closed her eyes against angry tears. "I'm your *daughter*, and you make me feel like my feelings don't matter. Is that your goal in life? Because it sure seems like it."

Her ever-composed mother was silent for a long moment, and Indi thought *maybe* there was a chance she'd finally open her eyes and see things from her point of view.

"Where is this coming from, Indira? Has that *man* been putting these ideas in your head?"

Infuriated, Indi spoke through gritted teeth. "That *man* is Archer Steele, one of the best winemakers in the country, and he is more supportive of me than you or Dad have *ever* been. *That man* listens to my hopes and dreams and my fears *and* my silliness. He sees *all* of me, and you know what? Sometimes I am dramatic with him, too, but he doesn't dismiss me for it. He listens closer, because that's what you do when you love someone." *Holy shit. He's never said he loves me. It feels like he does, but that doesn't mean it's true.* She couldn't get bogged down in that while arguing with her mother. "If you really want to know where this is coming from, all you have to do is think back to all the times you dismissed me over the years. All the times you disregarded my career and my success, calling it cute or asking when I'm going to stop my *nonsense*."

"We'd hoped you'd come around by now," her mother said, infuriatingly calmly. "Sweetheart, we're being practical. The business world is a man's world. It's fickle, and small businesses like yours are a dime a dozen. You never know *when* it will crumble, but it will likely end up fading away, as most do. Then you'll be left with no job and no husband, and you'll be too old to have a family. I just don't see why you couldn't make it work with James, so you'd be taken care of—"

"*Stop* it," she seethed, pacing the floor. "You need to get rid of that crazy idea you have about me and James. It's *never* going to happen, and I don't want to be taken care of in that way. Women have businesses and families all the time. I don't know why you make it seem like I can have only one or the other just because it's what you wanted. *If* my business fails, then it does, and that's on me. But I'll *never* regret having followed my dreams, because this is *my* life, not yours or Dad's, and I'm going to live it the way that makes me happy. You were hoping I'd come around? *Ha!* That's not happening." A sense of control came over her, and she lowered her voice. "I was hoping you and Dad would *come around* by now, but I can see that's never going to happen."

"We love you, Indira, and we want what's best for you."

"No, you don't. You want what's best for *you*." Tears slid down her cheeks. "And that's a shame, because I'm an amazing person, and one day you'll miss seeing me."

"What are you saying?"

"I'm saying that Archer was right to walk out of brunch. I don't want to spend my life dodging barbs and justifying my dreams just for you and Dad to accept me. I'm done trying to win you over. I want you in my life, Mom, but not like this. I don't want to feel like I'm not enough for you or anyone else, because I *am* enough." She paused, but her mom didn't even try to defend herself or even pretend she thought Indi was enough, and that silence drew tears from Indi's eyes. "I love you, and you know how to get in touch with me if you can ever see me, and love me, for who I am, with all my flaws and my dramatic outbursts and whatever else you find unappealing. Until then, goodbye, Mom."

Her heart raced and tears flooded her cheeks as she ended the call and lowered herself into her chair. She was breathing too hard. She felt like she'd been sliced open, but somehow she wasn't bleeding out. She was emptying herself of the weight of not feeling like she was enough for them. She'd carried it for so long, it was almost a relief to cut that umbilical cord. But with that severing came a new load of guilt, heavier than the burden she was expelling.

She knew she'd done the right thing, but how could she ever forgive herself for *this*?

Meredith hadn't known how right she was about Indi and Archer being two peas in a pod.

Maybe she and Archer could learn how to forgive themselves together.

Chapter Twenty-One

BY THE TIME Archer called to say he was on his way to pick up Indi, she'd already spoken to Meredith and Leni, had cried all her tears, and gotten the worst of her anger and hurt out. She told Archer what had happened with her mother, and he went silent, the way he did when he was trying *not* to go bananas. When he finally spoke, he didn't say anything bad about her parents, which she appreciated. She'd probably already thought anything he'd come up with anyway. Instead, he focused on *her*, saying all the right things, just as Meredith and Leni had. Although while Meredith had cried with her, Leni had said she'd like to kick Indi's parents' butts, and Archer had simply said, *We'll figure this out.* She was feeling a little better, until he told her that Ava had died, and that made her sad again.

Archer walked into the boutique like a man on a mission in his black winter jacket and boots. He drew Indi into his arms, holding her tight, and kissed her temple. "I'm sorry, darlin'."

"It's okay. I'm sorry about Ava. How are you? How's your mom?"

"We're fine. But I'm worried about you." He searched her eyes.

"I'm okay. It just hurts, and after hearing about Ava, I'm

not sure I did the right thing. Abby and her sister didn't have a choice about losing their parents, but I kicked mine out the door and slammed it behind them. Does that make me a monster?"

"You're no monster, babe." He pressed his large hands on her cheeks, gazing deeply into her eyes, like he needed her to hear every word he said. "You didn't kick them out the door. Your parents were never *in* your house to begin with. They were watchers from afar, trying to rope you into their corral. There's got to be a middle ground, and we'll find it. This is what needed to happen, but I can't believe it's the end. As I said, we'll figure this out together."

She loved him for wanting that, but she knew better. "There's nothing to figure out unless I want to sweep it all under the carpet. I think I just need to get out of my own head tonight and let it all go."

"Okay, then let's take a walk over to the park. Fresh air fixes everything."

"There's at least six inches of snow out there, and it's still coming down." The plows had been working hard all day, trying to keep up with the snowfall.

"What's the matter, city girl?" He cocked a brow. "Scared of a little snow?"

"*Hardly.*" He knew just how to lighten her mood, and boy did she appreciate it.

"Good, because it's gorgeous out, and I'd hate to have to dump your fine ass for a woman who doesn't mind snow."

She scoffed. "Good luck finding someone who'll put up with you."

He pressed his lips to hers. "Go get your things, smartass."

Archer pulled gloves and a black knit hat from his pocket

and put them on as she gathered her things and put on her pretty new cobalt-blue hat, scarf, and gloves. He'd blown her away when he'd given them to her and said the color looked *cool* with her eyes. He might not be eloquently romantic, but she'd had enough eloquent to gag on. She'd take real and raw over fake and fancy any day, and when Archer Steele was attached to those attributes, there was nothing more enticing.

As she locked the boutique, Archer put her bag in his truck.

"Ready?" He reached for her hand.

The snow crunched beneath their feet as they walked in silence toward the corner. Snow blanketed shop awnings, and little mounds of snow balanced precariously on tree limbs like precious gifts twinkling in the light from the old-fashioned streetlamps, giving the evening a romantic feel. She enjoyed walking with him like this, quiet and easy, in her new town.

They crossed the road, and when they stepped onto the curb, the snowy hill they stood upon spilled into the park below. The playground equipment and gazebo barely stood out against the snowy ground and white sky. The icy air stung Indi's cheeks, but it was a good sting. She tipped her face up to the sky and put her arms out to her sides, blinking away the constant stream of snowflakes. "You were right. Fresh air *does* make everything better." She filled her lungs with the cold air, caught up in a sudden rejuvenating sense of freedom that came out of nowhere.

"So does this."

She looked over just as he beaned her in the chest with a snowball. *"Archer!"*

He laughed, scooping up more snow and patting it into a ball. She shrieked and ran down the hill, laughing as she dodged the snowball. She grabbed a handful of snow, running as she packed it, and hurled it in his direction. He threw another, and she ducked, barely avoiding it. She turned around, scooping up more snow and packing it tight, and he pegged her in the back.

She spun around. "Your ass is *mine*, Steele!" She nailed him in the shoulder, and he sprinted after her.

Her shrieks and their laughter filled the air as they pelted each other, running around the gazebo and in and out of the swing set for cover. She sprinted around the slide, and he caught her around the waist, taking them both to the ground. He was on her in seconds, pinning her beneath his big body, his handsome red-cheeked face grinning down at her. She couldn't stop laughing.

"Whose ass is *whose*, Oliver?"

"Yours is mine," she said with a giggle. "I've got you *just* where I want you."

His arms pushed beneath her, and he pressed his lips to hers in a delicious kiss. "You don't suck at snowball fights."

"You don't suck at kissing." She leaned up and kissed his smiling lips. "I've never had a snowball fight before."

His brows slanted. "Get outta here."

"I'm serious. I grew up in the city, and my parents weren't exactly the *take the kids to the park and let them run wild* type of parents. We never went sledding or built snow forts or anything like that. Simon used to sneak me out sometimes to run around, but it was never like this."

"That might be okay for city dwellers, but you're a Silver Island girl now." He pushed to his feet, taking her hand and bringing her up with him, and brushed the snow from her clothes. "Let's go, city girl." He snagged her hand and headed back up the hill.

"Where are we going?" She hurried to keep up on whatever

new mission he was on.

"We've got some schooling to do. Your class, *Winters on Silver Island*, is now in session."

She loved the sound of that. "Do I get to seduce my professor?"

"Darlin', you already have." He tugged her into his arms and kissed her senseless.

Giddiness fluttered inside her as he chased her up the hill. It was funny how she'd never had butterflies or been a giddy girl until Archer came into her life and turned it upside down.

A little while later they pulled up in front of his parents' house. "What are we doing here?"

"You'll see." He came around and helped her out of the truck, flashing a grin as he took her hand. "This is where your lessons begin. Come on."

Archer took off jogging toward the backyard, pulling her with him. She loved seeing him this excited and carefree. He opened the shed, and as they stepped inside, she saw flashes of his youth hanging on the walls in the form of kites, baseball gloves, bats, toboggans, metal snow saucers, and sleds. She saw two funky bodysuits hanging on the wall with Jock's and Archer's names written in black marker down the sleeves. She'd heard the story of their homemade flight suits so many times, she knew it by heart. They'd always been risk takers, and when they were young, they'd thrown together flight suits, and Fitz and Wells had dared them to jump off the church roof. Jock had sprained his ankle, and Archer had broken his clavicle. Their father, being the incredible parent he was, didn't just punish them and shut down their hopes of skydiving. Once they were healed, he'd enabled them to tackle the challenge safely by taking them to learn to skydive with a proper instructor.

"Are those the infamous flight suits?"

"Sure are. I think we could fix them up now and make them work." He started moving boxes to clear a path through the middle of the shed.

"Please don't. I like you in one piece."

"Later you can show me just how much you like a certain *piece*." He laughed as he set a box down. It had a big square cut out of the front, and on the strip of cardboard above the square hole someone had written SILVER ISLAND NEWS in blue marker.

"What is *that*?"

"That was from Sutton's first reporting gig." He set down another box. "I made that for her when we were kids. It was supposed to be a television. We'd cover the dining room table with a sheet and set that on top of it, and then she'd pretend to do the news."

Her heart filled up with him even more. "And you'd watch?"

"Had to," he said as he moved more boxes. "No one else would." He motioned to a black minibike. "That was Levi's first bike."

"Your parents kept everything. I bet Joey would love that."

"Why do you think it's hidden behind boxes? I tried to take it out last summer, but he had a fit. He used to drive that thing all over Silver Haven, but I guess things change when it's your kid."

She didn't think her parents had kept anything from her childhood, and she wondered what they'd been like when they were young. They'd never talked about their childhoods, but she didn't want to get lost in that right now.

"Ah, here it is." He reached over the boxes, lifting out what looked like a homemade souped-up sled, with two skis as runners and handlebars with ropes tied to them as a steering mechanism. It was at least twice the size of a normal sled. "I made this when I was twelve and fine-tuned it over the years. This baby is wicked fast. I blew away everyone on the hill year after year."

Indi laughed. "But you're not *too* competitive."

"Hey, there's a reason you're with me. A powerful business-woman like you doesn't want to be with a low-key loser." He held the sled over his head as he carried it out of the shed, dropping a kiss on her lips as he passed.

She'd never been called a powerful businesswoman before, and that felt all kinds of amazing. "What if I'm with you for your *other* attributes?" she teased as they dragged the sled toward the hill at the far end of the yard.

"Don't kid yourself. There are no *what ifs* about it." He slung an arm over her shoulder. "You definitely climbed on for the ride, but who can blame you? I'm a good lay with a hard cock that gets the job done more than once."

She laughed. "You're *so* arrogant."

"Hey, do I speak the truth, or what?"

She rolled her eyes but couldn't help smiling, because it was that bad-boy confidence that had first roped her in, and she still adored it.

"But here's the thing. You're still here, and we both know I'm a difficult partner with a big mouth and an attitude. That makes me a hard pill to swallow. No pun intended."

God, she loved his honesty. "You're definitely more like a barrel of whiskey than a tall glass of champagne. You can be tough to swallow, but you're *so* worth the burn."

A smirk lifted one side of his mouth. "You've got that right." He leaned in and kissed her. "But I've got to believe you're with me for more than what I can do in the bedroom, or am I in for a rude awakening?"

"*Archer*," she said softly, touched by his vulnerability. "I wouldn't be here if behind that badass big mouth you weren't a kindhearted, generous man who shows himself in the most thoughtful ways, and I have a feeling we've only scratched the surface."

She leaned closer, lowering her voice. "But it's still about your skills in the bedroom, so don't let them slip." She smacked his ass, and he belted out a laugh.

ARCHER COULDN'T REMEMBER the last time he'd played in the snow, but whenever it was, it couldn't have been anywhere near as fun as this. Indi screamed each and every time they sledded down the hill behind his parents' house, and she trudged back up like a trooper, chatting and joking around like her heart hadn't been crushed just a couple of hours ago. He looked at her, bent over and rolling a basketball-sized snowball for the fort they were building. It had stopped snowing, and her cheeks and nose were bright pink, her brows knitted, and her lower lip was trapped between her teeth. Concentration sure looked good on her. Then again, what didn't?

Her attention shifted from the snowball to him, and a smile broke free. "This fort isn't going to build itself, Steele. Get a move on."

Did she know that she did him in with every little thing she said? As he rolled another snowball, he had the strange thought that he'd look back on this night years from now and remember it as one of the best nights of his life. He'd remember her exactly like she was, with that blue hat trapping her gorgeous hair as she got down on her knees to roll the enormous snowball toward the fort. That thought was followed by a sinking feeling. He knew the situation with her parents would knock the wind from her sails at some point, and though he was going to do everything he could to try to fix the mess he'd surely aggravated, when the time came, he'd be whatever she needed—the wind, the sun, her freaking *anchor*. Hell, he'd be her whole damn boat and the sea itself if that's what it took to get her through it.

She pushed to her feet and planted her hands on her hips. "Can I get some muscle over here?"

"Careful what you ask for." He waggled his brows, earning one of her killer smiles.

They rolled and stacked and built a chest-high wall and two knee walls on the sides. "That's one hell of a fort. You're shivering. Have you had enough?"

"What? *No.* I want to sit in it. You can't build a fort and then just go inside."

Loving her determination, he took off his jacket and held it up for her.

"*Archer*, you need that. It's freezing out here."

"I'm hot just looking at you." He tried to put it on her, but she pushed it away. "Indi, put it on or we're leaving."

She rolled her eyes. "You're so stubborn."

"Look who's talking." He helped her put his jacket on over hers.

She held out her arms, showing him that the sleeves hung several inches past her hands with the most adorable expression, like *What now, genius?* He laughed and rolled up her sleeves.

"I want to take a picture of our fort." She bit the tip of her glove to pull it off.

He lowered her hand. "I've got it. Keep your hands warm." He took off his gloves and pulled out his phone. "Stand in front of the fort."

"I want you in the picture, too."

"After I take one of you, I'll take one of us."

Her smile lit up the night as he took the picture. "Now get behind the wall."

She hurried around to the other side, and he took another picture. Then he went to her and put his arm around her shoulder, taking a selfie of the two of them.

"Take another!" she exclaimed.

He held up his phone again, and she went up on her toes, puckering up to his cheek as he took the picture, and then he took several more of them kissing, laughing, and holding up peace signs. It might be childish, but it was beyond fun and quite possibly his favorite moment of the night.

"I've got an idea. Stay right here. I'm going foraging for supplies."

She saluted. "Aye-aye, Captain."

He ran up to the house and went in the patio door. His parents were snuggling in front of the fireplace in the living room. "Sorry to interrupt."

His father grinned. "Did I forget to put the sock on the doorknob?"

"*Christ.* I don't want to think about that."

His mother giggled. "That's okay, baby. We thought that was you in the shed earlier. Where is your coat? What kind of trouble are you getting into out there?"

"The best kind. I'm hanging out with Indi. I gave her my jacket. Do you mind if I take a few blankets outside? And, Pop, can I borrow a jacket and steal some wood? I want to build a fire in our fort."

His father arched a brow. "Your *fort*? Do you want me to get out your G.I. Joes, too?"

His mother chuckled, and Archer shook his head. He returned to the fort wearing his father's Carhartt jacket, carrying several blankets and an armful of wood.

"Wow. You're a great forager. Your parents don't mind if the blankets get snowy?"

"I doubt they care about much right now. They're making out in the living room."

"Do you know how lucky you are to have parents who can't keep their hands off each other?"

"Yeah." He dug a hole in the snow for the fire. "I'm lucky all around where they're concerned." He pushed to his feet and gathered her in his arms. "I'm sorry about all the crap you're going through with your parents. I probably shouldn't have rocked the boat with your father, but I couldn't sit back and watch you be disregarded like that. You didn't ride your family's coattails or carry on someone else's legacy. You worked your ass off, and you're building your *own* empire. I don't mean to disrespect your parents, but there's something wrong with anyone who doesn't admire that."

She went up on her toes and kissed him, whispering, "Thank you."

He built the fire, and she laid out a nest of blankets. They lay by the fire, Indi on her back and Archer on his side, his arm draped across her belly. Flames from the fire crackled and sparked, their reflections dancing in her eyes. She couldn't look more beautiful if she tried.

"This has been the absolute *best* night." She ran her gloved finger along his jaw. "You guys must have had so much fun as kids, playing out here."

"We had a blast, but you know all about me and my childhood. I want to hear about that rebellious streak your parents mentioned."

"I never did anything *too* bad, just tested a few boundaries."

"Somehow I doubt that. Tell me about it."

"You might be disappointed. There are no flight suits in my past."

"Spill it, Oliver."

She smiled. "Okay, but you've been warned. The thing that stands out the most is that my mom always wanted me to look *buttoned up and beautiful*, as she put it, which really meant I had to dress prim and proper. At first I tried altering my outfits by cutting my shorts and skirts shorter, but after getting grounded for the umpteenth time, I found other ways. Sometimes I'd make my outfit a little cooler when I got to school by unbuttoning my shirt or hiking up my skirt so it didn't brush my knees. But then I got smart and started buying clothes with my allowance and giving them to my friends to take home. They'd bring them to school for me to change into. That worked for a while, until the principal, a good friend of my parents', called home and outed me."

He pictured her as a teenager, with that challenging spark in her eyes he'd seen a hundred times, wanting to break free from that perfect box her parents wanted her to live in. As much as he wished he'd known her then, he knew in his gut that he'd have been as intensely attracted to her as he was now, and he'd have gotten her into even more trouble. "So you've always been a temptress."

"I wouldn't say *that*. I didn't lose my virginity until I was a senior in high school. I just don't like being told how to act or what to wear."

"That's understandable. What else did you do?"

"Well, we had nannies a lot, and one time I was so sick of being watched all the time, I did something awful. I put laxative in my nanny's coffee so she would have to leave."

He laughed. "That's pretty smart. How old were you?"

"I don't know. Eleven, maybe. My friend suggested it. I never got caught, but I still feel bad about it."

"I'm sure you didn't do any permanent damage."

"I know, but I should've put it in my parents' coffee, not hers."

"Nah. Then they would have stayed at home with you. You mentioned sneaking out with Simon. Was that fun?"

"*Yes.* We just ran around the streets together, but sometimes he took me on the roof. That *felt* a lot more defiant because it was dangerous. I loved that feeling." She twisted her ring. "Simon gave me this ring for my sixteenth birthday."

"I wondered where you got it. I noticed you never take it off."

"It's a reminder of his faith in me. When he gave me the ring, he said I was going to do big things one day. That's driven me and given me strength every time our parents tried to get me to change."

He was relieved to know Simon had stood up for her in the ways he'd been able to. "That's great, babe."

"I really missed him when he went to college, but he'd given me *tools* to get through the rough days. When my parents pissed me off during the day, I'd go up on the roof alone at night.

That was my rebellion, but up there, it felt like Simon was with me, reminding me to be strong."

Her rebellious streak was mild compared to most kids, but he didn't tell her that, because her smile told him how much she'd loved doing those things. "I'm glad you had that space, but you're lucky you didn't get hurt."

"Says the guy who jumped off the roof of the church."

He chuckled and kissed her.

"When I was up there alone, I'd make all sorts of plans to become the *best* cosmetologist. I wanted all the girls and women who had been told they were too plain, their cheeks were too pudgy or too skinny, or their hair was too unruly, to come to me so I could show them how naturally gorgeous they were."

"Then how did you end up working with models and at fashion shows?"

"The reality of cosmetology is you either work at a salon or a department store, and I did them both for a little while, but it was too confining. I wanted to do more, something bigger. Leni suggested I try working with some of her clients on their commercial photo shoots, and it grew from there. At the time it sounded exciting, so I gave it a shot, thinking it might fill that gap. And I loved it at first. I was in control of my own schedule, and while models are tall and thin and beautiful, many of them were covering up their natural beauty like freckles, birthmarks, scars. The things that made them unique. When I worked with the same girls more than two or three times, I was able to get the person who hired them to allow some of those attributes to be seen. I got a lot of commendations for that, and the money was great. But as time wore on, I had to fight tooth and nail and won very few negotiations, and the models didn't want to make waves. Plus, the divas outweighed the nice girls, and that wore on me."

He loved that she'd remained true to the passion that had started with her sister, instead of taking the path paved with dollar signs. "I hear you on that. And now your big plans are coming true. All because you're a rebel at heart." She smiled, and he said, "How else did you rebel?"

"I skipped school with the *baddest* boy, and…" She snapped her mouth closed. "Never mind."

"You can't do that. What happened?"

"You probably don't want to hear this, but we had *sex*." She whispered *sex*. "He was my first."

He clenched his jaw. "Great. That's two guys whose legs I have to break."

"Two?"

"*James*, obviously."

She laughed. "Wait. You think I've only been with *two* guys?" More laughter bubbled out, and she touched his chest. "Okay, *yeah*. Let's go with that."

He lowered his face to a whisper away from hers. "I know damn well you've been with more guys than that to own your sexuality the way you do, but that doesn't mean I want to think about it." He brushed his lips over hers. "Don't destroy my fantasy world, babe. It keeps my monsters at bay."

She giggled. "Is there room for one more in your fantasy world? Because I'm living a fantasy of my own, pretending being with me made you forget every woman who came before me."

"Woman, you have *no* idea the ways in which you've messed with my head." *And my heart* was on the tip of his tongue, but he kept that to himself.

"Hope you kids are dressed in there!" his father called out.

He and Indi sat up as his parents came around the side of the fort. His father carried a bundle of blankets, skewers, and a bag of marshmallows, and his mother carried a thermos and four mugs.

"It wouldn't be the first time we caught you naked in the snow," his mother said.

"What? Is this your go-to move?" Indi asked. "Taking girls into a snow fort?"

"No, *Jesus*. I have no idea what she's talking about."

His parents laughed, and as his father spread out their blankets, he said, "He wasn't with a girl. When he and Jock were little, they woke up early one morning and wanted to play in the snow. Shelley went to get their clothes, and our impatient boys stripped naked and ran out the back door."

"I've never seen such tiny icicles," Shelley teased, and his parents and Indi laughed.

"Seriously, Mom?" Archer cursed under his breath.

"Oh, baby, you were only a little boy, and it *was* cold outside."

"Okay, *enough*." Archer scrubbed a hand down his face. "Did you come out here just to embarrass me?"

"No. That's just a nice side effect." His father chuckled.

Archer glowered at him, although in all fairness, he'd never brought a girl he was seeing over to warrant this particular type of torture, and in an odd way, it felt kind of cool being on the other side of it and bringing Indi further into their inner circle.

"We were just reminiscing about how nice it was to sit by a fire in the snow with you and the others when you were growing up," his mother said. "We didn't think you'd mind if we brought hot chocolate and marshmallows and sat with you for a bit. But if you would rather be alone—"

"It's *fine*, Mom."

"Wonderful." She handed them each a mug and filled them with hot chocolate.

"Thank you. This will definitely hit the spot." Indi took a sip and leaned against Archer. "I would love to hear more stories about what it was like to raise this amazing beast."

His father rubbed his hands together. "Where, oh where, do we start?"

"I can see this is going to be fun. Might as well get comfortable." Archer moved behind Indi, so she was sitting between his legs with her back against his chest, and covered her legs with a blanket. "A'right. Have at it."

"What do you want to hear about first?" his father asked. "Pranks, like the time Archer taped bait fish to the inside of Jock's dresser so he went to school smelling like dead fish for two weeks? Or the period when Levi was into boy bands and wanted to bleach his hair, and *this one* and his brother offered to do it for him? Only they dyed his whole head *pink*, except for the shape of a penis in the back of his head."

Indi laughed. "That's funny, but poor Levi. How long did it take for him to notice?"

"He saw the pink right away," Archer explained. "But we kept him away from Mom and Dad that night and told the girls they were next if they told on us. He went to school the next day, and after the kids started laughing and pointing, the teachers noticed and sent him home. It was *awesome*."

"He must have been mortified," Indi said.

"You can't feel too bad for him," his father said. "We had to shave his head, and then the girls were all over him. They thought he looked tough, and he quickly became the hottest bad boy in seventh grade."

Archer dipped his head beside Indi's. "See? He should thank me."

"Did they ever get you back?" Indi asked.

"Hell yeah. Plenty of times. One year Jock wrote love notes to my math teacher and signed my name every day for an entire week. I couldn't figure out why she kept telling me that she enjoyed having me in her class, but I had to stop flirting. I thought she meant flirting with the girls in my class until I got called into the principal's office and my parents were there. That was *fun*."

Indi laughed. "Now, that's a good one. Did your pranks ever backfire?"

"Not mine, but Jock's did. During our senior year, he told a bunch of girls I was going to ask them to the prom, and you know how gossip is around here. Half the girls in my class were pissed at me. When I realized what he'd done, I knew just how to get him back. I told the girls what was going on and asked them *all* to the dance. I was the only guy there with a harem."

They all laughed.

"Our boys *still* try to one-up each other to claim *king of the pranksters* status," his mother explained. "I'll never forget the time Archer…"

Archer listened as his parents took far too much pleasure telling Indi every embarrassing story they could think of. Indi laughed and teased him as they toasted marshmallows and finished the hot chocolate, all of which made hearing those age-old stories for the millionth time a hell of a lot more enjoyable.

A long while later, as the fire dimmed and Indi sat bundled up between Archer's legs, she was shivering again. He held her tighter and said, "Are you ready to take off?"

"Not yet. I'm having too much fun."

"Okay, but when we go back to my place, I'm going to draw you a hot bath, and we're sleeping by the fire in the living room."

"Really?" She popped to her feet. "This has been fun, but I'm ready to go now."

They all laughed, and Archer began gathering the blankets they'd used.

His father said, "I've got it, son. You kids can head home."

You've cleaned up my messes long enough. The thought came out of nowhere. The fucking guilt was inescapable, rearing its ugly head at the most unexpected moments. "You've got your own blankets to carry. I'll put these in the house."

"Thanks. Will we see you for breakfast tomorrow?" his father asked.

"I'd love that," Indi said, gazing up at him. "Okay?"

"Sounds good." It was funny how they'd fallen into the habit of sleeping at his place. Indi still offered to give him space, but that was the last thing he wanted. Getting out from under the guilt had trampled over his need for space, taking over the top of his priority list—right beside being there for Indi as she took her career to the next level and built a new life without the support of her parents.

"Terrific," his mother exclaimed. "I'll make Archer's favorite chocolate chip and walnut pancakes."

His mother looked like she'd won the lottery, and he had to admit that he felt that way, too. They hugged his parents goodbye, and he put his arm around Indi, pulling her closer.

"I can't wait. I had a great time tonight. I'm glad you joined us." Indi slid her arm around Archer. "We'll see you in the morning."

As they walked away, he heard his father say, "How do you

feel about a hot bath for two?"

His father still had it all going on, and Archer knew that if by some miracle he was ever able to get a handle on his guilt, and Indi stayed with him, he'd be the exact same way with her.

Chapter Twenty-Two

SATURDAY ARRIVED WITH gray skies and a solemn calm. The snow had melted, leaving the ground soggy and the landscape dreary for Ava's funeral. They'd done a good job of keeping Ava's death and the private service under wraps. The Remingtons and Silvers were there with Indi and Archer and his family to pay their respects. Leni was comforting Abby, who was in tears, while Deirdra was shrouded in resentment, as evident in her dry-eyed stare. Archer's mother had offered to host a gathering after the funeral, but Abby had politely declined, saying she knew she'd be a mess, while Deirdra had said the idea of reminiscing about her mother was about as appealing as having her fingernails ripped out with pliers. Archer couldn't blame her for releasing that venom. He was well versed in using anger to deal with unwanted emotions.

As the casket was lowered into the ground, Archer was thrown back to the awful day when they'd laid Kayla and Liam to rest. The memory and the pain were so vivid, he could barely breathe. He looked at Jock's grief-stricken face as he held Hadley in one arm, his other around Daphne, and knew he was suffering, too. Deep down he knew Jock blamed himself for their deaths. Jock glanced over, and their eyes held, their twin

289

connection not quite as powerful or secure as it had once been. How could it be when Archer's secret was still tightly wound around it like barbed wire, abrading every word they spoke and everything they shared, every damn minute of the day?

Indi must have sensed his discomfort, because she laced her fingers with his, her sweet voice whispering through his head, *I think you need to forgive yourself in order to let it go, and maybe the way to do that is to own up to the things that you feel you've done.* He swallowed hard. What if the truth didn't set him free? What if it was too little too late, or the last straw, giving Jock a reason to stop loving him once and for all?

He held Indi's hand tighter, hating that he felt like a villain in his own family as much as he hated needing help to turn it around. But he was equally thankful for his family's love and for Indi's support. He gritted his teeth against the conflicting emotions as the funeral ended.

Archer and Indi waited until the others had a chance to give their condolences to Deirdra and Abby before going over. Archer hugged them. "If there's anything I can do, please let me know."

"We appreciate that," Deirdra said. "But your family has done enough."

Indi hugged Abby. "I'm so sorry. I can't imagine how difficult this is for you."

"Thank you. I just wish we'd had some warning." Abby wiped her eyes. "There's so much we never got to say."

Deirdra looked at Abby like she was crazy. "I don't know why you're surprised that she was as selfish in death as she was in life."

"Because it's *such* a big thing to hide." Fresh tears fell from Abby's eyes as she and Deirdra went head-to-head about the magnitude of their mother's secrets.

They could have been talking about him. If he were to die tomorrow, Indi would be left holding all his secrets. He imagined Indi having a similar conversation with Jock about Kayla's texts, taking the brunt of his selfishness and weakness. Neither of them deserved that.

His sisters came over, but their voices were white noise to his thoughts, and something inside him snapped. *Fuck it.* He was *done* being selfish, regardless of the consequences.

He saw Jock talking with Brant a few feet away and squeezed Indi's hand. "I've got to take care of something. Will you be okay for a minute?"

"Of course." She studied his face. "Are you okay?"

He nodded and headed for Jock. "Can I talk to you alone for a second?" He pulled him away by the arm, not waiting for an answer.

Jock yanked his arm free. "What's going on?"

His words fell fast and hot. "It was my fault Kayla died."

"Archer, we went over this. It wasn't—"

"Shut up and let me finish." He fisted his hands as he gritted out the truth that had been slowly killing him. "The reason she was texting me that night was because she wanted me to meet you guys in the city. But I was out drinking, and...*fuck.* I was too selfish to get my ass on that ferry. That's all it would've taken. She never would've gotten into that car. She and Liam could be alive right now if I hadn't been so selfish." Tears burned, and he grabbed his head with both hands, turning away, trying to silence the guilt and ghosts as the texts came back to him like knives to his chest. "I fucking hate myself."

"Archer it wasn't your—"

"*Don't* placate me." He backed away, his mind spinning,

but forced himself to hold Jock's stare. "I'm an asshole, Jock. I should've told you, but I was too angry. I hated that I was alive and they weren't, and last fall when we fought and you told me she was in love with me, it messed with my head. Suddenly those texts took on new meaning, and I was afraid to tell you because I didn't want to give you another reason to hate me." He glanced at Indi, standing a good distance away with his sisters, watching them. "The truth is, I'm *still* a selfish bastard, because the only reason I'm telling you now is that I want to be with Indi, and I *can't* with this guilt hanging around my neck like a noose. I don't deserve her, Jock, and I don't deserve your forgiveness, but I'm asking for it, because I've never wanted anything in my life as much as I want that woman by my side."

Jock crossed his arms, his eyes narrowing. "Are you done?"

His voice was as serious as his stare. Archer stood taller, bracing himself for his brother's wrath, and nodded curtly.

Jock stepped closer, biceps flexing.

"You can hit me. I won't fight back." Archer squared his shoulders.

"Listen carefully to what I have to say, because this has gone on long enough."

Emotions clogged Archer's throat, and he lifted his chin.

"I knew about the texts, and it makes me sick to think you've been torturing yourself over them for all this time. I love you, brother, and there is nothing to forgive that hasn't already been forgiven."

Hot tears spilled down Archer's cheeks, and he swiped them away. "She and Liam might've lived if I'd gone."

"First of all, she knew how much you hated the city, and she knew you wouldn't come. How many other times had she asked you to come out with us or come see her?"

"Hundreds."

"Exactly. You've *got* to let this go. I had to learn to let it go, too. I had to forgive myself for going out that night. If we'd stayed home, she wouldn't have gotten in that car. You can't do that to yourself. Kayla would kick your ass if she knew you felt guilty at all, much less held on to it for so long."

In all these years, Archer hadn't thought about what Kayla would think of him now, but Jock was right. She never let him stew over shit. She had a way of showing him the things he didn't see when he was mad or sad or just fucking messed up. *Just like Indi does.* "Yeah. She would kick my ass."

"She knew you might not be in love with her, and she still wanted you to be happy, with or without her. I want that for you, too. I love you, Archer, and *nothing* will ever change that." He pulled him into an embrace. As they stepped back, Jock held his gaze. "I know it's hard because you want to place blame, and you've always tried to take the blame for everything anyone ever did. But I'm begging you, man. Let go of this shit once and for all before your life passes you by. You *deserve* Indi. Don't screw that up. Stop trying to save everyone else and save yourself for once."

Archer nodded, too choked up to figure out how to respond.

"Are you okay? Can I go hug my wife and daughter now?"

"I will be. Thanks, man." As Jock turned to walk away, Archer said, "Hey, asshole."

Jock glanced over his shoulder, brows raised.

"You could've told me you knew about the texts last fall."

Jock shrugged. "They weren't important then, and they're not now."

Archer felt the knots in his chest loosening, but that noose was still hanging around his neck, and he had a feeling there was only one way to free himself of that. He headed for Indi.

She hurried over to him, worry shadowing her eyes. "Are you all right? You guys looked like you were going to fight."

"I told him about the texts." He took her hand, telling her what had transpired as they walked across the grass toward the hill overlooking the water.

"That's great. Do you feel better?"

"Yeah, but it hasn't really sunk in yet."

"Okay. Where are we going?"

"To say goodbye to Kayla."

INDI WAS IN shock as they walked in silence past row after row of headstones. She couldn't tell if Archer was okay. His expression was tight, his brows knitted. His eyes were trained on the ground as they climbed a small hill, her heels digging into the damp earth. When they reached the crest, weathered headstones stretched out before them as far as her eyes could see, standing sentinel over the cemetery on one side and the deep-blue ocean on the other. Withered bouquets, weather-beaten toys, and a smattering of fresh flowers lay at their bases. How many of those graves were forgotten, no longer visited or thought about? How many storms had pummeled them? How many prayers had been said on this hill? She imagined buckets of tears had been shed, years of agonizing wails carried off in the wind.

Archer was staring off to his left. "She's down there."

Indi was so nervous for him, she felt like she'd sprinted up the hill. "Do you want me to come with you?"

He shook his head, meeting her gaze. "Would you mind waiting here?"

"No."

He drew her gently into his arms, so different from his usual eager self. He didn't say a word, just held her, then pressed a kiss to the top of her head before heading for Kayla's grave.

She watched him walk away, and when he knelt in front of Kayla's headstone, shoulders rounded, knees sinking into the earth, tears filled her eyes. She was far enough away that she couldn't hear him pouring his heart out to the first girl who had owned a very big piece of it, but she didn't need to hear those private sentiments. His body language was enough to make her want to run over and kneel beside him, but she remained where she was as his chin fell to his chest and his hands splayed on his thighs.

As time ticked by, his face fell into his hands, his shoulders rocking, breaking Indi's heart anew. She swiped at her tears, and after a few minutes, Archer lifted his face, saying something she couldn't hear. She looked out over the water, a cold breeze sweeping over her. The view was stunning. Indi didn't know what she believed about what happened after a person left this life, but she hoped Kayla was hearing every word he said.

Archer's voice grew stronger, and she looked over. What seemed like an endless string of words she couldn't make out were falling from his lips. His shoulders were no longer rounded, and though his hands were still perched on his thighs, he looked stronger and more in control. He remained there for a long time, kneeling in the wet grass by Kayla's grave, saying only *he* knew what. Indi heard him laugh a couple of times, and that was when she knew he was going to be okay.

When he finally pushed to his feet, the knees of his jeans wet and dirty, he touched his fingers to his lips, then touched the top of the gravestone and headed for Indi.

"Sorry that took so long." He sounded different, as if what he'd done had taken all his energy.

"It's fine. Do you want more time? I don't mind waiting."

"No. I've said everything I needed to say and everything she needed to hear."

She felt relieved, but he still seemed a little uncomfortable. "Are you okay?"

"Yeah." He kissed her and slung his arm over her shoulder as they walked down the hill. "Thanks to you, I think I really am. Or at least I will be."

Chapter Twenty-Three

INDI LOOKED DOWN at hers and Archer's joined hands as the cab drove through the streets of Boston on the way to the *Wine Aficionado* gala. She'd been noticing more about them lately. Every little thing, actually, like the way her fingers were thin and delicate, her skin soft and pale, while his fingers were thick and rough, his skin rugged and tanned, even in winter. Even the way they pushed each other and fought *with* and *for* each other was different, but it worked for them, as if they were meant to be.

Her gaze traveled from their hands, resting on one of his jeans-clad thighs, up the length of his arm. His biceps and chest strained against his denim-blue dress shirt and suede navy vest. He might not be dressed in a suit and tie, and he was wearing black leather boots instead of dress shoes, but he took her breath away. Not just for how great he looked, but also because of the effort he'd been putting into healing. He'd blown her away when he'd talked with Jock and even more so when he'd knelt in front of Kayla's grave and poured out his heart. In the week since, it was like he'd shed his skin and didn't know how to exist without it. He'd been agitated and twitchy for a day or two, rolling his shoulders and stretching his neck a lot. But then she'd noticed him starting to settle down, and the last couple of days she'd noticed other differences, too. They weren't as blatant as night and day. They were subtler, more like night and evening. He breathed a little easier, didn't seem as tense, and those shadows in his eyes were lifting. And all the while, through the discomfort and uncertainty, they'd grown closer.

"You've got that look in your eyes, like you want to get naked again." His lips quirked up, his silent offer hanging between them.

He hadn't wanted to attend the cocktail hour before the gala, and they'd made good use of that extra time exploring each other's bodies in his living room, his bedroom, *and* his shower. She had a feeling their pre-event tryst had been his way of trying to ease his anxiety over the event, and she was okay with that.

"What if I say I do?"

He started unbuttoning his shirt, and the driver glanced in the rearview mirror.

"*Stop*," she whispered. "What is with you lately?" They'd gotten caught making out at his parents' house Wednesday night when they'd gone for dinner with Lenore, Jules, Grant, Daphne, Hadley, and Jock. After dinner, Archer had said he wanted to show her something in his childhood bedroom, and then he'd tackled her on the bed. Just as they'd gotten lost in their kisses, Jock sounded a freaking *airhorn* in the hallway. Archer had sprung to his feet and chased him all the way outside. A wrestling match had ensued on the front lawn, while Indi and the rest of them watched through the windows, cracking up. Indi was relieved to see that Shelley seemed to be doing okay after losing Ava, and she had a feeling the craziness and laughter between Shelley's two sons who had been disconnected for so long had done her heart good.

"It's not just lately, darlin'. Need I remind you about all the places we've fooled around the past five months?"

"No, you don't, thank you very much. I have a very vivid memory for those things, and I *wasn't* looking at you like that."

He gave her a disbelieving look.

"Okay, I *was*, but I was also thinking about how amazing you are."

He put his mouth beside her ear, speaking low. "You mean because I already made you come four times tonight, and that was just a prelude?"

Her body tingled. Would she ever tire of his dirty talk? "*No.* I meant because of the things you've done, coming clean to Jock, saying goodbye to Kayla, and now you're going to the gala. That's a lot."

"Yeah, well, this hot little thing came into my life and made me realize I needed to get my shit together if I wanted to hang out with her."

"Where is she?" Indi looked around teasingly. "I want to thank her."

He hooked his arm around her shoulders, pulling her into a kiss as the car pulled to the curb in front of the hotel. Archer put on his bomber jacket and came around to help her out.

She looked up at the skyscraper and out at the busy road. Even though she'd gone back to New York twice this week to prepare for Fashion Week and to start packing up her apartment, it felt funny to be in a city, instead of the quaint small town she now called home. She hadn't fully moved in, but she was getting there. She'd brought more clothes and some of her kitchen supplies to her island apartment, and Simon had helped Archer carry one of her bedroom dressers, the living room chairs, and a few other things out of her apartment in the city to his truck, and then Grant and Jock had helped him move them once they got back to the island. She was having fun setting up her apartment, and doing it with Archer made it even more special.

Archer followed her gaze around them. "Missing the city?"

"Nope. I like the island better."

"That's because I'm there." He kissed her. "Let's get this over with." His tone matched the tension around his mouth and eyes and the rigidity of his body, so different from the way he'd been in the car.

They headed into the hotel. The scent of money hung in the air, with its marble floors, lavish furniture, and staff dressed to the nines. That was another thing Indi didn't miss, the pretentiousness that accompanied certain businesses and parts of cities. She'd dressed down in a white pinstripe blouse, black skinny pants, and high-heeled black ankle boots, and it was crazy how freeing it was not to play the games of the rich. She didn't feel uneasy showing up underdressed. She was too proud of Archer to worry about clothes. Even if he didn't win the award, he'd been nominated, and that was a phenomenal achievement.

"Were your parents okay with us missing the cocktail hour?" she asked as they followed signs for the gala toward the ballroom.

"I didn't tell them we wouldn't be there. They don't care about that stuff."

"But they might think you decided not to come."

"Then they'll be pleasantly surprised when we walk in."

She worried about his parents thinking he backed out, and she stopped walking and put her hand on his chest, which she'd learned was a good way to get his full attention, no matter what the subject—sex, business, or just because she wanted to look at his handsome face. She gazed into his tension-filled eyes and hoped he understood what she had to say. "I know it's stressful for you to be here, and I get that your mind wasn't on your parents earlier. Mine wasn't, either. But remember how the scary toothbrush morning could have gone better if you had told me you needed space in a different way?"

"Yeah."

"This is kind of the same thing. Sometimes the things we don't say can cause stress for other people, too. Your parents might not care about cocktail hour, but they care about you, and I have a feeling if they think you decided not to show up, they'd worry about you and what it meant."

"Shit. I hadn't thought about that."

"I know, and I might be overthinking, but I know how you feel about your family, and I wanted to point it out. Maybe the next time we blow them off, we can both try to remember to give them a heads-up."

"Yeah, definitely." He tensed up as they made their way down the hall toward the registration table outside the banquet room.

"I didn't mean to stress you out."

"You didn't. You're right. I need to pull my head out of my ass about stuff like that."

She lowered her voice. "Well, technically, your head was between my legs, but…"

They laughed, and he kissed her. Then they went to check in, and the attendants took their coats. The din of conversation rose around them as they stepped into the dimly lit banquet room, and what looked like hundreds of people dressed in tuxedos, dark suits, and fancy dresses sat at large round tables with several bottles of wine in the center. Strings of white lights were draped elaborately from the high ceiling, giving it a starry-sky feel. Along the sides of the room were large video displays showing various wineries, including one for Top of the Island, which showed a picture of the side of the winery, the courtyard and knee wall, and acres of gorgeous leafy vines. Archer stood within those beautiful vines, big and broad, looking off in the distance, outshining everything around him.

Indi reached for his hand. "Did you know the event was going to be this big?"

"These events are always big. People love to get dressed up and show off." He took her hand. "Let's find our seats."

They followed the directions they'd been given to their seats, and there with his parents sat Lenore, Jock, Daphne, Levi, Sutton, Leni, Jules, and Grant. Archer's eyes moved over their faces. "What are you all doing here?"

"We're here to support you, doofus." Leni rose to her feet, motioning to her taupe blazer, white blouse, and skinny jeans. "Why else would I dress like this on a Saturday night?"

As she sat down, Indi quickly scanned the others. The men were wearing open dress shirts without ties. Levi had on a brown leather vest. She leaned back to glimpse under the table and saw that the men were all wearing jeans. Indi's heart soared. She glanced at Shelley in a casual floral dress, and Daphne in a black sweater. Sutton wore a simple red dress, while Jules shined in a white blouse with yellow polka dots, her hair in her signature fountain hairdo. Even Lenore, a true fashionista, had dressed down, wearing an off-white blouse with a colorful chunky necklace.

"It's not every day our brother gets nominated as the best winemaker in the country," Jock added.

Archer squeezed Indi's hand, the muscles in his jaw bunching.

Shelley and Steve stood to greet them as Lenore held her hand out to Levi. "Pay up, biker boy. I told you he'd show."

Levi grumbled and pulled out his wallet, handing her a twenty-dollar bill.

"I knew I should've gotten in on that action," Sutton said, causing a few chuckles.

Steve put a hand on Archer's shoulder. "We're all proud of you, son."

Archer's eyes narrowed, and he breathed a little harder, reminding Indi of an animal backed into a corner. As happy as she was for him to have their support, he hadn't wanted to celebrate at all, and now it was an even bigger deal. He had such conflicting feelings surrounding his family, she realized this probably added to them.

"You look handsome, honey." Shelley embraced Archer. "And, Indi, you look beautiful."

"Thank you. So do you."

Grant pulled out the chair beside him. "Take a load off."

Archer was dead silent as they sat down. Indi put her hand on his under the table, hoping to ease his tension.

"This is *so* fun," Jules exclaimed. "I love that we're all here."

Sutton flipped her blond hair over her shoulder and lifted a brow. "I always thought I'd be the first one to be nominated for the best of *something* in the country."

"Too bad they don't give out awards for faking it until you make it." Leni sipped her wine. "Archer, did you see your picture over there?" She pointed to the video display Indi had seen on their way in.

"Yeah," he said gruffly. "Where'd they get that?"

"I had Tara take pictures of the winery last summer. You just happened to be in the field that day. It worked out perfectly." His mother reached for one of the bottles of wine in the center of the table. "Who wants to try this one?"

"Not me." Jock reached for a different bottle. "I want to try the one you had earlier."

As everyone chose their wine and glasses were filled, Archer sat silently stewing. Indi wished she knew what was going on in his head. She tried brushing her thumb over the back of his hand, hoping it might help.

Steve said, "Indi, I hear you hired a couple of employees."

"Yes. Noelle, who works with Jules, and Macie, a friend of Daphne's." She'd not only hired them, but the three of them had met for coffee, and they'd gotten along brilliantly.

"Macie's excited about working with you," Daphne said.

"Isn't Noelle hilarious?" Jules asked. "She has a dry sense of humor, but she cracks me up."

"She is funny. I'm looking forward to working with both of them. They're coming in Monday to help unpack the inventory that arrived this week."

"She also got the photographs of Bellamy that Tara took for the boutique," Leni said. "Wait until you see them. They're absolutely stunning."

"Archer and Jock already hung them up," Indi said. "They're so big, I was worried about how they'd look, but you know your stuff, Leni. They're perfect."

"I know." Leni sat back and blew on her fingertips, brushing them up and down the front of her blouse.

"You're so full of yourself," Sutton teased.

"Being full of yourself isn't a bad thing," Lenore said. "Your grandfather was about as full of himself as a man could get, and he was the best man *and* best winemaker I'd ever known."

Jock hiked a thumb at Archer. "Have you met my brother?"

"I was speaking in past tense. Who do you think taught Archer and your father everything they know? Your grandfather, that's who." Lenore set a loving gaze on Archer. "Your grandpa is smiling down on you right now, honey."

"Can you all just *stop*," Archer said sternly, and everyone quieted, turning their attention to him. He clenched his jaw, his hand curling into a fist beneath Indi's.

Indi held her breath, wondering if they were about to have a *bananas* moment and hoping not.

"What's wrong, honey?" Shelley asked.

"I want to say something." He drew his shoulders back, his gaze moving around the table, while beneath the table, his hand unfurled, and he laced his fingers with Indi's. "I can't sit here and listen to your praise."

"Oh, honey, you deserve it," Lenore said, and everyone agreed.

"No, that's just it. I *don't*. I was a prick for a long time, and while things are better between me and Jock, I never apologized to all of you."

Holy shit. You're going for it. Please go well, please go well, please go well.

"You don't need to apologize," Jules said, and the others agreed.

"Yes, I do," he bit out. "Especially to you, Jules. I'm sorry I wasn't there when you were sick, but I couldn't bear to watch you suffer."

"You *were* there for me," Jules said sweetly. "Don't you remember? When I was stuck inside, you told me you were going outside to fight the cancer monster, and you drew scary pictures on the outside of my windows with permanent marker and told me no monsters of any kind could get past them. You made me feel safe."

He'd forgotten about those drawings. "I should have been by your side," he said, rough and regretful.

Jules smiled. "You *were*, just in a different way. I've always felt like you were there for me, no matter what I was going through, and even more importantly, no matter what you were going through. You've let me cry on your shoulder a zillion times. After everyone else left the island, it was just you and me. We're like this." She held up her hand and crossed her fingers. "Nothing could change that."

Archer swallowed hard and nodded curtly.

Indi couldn't be prouder of him for getting years of guilt off his chest, or more thrilled that Jules had said there was no reason for him to feel guilty.

He looked at the rest of his family, holding Indi's hand tighter. "I'm sorry I divided our family. I never should have blamed Jock, much less taken it out on all of you. I have no idea why you didn't shut me out, but I'm thankful you didn't."

"Honey, we love you," his mother said. "We all deal with grief differently."

"Archer, you weren't alone in that fight for all those years." Jock set a serious stare on him. "Staying away from the island was on *me*, not you. That was my choice. If I'd fought harder to get through to you, or come back more often, maybe things would have been different or gotten better sooner." He reached for Daphne's hand. "But life is strange, man. If that had happened, I wouldn't have met Daphne and Hadley, so there's our silver lining."

"I never thought the fight was either of your faults," Sutton said. "It was a tragedy that affected all of us, and we were all devastated. We just handled it differently."

Indi felt tension easing in Archer's grip.

"Yeah, man," Levi said. "Don't sweat the past. We don't blame you. We just wish we could have helped you through it."

"I'm not very good at accepting help, but I'm trying to figure things out." Archer looked at Indi, relief welling in his eyes. "Thanks to this beautiful woman, I'm trying to learn not to be such a prick."

"She's not a miracle worker," Leni teased.

Everyone glowered at her, except Archer, who laughed.

Laughed!

"She must be." Archer pulled Indi closer. "I'm here, aren't I?"

RELIEF FLOWED THROUGH Archer like blood through his veins as they enjoyed dinner and lighter conversation. He couldn't believe he'd finally found the wherewithal to apologize. While he was relieved, he was also kind of still in shock. He'd carried a world of guilt on his shoulders, and his family hadn't blamed him for a damn thing. He had a feeling it would take some time for all of that to really sink in, just as his other confessions had. Indi must have said she was proud of him a hundred times already, and she was positively glowing, as were his parents and grandmother. Even his siblings were looking at him differently, or at least it felt like they were.

"Aren't you glad you came?" Indi asked for his ears only.

"Yes, *very*. Thanks for pushing me." But he was still itching to leave. Looking around the table, he didn't care if he won the award, because he already had everything that mattered.

Thankfully, they began announcing the awards. When they got to Winemaker of the Year, Indi squeezed his hand. His mother's hands were clasped in front of her chin, as if she were praying, and Jules's eyes were closed, and she was whispering, "*Please, please, please.*" Jock mouthed, *You've got this.* As Archer looked around the table at everyone's hopeful expressions, his feelings changed. He wanted to win the award for them.

"And the Winemaker of the Year is..." The announcer paused dramatically. "*Archer Steele,* with Top of the Island Winery and Vineyards," boomed through the room, and applause exploded.

Indi threw her arms around him, Jules squealed, and the rest of his family cheered and whistled as he got up to accept the award.

Jock hollered, "Way to go, Archer!"

He hated this shit, but his family sure loved it, and he was glad to make them proud. He shook the hands of all the officials onstage, and then they invited him to the podium to make an acceptance speech.

The crowd silenced as he looked out at them, his eyes drawn to Indi and his family, all grinning like his winning had been a gift to them. He felt that tug in his chest that had been happening a lot more often lately and said, "I don't make wine to win awards, and I don't like making speeches." There was a rumble of laughter. "I also wasn't going to come tonight, because I don't need to be praised for doing what I love. But this award, and this night, were important to my family, and I wouldn't be standing here without them. So, thank you for this honor." He held up the award. "This one's for you, Gramps."

Applause rang out as he walked off the stage, and his family stood up and clapped, and everyone around them rose to their feet, applauding.

As the announcer ended the ceremony and people began milling about, Archer handed his father the award. "A'right, let's get out of here."

"Can we do that?" Indi asked.

"Darn right we can," his grandmother said. "I'm with you. Enough of this hullabaloo."

"You guys can't leave," Jules pleaded. "It's a special night."

It was a very special night, for reasons other than the award, but that didn't change the fact that Archer had had enough of being around strangers.

"Once we leave, Leni and Sutton will go back to New York, and Levi will go home," Jules complained. "I want more time with everyone."

"Jules, I'm not leaving without my daughter," Levi said. "Joey's with Tara tonight, remember? I'm staying on the island."

"People are going to want to congratulate Archer," Leni pointed out.

"That's exactly why I'm leaving." Archer took Indi's hand, but he felt bad for Jules and didn't want to let her down. "Jules, how about we all go for ice cream, or find a deli with great desserts and hang out a little longer?"

"Yes!" Jules wiggled her shoulders and took Grant's hand.

"Archer, you have the best ideas, and we have an overnight babysitter," Daphne said.

"Ryan is having a sleepover for Hadley and Ritchie," Jock explained.

"You can't beat a cute policeman as a babysitter," Lenore

said.

"I'm in for dessert," Sutton said. "And I kind of wish I was staying at Daph and Jock's tonight so I could use my auntie status to pop over to Hottie McCoppy's house for breakfast with my niece."

Archer shook his head.

"Come on, twinnie. I'll buy you a sundae." Levi pulled Leni to her feet.

His father took his mother's hand. "Let's go, beautiful. Looks like we're blowing this taco stand."

Archer nuzzled Indi's neck and whispered, "I've got something you can blow."

She looked nervously around them, but she was grinning as they followed the others out of the banquet room. "Really? After the night you've had, *that's* what you're thinking about?"

"Darlin', have you looked in the mirror? If you were me, you'd be thinking about ripping your clothes off, too."

"You're *so* bad."

He kissed her. "And you wouldn't want me any other way."

They collected their coats and jackets, and as they headed out of the hotel with his family chatting happily around them, Archer knew he'd never forget this night, and he owed it all to the beautiful woman by his side.

Chapter Twenty-Four

WEDNESDAY MORNING, INDI lay in Archer's arms, her back against his chest, his legs curled behind hers. It was the opening day of Fashion Week, and they were in her apartment in New York City. In less than two hours, Archer would be back on Silver Island, and she'd be surrounded by the world's most prominent designers and teams of stylists and dozens of other people helping to get some of the most beautiful people in the world runway ready. She was scheduled to work until nine thirty for the next three nights, and this was the last time she would be with Archer until Saturday night, when she was getting off at seven, and he was coming back to see her. She was excited to work the show, but that excitement didn't compare to *this*.

It was the feel of him wrapped around her she was going to miss the most. The way their bodies fit so well together. The gentle press of his chest against her back when he inhaled, the way his arm circled her belly and he tucked his hand between her hip and the mattress, like he was afraid she might roll away in the middle of the night. It felt strange to be mourning their time apart when he was right there with her. She'd never missed any of the guys she'd gone out with. Not even James. She'd mentioned that to Meredith yesterday when they were scheduling their makeup video sessions, and her sister had said, *That's how love works.*

Love.

They hadn't gotten together looking for love, but here she was, happily falling head over heels for him. That was another feeling she didn't know what to do with, but one thing was for certain. She couldn't tell Archer any of that. He had gotten scared over a *toothbrush*, which gave her a giggle now that she had some distance from it. They'd come a long way since then, and they were doing great. Even better now that Archer had come clean to Jock and apologized to his family. In some ways they were plowing ahead at full speed, and in others they were taking their time. Talking about their feelings for each other fit into the latter, but they'd been staying at his place every night, which was wonderful. It hadn't happened because they'd talked about it or he'd cleaned out a drawer for her or made room in his closet. They just ended up naked in each other's arms every night. Indi lived out of her toiletry bag and brought clean clothes over every few days, which wasn't ideal, but it made sense for them. Not that she was complaining. There was no place else she'd rather be, and she especially loved that sometimes they lay tangled up for hours just talking. Well, she did most of the talking. Archer shared his thoughts in sound bites, but they were important sound bites.

He was definitely more a man of action than words, and *oh, how I love his actions.*

She snuggled deeper into the curve of his body, wishing she could slow time and make the morning last longer. It was Valentine's Day, after all. She'd spent an hour picking out the perfect card for him. On the front it had five gold stars and below them it read EXCELLENT. WOULD BANG AGAIN. On the inside of the card was a red heart and THERE'S BEEN A STAR-RATINGS INCREASE. WANNA GO FOR TEN? HAPPY VALEN-TINE'S DAY! But Archer hadn't mentioned the holiday, and she wasn't sure she should give him the card. They'd been so busy, she wondered if it had just slipped his mind. She'd almost said something last night, but then she'd thought better of it. He wasn't the romantic type, and she didn't want to make him feel bad if he hadn't thought about the holiday.

His entire body embraced her from behind. His beard tick-led as he kissed her shoulder. "G'morning, darlin'."

She'd miss his gravelly morning voice, too.

He rolled her onto her back, shifting over her, his sexy smile simmering in his eyes. "Are you nervous about today?"

He was warm, hard, and deliciously heavy, making her crave more of him. It took a second for her to rein in those desires and answer. "I've been doing Fashion Week long enough to know it'll be fine, but I'm always a little nervous."

He kissed her neck, whispering gruffly, "You're going to slay the whole fucking week."

She pressed her fingers into his back, his unconditional support drawing out her heart. "I'm going to miss this."

"Oh yeah?" He rocked his hips. "I'm going to miss *this*, too."

She smiled. So very *Archer*. "You know what I mean."

He cradled her face between his hands. "I'm going to miss you, too." He brushed a kiss to her lips. "But I'm going to leave you feeling so good, you'll feel me for days."

"I like the sound of that." Sex with Archer had been amaz-ing before, but it had gotten even more intense, heightened by their deepening emotions. She closed her eyes as he kissed her cheek and jaw, traveling slowly down her body, every touch of his lips lighting sparks beneath her skin. He took his time, licking and kissing, murmuring sexiness against her skin as he nipped and caressed, touching every inch of her and driving her out of her freaking mind.

"*Archer,*" she pleaded, trembling with desire.

His eyes blazed into her as he buried his face between her legs. The first slick of his tongue sent her hips off the mattress. He held them down, devouring her slowly at first, then quickening his pace, taking her right up to the edge, then slowing again, in a rhythm so exquisite, pleasure radiated through her core. She fisted her hands in the sheets, digging her heels into the mattress as fiery sensations chased over her skin. When he brought his fingers into play, she couldn't think, couldn't see, as she surrendered to his masterful ministrations, and cried out his name. Her orgasm went on and on, and when she finally collapsed beneath him, trying to catch her breath, he moved up her body, taking her in a merciless kiss as he thrust into her, burying himself to the root. Pleasure shot through her. She clawed at his back, bowing off the mattress, wrapping her legs around his, chasing the high only he—*they*—created. He intensified the kiss, slowing them down, and she felt every inch of his thick shaft sliding in and out at a torturous pace, magnifying every sensation to agonizing levels. He broke their kiss and brushed his lips along her cheek, whispering, "Oh *yeah*, baby. I want to *live* inside you."

The emotion in his voice sent beats of ecstasy pulsing through her. She grabbed his ass with both hands, earning a sexy growl and a quickening of his efforts.

"*Harder,*" she demanded.

"Fuck, baby." He buried his face in her hair and sealed his

teeth over her neck, sending a mix of pleasure and pain slicing through her.

"Come *with* me," she pleaded, wanting even *more* of a connection.

He grabbed her legs behind the knees, pulling them up to her waist, thrusting harder and faster, until his name flew from her lips, unleashing the last of his restraint, and he roared out her name, catapulting her into a world so full of them, she never wanted to leave.

THE MORNING PASSED too quickly, and as Archer put on his bomber jacket and pulled Indi into his arms, she wondered why all good things had to come to an end. She wished they could disappear into one of those time warps they made movies about when the characters relived the same scene over and over.

"I hate that I've got to roll, baby, but the ferry won't wait." He kissed her forehead. "You sure I can't drop you off?"

"Yeah. I wish you could, but Josh and Riley Braden, one of the designers I'm working for today, are sending a car to pick me up."

"Braden? Any relation to Sutton's boss, Flynn?"

"Yeah, they're cousins, and tomorrow I'm working for another of their cousins, Jillian Braden. Oh my *gosh.* You know what I just realized? Jillian's partner for Silver-Stone Cycles' Leather and Lace clothing line she's featuring tomorrow is Jace Stone, and he's Josh's assistant Mia's older brother."

Archer blinked several times. "I don't know how you keep that shit straight. I'll stick to winemaking." He pressed his lips to hers. "I'm proud of you."

"Thank you. That means a lot to me."

"I know you'll be slammed today, so I won't call. Is it okay to text?"

"Yes, I'd like that, but I might not be able to respond until I get a break."

"I get it. That's cool." He lowered his lips to hers in a slow, deep kiss that lasted so long she got lost in him again. Then he lifted her chin, gazing into her eyes. "See you Saturday?"

She nodded.

He tenderly touched his lips to hers, and then he embraced her, holding her tight, and rested his cheek on her head for a long moment, as though he were memorizing the feel of her just as she was with him. The longer he held her, the more emotional she became. When he loosened his grip, it felt reluctant, and when he lowered his arms, he looked as torn as she was. He reached into his pocket, and the arrogant grin she loved took over. "Happy Valentine's Day, darlin'."

He handed her a card and a small box of candy conversation hearts, the kind kids give out at school. She filled with joy. "You remembered?"

"I told you it might not seem like I'm thinking about you all the time, but you've planted yourself in my head like a wild vine."

She was wrong about Archer not being romantic. That was the most romantic thing anyone had ever said to her. "I love that, and I got you a card, too." She ran to get his card and handed him the envelope. "I'm sorry I didn't get you a present."

"You're all the present I need. I'll read this on the ferry. I have to go before I miss it." He kissed her again. "I'll text you later." He opened the door but leaned in for another kiss, and one after that. He groaned and kissed her again. "Shit. I gotta go."

She laughed, and when she closed the door behind him, she leaned against it, pressing the envelope and the candy box to her chest, grinning like a fool. Who knew a card and candy could mean so much?

She pulled the card out of the envelope, and scrawled across the front was AS LONG AS I HAVE A FACE, YOU'LL ALWAYS HAVE A PLACE TO SIT. There were two red hearts with PS: NICE BUTT beneath them. Indi laughed, shaking her head as she opened it. The card was blank inside, but Archer had written, *There's no one else I'd rather have as my valentine*, and signed his name. Her heart beat to a new, happier tune, and she read it again. His handwriting was messy and slanted to the right, his signature a large *A*, the rest nearly illegible. She liked his messy writing—it was very Archer-like—and she loved what he'd written, which wasn't Archer-like at all, and that made it even more special. She looked at the small box of candy and read the hearts printed on the outside. *Bend Over. Spank Me. Suck It. Spread 'Em.*

Laughter tumbled from her lips, and she whipped out her phone, thumbing out a text. *Looking forward to playing our candy-heart game Saturday night. Xox*

Her phone vibrated a few minutes later with his response— a devil emoji.

Saturday night couldn't come fast enough.

Chapter Twenty-Five

WORKING BEHIND THE scenes at Fashion Week was like trying to wrangle a gaggle of swans while dodging land mines and being chased by tigers in a blinding snowstorm. It took droves of people working as fast as they could under insurmountable pressure and thinking ten steps ahead at all times to pull it off. It was after seven in the evening, and Indi had spent the last twelve hours working at breakneck speed as models came and went from her styling chair, often running in at the last minute covered in body glitter, makeup, and hair spray from other shows, making Indi's job that much harder, while around her, designers and stylists made last-minute fixes, photographers, managers, and publicists milled about, trying to pimp their crews, and lucky fans who had scored backstage passes vied for selfies with the fashion-famous elite. The energy in the room was off the charts, but even with all that madness, people were having fun. Models and PR reps took to social media with as many glamour shots as funny selfies. Leni was right there with them, pimping out her designer clients and getting pictures of Indi while she worked. Her bestie's marketing brain never turned off.

The event was unparalleled, but as much as Indi loved it,

she wouldn't miss the constant pressure or exhausting days. When she'd first secured the gig five years ago—*thank you, Leni*—she'd felt like she'd *made it* and had thought her parents would finally recognize all her hard work. She should have known better. As she applied model Dusty Kincaid's makeup, she realized she no longer felt the sting of disappointment or resentment that usually accompanied those thoughts. As sad as that was, it was a big relief to allow herself to stop wishing for something her parents weren't capable of giving.

"You okay?" Dusty was looking at her curiously, one blue eye heavily made up, the other halfway there. "You look like your mind is someplace else, which is tough to accomplish with all that's going on around here."

"Sorry. I was just thinking about something." She silently chided herself and refocused on applying his makeup.

"About your boyfriend?" He cocked a grin. "Because if he's making you look like that, maybe he's not the right guy."

"What do you know about being the right guy?" she teased. She'd worked with Dusty at several events over the past few years. He was in his early twenties and about as flirtatious as Wells Silver. "I was just thinking about work."

"Indi!" Model Penelope Price rushed over with an assistant on her heels, frantically pointing to her hair. One side of the updo Indi had styled for her was all messed up. "I'm sorry. It happened when I dressed."

"It's okay." Indi quickly began fixing her hair.

"Lightning fast," the assistant warned. "She walks in four minutes."

"Not a problem. Almost done." Indi secured the last wayward strand. *"Go."*

As they rushed away, she went back to Dusty. "Sorry."

"You can make it up to me by letting me take you for a drink after the show."

"Are you even old enough to drink?" she teased. "I'm seeing someone, but there are plenty of gorgeous women in here who would probably love to join you."

He lowered his voice. "I'm sick of fake women who exist on kale and smoothies and expect to be wined and dined."

Indi was not going to miss that, or the higher-than-thou personalities she'd been dodging all day. "It kind of comes with the territory."

"That's one thing I miss about the girls back home in Oak Falls, Virginia. They give you shit if you're too uppity and think a barn dance is the best thing under the sun."

"A barn dance? That sounds fun."

"Yeah, they are fun. Where's your man taking you for Valentine's Day?"

She thought of Archer's naughty texts from earlier, in which he promised all sorts of delicious activities for Saturday night. "Actually, I'm working late and he's out of town. After being on my feet for fourteen hours, the only place I'm going is into a nice hot bath."

"That sounds good to me. What time?"

She shook her head as Mia Stone, Josh and Riley Braden's assistant, hurried over. Mia was a petite brunette, and she moved in her heels like they were sneakers. Indi didn't know how she did it. She'd worn her most comfortable flat-soled ankle boots, and her feet had been aching for the last two hours.

"There's been a change for the last two girls. They want middle parts and big hair instead of slicked back and tucked behind the ears. Fair warning, one of the models has stick-straight hair." Mia was as unflappable as always.

Indi had a feeling if the roof caved in, Mia would still be calm, cool, and collected as she directed the models and guests to the parking lot and tried to continue the show. "I love a challenge." She finished Dusty's makeup, thankful she was almost done for the night. "You're done, Casanova. Go make the girls drool."

"I'm on it. But first…" He climbed out of the chair to his full height of six-plus feet and draped an arm around Mia. "Hey, beautiful. Care to go for a Valentine's Day drink with the hottest guy in New York City?"

"Show him to me, and then I'll decide." Mia moved out from under Dusty's arm.

"Dusty, you're up!" an assistant called out, and Dusty hurried away.

Mia crossed her arms, drumming her fingers on her forearms. "If I were a decade younger and not hung up on a certain PI who can't see what's right in front of him, I'd take him up on that drink." She'd been hung up on Archer's cousin Reggie for years.

"I was going to ask if there was any news in that department." Indi began organizing her supplies.

"Nope. Not since that one date we went on when he kissed the hell out of me and then told me it was best if we remained just friends." Mia rolled her eyes. "Maybe your man should talk with his cousin about how great it is to be friends with benefits who turn into more."

"I'm not sure putting together a guy who doesn't want to label us and doesn't talk about his feelings for me with a guy who investigates liars and cheaters will have a good outcome for either of us."

"You're right. Keep Archer away from Reggie. I'll figure

something out."

Another assistant brought a male model over and asked Indi to give him smoky eyes with neon blue eyelids. Indi made quick work of fixing him up and let out a breath as they hurried away. "Is it nine thirty yet?"

"Not quite, Cinderella."

"Indi! Mia!" Leni called from a few feet away, where she was standing with a photographer. "I want a shot of you two exactly like the one we took when you first worked Fashion Week together. Arm in arm, big smiles."

They posed for the picture, and when Leni and the photographer moved on, Mia said, "That woman amazes me. And so do you. Are you sure you don't want to do big-city events anymore? I'm going to miss working with you. Who will I talk to about my nonexistent love life?"

"We have a whole week to talk, and after that you'll just have to visit me on Silver Island. I know you're a big-city girl at heart, but you'd love the down-to-earth community and the cute towns."

"It would be a great break from all of this. Did I tell you that Jace gave Jennifer a free trip to the island?" Jennifer was Mia's sister.

"No. Did she love it?"

"She hasn't gone yet. Maybe I'll confiscate her gift certificate and find someone to do the pretzel dip with. Jen says it's the best sexual position she's ever tried."

"I have no idea what *that* is, but confiscating the gift certificate sounds like a good plan." Thinking of surprising Archer with something new on Saturday, she made a mental note to look up the pretzel dip. She glanced over Mia's shoulder at another model making a beeline for her. "Break's over."

"Don't forget, middle part, big hair," Mia said as she walked away.

"Got it!" Indi said as the leggy model sat in her chair. The model gave her the lowdown on what she needed, and Indi checked her list from the designers. She'd been given different instructions, so she quickly called the cell number on the list for the designer's assistant.

Two hours later, she stowed her supplies in the allocated area and made her way out to the car waiting for her at the curb. Everything hurt, from her hands and forearms to her legs and feet. She was also starving, and her pulse was still racing from the frantic pace of the event. But she couldn't let herself relax just yet, because once she did, she'd crash like a boulder off a cliff. She needed to check her messages and text Archer first. She'd gotten several texts that morning in addition to Archer's. Meredith had wished her good luck, Jules had sent a group text to Indi and her family telling her to *break a leg (but not really)*, and Indi had been pleasantly surprised when Simon had texted to say he was thinking of her and hoped she had a great day. She and Simon rarely texted, but he'd messaged her the day after he'd come to the island, and they'd had a nice conversation.

She took a deep breath and blew it out slowly as she pulled out her phone. There was a missed text from Archer, one from Simon, and several responses to the group text.

She read Archer's first. *Still kicking ass and taking names?* She thumbed out, *On my way home. So tired. How's your night?*

While she waited for his reply, she read Simon's message. *How'd it go?* She typed, *Great. I'm exhausted. Thanks for checking on me. Love you.* His response rolled in seconds later. *Love you too. Proud of you.*

A message from Archer popped up, and she opened it. *I'm*

hanging out with Brant. He's not as hot as you. Is it Saturday yet? He added a devil emoji. She smiled and typed, *Almost. Miss you.* His response was immediate. *Miss you too. Get some rest. You're going to need all your energy for this weekend.* She knew she'd be even more exhausted Saturday than she was tonight, but with him, she always got a second wind. She sent back a heart emoji, wishing she could fall asleep in his arms tonight and every other night.

She read the group text responses from Archer's parents and every one of his siblings, including Leni. As she scrolled through their well wishes, her mind tiptoed back to her parents. Unwilling to be brought down, she closed her eyes and tipped her head back, willing them away with thoughts of Archer.

When the driver dropped her off, she trudged up the stairs to her apartment, thankful to be home. She unlocked the door and stepped inside. For a split second her exhausted mind had her thinking she was in the wrong apartment. Candles danced on every surface, and strings of twinkling lights were draped over the pictures on the walls and around the windows and shelves. Bouquets of red roses decorated the counters and the coffee table, on which were plates, a bag from her favorite taco shop down the street, and two champagne glasses filled with mojitos, complete with a slice of lime and a sprig of mint. She'd know her favorite drink anywhere. She saw more bouquets in the bedroom, and as her big, thoughtful man pushed to his feet from the couch holding an enormous heart-shaped box of candy and an adorable stuffed bear, she thought her heart might burst from her chest.

"Happy Valentine's Day, darlin'."

She dropped her bag and threw her arms around him, tears welling in her eyes. "I can't believe you're here! I was *just* wishing I could see you. This is amazing." She went up on her toes and kissed him. "You didn't have to do all of this."

"Did you really think I'd let you spend Valentine's night alone?"

"I don't know. I guess I did because we're both so busy and you were back on the island, and it's a long trip."

I'D TRAVEL A thousand miles to see you. "Haven't I told you not to underestimate me?"

He'd been planning this night for a week. She might have downplayed how grueling Fashion Week was to him, but he'd listened when she talked with his sisters about it over dinner at his parents' house, and it sounded like *grueling* didn't even begin to describe the magnitude of effort she'd be putting in over the next week.

He kissed her again, and her stomach growled loudly, making them both laugh. "I had a feeling you hadn't eaten. Why don't you go change into comfy clothes and I'll get dinner ready."

She sighed gratefully. "You're the *best*." As she headed into the bedroom, she said, "How did you get into my apartment?"

"A gentleman never tells." He put the food on their plates and set out napkins.

"Did you borrow Mare's key?"

"No."

"No one else has a key," she called out as she changed.

He knew she'd keep picking away until she figured it out. "If I'd thought of borrowing your sister's key, it would have made me feel like less of a creeper, but I borrowed yours the other morning and made a copy while you were working. I put the original back on your key ring that night, and my copy of your key is on your nightstand."

"You're sneaky," she said as she came back into the living room, looking adorable in pink sweatpants and one of his T-shirts. The sleeves hung past her elbows, and she'd tied it at her waist.

He had no idea how a piece of clothing could make him fall harder for her, but he'd noticed the same thing when they'd built the snow fort and she'd worn his jacket over hers. "You look cute as hell. When did you steal that?"

She shrugged and climbed onto the couch, tucking her legs beside her. She looked so tired, he wanted to take her in his arms and hold her until she fell asleep, but he knew she was hungry, and he'd been looking forward to pampering her for days. He handed her a plate of three tacos and sat at the far end of the couch. "Give me your feet."

She tilted her head, stretching her legs toward him. "Is this a new type of foreplay?"

"Tonight's not about sex." He pressed his thumbs into the sole of her foot, massaging along its center and outward.

She moaned appreciatively. "That feels *so* good."

That filled him with all kinds of pleasure. "Tell me about your day."

"Aren't you going to eat?" she asked.

"Don't worry about me." *The only thing I'm hungry for is more of that smile.* "You spent all day taking care of others. Tonight's all about taking care of you, and this is only the beginning. I'm going to do your legs, which I'm sure are aching, and your hands and wrists, which have to be sore, and then you're going to lie down so I can give you the best neck and back massage you've ever had."

Her gaze softened, but there was a lot more than appreciation looking back at him. "When did you get so thoughtful?"

When I started falling for a girl who made me want to give more than I received, to take care of her, and put her first. He skipped the question and said, "Now, enjoy your dinner and tell me all about your day of divas."

He continued massaging as she described a day of constant commotion and fast-paced activities that sounded like hell to him, but the passion in her voice was unmistakable. She ate as she talked, appreciative sounds slipping out between stories.

"You know how much I love these tacos." She finished the first taco and licked her fingers. "But tonight they taste even better, and I know it's because you're giving me the best foot massage I've ever had."

"Yeah? Do you get many foot massages?"

"Only here and there, when I get pedicures, but they're *nothing* like this. You have the *best* hands. The best *everything*." She picked up another taco and took a bite, her eyes dancing happily.

He'd never pampered anyone, but from that day forward, he was going to pamper her. Not only was she enjoying it, but it brought him immense pleasure, too. He began massaging his way up her leg and kneaded her calf.

She closed her eyes. "Sweet mother of…That feels *incredible*." She took another bite and set the plate on the table. With her cheeks full of tacos, she pointed to the box of chocolates. He handed it to her and reached for her glass.

"*No.* I'm okay." She waved to her legs. "Keep doing what you're doing, *please*."

He chuckled and continued working the knots out of her muscles as she plucked piece after piece of chocolate and bit into them, putting some back in the box and exclaiming with others, "*Ohmygod! You have to taste this*," then feeding him the other half. "Isn't it good?" she asked after each one, but she didn't wait for answers as she stuffed more candy into his mouth.

"Are those rejects?" he asked as she placed another half-eaten chocolate in the box.

"Not all of them. Some are my favorites and I'm saving them for later."

"Ah, so I get the not-so-great pieces?" he teased.

Her eyes widened. "Uh-oh. You're right. Here." She handed him the box.

He laughed and pushed it back toward her. "Babe, I don't want them. I was kidding, and I like watching you enjoy them, so eat up."

"Okay. *Sorry.*" She bit into another piece. "*Mm. So* good. You'll love this one."

She had chocolate on her cheek, lips, and fingers, and leaned in to give him the other half with a vibrant smile that reached her tired eyes. She'd never looked happier or more beautiful, and as she put the chocolate in his mouth, he realized he wasn't just falling for her. He was tumbling down that rocky slope faster than the speed of sound with no desire to stop. Was this what he'd seen in his grandfather's eyes when he was around his grandmother? What he saw in his father's eyes every second he was with or talking about his mother? Was it what Jock had felt for Daphne that had finally brought him back to the island and given him the strength to confront Archer? What Kayla had felt when she'd been texting him that fateful night? Because holy shit, this feeling was phenomenal, but it was also nerve rattling. Was it too much too fast? What if Indi didn't feel the same? Those three sacred words vying for release were too damn powerful. They'd change everything. Were they ready for that? Was *he*?

"What do you think?" she asked excitedly. "Did you love it?"

Indi's voice brought him back to the moment, the taste of coconut and chocolate melting in his mouth. He swallowed the candy, trying to push his whirling emotions down with it, but they refused to go. He grabbed her beautiful face between both hands, gritting out, "I do. I fucking *love* it," and crushed his lips to hers before the rest of his heart fell out.

Chapter Twenty-Six

"WE'RE ALL SET. The driver's picking us up at the coffee shop, but we have to hurry." Indi put on her sunglasses as she and Archer hurried out of her apartment Thursday morning. Last night after eating the chocolates and drinking their mojitos, he'd stripped her naked and proceeded to give her the full-body massage he'd promised, putting her in such a deep state of relaxation, she'd fallen fast asleep. She'd woken up this morning to Archer kissing his way down her stomach, and what a glorious alarm that was! But they'd gotten carried away and had lost track of time. It was worth having to rush, but she couldn't afford to be late. She was working with Jillian Braden today, and the car Jillian was sending was also picking up two other members of her team. It was barely acceptable for the models to show up late if they were coming from other events, and it was definitely not okay for the team to show up late.

"I'd say I'm sorry, but I'd be lying. I enjoyed every second of breakfast in bed, and that pretzel dip was hot. You need to ask Mia's sister for more recommendations."

"You're not kidding." Indi had looked up the position last night while they'd finished their mojitos, and she'd been half kidding when she'd suggested they try it. But *wow* was she glad they had. It sounded more complicated than it was, with Indi lying on her right side, and Archer straddling her right leg, curling her left leg around his left side. The position allowed him to thrust as hard and deep as doggy style, but they had eye contact, which made it much more intimate, and the angle made everything more intense.

They turned the corner, and the green awning of the coffee shop that had fueled her mornings since the first day she'd moved into her apartment stood out like a beacon in the middle of the block.

"Thanks again for coming to surprise me. I think I'm still in shock."

"That's just an orgasm hangover."

He opened the door, and she was glad to see there wasn't a big line. The barista gave Archer a once-over as she made their coffees, but Archer paid her no mind, leaning in to kiss Indi.

He glanced out the window as the barista set their coffees on the counter. "Your car is out there. I'll pay. You go ahead so you're not late." He pulled her into a quick kiss. "I'll text you later."

She hurried out the door and plowed into someone on his way in. "Sorry." She looked up just as James's face came into view.

"Indi?"

"James. Hi. *Sorry.* I was rushing, and I didn't see you." She stepped out of the way to let a couple walk inside.

"It's okay. It's great to see you." He hugged her as Archer came out the door, a silent question in his eyes. "I've missed you. You look beautiful, as always. I guess island life agrees with you."

"It does. I'm happy there." Archer came to her side as the

driver got out of the car and opened the back door, making her even more nervous. She motioned to Archer. "You remember me talking about Leni's brother, Archer? Archer's been helping me get my boutique together. Archer, this is James."

"Nice to meet you." James held out his hand.

Archer ignored his proffered hand, jaw tight, and lifted his chin in acknowledgment.

James lowered his hand, giving Indi an awkward look. "I'll call you. We'll catch up."

"Okay, sure. Good to see you." As James went into the coffee shop, Archer looked like he was ready to explode.

"Leni's brother? *Seriously?*" Archer said harshly. "Is that all I am to you? Just a guy who's helping you get your shop ready?"

Her heart sank at the hurt in his voice. "*No,* of course not. He caught me off guard. I barreled into him and got flustered, and I haven't talked to him since Winter Walk. I didn't want to rub our relationship in his face."

"You're *that* worried about him? How would you feel if I introduced you as Leni's *friend* to a woman I went out with for years?"

Shit. I really screwed up. "I'd hate it, and I'm sorry." The driver cleared his throat, as if she weren't frantic enough. "I *really* have to go. Can we talk about this tonight?"

"Yeah, whatever. *Go.*" A storm of conflicting emotions brewed in his eyes as he turned and walked away.

She climbed into the car, watching him disappear around the corner, and suddenly she knew how it felt to be Archer and have shit come out of her mouth that she couldn't take back.

FASHION WEEK DIDN'T slow down just because Indi had put her foot in her mouth and hurt the man she cared most about. But even the chaos around her was nothing compared to the worry raging inside her. She'd texted Archer three times and he hadn't responded. She was a nervous wreck, and it didn't help that she felt like a big jerk. Leni's brother? What was she thinking?

The model she'd just prepped left her chair, and it took everything Indi had not to say *the hell with it* and leave the show to go to the island and find Archer. As if leaving the show was even an option. Besides not being the type of person to screw over the designers, Leni was walking toward her with Dixie Whiskey-Stone, the wife of Jace Stone and the face of the Leather and Lace clothing line. Leni had known the second she'd seen Indi walk in that something was wrong, and Indi had explained how badly she'd messed up with Archer. Now concern brimmed in Leni's eyes.

"Hi, Indi." Dixie gave her a quick hug. "It's good to see you again."

"You too." They'd worked together several times, and Indi really liked her. She was a tough but feminine biker, with gorgeous, naturally wavy red hair and a strong personality.

As Dixie settled into the chair, Leni took Indi by the arm, turning their backs to Dixie. "Are you okay?"

"Not really." She turned around to get started on Dixie's hair, which was almost perfect. "He isn't responding to my texts."

Leni sighed. "What is it with men not being able to communicate?"

"My husband was the *worst* communicator when we first got together." Dixie had never been shy about jumping into conversations. "But I fixed that."

"This time I don't blame him." Indi primped Dixie's hair. "I put my foot in my mouth and said some hurtful things. But now I'm curious, Dixie. How did you fix the communication issues? Maybe I can try it."

"Well, my guy went *days* without contacting me. I tried drowning my sorrows in ice cream and whiskey," Dixie answered as Indi started applying her makeup. "And when that didn't work, I punched him in the face."

Leni laughed. "Girl, I love you."

"You *punched* him?" Indi had never punched anyone in her life, and she wasn't about to start.

"Sure did, and it worked. He's a much better communicator now." Dixie looked across the room at Jace, who was towering over Jillian as a photographer took their picture. Jace's dark hair brushed the collar of his leather jacket, and with his serious expression and deep-set eyes, he looked as broody as burgundy-haired, bright-eyed Jillian looked chipper. "I still can't believe that gorgeous man is *all* mine."

Commotion erupted by the doors, and Dixie said, "Sounds like someone's catching hell."

"I'd better see what's going on," Leni said. "The last thing I need is one of my clients getting bad press."

As she walked away, voices escalated, and Archer came into view, wrenching his arm away from a security guard. The air rushed from Indi's lungs as he plowed through the crowd, arms arced out from his body, eyes locked on *her*.

Dixie mumbled, "Holy shit," just as Leni shouted, "He's with me! It's okay!"

Leni hurried over to Archer as he closed in on Indi and asked through gritted teeth, "What the hell are you doing?"

Eyes blazing, Archer said, "Setting the fucking record straight."

Everyone was watching them, and Jillian's assistant was glowering at Indi, tapping her watch, reminding her that Dixie had to get ready. *Shitshitshit.* Indi frantically began applying Dixie's makeup. Her heart hammered against her ribs as Archer stepped beside her, emotions billowing off him.

"I'm *working*," she said lamely, wanting to say so much more but afraid she'd make things worse.

"No shit. I just need to clear a few things up, and then I'll get out of your hair." His tone was angry but low, which told her how hard *he* was trying not to make more of a scene, too. "What happened out there *sucked*. I know you got flustered, and you didn't want to hurt that guy, but it stung. And maybe that's on me—"

"*No.* It was me. I said the wrong thing." She struggled against tears. "I didn't mean to hurt either of you."

"I know you didn't, but I didn't help. I'm not the best at telling you how I feel. But I'm here to set the record straight, so the next time you're in that situation you'll know *exactly* what to say. I don't know how we got here, but it doesn't matter, and there's no going back."

Tears welled in her eyes. *"Wait..."*

"I can't wait. I need to tell you." He threw up his hands. "I fucking *love* you, Indi. I can't help it, and I don't want to slow down. I've fallen in love with *everything* about you, from the way you touch me to your dirty mouth. I *especially* like that, but this is *love*, baby, not just sex. It might have been just sex at first. I don't even know anymore because you've become such a big part of me, and I don't want to go back to figure it out." His words fell fast and vehement. "I've been tied to the past for too long. I want to keep moving forward with you. You're the most amazing person I know, with your confidence and your fearlessness. I love that you're rebellious, like me, and you're passionate about everything you do. You know what else I love? That you're so damn headstrong, you never hesitate to give me hell, and the way you are with our friends and family." He banged his fist over his heart. "You get me right here, baby."

Her jaw dropped in disbelief, her heart sprinting in her chest. "You...you *love* me?"

"*Yes.* I *love* you." His tone softened as tears spilled from her eyes. "I don't know what's going to happen with your parents, but I love that you're not willing to let your dreams go up in flames for them. I want to shield you from their fire and try to fix that mess, but I know the best you'll let me do is to walk through those flames *with* you, and I want to be there every step of the way, Indi. I want to be your man more than anything in this world. I know I can be a jerk, and I say things I shouldn't, but I'll work on that. I will protect your heart with everything I have. I realize that you got flustered with James because you hate to hurt people, so I'm going to take that out of your hands from now on. The next time we run into one of your exes, all you have to say is, 'This is Archer,' and *I'll* tell them I'm the guy giving you orgasm hangovers and full-body massages and that I'm wildly, passionately in love with you."

She laughed through her tears as chuckles rose around them, but she was so choked up, it sounded more like a bark.

"Or I can just say that I'm your boyfriend. We'll work on that." He took her trembling hand, gazing deeply into her eyes. "I'm not asking you to love me back. Lord knows I'm not easy to love—"

"I call *bananas* on you, Archer Steele." Her voice cracked. "I may not always like the things you say, and that's okay, because you don't like everything I say, either. But you're easy to love, and I'm pretty sure I've been falling in love with you all along."

He pulled her into his arms and kissed her as cheers and applause rang out around them, and salty tears slipped through their lips.

"Now, *that's* a love I can relate to," Dixie said, causing a rumble of laughter.

"I'm so sorry for what I said," Indi whispered.

Jillian came through the crowd and planted a hand on her hip. "*Great.* Two more people in love, and neither one of them is *me*. Story of my life." She sighed, but she was smiling. "Indi, I'm *really* happy for you, and you"—she pointed at Archer—"if you've got a single, hot brother, send him my way, but Dixie needs to get her butt onstage. Can we get on with the show, please?"

"Yes, sorry." With her heart in her throat, Indi turned back to Dixie.

Archer raised his hands to the crowd, announcing, "Sorry, folks, but it's not every day a man gets caught by love. My apologies for the disruption. There's nothing more to see here."

As the crowd murmured and dispersed, chaos once again ensued. Leni sidled up to Archer and said, "I have no idea who you are right now, but I freaking love you. You guys probably have about ten seconds before all of this goes viral, so brace yourselves. And if you hurt Indi, you'll have me to deal with."

She stalked off, and Archer put a hand on Indi's back as she finished Dixie's makeup. "I hope I didn't get you in trouble."

"I don't care if you did. You love me, and I love you, and that's what matters."

"We'll talk later. For now, your capable and *willing* assistant is here to serve you." The seduction in his voice was unmistakable.

Dixie smirked. "Just keep your clothes on long enough to finish my makeup."

Indi and Archer laughed, and Indi finished applying her makeup and stepped back. "You're done, Dix. *Go.*" As Dixie hurried away, Indi turned her attention to the man who she knew would never stop surprising her. "And we, Archer Steele, are just getting started." She grabbed the front of his jacket, pulling him into a long slow kiss.

Chapter Twenty-Seven

THE TRUCK RUMBLED as Archer drove off the ferry's ramp onto Silver Island. Indi looked over her shoulder at her furniture and boxes in the truck bed and, just beyond, at Levi's truck, also filled with her belongings as he followed them toward her new apartment. It was strange to think her entire life could fit in two trucks. But somehow she knew that even if she moved away from the island today, the life she'd already built there was too big to fit in any number of trucks, because the amount of happiness she felt couldn't be boxed up and packed away.

It had been two weeks since Archer had stormed into the back room at Fashion Week and proclaimed his love for her. Leni had been right about his outburst going viral. Not only were there several different videos making the rounds, each with millions of views, but *Page Six*, *TMZ*, and a handful of other media outlets had also picked up the story. She hadn't heard a peep from her parents, but Meredith and Simon had enjoyed teasing Archer about it, although they were thrilled for them. Needless to say, Archer was not happy with his newfound celebrity. Indi had thought he'd blow a gasket when she'd shown him some of the many memes and GIFs people had created of him throwing his hands up as he said he loved her for the very first time, with declarations like IF I CAN'T HAVE THIS, I DON'T WANT ANYTHING captioning them.

Indi might be leaving her old life behind, but that day would live on in infamy. Just as she knew their love would.

Archer put his hand on hers, drawing her attention. "Don't look back, darlin'. Your future is this way."

"Yes, it is." Her phone vibrated with a text, and she glanced at the screen. "It's James."

"What's that a-hole up to?" Archer winked.

She loved that wink and everything it stood for. She'd called James the morning after they'd seen him, and she'd told him all about Archer and apologized for their awkward interaction. He was as kind and warm as always, and being the gentleman he was, he invited her and Archer to meet him for dinner and drinks. They took him up on it the following weekend. James had explained that he wasn't pushing a relationship with her. It had been her mother all along, and her mother had been hinting to James that Indi was interested. Indi had been tempted to call her mother out on it, but she and Archer had talked and decided it wasn't worth her energy. Something good came out of that dinner. An unexpected friendship between Archer and James. They'd gotten along so well, Archer had suggested they all have dinner a few days later, and James had even brought a date, Eden Jalespy, who was kind and beautiful and obviously very taken with James. They'd come to the island last weekend, and Indi and Archer had shown them around. They'd had a really good time, and they'd hung out with Indi and their friends at Rock Bottom Saturday night. James fit right in with Jules and Grant, Jock and Daphne, Wells, Fitz, and the others. He was funny and charming and attentive to Eden, reminding

Indi of why they'd been such good friends in the first place.

As she opened James's text, she realized she wasn't leaving *all* of her old life behind. She had a feeling he would always be part of their lives, and she was glad about that. She read his text aloud. "The city is already duller without you. Good luck with your move. See you at the grand opening, if not before."

Archer squeezed her hand as they came to the stop sign on the corner of Main Street and Bayview Avenue. "He's a good guy. I'm glad I didn't have to break his legs."

Indi laughed. "I'm sure he is, too." She looked at Jules's shop to her right, with its red-framed picture windows and iron giraffes out front. The giraffes wore red bows around their necks and white knit hats. Her new apartment was a few doors down. She wondered if Archer would stay there with her sometimes, or if they'd continue to stay at his cottage. She realized what she wasn't thinking was about staying in separate places. She'd had enough of that during Fashion Week.

Archer drove through the stop sign instead of turning onto Main Street.

"Where are you going?"

"I need to stop at the cottage first."

"Okay." She glanced behind them. "Should we text Levi? He's still following us."

"I already told him."

She settled back in her seat, taking in the park and the cute cottages along the road as they wound through the quiet streets, making their way toward Archer's cottage. She opened her window as they neared the marina, enjoying the crisp scents of winter and the sea. The scents of her new home.

"What's that smile for?" he asked as he turned into Seaview, the community where he lived.

"I was just thinking about being home. Silver Island feels like home to me, and I love everything about it."

He cocked a grin. "Even the gruff winemaker?"

"*Especially* the gruff winemaker."

"I'm glad to hear that."

As they neared his cottage, she saw a silver car she didn't recognize in the driveway. "Whose car is that?"

"It belongs to the girl who's moving in." He parked the truck and climbed out, leaving her dumbfounded as he came around to help her out.

She took his hand as she stepped down. "I don't understand. You rented your cottage?"

"No."

"Okay. Did you rent out a room?"

"*No.*" He reached for her hand, but she crossed her arms.

"But that's a *girl's* car, and she's moving into *your* cottage?" She narrowed her eyes. "What the hell, Archer? Where is she going to be *sleeping*?"

Levi climbed out of his truck, heading their way.

"In my bed, babe. Where do you think?"

She gritted her teeth, trying not to explode. "What the everloving hell are you talking about?"

Levi held up his hands and backed away. "I'll go measure the neighbor's yard."

Archer reached for her again, but she took a step back. "*What* is going on, Archer?" She looked between the car and him. A devilish grin brought a familiar wickedness to his eyes, and understanding dawned on her. "You're messing with me, aren't you?"

"Maybe." He laughed.

"*Archer!* You were *this close* to getting slapped in the face, you big pain. I knew you'd never cheat, but I was so confused. Who's really here?"

He put his arms around her waist, smiling from ear to ear. "That's your car, babe, and I'm hoping you'll want to move in with me."

Her eyes nearly bugged out of her head. "You did *not* buy me a car."

"Yeah, I did. It's a Nissan Rogue. The perfect car for my rebellious girl, don't you think? It's all-wheel drive, and the next time it snows, we'll go for a ride, and I'll teach you how to keep from spinning out."

"Archer, you cannot buy me a car. I'm paying you back."

"*No*, you're not."

"*Yes*, I am. You can't just buy me a car." Her voice escalated, torn between the incredibly kind gesture and the knee-jerk reaction caused by years of fighting for her independence. "I have money. I can buy my own car. I don't need to be taken care of like that."

"It's *done*, Indi. I already bought it. It's just a fucking car," he said angrily, pacing the grass. "Is it a crime to want you to be safe and not spend a fortune on rentals? Jesus, Indi. It's not like I'm asking you to quit working and have my babies."

"*Good*, because that's not happening." She hated herself for arguing but couldn't seem to stop.

"*Great.*" His nostrils flared. "You're driving me fucking bananas."

She looked at him, and suddenly she saw the ridiculousness of their argument, and she laughed. "I am fucking bananas. I'm sorry."

Archer stopped pacing and shook his head, laughter rumbling out. He tugged her into his arms, both of them laughing.

"You're *both* bananas." Levi pointed at Archer. "You should have listened to Leni when she told you that Indi would tell you to shove that car up your—"

Archer silenced him with a stare.

"Okay, then." Levi grabbed a box from the truck and headed up the walk. "I'll just take this inside. I assume she's moving in, because you two are made for each other."

As Levi headed inside, Indi winced. "*Uh-oh.* I skipped right over you asking me to move in. Do you still want me to?"

"Only if you take the car." He cocked an arrogant grin.

Oh, how she loved him! "Only if you let me pay you back."

He tightened his hold on her, his eyes smoldering. "You can pay me back, all right, but not with money."

"*Archer.*" She laughed softly. "How am I supposed to argue with *that*?"

"You're not, but I'm sure you'll think of a way." He crushed his mouth to hers. "Do me a favor, babe. Don't ever doubt my love for you. It's unconditional. You can be as argumentative as you want, and it won't change how I feel about you."

She felt a rush of unexpected emotions and kissed the center of his chest. "Thank you. I'm holding you to that. But I don't need big gifts. I only need your love."

"I'm sorry I didn't ask you about the car, but it was bought out of love." He glanced at the car. "I've got to tell you, in my head the whole thing played out a lot differently, with accolades like, *Oh, Archer! A car? You're my hero!* and lots of kisses, and *other* sexy thank-yous."

She laughed. "You're such a goof. Don't you know you *are* my hero? You freed me from futilely trying to win over my parents better than Johnny Castle."

"Who the hell is Johnny Castle?"

"*Dirty Dancing? Nobody puts Baby in a corner?* Never mind. You're my hero, all right, you loved me enough to figure out how to forgive yourself for us, and knowing how hard that was for you tells me that your love for me must be bigger than anything else in the world." She lowered her voice and ran her finger down his chest. "Who else can give me orgasm hangovers? And about those *other* thank-yous? I'll make them up to you tonight."

"I look forward to it." He touched his forehead to hers, holding her against him. "You have no idea how much you mean to me. I never knew I could love someone as much as I love you, and I will do everything within my power to exceed your hero expectations."

He kissed her again, and she teased, "Everything's a competition."

"Damn right. Come on. Let's check out your wheels."

The thrill of the whole situation hit her as they walked over to the car. "I can't believe you bought me a *car*. You're crazy, you know that?"

"Crazy about you, babe." He handed her the keys and kept hold of her hand. "You know I'd never try to take over your life or tie you down."

"That's a shame." She went up on her toes and whispered, "I'd like you to tie me down."

He growled and hauled her into a kiss.

"Aw, come on," Levi hollered as he came outside. "Save it for the bedroom."

They cracked up, and then he kissed her again.

"Let's get this furniture inside, bro," Levi called over.

"A'right. I'm coming." Archer gave her another quick kiss. "Take your time, babe."

As he went to the truck, she climbed into the car, repositioned the seat, and checked out all the gadgets, overwhelmed by his generosity. It really was perfect, with plenty of room for her cosmetics cases and supplies, and the name—*Rogue*—was perfect, too.

She got out of the car to tell him so, as they were setting the dresser on the grass by the truck. She sauntered over and couldn't resist teasing him. "You sure you want to move that in? Because you thought the toothbrush was scary, and I can't just pick up my dresser and leave."

Archer stalked toward her, eyes narrowing. "You think you're funny, don't you?"

She stumbled backward, laughing. "I'm just sayin'."

He bolted toward her, and she squealed, trying to run, but he caught her and hauled her over his shoulder. "I think it's time to get started on that tying up."

"Levi, *help!*" She cracked up.

Levi held his palms up to the sky, laughing as Archer charged around the yard with her over his shoulder.

"Nobody can save you now, baby." Archer headed for the house. "You're *mine*."

"Archer Steele, you are *not* tying me up with your brother here."

He stopped and uttered a curse as he lowered her to her feet, and Levi hollered, "Sorry, bro."

"You're lucky he's here." As he lowered his smiling lips to hers, he said, "We'll pick up where we left off later."

"I'm counting on it." She went up on her toes, meeting him in a sweet kiss.

"Let's go, babe. The sooner we get you moved in, the sooner we get down to business." He smacked her ass, and they headed over to the truck.

The three of them joked around as they moved her furniture and all her boxes into the cottage. They piled her clothes on Archer's—*their*—bed. That felt all kinds of good! Maybe she should be nervous about agreeing to move in so fast, but she loved Archer and all his rough edges, and after everything they'd been through together, she knew there was nothing they couldn't handle.

When they finished moving everything inside, they ordered pizza and ate in the living room. Indi sat beside Archer on the couch, taking in the plethora of boxes and various other belongings scattered around the living and dining rooms. "I didn't realize I had so much stuff. I'm going to be unpacking boxes all night."

"I'll help you, babe." Archer grabbed another piece of pizza.

"I don't know how you'll fit all this stuff on your boat when you rent this place this out," Levi pointed out.

"Oh gosh. I didn't even think about that." Indi looked at Archer. "Do you have closet space on your boat? If you don't, I can store my stuff in my apartment. I don't need all that much on a day-to-day basis."

Archer put his hand on her leg. "It's a yacht, babe. There's plenty of closet space. Besides, you'll want to do something with your apartment, won't you?"

"I haven't thought about it, but probably. I could sublet it out or use it for the shop if things go well. Or maybe I'll eventually hire someone to do facials and that sort of thing and make it into a mini spa. How fun would that be?" She got a little excited thinking about it. "There's so much potential."

Levi looked at Archer. "Sounds like we're in for more renovations."

"Whatever Indi wants." Archer kissed her, and she warmed all over.

"At least you brought pictures," Levi said. "Maybe you can brighten this place up and make it feel less like a Motel 6."

"*Dude*," Archer complained. "It's a rental."

Levi shook his head. "Not anymore, it's not. This is yours and Indi's *home*, at least until the weather warms up."

"You think I don't know that?" Archer pushed to his feet and headed into one of the guest rooms.

"You just said it was a rental," Levi pointed out.

Indi wondered if the word *home* had been a little scary for him. She didn't think it had after all the nice things he'd said and done, but they *were* taking a huge step.

"Because it's always been a rental for half the year," Archer said as he came out of the guest room carrying a box with several large framed photographs in it and set it on the coffee table beside the pizza box. "But now it's our home."

Shocked, Indi said, "What do you mean? I love your boat. That's where we first came together. I want to live there with you."

"And we will, but if we're building a home, there's no sense pussyfooting around when we can jump in with two feet."

Indi was floored. The man she'd thought would never settle down wanted to build *two* homes for them. Boy, she loved his brand of romance.

He took one of the pictures and set it on Indi's lap. Her heart swelled at the photograph of her and Archer standing by their snow fort, all smiles and pink, cold noses, in a beautiful distressed pale-blue frame. "You got it printed out. I *love* it."

"Me too." He handed her another one, this one a photo of them kissing in a seafoam-green frame, and another of them making bunny ears, in a navy-blue frame. Then he handed her a picture in a distressed aqua frame of Indi talking with Simon and Meredith, inside her boutique the day they'd come to the island.

Indi was so touched by all of them, she felt like she might cry. "Who took this?"

"I did," Archer said.

"Why didn't you tell me you took it?"

"What kind of surprise would that be?" Archer winked at her.

"Damn, bro," Levi said. "You really *do* know about making a home."

"No shit. We'll make a home here and on the boat, and we'll stay wherever my girl wants." He took out another picture. This one was in a wine-colored frame, and it was taken at the ice cream shop they'd found after the awards banquet, of his entire family and Indi and Grant. Archer sat between Indi and Jock, his arms around both of them. Everyone was smiling, half-eaten ice cream sundaes on the table in front of them.

"Archer…" She ran her fingers around the picture. "This is so special."

"I want a copy of that one," Levi said. "What else have you got in there?"

"Just a few more." Archer smirked and handed Indi the picture Tara had taken of him that she'd called *Man on Fire*, in a heavy black frame with pink hearts all over it. "I thought you might want this one in your office."

Her heart felt like it might burst. She pressed it to her chest. "I couldn't love it more. Thank you."

He winked and pulled another picture out of the box. This one was in a pink wooden frame, and when he turned it toward them, she saw it was of Archer cradling a tiny baby in his muscular arms. He looked young, clean shaven, and so very handsome. He was smiling, even though his eyes looked tired. Indi didn't think anything could soften her man's rough edges, but that baby sure did. She felt an unfamiliar tug low in her belly, and her mind tiptoed to a future of Archer holding their babies. She might not want to give up her career, but she definitely still wanted a family, and she was looking at the only man she wanted to have that family with.

"That's Joey," Levi said, taking the picture from him. "She was only about two weeks old in this picture. I remember when Mom took it. You'd been up walking Joey for hours. She was the cutest baby, wasn't she?"

"She was," Archer said. "And the noisiest."

Levi laughed. "You saved my sanity, man."

Archer's jaw twitched, and he took out a picture of him and Hadley in a pretty red frame. He was standing by a Christmas tree holding Hadley. Her tiny arms were wrapped around his neck, her head resting on his shoulder, brows knitted, lips pursed. Indi had never seen two people with such serious matching expressions.

"That might be my all-time favorite picture." Indi laughed. "You are two peas in a pod."

Archer smiled and looked at the picture. "Our family's been through hell, but Jock was right when he said if we hadn't gone through it, he'd never have met Daphne and Hadley, and I don't want to imagine our lives without them."

He put the picture back in the box and pulled out the last one, studying it, his jaw tightening as he turned the gray wooden frame toward them. It was a picture of Archer and his grandfather standing among the vines in full bloom, bunches of plump grapes poking out between green leaves. Talk about two peas in a pod—both Archer and his grandfather wore jeans, the knees brown with dirt, blue T-shirts, also smeared with dirt, and matching work boots. Archer was holding a pair of clippers in one hand, and his other hand was engulfed in his grandfather's large hand. His grandfather was looking down at him, not at the camera, and Archer was peering up at the man, who looked giant compared to his grandson. The love in their eyes practically jumped off the picture.

"I miss Gramps," Levi said. "What were you, six in that picture?"

"Yeah." Archer nodded.

Indi put her hand on her chest. "I was wrong. That one is my favorite. Archer, they're all so special. They really make this place our home. Thank you for going to all that trouble."

"They're *all* my favorites." Archer put the other pictures back in the box. As he moved the box to the floor, he eyed Levi. "Done giving me shit now?"

Levi pushed to his feet. "Yup. You kind of just blew me away. I'll help you hang them up." He reached into a box and pulled out one of Indi's pictures. "We're hanging these, too, right?"

Archer said, "Yes," as Indi said, "No."

"What do you mean, *no*?" Archer asked tightly.

"We don't need to hang my work pictures."

"Like hell we don't," Archer insisted.

"Archer, I don't need the validation anymore. You give me more than the pictures ever could."

"You worked your ass off, and we're going to hang them up."

"Don't be silly. We have a bunch of family pictures. That's

enough."

"No, it's *not*. We're *hanging* them up. You can take some to your office if you want, but I want to walk into *our* cottage and onto *our* boat and see you beaming at the fucking camera during your *first* Fashion Week or your *first Cosmo* cover or whatever the hell else you've got."

"Man, you two." Levi shook his head. "Dad was right when he said passionate people can get heated up over nothing. You know it's always going to be like this, right?"

Sparks flew hot and wild between Archer and Indi, but in the next breath, laughter tumbled from their lips. Archer pulled her into his arms, and they both said, "I wouldn't want it any other way."

Chapter Twenty-Eight

PRACTICALLY THE WHOLE island showed up for the grand opening of Indi's boutique. Nobody could have anticipated the hordes of people who had come from the mainland. Indi hadn't heard anything from her parents after the phone call with her mother, but she'd come to terms with that, and she wasn't going to let their absence ruin this incredible day. Between her personal invitations, Leni's marketing efforts, Bellamy's videos and influencer connections, and good old word of mouth, the place was hopping. There were lines out the front door as people came and went, buying products, watching Indi's cosmetic and skincare demonstrations, and asking so many questions, Indi was sure she'd be hoarse by nightfall. Bellamy, Meredith, Shelley, and even Anika had volunteered to model for the demonstrations, and Noelle and Macie were doing a fantastic job. They were informative and professional, and the customers loved them. But Indi had grossly underestimated how busy they'd be, and she couldn't have managed the crowd without help from Sutton, Daphne, Jules, Lenore, Margot, and Gail, who had been taking turns jumping in to help customers and restock displays.

As Indi put the finishing touches on Shelley's makeup for

her current demonstration, she explained every step of the process to the crowd. She couldn't believe all those eager women were there for *her* products. Other than loving Archer, which was the best feeling in the world, there was no greater high than being surrounded by the products she'd developed, in the boutique born from her own ideas, knowing she got there with hard work and help from friends.

"And that is how you take your makeup from afternoon to evening. I hope you enjoyed this demonstration," Indi said to the crowd. "The next one will begin in an hour and will cover a fifteen-minute morning makeover. You can find all the products that I used on Shelley on the display table to my right. We're here to help if you have any questions."

As the crowd pushed forward, Noelle and Margot hurried over to the table and began helping customers as Macie sidled up to Indi. "I can answer their questions. Leni's looking for you. She said something about an interview."

"Okay. I'll find her."

Shelley said, "Macie, honey, I want to buy one of everything Indi used on me, but I have to hit the ladies' room. Can you please set them aside for me?"

"You've got it." Macie went to help the others.

"Shelley, you're not *buying* anything," Indi insisted. "I'll give you the products. You and Steve have already done so much for me. I could never take your money."

"Sweetheart, my sugar daddy would never let you do that." Shelley giggled.

"Your *sugar daddy* is not here, so he'll never know." Steve had taken Meredith's husband, Bruce, and the kids on a tour of the island.

"But *I'd* know." Shelley patted Indi's arm and hurried off

toward the bathroom.

Indi went in search of Leni, admiring the gold and silver balloons dancing above displays, giving the boutique a festive touch of joyous, understated *island* class. She and Archer had also tied gold and silver balloons to the awning out front, and they looked gorgeous with her gold sign. Archer had surprised her with an enormous planter overflowing with lush greenery and colorful flowers and INDIRA written across the front in gold, in Indi's handwriting. They'd put it by the entrance, making the boutique even more inviting.

As she made her way through the crowd, she stopped to answer questions and spotted Tara taking pictures, as she'd been doing all day, and Joey, her loyal assistant, flashing her PRESS badge and handing out Tara's card. They really did make a great team. Indi stole a glance at Archer standing by the front doors, and her heart beat a little faster. He had insisted that he and his brothers keep their eyes peeled for shoplifters, even though everyone had assured her that there was almost no crime on the island. Indi had told him that she had anti-theft stickers on every product, but he'd said, *Better safe than sorry.* She loved that he cared so much, and he and his brothers were taking their charge seriously. Levi and Jock stood watch on opposite sides of the room, while Archer stood by the doors, feet planted hip distance apart, arms crossed, chin low, his eagle eyes scanning the room as he talked with Simon.

His gaze found her, sparks burning up the space between them, stirring butterflies in her belly. His lips tipped up. Between training her employees, getting the shopkeeping software installed and learning to use it, and what seemed like a million other things she'd needed to finalize for the grand opening, and Archer's busier schedule as they geared up for the new season, pruning the vines and planting new ones, they'd had a busy, wonderful first month of living together. It wasn't without the need for both of them to count to ten, but they'd come up with an even better system. Whenever one of them started to raise their voice, the other kissed them. It worked so well, they often ended up laughing or making out. She wished they'd thought of it months ago.

"Stop drooling over my brother. I need you right now for a quick interview with a reporter from the *Cape Cod Times*," Leni said, tugging Indi toward a tall blond man.

The quick interview ended up taking half an hour, but Indi had a good time talking about her products, and Leni seemed pleased.

"Babe." Archer waved her over. He was holding a gigantic bouquet of red roses.

She hurried across the room. "Where did those come from?"

"They were just delivered for you. There's a card."

She reached for the card as Meredith walked up and said, "Now, *that's* a beautiful bouquet. Who are they from?"

Indi pulled the card out of the envelope and read it. *Indira, best of luck with your new endeavor. Love, Mom and Dad.* Her pulse quickened nervously, and her throat thickened. "It's from Mom and Dad." Archer put his hand on her back, and she was thankful for that support. She read the card again, unable to believe it and unsure what to think. "I don't get it. I haven't heard from them in weeks. Do you think they mean it, or do you think it's just their way of checking off a to-do list?"

"Babe, they reached out and wished you luck," Archer said. "That sounds like a step in the right direction."

"I want to believe that, but I'm afraid to get my hopes up."

"I think they regret the way they've treated you," Meredith

said. "They've been asking about you a lot the past few weeks."

"Really?" The little girl in her clung to that, but the adult in her tamped that eagerness down.

"People can change," Archer said.

She looked at the man who had changed in so many ways and had unknowingly helped her to change, too. She'd become stronger and also softer. After the way she'd reacted to Archer giving her the car, she'd realized she had a chip on her shoulder about being taken care of, and she'd been learning to let her guard down in that respect.

"You're right. People can change." She looked at the card again. "I'll take this for what it appears to be. It's not an apology, but maybe it is an olive branch, and things will start to get better. But even if it's not, it won't derail me. They don't have that power anymore, and either way, it's nice that they sent it."

"I agree," Meredith said. "And speaking of changes, I wasn't going to say anything until after you had your big day."

"You're pregnant?" Indi exclaimed.

"God no." Meredith laughed. "I love my children, but I don't need more right now. I decided to apply to law school."

"What? That's fantastic!" She hugged her. "What about Bruce and the kids?"

"Bruce supports me one hundred percent. He's never asked me not to work, and the kids are excited for me. Mom and Dad aren't happy about it, but I can deal with that. I never would have been able to find the courage to do it if you hadn't stuck to your guns with them." Meredith looked at Archer. "And the way you stand up for Indi is what every woman hopes for. Seeing you with her has changed my life and made my marriage stronger. Thank you for loving my sister the way she deserves to be loved."

"*Ohmygosh.* Now I'm going to cry." Indi fanned her face.

Archer pulled Indi closer, holding the bouquet in one arm, and kissed her temple. "Your sister changed my world, Mare. She made me a stronger, better man. She's the one who deserves the thanks for putting up with my ornery ass."

"I happen to love your ornery ass," Indi said.

"You guys are so cute." Meredith reached for the bouquet. "How about I take these flowers, and you two go find a dark corner to make out in or something."

"Now, that's a plan I can get behind." Archer cocked a grin, tugging Indi toward the office.

THEY NEVER MADE it to a dark corner. After a few stolen smooches, Indi was pulled away to tend to customers. Archer watched in awe as she worked the crowd all afternoon and into the early evening. She held customers' rapt attention as she demonstrated different skincare and makeup routines. She was fascinating, with her easy smile and professional demeanor, so different from the sexy vamp he loved through the nights and the sweet cuddler he woke with each morning.

As the evening wound down and the place emptied out, Archer's father sauntered over. "Hey, Pop."

"What a day, huh? I think it's safe to say Indi's boutique will be a success."

"I'm damn proud of her."

"We all are." His father motioned to Meredith and Bruce chatting with James and Eden. "They're good people."

"Yeah. Does something seem off to you with James and Eden?" He'd noticed James wasn't doting on her the way he had the other times he'd seen them.

"You noticed too, huh? There's definite tension there. Think I need to teach them the ten-second rule?"

They both chuckled.

"Can I get a picture of you two?" Tara asked.

"Why not?" Steve slung an arm over Archer's shoulder and Tara took the picture.

Joey came running over with Levi on her heels. "Can we get in the picture?"

"Sure," Tara said. Levi stood beside Archer, and Joey wiggled between Archer and his father, beaming as Tara took the picture. "Got it."

"Thank you!" Joey exclaimed. "Aunt Tara, can you babysit me over spring break at our house? Dad has a big job to do, and I don't want to miss my skateboarding club practices and tournament."

Tara looked at Levi, a little shy and a little longingly. "When is it?"

"In a few weeks," Levi answered. "If you're tied up, don't worry about it. We'll figure something else out."

Tara smiled, and Archer recognized that special smile as the one that only appeared for his brother. "It's okay. I can do it."

"Yay!" Joey hugged her. "Come on. The last people just left, and you promised I could get a picture with Indi after everyone was gone."

As they walked away, Archer nudged his brother. "When are you going to finally make a move on her?"

"What are you talking about?" Levi looked at him like he was nuts. "It's *Tara*."

"Yeah, a gorgeous blonde who totally digs you. Dad, back me up here."

Their father chuckled and stepped away. "I think I hear your mother calling."

"Dude, Tara's like family, and she's Amelia's *sister*." Levi said it like it was the only answer he needed. "I know better than to get tangled up in that hornets' nest."

"Whatever, man. For the record, I think you're making a big mistake." Archer's phone vibrated, and he read the text. "Come on. Wells just got here."

They headed up to the front of the store as the door flew open. Wells walked in and held the door as the rest of his family paraded in, followed by the Remingtons, carrying trays of food, coolers full of drinks, and folding tables. Wells said, "Set everything up wherever it'll fit!"

Indi rushed over. "What's going on?"

Keira held up a tray of Indi's favorite pastries and desserts. "Your man sure knows how to do it up right." Behind her, the others were setting out trays of barbecued ribs, tacos, and chicken, bowls of salad and vegetables, and platters of fresh fruit.

Indi's jaw dropped as Archer swept an arm around her waist. "Surprise, darlin'. I wanted to honor your big day with a special night."

"Archer? This is too much. It's—"

He silenced her with a hard press of his lips, and everyone laughed.

She whispered, "Thank you," and turned to the others. "Thank you all so much. I love this island and the life we're building here. I know this is where I was always meant to be."

"I can't do this anymore!" James stalked over to them. "I

can't watch this happen and not step in. I've been living a lie, Indi."

"James, no!" Eden cried.

"I'm sorry, Eden." He looked at Indi, brow wrinkled in anguish. "You're not supposed to be here on the island, Indi. You're supposed to be with *me*. I'm sorry, Archer, but I *love* her!" James sank down on one knee.

"James, what are you doing? Get up," Indi said frantically.

Rage pounded through Archer. "Dude, what the hell?"

James threw his hands up dramatically. "Marry me, Indi! Be my wife; have my babies! We'll sell this place and travel the world!"

"What the *fuck*?" Archer grabbed him by the back of his shirt, adrenaline surging through him as he lifted James off his feet and tossed him aside. "Stay the *hell* away from her. If she's marrying any asshole, it's going to be me!"

"Archer! Don't hurt him!" Indi yelled.

James stumbled backward, holding his hands up. "Okay, man, don't go bananas on me."

Archer stalked toward him, seeing red, hands fisting. "What the hell did you—"

"*Whoa! Stop!*" Levi grabbed one of Archer's arms and Grant grabbed the other, dragging him away from James.

"What the—" Archer yanked his arms free and spun around, ready to tear someone apart, but every person in there other than Indi was biting into a banana and laughing. *What the...?*

Hadley held up her banana and said, "Nana, Unca Archer!"

"Are you shitting me?" Archer chided himself. "*Kidding* me. Are you kidding me?"

Jock's hands shot up into the air and he shouted, "We are

the reigning prank kings!" and high-fived Levi. The other guys, even Roddy and Steve, got in on the high-fiving.

Archer looked at James. "I can't believe you were in on this."

"Sorry, man," James said. "They said it was an initiation."

Archer cursed under his breath and looked at his father. "*Tension* between them, huh?"

His father laughed.

"Sorry, Indi. They made us do it," Eden said as she ran to James's side. "I'd never let him go that easily."

"I love these people!" Meredith said loudly, making everyone laugh again.

"Y'all suck," Archer said, laughing as he stalked over to Indi. "But the joke's on you." He dug out the ring he'd planned on giving her later in the evening, and with his heart hammering against his ribs, he dropped to one knee.

There was a collective gasp, along with some *ohmygod*s and *holy crap*s.

Indi's eyes widened. "What are you doing?"

"Hopefully making you my fiancée." He took her hand and gazed up at the most beautiful woman in the world. The din of the others fell away as he said, "I was going to do this later tonight, when it was just the two of us. But after this fiasco, I don't want to wait another second. I love you, darlin', and I love the life we're building together. Don't freak out, but one day I want to see your belly round with our babies, and I want to raise our bullheaded little boys who'll do stupid things and drive us crazy and our rebellious little girls who will probably drive us even crazier."

She laughed, tears sliding down her cheeks as the other women *aww*ed.

"I want to walk with our children and grandchildren through the vineyard and teach them about life and love, and I want to watch your company soar to whatever heights you want it to. But most of all, I want to live every day of my life by your side. I want to see your beautiful face every morning and hold you in my arms at night. And when you yell at me for making mistakes, which you know I will, I want to kiss you into silence and remind you of all the reasons you fell in love with me in the first place. Maybe we should make a list now, so when I'm old and losing my memory but still doing stupid things, I can use it."

She laughed even as tears spilled from her eyes.

He held up the two-carat engagement ring he'd designed and had Alexander Silver's cousin, Sterling, make for her, with halo diamonds set in a floral motif around a central canary diamond set in rose gold, with more diamonds cascading along a white-gold band. Her jaw dropped, fresh tears streaming down her cheeks.

"Indi, baby, will you marry me and let me drive you bananas and love you for the rest of our lives?"

"Yes!" She nodded vehemently as he pushed to his feet, and she launched herself into his arms. Cheers and applause rang out as they murmured *I love you*s between kisses.

Archer put the ring on her trembling finger, and everyone converged on them. They were passed from one set of loving arms to the next, as congratulations and more whoops and cheers rang out.

When Indi finally landed back in his arms, the others' elated voices sounding around them, she was absolutely glowing. "I love you, babe. I hope today was everything you could have hoped for."

She gazed up at him with so much love in her eyes, he could drown in it, and what a glorious death that would be. "*You're* everything I could have hoped for, Archer, and *so* much more."

Ready for More Steeles?

I hope you loved Indi and Archer's story. If this was your first Steele family novel, grab Levi and Tara's book below, and then go back and read the first two books in the series, starting with Jock and Daphne's story, TEMPTED BY LOVE. If you'd like to read Dixie Whiskey and Jace Stone's love story, pick up TAMING MY WHISKEY, and to read about Josh and Riley, buy FRIENDSHIP ON FIRE.

Some fates are too tempting to deny

When single-father Levi Steele offers to help his daughter's beautiful aunt Tara find a home on Silver Island, their intense connection makes it even harder to resist the one woman he and his daughter can't afford to lose.

WANT MORE SILVER ISLAND?

Join Abby and Deirdra de Messiéres as they heal from their pasts and find love—and family—in the Silver Harbor Series.

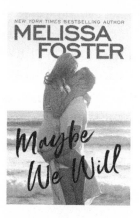

When chef Abby de Messiéres returns to Silver Island with her sister to get their late mother's affairs in order, she expected to inherit her mother's bistro along with their childhood home, not to discover a half sister they hadn't known existed and a handsome vacationer camped out on her mother's patio.

The Silver Harbor series is published by Montlake Romance and will be available in paperback and audio formats at all book retailers and exclusively in digital format for Kindle and Kindle apps.

Have you met the Bradens & Montgomerys?

Fiercely loyal, wickedly naughty heroes and smart, sassy heroines.

No cheating, no cliffhangers, and always a happily ever after.

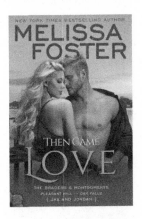

What happens when you find your soul mate but she belongs to someone else?

Famed wedding gown designer Jax Braden faces his toughest competitor yet—his heart. Passion ignites between Jax and soon-to-be bride Jordan Lawler. But honesty is everything to both of them, and neither will cross those lines. Loyalties are tested and hearts are frayed as Jax and Jordan are drawn into a love too strong to deny.

Have you met the Wickeds: Dark Knights at Bayside?

If you think bikers are all the same, you haven't met the Dark Knights. The Dark Knights are a motorcycle club, not a gang. Their members stick together like family and will stop at nothing to keep their communities safe, and their emotional stories will touch your heart and leave you wanting more.

Can you handle DWAYNE WICKED?

He's the ultimate player. She wants him to teach her the game in hopes of scoring his cousin. Practices heat up as roommates become teammates and rules are broken. Let the wicked fun begin.

No cheating. No cliffhangers. Guaranteed to leave readers hopelessly in love with the sinfully delicious Wickeds.

About the Love in Bloom World

Love in Bloom is the overarching romance collection name for several family series whose worlds interconnect. For example, *Lovers at Heart, Reimagined* is the title of the first book in The Bradens. The Bradens are set in the Love in Bloom world, and within The Bradens, you will see characters from other Love in Bloom series, such as The Snow Sisters and The Remingtons, so you never miss an engagement, wedding, or birth.

Where to Start

All Love in Bloom books can be enjoyed as stand-alone novels or as part of the larger series. If you are an avid reader and enjoy long series, I'd suggest starting with the very first Love in Bloom novel, *Sisters in Love*, and then reading through all of the series in the collection in publication order. However, you can start with any book or series without feeling a step behind. I offer free downloadable series checklists, publication schedules, and family trees on my website. A paperback series guide for the first thirty-six books in the series is available at most retailers and provides pertinent details for each book as well as places for you to take notes about the characters and stories.

See the Entire Love in Bloom Collection

www.MelissaFoster.com/love-bloom-series

Download Series Checklists, Family Trees, and Publication Schedules

www.MelissaFoster.com/reader-goodies

Download Free First-in-Series eBooks

www.MelissaFoster.com/free-ebooks

More Books By Melissa Foster

LOVE IN BLOOM SERIES

SNOW SISTERS
Sisters in Love
Sisters in Bloom
Sisters in White

THE BRADENS at Weston
Lovers at Heart, Reimagined
Destined for Love
Friendship on Fire
Sea of Love
Bursting with Love
Hearts at Play

THE BRADENS at Trusty
Taken by Love
Fated for Love
Romancing My Love
Flirting with Love
Dreaming of Love
Crashing into Love

THE BRADENS at Peaceful Harbor
Healed by Love
Surrender My Love
River of Love
Crushing on Love
Whisper of Love
Thrill of Love

THE BRADENS & MONTGOMERYS at Pleasant Hill – Oak Falls
Embracing Her Heart
Anything for Love

Trails of Love
Wild, Crazy Hearts
Making You Mine
Searching for Love
Hot for Love
Sweet, Sexy Heart
Then Came Love

THE BRADEN NOVELLAS
Promise My Love
Our New Love
Daring Her Love
Story of Love
Love at Last
A Very Braden Christmas

THE REMINGTONS
Game of Love
Stroke of Love
Flames of Love
Slope of Love
Read, Write, Love
Touched by Love

SEASIDE SUMMERS
Seaside Dreams
Seaside Hearts
Seaside Sunsets
Seaside Secrets
Seaside Nights
Seaside Embrace
Seaside Lovers
Seaside Whispers
Seaside Serenade

BAYSIDE SUMMERS
Bayside Desires
Bayside Passions

Bayside Heat
Bayside Escape
Bayside Romance
Bayside Fantasies

THE STEELES AT SILVER ISLAND
Tempted by Love
My True Love
Caught by Love
Always Her Love

THE RYDERS
Seized by Love
Claimed by Love
Chased by Love
Rescued by Love
Swept Into Love

THE WHISKEYS: DARK KNIGHTS AT PEACEFUL HARBOR
Tru Blue
Truly, Madly, Whiskey
Driving Whiskey Wild
Wicked Whiskey Love
Mad About Moon
Taming My Whiskey
The Gritty Truth
In for a Penny
Running on Diesel

THE WHISKEYS: DARK KNIGHTS AT REDEMPTION RANCH
The Trouble with Whiskey

SUGAR LAKE
The Real Thing
Only for You
Love Like Ours
Finding My Girl

HARMONY POINTE
Call Her Mine
This is Love
She Loves Me

THE WICKEDS: DARK KNIGHTS AT BAYSIDE
A Little Bit Wicked
The Wicked Aftermath

SILVER HARBOR
Maybe We Will
Maybe We Should

WILD BOYS AFTER DARK
Logan
Heath
Jackson
Cooper

BAD BOYS AFTER DARK
Mick
Dylan
Carson
Brett

HARBORSIDE NIGHTS SERIES
Includes characters from the Love in Bloom series
Catching Cassidy
Discovering Delilah
Tempting Tristan

More Books by Melissa
Chasing Amanda (mystery/suspense)
Come Back to Me (mystery/suspense)
Have No Shame (historical fiction/romance)
Love, Lies & Mystery (3-book bundle)
Megan's Way (literary fiction)
Traces of Kara (psychological thriller)
Where Petals Fall (suspense)

Acknowledgments

I hope you enjoyed Indi and Archer's book, and I'm excited to bring you more Steeles on Silver Island love stories. My Silver Harbor series is also set on Silver Island and features the de Messiéres family. As with all my series, characters from this series cross over to other series. If you'd like to read more about Silver Island, pick up *Searching for Love*, a Bradens & Montgomerys novel featuring treasure hunter Zev Braden. A good portion of Zev's story takes place on and around the island, as does *Bayside Fantasies*, a Bayside Summers novel featuring billionaire Jett Masters.

If this was your first introduction to my books, you have many more happily ever afters waiting for you. You can start at the very beginning of the Love in Bloom big-family romance collection with *Sisters in Love*, which is free in digital format at the time of this publication (price subject to change), or if you prefer to stick with the Cape Cod series, look for Seaside Summers and Bayside Summers. I suggest starting with *Seaside Dreams*, which is currently free in digital format (price subject to change). That series leads into the Bayside Summers series, which leads to the Steeles at Silver Island.

I am blessed to have the support of many friends and family members, and though I could never name them all, special thanks go out to Sharon Martin, Lisa Posillico-Filipe, and Missy and Shelby DeHaven, all of whom keep me sane. Special thanks go out to John "KZ" Kondratowicz, aka Agador Spartacus and/or Batman, retired Captain Vice Commander for the US Coast Guard, for patiently answering my nautical questions and always happily providing sophisticates for me and the rest of our beloved beach family, and to Will Sullivan, Wellfleet Harbormaster, who also took the time to answer my many questions about marinas in the winter.

I thoroughly enjoy chatting with my fans. If you haven't joined my Facebook fan club, I hope you will. We have loads of fun, chat about books, and members get special sneak peeks of upcoming publications.
www.Facebook.com/groups/MelissaFosterFans

Loads of gratitude go out to my editorial team, Kristen, Penina, Elaini, Juliette, Lynn, Justinn, and Lee, for all you do for me and for our readers. And, of course, a world of thanks goes out to my four incredible sons and my mother for their endless support.

Meet Melissa

www.MelissaFoster.com

Melissa Foster is a *New York Times* and *USA Today* bestselling and award-winning author. Her books have been recommended by *USA Today*'s book blog, *Hagerstown* magazine, *The Patriot*, and several other print venues. Melissa has painted and donated several murals to the Hospital for Sick Children in Washington, DC.

Visit Melissa on her website or chat with her on social media. Melissa enjoys discussing her books with book clubs and reader groups and welcomes an invitation to your event. Melissa's books are available through most online retailers in paperback, digital, and audio formats.